PRAISE FOR *WHERE THE FOREST MEETS THE STARS*

"Vanderah's beautifully human story reminds us that sometimes we need to look beyond the treetops at the stars to let some light into our lives."

—New York Journal of Books

"Enchanting, insightful, and extraordinary."

—*Novelgossip*

"*Where the Forest Meets the Stars* is a magical little gem of a book filled with lots of love and hope."

—*HelloGiggles*

"A captivating fantasy tale of mystery and intrigue . . ."

—*Fresh Fiction*

"A skillfully written and thoroughly entertaining novel by an author with a genuine gift for originality and a distinctive narrative-driven storytelling style . . ."

—*Midwest Book Review*

"Though the novel appears to start as a fantasy, it evolves into a domestic drama with murder-mystery elements, all adding up to a satisfying read."

—*Booklist*

"*Where the Forest Meets the Stars*, by Glendy Vanderah, is an enchanting, heartwarming, not to be missed novel that is bursting with love and hope."

—*The Patriot Ledger*

"A heartwarming, magical story about love, loss, and finding family where you least expect it. This touching novel will remind readers of a modern-day *The Snow Child*."

—Christopher Meades, award-winning author of *Hanna Who Fell from the Sky*

"*Where the Forest Meets the Stars* is an enchanting novel full of hope and the power of love that will pull at your heartstrings. Perfect for fans of Sarah Addison Allen."

—Karen Katchur, author of *Spring Girls*

"*Where the Forest Meets the Stars* will grab you from the very first page and surprise you the whole way through. This is an incredibly original, imaginative, and curious story. Glendy Vanderah has managed to create a world that is very real and, yet, entirely out of the ordinary."

—Taylor Jenkins Reid, *New York Times* bestselling author of *Daisy Jones & the Six*

"In *Where the Forest Meets the Stars*, Glendy Vanderah weaves a deft and poignant story with well-drawn characters, including clever Ursa. With an unexpected and heart-racing climax, readers will wait breathlessly to find out what happens. A beautiful story of love, resilience, and the power of second chances."

—Susie Orman Schnall, award-winning author of *We Came Here to Shine*

"*Where the Forest Meets the Stars* is a lovely, surprising, and insightful look at the way bonds are formed—both the ones that we choose and the ones that seem to choose us."

—Rebecca Kauffman, author of *The Gunners*

The
LIGHT
THROUGH
the
LEAVES

ALSO BY GLENDY VANDERAH

Where the Forest Meets the Stars

The LIGHT THROUGH the LEAVES

a novel

GLENDY VANDERAH

LAKE UNION
PUBLISHING

Text copyright © 2021 by Glendy C. Vanderah
All rights reserved.

No part of this book may be reproduced, or stored in a retrieval system, or transmitted in any form or by any means, electronic, mechanical, photocopying, recording, or otherwise, without express written permission of the publisher.

Published by Lake Union Publishing, Seattle

www.apub.com

Amazon, the Amazon logo, and Lake Union Publishing are trademarks of Amazon.com, Inc., or its affiliates.

ISBN-13: 9781542028103 (hardcover)
ISBN-10: 1542028108 (hardcover)
ISBN-13: 9781542026208 (paperback)
ISBN-10: 1542026202 (paperback)

Cover design by Shasti O'Leary Soudant

Printed in the United States of America

First Edition

For my family

Prologue

The first words Ellis wrote to the woods were *Please come back*. She was nine years old, sitting on the bank of the river in the Wild Wood. Zane had named it that. When she came home with muddy shoes and wind-tangled hair, he'd say something like, "Has the hobgoblin been to her Wild Wood again?" And she'd reply, "Yes," because it *was* wild and it *was* hers.

No one but Ellis went in the forest that bordered the trailer park and stretched far beyond the other side of the river. Other people thought that bit of water and trees was just a lot of nothing. They couldn't see how pretty it was. To get in from the trailer park, they would have to know how to crawl through a thicket of rose and blackberry thorns. Ellis knew the exact spot. It was like a magic door.

The day she wrote the first note, she'd gone straight in from the school bus. She'd done that most days for the last few months since her mother had gotten worse. She liked to sit by the river to do her homework, but that day the math problems sat unsolved in her lap. All she wanted to do was watch the river.

The water was high from spring rains, all kinds of stuff floating past fast. Leaves, branches, a paper cup. A ghostly white cloth that might be a T-shirt slithered over a riffle of rocks. It caught on a submerged branch for a while, but the river worked at it, pulling and fretting, until the cloth jerked away from the branch. Ellis sat up to see if it would get caught again. But the ghost shirt disappeared, sucked by swirling currents into the deep black water. For some reason, she felt as if her insides had sunk down with it.

She ripped a little square from her notebook paper and wrote the three words. *Please come back.* She stared at them for a long time, then added two more. *From Ellis.*

She folded the paper in half and tossed it into the river. She watched the little boat glide swiftly away on the gray glass of water. She imagined her words as five staunch sailors who would endure the hazards of rough water to deliver her message. She watched those words until they disappeared around the river bend.

Sending the message felt satisfying. As if something important had transpired between her and the river.

When her note hadn't brought results a few days later, she decided to be more specific. That blustery April day, she wrote in careful script, *Dear Wind, Please bring Zane back. From Ellis.* She scaled her climbing tree to the usual high branch, waited for a strong gust of wind, and let the tiny letter go. It flew out of sight much faster than the first message. She hoped that was a good sign.

It wasn't, not for bringing Zane back, but she kept writing to the woods anyway. She sent more words downriver and into the wind, tucked tiny messages into tree roots, laid them under rocks, sank them into the soft punk of rotting logs.

She didn't know why she kept doing it. It just felt good, maybe how some kids felt when they talked to God in their prayers. After a while, you figured out no one was going to answer. That made it better, really, because you could say any secret thing you wouldn't say to someone who was listening. That was all that mattered, getting some of the words out before they piled too full inside you.

PART ONE

DAUGHTER OF THE WILD WOOD

1

Ellis saw a dark hollow at the base of an oak. It would be a good place to put a message.

What would she write? How would she word what she'd seen when she still couldn't comprehend it?

She tried to imagine how her nine-year-old self would say it. Concisely, on a small shred of paper: *Dear Tree, Jonah has betrayed me. I don't know what to do. From Ellis.*

What she wanted to write was, *What should I do?* But other than the day she'd asked the wind to bring Zane back, she usually didn't ask for something directly. Writing the notes had mostly been a way to work through events that troubled her. She did it for years, the messages increasing in length as she got older.

Dear Rock, I wonder where Zane is and if he misses me.

Dear Tree, Mom won't get up and I have no food. Maybe I should ask Edith for supper.

Dear Salamander, Today Heather told me I should wash my clothes. She said it in front of everyone on the bus. I wish I lived under this log with you. You get to be as dirty as you want.

Jasper and River had run ahead. They were almost at the little pier that jutted over the forest pond.

Ellis had to pull her mind back to where she was.

"Careful!" she called. "Don't get too close to the water." The boys were four and a half and had been taught how to stay afloat in swim lessons, but she still feared their nearness to the deep black water.

When she arrived at the dock, they were stretched out on their bellies, fishnets in hand, looking for tadpoles. The muscles in her arms and shoulders released their aching tension as she set down the baby in her car carrier. She gave the boys the two mason jars from the bag in her other hand.

"Shore will be a better place to find them," she said.

She showed her sons where to find tadpoles, in the muck along the shoreline. In his knee-high rubber boots, River stepped into the water to block Jasper. He wanted to be the first to capture one.

Jonah and Ellis secretly joked that the twins had taken their names too literally: River as loud and impetuous as rushing water, Jasper as quiet and forbearing as a stone. River was born three minutes before his twin, and he'd been three steps ahead of Jasper ever since.

Thinking about Jonah made her physically ill. She sat on the ground next to the baby.

She had to divorce him. Obviously.

He'd probably been with Irene since early in Ellis's pregnancy. That was when he'd started the lessons. All those months, he'd been sleeping with his hard-bodied tennis instructor while his wife got softer growing his baby. She suspected he'd been lying to her about that tough case at his law firm. Lying to his boys. On Saturday, he wouldn't even take them to the park. He'd probably been with Irene.

Ellis kept seeing it, Jonah getting into her sporty white car near his work. The passionate kiss. At eleven thirty in the morning. Tennis wasn't the only reason he'd gotten in shape lately. Apparently, he was doing intense workouts over his long lunch hours.

The boys had been in the van when Ellis saw the kiss. If she hadn't quickly said something to distract them, they might have seen. Any of her friends might have. Probably some of their mutual friends had seen them together or knew about the affair. Ellis felt betrayed by them, too.

"I found a whole bunch!" River said. "Mom! Come see!"

She glanced at Viola asleep in her carrier. She'd nodded off during the jostling walk through the woods. Ellis left her at the pier to look at the tadpoles.

"Do you see them?" River said. "Mom? Mom?"

"I see."

"You're stepping on them," Jasper said. "River, stop it!"

"I'm not! They swam away."

"Mom, he's killing them."

"Guys, let's just calm down, okay? Put some pond water in your jars and try to catch a few."

"How many?" Jasper asked.

"You can each catch about ten. Twenty's a good number for the big fishbowl, don't you think?"

"I want to keep mine in a different place from Jasper's," River said.

"No, they all go in the bowl. And once they turn into frogs, we'll bring them back here."

"Why?"

"This is their home. They're adapted to this environment."

How would the boys adapt to the new life ahead of them? Now they'd be living between two parents and two homes. Would she keep the house or would Jonah? Would she have to get a job? What kind of job would an undergraduate degree in plant biology get her—especially when she had zero experience in anything but babies?

She returned to her daughter and tucked the blanket beneath her cherubic face. Even through Viola's baby fat, Ellis could see she was going to look like her. She had the brown eyes and tan olive complexion, and she already had a lot of curl to her dark hair. Her daughter would be the first relative she knew who looked like her. The boys took after Jonah and her mother, both with fairer skin, blue eyes, and straight hair. Ellis assumed she and Viola must look like her father, but she knew nothing about him other than a name on her birth certificate. But she even questioned that because her mother said, "I don't know who your father was," the one time she'd responded to Ellis's questions about him.

She dabbed a dribble of breast milk on the side of the baby's lips with her finger. Viola reacted to her touch, turning her mouth instinctively toward it, but stayed asleep.

Even now, more than two months postpartum, Ellis sometimes couldn't believe Viola was there, another being she'd created, another little person who depended on her. Just when she'd finally gotten used to her routine with Jonah and the boys, when she'd almost come to terms with the strange future the unplanned twins had thrust upon her and Jonah. Thrown from campus life into suburbia. Botany texts traded for parenting books. Singles' parties replaced by playgroups. Graduate school applications buried beneath research into preschools.

Ellis suspected the sudden reality of another baby had been as much of a shock to Jonah. Maybe that was why he'd escaped into the affair with Irene. Yet, he'd been the one who pushed for another baby. As the boys approached four, when they looked more "little boy" than toddler, Jonah had said he wanted a baby in the house again. He missed the infant stage, hoped for a girl.

And here was his little girl, left mostly to Ellis—an exhausted, milk-dripping matron, also juggling two active boys, while Jonah got to act his twenty-nine years, talking to adults at work, going out for drinks, feeling attractive with a beautiful young woman.

"Stop it!" River said. "Mom!"

Tadpole catching was not going well. None of it was. Ellis had come to the woods to calm herself, but she felt worse than when she'd arrived and still been in shock. Now she was angry.

And she felt guilty, she realized, because that inkling she'd had from the start, that she and Jonah weren't meant to be, must have been real. Even months after they'd been together, she'd sensed an absence of passion in him, though he frequently proclaimed his love for her. She'd mistrusted her doubts, assuming the deficiency—if there was one—had to do with her. She had plenty of proof that she was to blame. Her mother hadn't wanted her. Zane had left her, hadn't even said goodbye. Ellis wasn't like regular people. She was unsociable and peculiar, not the kind of person anyone wanted to stick with.

She had to get out of the forest. For the first time in her life, her favorite environment felt all wrong, as if it had also betrayed her. The trees and rocks, the dark water, whispered about her, telling the story of the needy little girl who'd written notes to no one.

She hastened the tadpole catching. The boys complained about her helping, but at the rate they were going—Jasper with two tadpoles in his jar, River with four—they would be there for hours. Ellis scooped tadpoles into the net she'd taken from Jasper and dumped them into their jars. When she tried to get them moving, River complained that Jasper had more in his jar.

"It doesn't matter. They're all going into one tank," she said.

"It's not fair," River said.

She dropped another net of the wriggling creatures into River's jar, increasing his catch by at least half a dozen. He shot Jasper a triumphant grin.

"Mom . . . ," Jasper began.

"Enough," she said, screwing the lids onto the mason jars.

Viola was still asleep. Ellis wrapped her arm around the carrier handle, picked up the bag with nets, and headed down the trail. Every step closer to the van was like heading for a cliff edge. When Jonah got home, she'd tell him what she'd decided. She had to step off the precipice, end this charade they were calling a marriage.

No, she wasn't ending it. Jonah already had. She had to be firm with herself about that.

A raven called its guttural croak from the direction of the trailhead parking lot. Something had it riled up, maybe a hawk near its nest. As Ellis arrived in the parking lot, she saw the raven. It was perched on a branch over her van, calling with strange urgency, voicing the wretchedness of her situation. She wished it would shut up.

River and Jasper were already arguing about who got middle and who got back. Ellis hated to do it, but she gave easier-going Jasper the short straw as she often did to minimize conflict.

"But River got middle on the way here," Jasper said.

"Did he?" Ellis said. "Go on, get in."

"But, Mom, it's not fair. It's my turn."

Of all days for him to start challenging River's authority. But Ellis liked his sudden confidence.

"Okay, River in back."

"I don't want to sit in back!" he said.

"She said!"

"But first she said I had middle!"

The raven added its throaty *kraa, kraa, kraa!* in quick succession.

"Get *in*!" Ellis shouted.

River climbed in back. Jasper went to the middle. Ellis put the bag with the nets on the floor and held Jasper's jar while he buckled his seat belt.

A howl rose out of the back seat. "My tadpoles!" River screamed.

Ellis set the baby carrier on the ground and leaned into the van, seeing River's entire jar poured over the back seat, tadpoles wriggling in the thin veneer of water left.

"Why wasn't the lid on?" she said.

"I was trying . . . I was trying to get that other thing out of there. That big, scary bug!" River cried.

Probably a dragonfly larva. The predatory insect *was* scary looking.

"Mom, they're dying!" Jasper said. "Mom! Help them!"

Jasper's pronouncement made River wail louder.

Ellis ran around to the other side of the van so she didn't have to lean over Jasper. She grabbed Jasper's jar, crawled over the middle seat, and tried to pick up the tadpoles. But she couldn't get a grip on them.

Both boys yowled, the raven squawking along with them.

Using a rag from the supplies, Ellis swiped as many tadpoles as she could into Jasper's jar. But some were beyond sight on the dark carpet. And one was wedged in the crack of the seat. If she tried to get it out, she'd probably squish it. Seeing it dead in the jar would upset the boys more. They protested loudly when she closed the jar.

"You didn't get all of them!" River said.

"There's one stuck in the seat!" Jasper said. "It's dying! You have to get it out!"

"We'll try to get it at home," she said.

"It'll die!"

"I want to go back and get more!" River said.

"No! You shouldn't have taken the lid off. We're going, and we still have plenty."

"We don't have enough!"

"There're two on the floor!" Jasper shouted.

"Mom!"

The raven was still croaking along with the boys as Ellis started the van. When she turned out of the lot, River burst into melodramatic sobs.

"It's okay," Jasper told him. "Maybe they'll still be alive when we get home."

"They won't!" River cried.

"If Dad is home, he'll save them," Jasper said with certainty.

Ellis could almost taste the bitterness of her thoughts. Why was Jonah their hero? How did being so rarely at home bestow him with noble qualities? Jasper wouldn't be glorifying his father if he'd seen the son of a bitch kissing another woman that morning.

Ellis was dizzy thinking about what he'd done, what he'd been doing.

River's crying ebbed by the time they came to the main road.

"Mom?" Jasper said.

"What?"

"You forgot Viola."

Ellis pushed the brake and looked back. She stared at the empty seat next to Jasper. Not possible. She wouldn't have left her baby behind. But the carrier wasn't there. She'd forgotten to put the baby in the van when the tadpoles spilled.

Everything inside felt frozen. But it was more like she didn't have a body. She couldn't feel the steering wheel in her hands. She didn't have a face or arms or legs.

Somehow, she'd turned the van around, and her foot must have been pressing the accelerator.

It's okay. She'll still be there, still sleeping. It's okay. It's okay.

She pressed harder on the pedal.

What she'd done was normal. She wasn't used to putting a third child in the van. For more than four years, there had been only two. New parents did this. She'd heard stories about leaving the baby in the house. In the car. Just for a few minutes. Nothing dangerous. It would be okay.

The one and a half miles of winding road felt like ten.

What if she'd run her over as she pulled out? She might have killed her. What kind of mother did that?

She slowed at the sign for the forest preserve, turned into the trailhead parking lot. All was quiet, the raven flown from its branch. There were two cars in the lot, parked far from where the van had been. Ellis stared at the empty space her van had occupied.

No carrier. No baby.

She had a brief thought that she'd never had a third baby. Hadn't it felt like that sometimes? As if this life, three kids, was all a dream? She shut her eyes, certain everything would return to whatever was normal, two kids or three, when she opened them.

"Mom?"

She opened her eyes.

"Where's Viola?" Jasper asked.

The baby was gone. Someone had taken her daughter.

2

The jangle of curtain rings woke Ellis. She sat up in the bed, muzzy from a sleeping pill, unaware of the time of day until the shades started going up. She used her forearm to protect her eyes from the light slicing into her vision.

"What are you doing?"

"Oh!"

The woman hadn't known anyone was there. Ellis squinted at the unfamiliar person, a silhouette surrounded by painful brightness.

"I'm sorry, ma'am," the young woman said. "I was told to clean this room."

"Who told you?"

"Mrs. . . . uh . . . Bauhammer. Do you want me to leave?" Before Ellis responded, the woman added, "I was told to do everything in here. The bathroom. Strip the bed . . ."

The woman was afraid to bring The Hammer down on herself. Most people were. Ellis and Jonah used to joke about the nickname Ellis had given his mother. But it was no joke since his mother had moved in to "help" with their crisis.

Ellis wouldn't give the cleaning woman more trouble when she'd already had to deal with Mary Carol. She dragged herself out of bed. Then the other hammer hit. The colossal one.

Her baby was gone. Two weeks. Almost no hope of finding her now. She might be dead. Abused. Because Ellis had left her in a parking lot, offered her like a lamb to the slaughter to some crazy person.

She fractured beneath the weight of it. Being hit with it over and over had changed her. She was broken pieces of the woman who used to be Ellis Abbey Bauhammer, wife of Jonah, mother of three children, leading a perfectly ordinary life in the suburbs.

She pulled on her robe. Her breasts still hurt, but the milk was mostly gone now.

The cleaning woman hadn't moved. She stared at Ellis, her expression a mixture of curiosity and sympathy. No doubt she knew the whole story, as did most people who lived anywhere near that part of New York. Ellis couldn't stand that look in people's eyes, but she wouldn't hold it against the woman.

"Go ahead," Ellis told her. "I'll use another bathroom."

There was another cleaning woman in the boys' bathroom. She would have to use the bathroom attached to Viola's nursery.

No, she couldn't go in there. She never did anymore.

She went downstairs, where two more cleaning women were dusting and vacuuming. She used the half bath, then entered the kitchen. Mary Carol was there, her shoulder-length, chestnut-dyed hair perfectly sleek, her jeans and button-down shirt close fitting to show off her figure. She was at the stove cooking breakfast—or was it lunch? The boys were seated at the table, absorbed in the new video gadgets their grandmother had given them.

Before either woman uttered one word, The Hammer, the human one, hit Ellis with a look of crushing blame.

"Finally up?" Mary Carol said.

"The cleaning woman woke me."

"Did she?"

"I didn't get to sleep until past six in the morning."

"The sleeping pills don't work?"

She could only know Ellis's doctor had prescribed sleep medication if Jonah had told her. Mary Carol looked at Ellis smugly, as if to verify that her son was now more in her confidence than in his wife's.

Ellis went to the boys and touched their soft, dark hair with both hands. "Hi, guys."

"Hi, Mom," Jasper said, glancing up from his game.

"Hi," River said, keeping his eyes on his screen.

Her boys didn't even want to look at her now—because of what she'd done.

She pushed away the thought, told herself they were preoccupied with their games.

She poured a cup of coffee and turned to face her mother-in-law. "I can clean my own house, you know," she said in a quiet tone.

Mary Carol put on a wounded countenance. "I was only trying to help. I know it's difficult for you—to keep up—under the circumstances." As proof, she said, "The boys said they were hungry. I'm making grilled ham-and-cheese sandwiches. Would you like one?"

Ellis looked into the frying pan. "Ham? You know this house is vegetarian!"

"Jonah isn't."

"He is when I cook. And River and Jasper are."

"But you aren't cooking, are you?"

The little thread that had been keeping Ellis attached to civility broke. She grabbed the grilling sandwich out of the pan and threw it in the trash can. She burned her hand, but the pain hardly registered. She opened the refrigerator and found the deli ham.

"That's expensive meat," Mary Carol said.

"I don't care," Ellis said, thumping the wad of flesh into the can.

"Boys, I'm sorry to say your lunch is gone," Mary Carol said.

The boys had stopped playing their video games. They looked almost as if they were frightened of their own mother.

"I'll make grilled cheese, okay?"

"Okay," Jasper piped up.

River said nothing. He had that new look in his eyes, the resentful stare that made Ellis want to weep. He was angry that everything had changed. All the crying. Police. Detectives. Everyone in the house on edge—especially since Mary Carol had arrived. Almost daily, friends and neighbors came over with food or just to lament with them. River hated it. He hated her. He hated her for losing Viola and ruining his perfect life.

Ellis turned away from the three piercing gazes. She was dizzy from lack of sleep and near vomiting, but she got to work on the sandwiches. "Where is Jonah?" she asked.

"He had to run to the office," Mary Carol said.

On a Saturday. He was probably with Irene. Being consoled by her. Because he got no comfort from the increasingly deranged wife who'd left his baby daughter in the woods.

Mary Carol took a seat at the table with a cup of black coffee. She drank coffee all day to keep her appetite low. Attendance to her figure, to anything related to her appearance, had been Mary Carol's main occupation most of her life. Ellis could imagine how her mother-in-law viewed her current state. Ellis didn't even look in the mirror anymore.

She added apple slices to the boys' lunches, set the plates down, and sat across from them. "Put the games away and eat," she said. When they continued playing, she said, "Now."

River shot her another look. Ellis wondered what poison Mary Carol fed them when she wasn't around. And Ellis often wasn't around lately, she had to admit. She tried to keep herself, her increasing instability, away from the boys. She knew how it felt to see a parent lose her mind.

"Tomorrow the boys and I are going to church to pray for Viola," Mary Carol said. "You're welcome to come with us. If you get up in time. Service is at eight."

Talk about kicking someone when they were down. Mary Carol was unloading all her ammo on her this afternoon.

Ellis set down her coffee, looked into the steely-blue gaze of the woman who had accused her of deliberately "trapping" her son with pregnancy. She and her husband had bitterly opposed Jonah marrying a plant biology student who'd grown up in a trailer. With an addict mother and unknown father, no less. Ellis assumed his mother often used the words *trailer trash* to describe her, though Jonah would never have told her. Mary Carol even warned Jonah that his marriage to a woman who'd taken part in Pride marches might bring negative attention from the media and cause trouble for his father, a renowned conservative senator.

Ellis held The Hammer's challenging gaze. She saw it clearly. The woman who'd waged battle against Ellis since the day Jonah told her of their engagement would now do everything in her power to win that war. Ellis's shield wall was down, and Bauhammer was charging at her in full armor.

Ellis rose, pushing off the table with shaking arms. "Will you please come talk to me in the office?"

"Jonah's office?" Mary Carol said. "He prefers that room to be private."

"It's my goddamn house, *my* office!"

Mary Carol raised her eyebrows at her language, or perhaps to remind Ellis that she and her husband had given Jonah the down payment for the house as a wedding gift.

The boys had stopped eating, distressed by the conflict.

"Will you talk to me in private or not?"

Mary Carol saw that she was shaking, and Ellis thought she looked pleased. "If you insist," she said, rising from her chair. "Don't worry, boys. Everything is fine."

Ellis closed the door behind them in the downstairs study and faced her adversary. "You aren't going to do this," she said.

"Do what?"

"Erase me."

She looked amused. "I think you've taken a few too many of those pills, Ellis."

"Have I? Why did you give the boys video games when it's against our rules? Why are you feeding them meat when you know I don't want that? Why would you take them to your church when you know they already have one?"

She made a skeptical face. "What's it called, the Unitarian Universe . . . ?"

"The Unitarian Universalist Church."

"The boys told me what they do in their so-called Sunday school. Learning about Buddha, Jews, Muslims . . . Jasper even has a picture of an elephant god in his room! This is not a 'church.' It's more like a cult!"

"You'd better not be telling that to my children. Jonah and I decided this together. We want them to find their own way with spirituality."

"Don't involve Jonah in it. It was your idea, and you know it. If he'd married a Christian woman, those children would know Our Lord Jesus Christ as their one and only Savior!"

Ellis supposed that was true. Raised by parents with implacable beliefs, Jonah had learned to go with the flow. If he'd married a woman with strong convictions about her children attending church—or synagogue, mosque, or temple—he'd have let her take them. His feelings about organized religion were ambivalent, and he was used to being steered.

"Don't you see what you've done?" Mary Carol said.

Ellis certainly saw what she'd done. She saw it a hundred times a day. A little baby in a car carrier all alone in a forest.

"This terrible thing happened because you have no faith in the only God that can keep those babies out of Hell! Because you steered Jonah into your impiety! God took your baby to punish both of you." Tears, real ones, swelled in Mary Carol's eyes. "God is punishing me, too.

And my husband. We should have tried harder to stop our son from marrying you. We'll never see our only granddaughter again. What she suffered in life or death will forever torment us. We're all going to be punished for the rest of our lives!"

Ellis could scarcely breathe.

Mary Carol's blue eyes blazed with anguish. Ellis had never seen her reveal raw emotion so openly. But her mother-in-law quickly turned away, weeping as she returned to the boys.

When Ellis entered the kitchen, River and Jasper looked at their mother as if she were an evil witch. What else could transform their iron-willed grandma into that blubbering mess?

"It's okay, Mom. I don't mind going to church with Grandma," Jasper said, playing mediator. "She said we have to pray for Viola to bring her back."

"That won't bring her back," River scoffed.

"River! Have faith!" Mary Carol said.

"Why?" he said. "I don't want her back. I hated her."

"She's your sister!" Ellis shouted. "How could you say that?" Silver dots filled her eyes. She lunged at a chair to slow her fall, but her head hit the side of the table, knocking her into darkness.

3

Jonah strode into the bedroom with her new prescription. Some kind of sedative. He sat on the side of the bed, holding out a pill and a glass of water.

"I told you I'm not taking that," she said.

"The psychiatrist said you have to sleep and start eating. You have to reduce the stress."

Ellis looked into his eyes. "A pill can't fix what I'm going through, and you know it."

The coldness of his gaze made her want to cry. But she tried to understand. He was grieving for his daughter as much as she was. And she was the one who had left their baby in the forest. The media certainly hadn't left out that part of the story: Senator Bauhammer's Granddaughter Taken When Mother Leaves Her in Forest.

Ellis tried to imagine what it was like for Jonah to go to the law firm every day. What could his coworkers say to him when his own wife had lost his baby? Maybe they avoided him because offering sympathy was too awkward.

Jonah held out the pill. "You have to take it. What if you'd passed out while you were driving with the boys?" He gestured with his chin at the bandage on the side of her forehead. "They said you're lucky you didn't hit harder."

"I controlled the fall. I was only out for a few seconds."

"My mother said it was longer."

"She's only saying that to justify calling 911. She shouldn't have done that!"

"You fault her for that?" he said, an incredulous tone seeping through.

"Yes! Don't you see? She's trying to make it seem like I can't handle my house and kids. You need to make her leave!"

"The boys told me everything that happened. You yelled at River. You made my mother cry. You threw the lunch she'd made into the garbage. Who's the villain in this story, Ell? You or her?"

"Oh my god! Did you call me a 'villain'?"

And he'd just come from Irene's bed. Ellis was sometimes certain she could smell his lover on him, a scent that hung over him like a cloying cloud.

His expression softened when he saw her tears brimming. "I'm sorry. I shouldn't have used such a strong word."

"What word would you use?"

"I'm just saying, she had every right to call 911. You were acting irrational, you passed out, and your head was gushing blood. The boys were terrified."

"She scared them more by calling the paramedics."

His blue eyes went cold again.

"She's making everything worse. Did you know she's taking the boys to her church tomorrow?"

"So what? Maybe they need the comfort of church right now."

"They have a church! I decide what my children need. I'm their mother. Do you remember that, Jonah? I'm their mother!"

The coldness remained in his expression, and it froze her down deep. She understood what it meant. She couldn't be trusted. He thought the boys were better off with Mary Carol.

"I'm begging you to make her leave, Jonah."

"I need her help while I'm at work. She'll leave when you're able to care for the boys alone."

"I am!"

"I'm not seeing it, Ell."

"It's only been two weeks! They've just told us finding her is almost impossible now. Give me a chance to work through it."

"That's what this medication is for. To help you recover."

She looked at the little pill that would "help her recover." Two weeks ago, she'd been certain she and her children would never recover from Jonah's betrayal. Now all of that was submerged beneath much deeper grief. She was being consumed by it, sinking too fast. She was trying to grab on to something, anything—even on to him, the one who had opened the abyss in the first place.

"Take it," he said, pushing the pill into her lips.

So this was all he had to offer. Why did he not take her in his arms? Hold her, give her real security when she was so obviously going under?

She tasted salty tears with the drug's bitterness. But if it could dull the pain of his treachery, she would welcome it.

He pressed the water glass to her lips. She drank, swallowing the medication.

"Good," he said, patting her cheek like she was a child. "Now, get some sleep. We've got dinner covered. The boys are making pizzas with my mother."

"No meat! Don't let her put meat on them," Ellis said.

He sighed and closed the door.

4

Taking the pills got easier and easier. The medication didn't so much counteract her anguish as smear it. The brutally sharp photographs of her days became impressionist paintings. Pills, plural, because when she couldn't sleep again, they gave her another one.

The combination of the two drugs worked. After little more than a week, Ellis believed in them without question. The pain of existence was not something a person should have to feel.

Of course, she wasn't allowed to drive when she was taking the drugs. Mary Carol and Jonah took charge of the house. Sometimes the eminent senator Jonah Bauhammer II visited, spouting his intolerant opinions in front of the children, stoking the tension igniting in the house. Ellis frequently lost control of her temper with him, even when the boys looked on.

Jonah III would make her go upstairs to stop the fight. He'd been doing that for years, acting as a human barrier between her and his parents. He didn't support her or contest his parents' bigotry.

What a coward Jonah was. He'd often told Ellis it was a relief to be with someone who shared his deepest beliefs, yet his parents still didn't know he opposed their views. But even if they did find out, they'd blame Ellis for corrupting him.

Weeks passed. Mary Carol took the boys to her church every Sunday. Gave them meat. The cleaning ladies came every week.

Ellis wasn't getting better. She knew she wasn't because Jonah and Mary Carol no longer trusted her alone with her children. River and Jasper perceived the shift in control. More and more, they sought out their grandmother for their needs. The pain and fury were too much. Ellis took more medication, adding doses of the opioids she'd been prescribed for her back pain. She did have back pain—probably from staying in bed too much—but she'd made it sound worse than it was to get a refill.

Eventually, her five prescriptions weren't enough. She was secretive when she drank early in the day. But once the clock hit five, she felt no need to hide the martinis and old-fashioneds from her family. That was when she was in her best mood and at her finest with her boys. Joking with them, sometimes playing a board game. Though usually she was too stoned to play the game right.

Ellis learned how to vacate her past. Dissociate from her fears of the future. She could even slip away from the present. She was a ghost drifting around a prison that smelled of floor wax and dusting spray. Sometimes she swore her hands went right through the furniture when she tried to touch it.

Jonah stopped sleeping in the bedroom with her. Ellis understood. She disliked trying to sleep with the person she'd become as much as he did. And her bitterness toward him had grown almost as strong as her self-hatred. When he was in bed with her, keeping to the far side of the king mattress, his presence felt intrusive, as if she were sleeping with a stranger, some shitty guy who was cheating on his wife with his tennis instructor.

Almost six months after Ellis left her baby in the parking lot, the case of Viola Abbey Bauhammer's abduction was essentially closed. Her recovery was deemed *very unlikely* by the detective supervising the case.

After Jonah gave Ellis that news, she took an extra dose of her back medication. She didn't wait until five o'clock to pour a whiskey on ice while her husband aimed his usual reproachful glare at her.

"Do you want some?" she asked. "You look like you need it."

"That is not what I need, Ellis," he said bitterly.

He went to the kitchen, told his mother he had to go to work and wouldn't be home for dinner.

Apparently, what he needed was Irene.

"Go ahead, honey," Mary Carol said. "I have everything under control here."

Ellis drowned her shrinking ice cubes in more whiskey and watched Jonah pull his car out of the driveway. She didn't recall much more of that evening. She remembered hearing River and Jasper fight over the TV. She looked out her bedroom window, watching a raven flap its darkness across the ashen sky. She had a bottle of pills in her hand.

She woke in the emergency room. They told her she'd overdosed.

The same psychiatrist who'd prescribed the pills told her she had to stop taking them. She said she needed them. She begged. She cried. But they wouldn't let her have anything.

It hurt. God, it hurt.

Two days later, her first day back home, Jonah came to her in the living room. When Ellis saw the look on his face, she understood why Mary Carol had taken the boys out of the house. She was grateful for the drink in her hand. Jonah hadn't found the bottle she'd hidden in the laundry room when he'd cleared the house of alcohol and pills.

He glanced bitterly at the drink as he approached. "I'm not going to draw this out," he said. "I think we both know this isn't working."

"I agree," she said. "Your mother has to go. She's wrecking our family. Your father, too. Let's tell them they can never come here again."

His bold stance crumbled into perplexity.

She wanted to laugh at his dismay, but if she had, she'd have ruined the humor. Jonah was such an ass. He truly didn't know she was jesting.

"I'm talking about us," he said.

"I know," she said. "They've come between us. It's time we take a stand."

"Ellis . . ."

"What?"

"I'm trying to say I want to leave you."

She let herself laugh. And laugh and laugh. She was aware of how out of control she looked. She didn't care.

"Stop it."

"Stop what?" she said, wiping at the tears.

"Laughing. This isn't funny."

"What's funny is you don't know why it's funny. You don't know the half of it—as they say."

"What don't I know?"

"You don't know I took the kids to have lunch with you the day Viola was taken. You don't know we were going to surprise you with a picnic in the park like we used to do. You don't know I saw you get in Irene's car and kiss her. You don't know I said something to distract the boys and drove away fast so they wouldn't see you. You don't know how I felt at that moment, to know you'd been with another woman all that time, even while I was screaming and pushing your baby out."

Jonah stood in jaw-dropped silence.

"You don't know that was why I had to go to the woods that day. But you know that's what I do, go to the woods when I'm upset. To try to figure out what to do."

"Ell, I'm—"

"Quiet! I'm not done."

He clamped his mouth shut.

"You don't know I told the boys they could catch tadpoles so they'd want to go to the woods with me. You don't know I decided I had to divorce you, and it was the hardest decision of my life. You don't know River spilled his tadpoles in the car and both boys were screaming, and

I was so crazy about what you'd done to all of us that I forgot about the baby."

Ellis stood, suddenly strong.

"You don't know jack shit, Jonah! You don't know what it was like when I realized I'd left Viola. You don't know how I wanted to die when I saw someone had taken her."

Jonah pressed his palms to his temples, as if trying to squeeze everything he'd heard out of his brain.

"I'm leaving *you*!" she shouted. "Tell that to your lawyer! I'm leaving you because you've betrayed our marriage vows! I'm leaving you because you're at least half-responsible for Viola's abduction! I'm not taking this on by myself anymore! You're as guilty as I am!"

Jonah started crying. Ellis had never seen him do that, not even the day Viola was taken.

He was sobbing, all red in the face, his nose running, and she was struck by how much she had loved him. Or was it only his beauty that she'd loved? His thick nut-brown hair, eyes the color of clear sky, cheekbones as sculpted as smooth stones.

She hoped his looks weren't all that had drawn her in. But what was it; what had she loved about him? His gentleness? His calmness? Was it only that he'd said he loved her, and she thought she had to love him back? She once thought she loved his goodness, but now she knew he wasn't good. That hurt the most.

"Ell . . . Ell . . . ," he said at last, "I can't explain. I can't tell you. You don't understand . . . you don't know why . . ."

"I know what I saw. Do you deny it?"

"No."

"Are you still with her?"

He didn't reply, but she saw the answer. Guilt hung over him like a haze. Of course he was still with Irene. He was rarely home. He'd let his mother take over, just as he had when he was a boy.

Ellis slid down to the couch, sapped of her momentary strength. "I'm leaving you, Jonah. I want half of everything. But not the boys. I have to leave them."

He quit crying, his eyes wide. "You won't contest my custody?"

"Do you know what I see in the boys' eyes when they look at me? I see my eyes looking at my mother. I'm damaging them. I can't do them any good like this."

"That's not true! We're all still grieving Viola. But someday we'll recover. And when you're better, I hope we can share custody of the boys. They need you, Ellis."

"When will I be *better*? A month? A year? Three years? I don't know how long it will take me to get over this. All I know is I've become my mother, and it's the worst nightmare I can imagine. I have to leave them to stop hurting them. I'm begging you to be who you truly are with our children. If you can do that, I know they'll grow into good men."

5

They signed the papers within the week. Jonah gave her things he never would have if she'd fought. He wouldn't make her pay child support for the boys. He gave her money for her half of their belongings. He would deposit a monthly stipend into her bank account in lieu of giving her half the house. He wanted to live there. With Irene.

Ellis liked to imagine Mary Carol meeting Irene. The Bauhammers would probably judge a tennis instructor as they had Ellis: beneath their standards. Sparks certainly would fly when The Hammer met the steel-bodied tennis lady.

When Jonah heard Ellis planned to travel with a tent rather than rent or buy a home, he insisted she at least take the new SUV he'd traded for the van. He let Ellis take all the camping supplies. She'd bought most of them long before they married.

There was only one condition Jonah fought. He wanted contact with Ellis, and she wanted none. She had to cut off her life in New York like an umbilical cord. She'd either survive without Jonah, River, and Jasper, or she would not. In between was not possible.

Knowing Jonah would be tempted to find her, Ellis had to route her bank statements somewhere unknown to him. To someone she fully trusted.

Ellis stalled calling Dani to the last possible day. She'd last seen Danielle Yoon, her best friend from college, a week after Viola was abducted. Dani had found out about the abduction through mutual friends, and she'd immediately hopped on a plane to come help.

Dani was working with one of the most prestigious plant geneticists in the country, and Ellis knew she must have gone to extreme measures to leave behind her doctoral studies at the University of Florida. Ellis hated that her shameful mistake was making a mess of someone else's life. And Dani's hugs, tears, and repeated offers to assist with the boys had only made Ellis feel worse.

Dani was all those memories from before Jonah: botany labs and field trips, late-night dorm chats, study evenings, camping, cheap beer, and laughter—always laughter because Dani was one of the funniest people she knew. She didn't belong in Ellis's housewife life. She wasn't supposed to be sitting in her big suburban house weeping for Viola. Having her there—bringing all those memories with her—only cleaved open Ellis's pain. Ellis had found herself submerging her grief in stoicism to get her friend to leave. Dani stayed for two days, and after she left, Ellis retreated to her bed, wholly exhausted from pretending she had the strength to handle losing her daughter.

Calling Dani would be difficult. Ellis had stopped answering her texts long ago, and Dani surely had been hurt by that.

But the bank needed an address before she left town. She called next to the packed SUV.

Dani picked up on the second ring. "Ellis! How are you?"

"I'm okay. How are you?"

"I got so worried when you stopped answering my texts and calls. Have there been any new leads with finding Viola?"

"No," Ellis said. "How's your research going?"

"Really well." After a pause, she said, "What's going on? There's something wrong. I can tell."

"There is. I'm leaving Jonah . . . or I guess we're leaving each other."

"What? Divorce?"

"Yes."

"Ellis, no! You guys are still grieving Viola. Have you tried counseling?"

Neither Jonah nor Ellis had taken their friends' advice and seen a therapist. Ellis didn't see the point when Jonah had been cheating on her long before the abduction. And Jonah apparently had no intention of giving up his lover. There was nothing left in their marriage to salvage.

But Dani knew nothing about Jonah's affair, and Ellis wanted it to stay that way. She couldn't bear more of Dani's sympathy. It simply made the pain worse.

"Yes, we went to a therapist," Ellis lied. "It didn't work."

"But this is a terrible time to make a decision like this. Just half a year after your baby was abducted—"

"I really can't talk about this, Dani. I called because I have a huge favor to ask."

"Sure, anything!"

"Can I have my mail sent to your address for a little while?"

"Why do you need to do that?"

"I'm going on a road trip. To clear my head."

"Where? For how long?"

"I don't know."

"You're leaving the boys behind?"

"I have to. It's a mess."

"Did he get custody?"

"Yes."

"Full custody?"

"Yes," Ellis said. "I need to get on the road. Can I give your address to the bank?"

"Ell, you're freaking me out. If you're leaving your kids, something really bad happened. Does Jonah blame you for what happened? He better not, or I'll—"

"No, it's nothing like that."

Another lie. Obviously Jonah—and everyone else—blamed her. She deserved the blame.

"Please just answer," Ellis said. "All you have to do is throw my mail into a box. There won't be much. Just a few bank statements."

"Of course I'll keep your mail. But when will you come get it?"

"I don't know. Are you at the same address I sent the baby announcement to?"

"Yes."

"Thank you. I have to go—"

"Wait!" Dani said. "Will I still be able to call you at this number?"

Tears streamed down Ellis's cheeks. Getting rid of the phone would be cutting the last cord that connected her to Jonah and the boys. And Viola. "No, I won't have a phone for a while."

"Ellis, what's going on? You need to have a phone. I have to know you're okay!"

"I'll let you know when I get a new number. Bye. I love you."

Ellis ended the call.

Her phone service would turn off by the end of the week. Jonah had wanted her to keep it on, even said he would pay, but Ellis had to dump it along with everything else.

With shaky hands, she opened a new bottle of pills and popped one into her mouth. She'd found a doctor at a small clinic who'd given her prescriptions. To help with the stress of her divorce. And her baby's abduction. If she had to spill the gory guts of her life to get the meds, she would.

She entered the bank to deliver her new address. A house in Gainesville, Florida, a town in a distant state she'd never visited.

By the time she left the bank, the pill had taken the edge off. But no amount of pills could prepare her for her last task.

She drove to the first real house she'd ever lived in. She wouldn't miss it. It had always seemed ridiculously large to her: 4,200 square feet, four bedrooms plus an office, four and a half bathrooms, three-car garage. It was surrounded by an acre of lawn and plants that needed too much water, fertilizer, and trimming. Jonah had wanted the house—he'd said they needed a big place because they were having twins—and his mother had agreed. The down payment had been arranged in secret, as a wedding present, which meant Ellis couldn't decline.

Ellis pulled the SUV into the driveway. She was relieved to see Mary Carol's car was gone. She had told Jonah she wanted her gone when she came to see the boys, and for once he had let Ellis have a little bit of control.

Jonah met her on the sidewalk. "I've told them you're leaving. As you asked me to." He needed to remind her it was her idea and not his.

"Thank you," she said.

"Please don't do this," he said.

"You know I have to. You've seen the damage I've done to them."

He didn't disagree. "Why not stay here and check yourself into a recovery program?"

"And have them visit me there, seeing their mother in such bad shape that she had to lock herself up?"

"That's better than *not* seeing their mother."

"Is it?" She thought of those times she'd seen her mother passed out in a pool of vomit, or worse.

"Of course it's better!" he said. "And when you recover, you can buy a place nearby and see them whenever you want. I promise I'll let you."

"How kind of you."

"Ell, come on. You can't leave them."

"I can and I will. I couldn't stop you from wrecking our life, but I will control how it ends. I won't come begging to see my boys with Irene and Mary Carol hovering. I've seen how that goes, and so have you. All the fighting over the kids. The new partners of the divorced couple getting involved. The kids confused by their loyalties. Kids shouldn't be consigned to Hell because their parents made mistakes."

"It doesn't have to be Hell!"

"It will be, the slow-burn kind. And that's almost worse. I've lived it. I know."

"Goddamn it, Ellis! This is not your childhood! It's theirs! You need to get help to see that!"

Tears burned in her eyes. She'd promised herself she wouldn't cry. Not in front of the boys. Not the last time they saw her.

He came closer. He looked about to comfort her with an embrace, but his arms stuck at his sides as if they didn't know how to hold Ellis anymore. Or didn't want to.

"I'm sorry I yelled," he said. "Just . . . please don't go. You'll regret it. You know you will."

"I don't need you to tell me that!" she said. "I left my baby in the woods. I know the regret of leaving a child behind very well. I feel the agony of it in every moment."

"This isn't the same! You don't have to leave your boys to punish yourself. You have to forgive yourself for what happened to Viola."

"Have you? Have you forgiven me?"

Every second that he paused was a knife that drove deeper into her chest.

"I have forgiven you," he replied. "And I have to forgive myself. Now I know how much I was to blame for what happened that day."

"You could only forgive me when you discovered your part in it? Thank you, Jonah. Thank you for the unconditional support for the woman you married."

She pushed past him and strode to the front door.

The boys stood like little soldiers as she entered. She suspected they'd been watching their parents argue from the window. The anxious looks on their faces, the damage already done, reminded her to be strong. If she left now, they could recover.

"Hey, guys," Ellis said, stroking their hair as she often did.

"Hi, Mom," Jasper said.

River said nothing, his lips pressed so tight they were nearly blue. He wouldn't greet her because he was afraid he would cry.

She knelt to their eye level. "I'm going now. I want you to know I love you forever and ever. You know that, right? No matter where I am or where you are, I love you."

"Where will you be?" Jasper asked.

"I'll be in pretty places, getting better. And everything I look at will be for you. Every little flower and tree and bird. I'll be sharing it all with you."

"No you won't," River said bitterly. "Not if we aren't there."

"People who love each other can stay together in other ways. In their hearts."

"A heart is just an ugly lump in our bodies. Grandma showed me the turkey's heart before she cooked it for Thanksgiving."

Ellis put her hand on River's cheek. "I'm sorry you had to see that. Remember, you don't have to do anything you don't want to do. If you don't want to eat animals, say so."

"I don't eat animals," Jasper said. "I didn't want the turkey. I felt sorry for it."

Ellis took him in her arms and held him tight. The sweet smell of him made her dizzy with need. Nothing had ever hurt as much. Might that ugly lump in her body stop beating?

"I love you more than anything," she said into his ear.

"Me too," he said.

When she pulled away from his arms, tears ran down his cheeks. River's tears spilled, too, and he looked angry.

Ellis reached for him. He backed away.

"River, please let me hug you," she said.

"No!" he shouted. "This is all just stupid! I hate you! I hate you!"

He ran away, his little feet pounding up the stairs.

He wanted to do the leaving. To take control as much as possible. She understood. Oh, yes, she understood.

She put a kiss on her palm and placed it on Jasper's wet cheek. "Forever and ever," she said. And she walked out the door.

6

Ellis laid the package of butterscotch candies on Samuel Patrick Abbey's grave. She didn't put anything on his wife's stone. She wouldn't know what to bring her. As with her father, Ellis knew nothing about her grandmother. She'd died long before Ellis went to live with her grandfather at thirteen, and Samuel never talked about his wife. Other than one photograph of her on her wedding day, Margaret Anne Abbey, née Swanson, was thoroughly absent from the small apartment where Samuel had lived for the ten years since he'd become a widower.

Ellis wondered if she'd stop thinking about her children in ten years, if they would be as absent from her world as her grandmother had been for Samuel. It was probably different if the person you were separated from was still alive. Maybe that made it harder to let go.

But for all Ellis knew, Viola was already gone from the earth.

No, Ellis had to believe her daughter was alive. To keep the darkness from overcoming her. The baby was presumed to have been stolen by a woman—and naive or not, Ellis doubted a woman who wanted a baby would have motive to kill her.

A woman was the only lead the detectives had. A couple who'd been hiking saw a woman walking off-trail, and when she'd seen them looking at her, she'd quickly disappeared down a forested ravine. They had no description except that the woman was middle aged and had a blonde ponytail. The couple also said there was a blue sedan in the lot when they arrived, a car that wasn't there when Ellis went back for Viola. Unfortunately, she had been too distracted to notice if the blue car was in the lot when she'd initially come out of the forest with the children.

Ellis took one of the candies out of the bag. She sucked on its buttery sweetness, remembering the day her grandfather had gotten her at the police station after her mother died. She hadn't known anything about him; he'd parted ways with his rebellious daughter long before. Even in his seventies, he was robust, tall and unbent, a former construction worker, and all the more intimidating because he rarely talked. His first real communication with Ellis was handing her a butterscotch candy from his pocket as they left the police station.

During the five years Ellis lived with him, his candy offerings continued, a common communication between them. At first, Sam, as he asked her to call him, acted wary around her, often scrutinizing her silently, probably afraid she'd be like his daughter. But when he saw Ellis mostly kept to herself, did well in school, and helped clean the apartment, he gradually warmed. Ellis knew he'd accepted her when he started inviting her to watch football and baseball games with him. Though a lifelong resident of Youngstown, Ohio, he'd inherited his Pittsburgher father's dedication to the Steelers and Pirates, but he also followed Ohio State football.

Two of Sam's construction friends, Mick and Harry, often came over to watch the games, and when they saw Sam wouldn't, they took it upon themselves to teach Ellis the rules. Ellis liked those times, sitting on the couch with the three men watching sports. Mick always joked, Harry had almost poetic insights about life, and Sam made terse comments that were often unintentionally hilarious.

Ellis had never felt anything like that camaraderie with her mother. Usually she had been too drunk or stoned to share anything real with Ellis, especially during her last years. She mostly alternated between silence and ranting about nothing. Sometimes she'd say strange things she believed to be great wisdom, though they were nothing of the kind. Most of the time, Ellis and her mother had lived in unconnected parallel worlds.

The day before Ellis left Youngstown to attend Cornell University on scholarship, Sam, Mick, and Harry sent her off with a little party. By then, the men were in their eighties. Harry had been diagnosed with lung cancer, and he was soon leaving Youngstown to live with his son. The farewell cake had Steelers and Pirates logos, and Mick and Harry gave Ellis money to help her at college. Sam gave her quite a bit of money, and that week he'd surprised her with an old Chevy sedan to take to Ithaca.

Ellis cried and hugged the three men, and for the hundredth time, Mick said there was no way a girl that sweet could be related to mean old Samuel Abbey.

When Ellis said goodbye to Sam the next day, he said in slow words, "Well . . . I want to say something to you . . ." He paused before he continued. "When you first came here, I didn't know about you. I really didn't. But I soon saw. You're a quality person, Ellis. I'm proud of you. Real proud. I guess I'm going to miss you. I'm going to miss you a lot."

That was possibly the most words he'd ever said to her all at once. And the closest he'd ever come to saying he loved her. Ellis didn't say it either.

But now she knew she had loved him. She'd loved Mick and Harry, too. She wished she'd known how to tell them. All three were dead now.

Ellis swallowed the last tiny sliver of butterscotch candy. "I love you, Sam," she whispered to the grave.

But you were right not to trust me. I'm sorry you can't be proud of me anymore. I'm sorry.

She turned away from Sam. She walked back to the car as light snow began to flutter down. She needed a drink but wouldn't until she returned to the campground. She never drove drunk. She wouldn't risk an accident that might kill someone. A baby, a mother, a grandfather. She'd done enough damage already.

7

"Hello? Hey there!" a man called.

Whoever he was, he was in her campsite. Close to her tent.

"Hello?" he said again.

Ellis shook herself out of the stupor she'd been in for three days. Or was it four?

"If you're in there, please answer," the man said.

"Yes, I'm in here." She fumbled for the hunting knife she'd inherited from Sam. It had been his father's. She kept it in its sheath inside the sleeping bag when she slept.

"I'm a park ranger," the man said. "Are you aware you haven't paid for this campsite for the last three days?"

That meant she'd been there for four days. She'd paid for one day when she arrived.

Ellis kept the knife in her hand just in case. She unzipped the opening enough for them to see each other. He was a tall, dark-eyed man in his late twenties, wearing full ranger gear.

"I'm sorry about that," she said. "I'll pay. I wasn't trying to pull anything."

The man nodded. "I'm relieved to see you're okay. When I first walked up here and no one answered, I was afraid . . . well, you can imagine. Very few people camp here in winter."

Ellis loved that about winter camping. She'd taught herself how to do it when she'd started driving up to the Adirondacks, and she'd taken Jonah when they were dating. Cold camping with a lover was the best. Snuggling under warm blankets while the snow fell outside. The soft walls and warm interior felt like a tiny world born of their two bodies. To make love in a tent in winter felt deliciously primal.

The man wasn't leaving. She slipped on her coat and boots, unzipped the tent door, and clambered into the cold gray morning. She put up her hood to hide her snarl of hair.

The man scrutinized her. She must have looked bad because he appeared concerned. At least that was how she interpreted his gaze.

"Do you need me to pay for the campsite right now—before you leave?"

"No. I'll check the box later today."

"I'm heading out soon. I'll put it in when I leave."

"Sounds good," he said.

He walked toward his truck, turning around halfway. "Would you like a cup of hot coffee? I have a big thermos in here."

"Oh . . . no, but thank you."

"Have some. I promise the cup is clean." He walked away briskly before she could decline again.

She suspected he wanted to make sure she was okay. Maybe it was part of his training: *A winter camper alone could be a bad sign. Could be running from the police. Maybe suicidal. Keep your eye on them.*

"Sugar?" he called out.

Why not accept the coffee? She was dying for a cup. And if he needed to do his good deed for the day, she wouldn't filch his halo.

She replied, "Yes," to the sugar and walked toward him.

"Over there," he said, gesturing at the picnic table in her campsite.

She dusted an inch of snow off the table with her bare hands, and he set down the thermos and two cups. He handed her a few packets of sugar from his pocket.

"Thanks," Ellis said.

She stirred the sugar in with her finger, and he smiled. She dusted more snow off the table and sat on top with her boots resting on the snowy bench. She wrapped her wet hands around the warm cup, thawing their stiffness.

The ranger sat next to her. "I see you're from New York," he said, looking at the plates on her SUV.

"Yes."

He sipped his coffee, waiting for her to say more. "Just passing through Ohio?"

"I am."

They drank in silence for a minute.

He faced her. "I don't mean to pry, but is everything okay? I never saw a woman stay here for four days in winter." He added, "Alone, I mean."

"You usually get groups of women in winter? They come here for a really entertaining ladies' night?"

He smiled. "No."

He seemed like a nice guy. She should go easy on him. Give him something to allay his fears.

"I didn't mean to stay for four days. I came to Ohio to visit two family graves. After the first one . . . I guess I needed some downtime. Before I go to the next."

Next was her mother, a few towns over.

"I'm sorry," he said.

She nodded and huddled over her coffee.

"It's interesting you camp instead of stay in hotels when you're doing that."

He probably thought it odd that a person would stay there when they had enough money to own a fancy new SUV and nice tent. Ellis had purchased her camping equipment with gifts of money from her grandfather throughout college. She had some quality gear she'd gotten on sale. She wondered if the ranger would have offered coffee if she had a crap tent and beater car.

"I don't like hotels," she said. "I prefer the woods."

"I guess I can see that. But be careful. Sometimes we get some odd ones in campgrounds."

"There are odd ones everywhere."

"I know. But here you're completely alone."

She'd heard these warnings since she started camping alone during her college years. Her first roommate fretted and lectured every time Ellis disappeared from the dormitory for the weekend. But Ellis had to get outside and away from people sometimes. She'd needed that since the Wild Wood. During the years she lived with her grandfather, she'd gone to a nearby park to get her green fix.

She slid off the table and handed the empty cup to the ranger.

He smiled at her. "You look more awake now."

"I am. It was good coffee."

"I grind the beans fresh every morning." He held out his gloved hand. "I'm Keith Gephardt."

She shook his hand and said, "Nice to meet you," but didn't give her name.

He got the message. "I'd better get going."

He pulled his wallet out of his back pocket and took out a card. "Here's my cell number," he said. "Maybe if you need to talk after that second grave."

She tried to think what to say. It had been a long time since a man had given her his number. And she didn't know what it meant in such strange circumstances. Was he offering her his number as a park authority who was worried about her or as a man who wanted to have a drink with her?

She felt like she'd been looking into his eyes for too long. Not because his brown irises were beautifully colored or anything like that, but because they had to be the warmest eyes she'd ever seen.

She looked away and took the card.

"You stay safe now." He walked away.

"I will," she said to his back.

He waved before getting in the truck.

As the ranger's truck rumbled out of the campground, Ellis entered the tent and cleaned up with cloths, soap, and water she'd stored in jugs. She detangled her hair as best she could. Since she'd been with Jonah, she'd worn her hair short the way he liked it. Now she was growing it. She hadn't cut it since early in her pregnancy, and it was already down to her shoulders. But it was thick and wavy, would be too difficult to care for while camping. She should cut it off.

No. She wanted to keep growing it. She didn't want to see the woman who'd been deceived by Jonah every time she looked in the mirror.

She went outside to the spigot and washed it. The temperature was in the thirties, and her head felt like a block of ice beneath the frigid water. But the shock of it was oddly satisfying. Strengthening.

She was ready to go home.

8

Ellis had last seen Forest View Trailer Park the day she scattered her mother's ashes in the river behind the trailer. Sam had stood watching, silent as always, his rigid expression betraying nothing of how he felt about his daughter's death. Afterward, they got in his truck, packed with Ellis's few belongings, and left for Youngstown.

The end of her drive was the same route the school bus had taken. She knew it well, but a lot had changed. A new gas station. A strip mall where a woodlot had been. Her favorite ice-cream shop had become a nail salon.

She stopped the car where the entrance to the trailer park should have been. There was a new sidewalk and bus stop with a glass-sheltered bench where the potholed road used to be. Three tall apartment buildings rose up beyond the bus stop.

Ellis drove on until she found an entrance. **River Oaks Apartments. Studio, 1, and 2 bedrooms available. Beautiful river views. Pets welcome. Come take a tour of your new home!**

She wanted to believe she was in the wrong place. It couldn't look this different.

She turned the car into the apartment complex, following the curved road to an asphalt parking lot next to Building One. Where had her trailer been? Where was the forest?

She saw distant bare oaks beyond a large expanse of mowed lawn. The thin strip of trees grew in a sinuous line. That had to be the river.

She drove to the end of the asphalt, parked, and got out. The lawn was planted with a few young trees bound with ropes and stakes. Forest View was really gone. Even the forest. And Edith and Ed, who'd often fed Ellis when she was hungry. Libby and her two little boys. Larry, the Vietnam vet who had a ramp to his trailer for his wheelchair. He used to dump a whole bowl of Halloween candy into Ellis's bag every year. Where had they all gone?

She stepped into the short, snow-dusted grass. She had to see the one thing they couldn't erase. The river.

She walked across the long expanse of mown grass. She didn't understand why they hadn't left more of the forest. A big lawn was expensive to maintain. She supposed the developers had worried the forest would look too wild. Too scary. A place with snakes. A place where criminals might hide.

Ellis almost cried when she saw how few trees the developers had left around the water. They had been removed on the opposite side of the river, too. More lawns, parking lots, and apartment buildings. Over there, the buildings were a different color, probably built by another company.

The river looked much smaller than it had when she was a girl. It was shallow, as it often was in the winter. The water that coursed through the middle of its flat exposed banks was more like a stream than a river. The weak trickle over the rocks sounded sad to Ellis. As if the river knew what it had lost.

She climbed down the bank into the riverbed. The trash was worse than when she'd lived there. More beer bottles and cans. There was more algae on the rocks from pollutants. She walked downstream, hoping to find the place where she'd poured her mother's ashes. A bend to the left, a big log.

She stepped ankle-deep into the water, letting it soak into her hiking boots. The frigid water on her skin felt good. She was with her kin.

The river felt like a father to her. Her firstborn son was named for him. Jonah didn't know how Ellis had chosen the boys' names. He wouldn't have understood. Jasper was named after the only mother that had felt true to Ellis, the wooded earth around the river, especially the stones of the riverbed. So often she had touched, collected, and meditated on those varicolored stones.

Ellis looked around as she walked, hoping to glimpse any of her favorite plants that might have survived the first freezes of the year. She especially wanted to see the heart-shaped leaves of the violet species that used to grow there. There had been purple, lavender, white, and yellow. In college, she'd learned the genus of violets was the beautiful Latin word *Viola*—the only name she'd considered for her daughter.

Jonah had loved the name, too. He'd associated it with the protagonist in *Twelfth Night*, one of his favorite Shakespearean plays. He'd gladly given Ellis full responsibility for naming the boys, as well. His parents had expected their firstborn male would be Jonah IV, but Ellis and Jonah hadn't wanted another child named for the legacy of intolerance associated with the two elder Jonahs. When Ellis had chosen the names River and Jasper, Jonah's parents had been incensed. Mary Carol even caused a scene in the hospital the day Ellis filled out the birth certificates. She'd said Ellis had coerced her son into abandoning family tradition for "her ridiculous hippie names." Ellis hadn't minded taking the blame. She'd told Mary Carol, "If their names upset you, you know where the door is." A nurse had high-fived Ellis when Mary Carol strode out of the room.

Ellis couldn't find any violet plants. They'd gone dormant for the winter or had perished with the removal of the forest.

She'd come to a left bend. She was quite sure that was where she'd scattered her mother's ashes, though the log that had marked the location was gone. She sat down in the river stones and took a few in her fingers. She looked at the river's curve, seeing her first note sail out of sight. *Please come back.*

She thought of Viola, who would never come back. Ellis knew it was true. She would never see her daughter again. No one returned once they disappeared around that bend. Zane had been the first to show her that. From him, she'd learned to be careful of how much she loved anyone.

Ellis didn't remember much about her life before Zane. Before she was in school, he visited the trailer but never stayed overnight. He was a chef, one of her mother's many restaurant friends who came over for parties. But back then, Ellis mostly saw him as her favorite babysitter. A group of friends—six or more—used to take care of Ellis while her mother waitressed, but Zane was the only one who knew how to make the magic.

"What shall we do today, my queen?" he asked when her mother left.

"I don't know."

"You don't know when there are a zillion cool things we can do?"

"What cool things?"

"We can live in the Sahara Desert in a tent. We can go on a safari riding a zebra. We can sail a ship on the stormy Atlantic . . ."

"Okay," Ellis said.

"Which one?"

"All of them."

And so they did. The Sahara was a tent they made with sheets in the backyard. Safari by zebra was her riding on his shoulders as they walked the neighborhood looking for birds and squirrels. And sailing the stormy Atlantic was little boats they made and pushed around in rainwater that collected in the big ditch out front.

Her mother was angry when she came home and saw how muddy Ellis was. "What the hell, Zane? I'm dead tired and those were her last clean clothes. Now I have to go to the Laundromat."

Ellis didn't understand why she said that. Usually she let Ellis wear dirty clothes for weeks.

"I'll take the laundry over," Zane said.

Her mother lit a cigarette, inhaled the smoke deep. "I'm sure you have better things to do on your day off after you watched my kid all day."

He got very close to her. He did that a lot. "I don't," he said. "And when I come back, I'll bring a pizza for all of us. Go put your feet up."

Her mother put her feet up and drank whiskey. Ellis sat on the steps, waiting for Zane to come back. She was afraid to go near her mother when she was in a bad mood. But when Zane returned, he'd make her happier. He'd say, "Come here, gorgeous," and massage her sore feet while they watched TV. Sometimes she took off her shirt and he rubbed her back.

Zane first stayed overnight when Ellis was in kindergarten. That was when he started saying, "I love you, baby," to her mother. Nothing made Ellis happier, because when he said that, he stuck around. He took Ellis and her mother for ice cream and to go swimming at the big lake. Sometimes he brought Ellis fun places when her mother was working, like the night they went to the county fair and rode the Ferris wheel.

He started doing things her mother used to do. When he took Ellis grocery shopping, he let her put things in the cart her mother would never have allowed.

"Oh, we're having Bugles and Cap'n Crunch for dinner?" he'd ask.

"Can we?"

"Why not? That's all the important food groups covered."

He drove her to school all through kindergarten because he said she was too little to ride the bus. One morning, Ellis overheard a teacher ask her kindergarten teacher, "Who is that?" when Zane dropped her off. Her teacher replied, "He's sort of her father."

That had been one of the best moments of her life. To know someone else saw funny, sweet Zane as her sort-of father. From that day on, that was what he was. Almost her father. And that was more than enough for her.

But everything started to change after the accident. When Ellis was six and a half, her mother fell down a stairway while waitressing, breaking her ankle and hurting her back. The restaurant manager fired her and wouldn't let her claim workers' compensation because he said she'd fallen because she was stoned. Ellis's mother hired a lawyer, who said she fell because she worked in hazardous conditions. She carried big trays, and the stairs to the upper dining room were narrow and steep.

The lawyer won, and her mother got money. She could stay home all the time if she wanted. At first, that had seemed good to Ellis. But within a few months, it was bad. Her mother drank more and did more drugs when she didn't have to stay sober for work. She and Zane fought more than usual.

"What did you do all day yesterday?" he asked, sorting through laundry, trying to find clean pants for Ellis.

"You know my back hurts too bad to carry laundry baskets."

"But it didn't hurt too much to drive to the liquor store?"

"Are you accusing me of lying?"

"She has no clean clothes, goddamn it! You're home all day. I've worked five double shifts straight."

"I never asked for your help."

"I know. You just dump this dad shit on me every day!"

Ellis wanted to cry. But if she did, he would get more upset when he saw he'd made her sad. He might leave forever. She clenched every muscle in her body to stop the tears.

"Just get out if you don't like being here!" her mother shouted. "Get out and don't come back!"

"Maybe I will!" he yelled. "I'm tired of this bullshit!"

Those threats always made Ellis feel like her heart was falling out of her chest. She found dirty leggings under her bed and held them up. "I found clean ones, Zane! Will you drive me to the bus stop?"

"Your mother just told me to leave."

"Don't go!" Ellis said, tugging the dirty leggings up her legs. "I'm ready. We can go."

He shot a questioning look at her mother.

"Just take her," her mother grumbled. She wanted to get high rather than do it herself.

In the beginning, her mother could control Zane with the threat of making him leave. He would apologize, nuzzling her, and he would stay. But after the accident, the more her mother got stoned and yelled, the more Zane walked out the door. Once he was away for nine days. But he came back, saying, "I love you, baby," in her mother's ear as he always did, and they went in the bedroom. Ellis heard them laugh and make those other sounds that were a relief, because that meant Zane would stay.

Ellis was eight when her mother started using a new drug she put in her arm with a needle. Zane didn't want her to, and the fighting got even worse. Ellis was afraid Zane would leave for good. He stopped saying, "I love you, baby."

"You need to get help with this," Zane said when he found her mother sprawled in a stupor in her bed.

"With what?" her mother said.

"You know what! You're killing yourself with that shit! And you don't even pretend to take care of Ellis anymore!"

She staggered to her feet. "Get the hell out if you don't like it."

"No, don't," Ellis said, pulling on Zane's hand. "I can take care of myself. I made strawberry Jell-O and put peaches in it. Come see."

He was too upset to look. He gripped her hand and said, "Come on. Let's get a hamburger."

"I didn't say you could take my daughter," her mother called as they went out the door.

Zane muttered curses. He didn't try to make Ellis feel better like he used to. He just stayed quiet and drove her to get food at the drive-through.

"Zane . . . ?"

"What?"

"Are you coming to my play at school tomorrow?"

He paid the woman in the fast-food window. He didn't answer.

"I'm a flower that talks about why people should compost. Are you coming?"

"I don't know, Ell."

"Please?"

His heavy sigh felt like a weight on Ellis's heart. "I'll try to be there," he said.

The next day, Ellis almost couldn't say her lines when she saw Zane wasn't in the audience. She didn't care about the play. She was afraid Zane was gone for good, and all she wanted to do was cry. Her mother wasn't among the smiling parents either. But she'd expected that.

Zane stuck around for another month. A few days after Ellis turned nine, after one of the biggest fights ever, Zane left and never came back. He didn't say goodbye, not to Ellis or to her mother. He just disappeared. Ellis had to listen to her mother say every mean thing she could think of about Zane. Ellis didn't want to hear those things, but her mother never stopped hating him until the day she died.

Her mother died the last month Ellis was in seventh grade. On a Sunday in May, the best month in the Wild Wood. That was when the wildflowers bloomed, and leaves, birds, frogs, and everything else came back. Ellis took a baggie of cereal to the river for her breakfast that morning. As the clouds from the overnight rain cleared away, the rising sun slanted through the newly leafed branches, casting misty shafts of golden light all over the forest. Ellis was too old to believe in magic anymore, but for a little while, she did again. She sat very still and focused. She wanted to make a picture of the sunbeams in her mind. It was all too perfect to forget. When she went home an hour later, her mother still hadn't gotten out of bed. Ellis peeped into her bedroom to ask if she should make a pot of coffee. Her mother lay still and gray in her bed. Dead. Next to her, an empty heroin syringe gleamed in a pool of sunlight coming in through the window.

Ellis sorted through the river stones while reflecting. The one in her hand looked like a face. An old wizened woman, her eyes sunken into folds of skin, her nose grown globular with age. Ellis carefully set down the crone, one of many stones to mark the spot where her mother's ashes had been poured.

She stood and returned to the reality of her missing forest. Her piece of earth, her one true mother, had left her, had disappeared around the bend with everything else. With the ashes. With her paper notes. With Zane and everyone else.

The Wild Wood would never come back, maybe not even *Viola striata*, the common white violet with purple stripes that had been her favorite. All that was left was river and stone. She had named her boys well. They would endure. They would persist without her.

Ellis had one last note to give her woods. She took her phone out of her pocket. She'd planned to bury it under a log or large rock near where she'd poured her mother's ashes. But there were no more logs or big rocks.

Ellis opened her photos. The last one she'd taken was a close-up of Viola's face. Two months old. Then one of Jonah holding her. And River and Jasper cradling her between them on the couch.

She had to stop. If she kept inflicting pain on herself, she might sink too far into it. She might want to disappear down the river, too.

With a touch of her finger, the screen turned black. The glass reflected her face and the few trees that were left to witness her last message. She chose a large rock in the middle of the streaming water.

She lifted it and wedged the phone into the bottom of the streambed. She watched water course over the phone, little bubbles dancing like stars on the black night of the screen. Then she dropped the rock, and it disappeared.

She was not one to pollute waterways, but she didn't see it like that. It was a water burial. The closure of her family. Of her past. Of the future she used to see. Everything she'd ever lost was forever merged in this one piece of earth she'd loved. Even that piece of earth, and her love for it, was now buried there.

She climbed up the riverbank. She was acutely aware of the absence of who she'd been, and the sickening, visceral emptiness expanded with every step away from the river. She was like a cavernous tree, dying from the inside out.

A fortyish woman in a blue beret walked briskly toward her with a dog on a leash. "I saw you come up from the river," she said breathlessly.

"Yes, I was walking," Ellis said.

"Have you heard their plans? They're going to put a fence between us and the river."

Ellis supposed *us* referred to the people who lived in the apartment buildings.

"Some stupid woman from Building Two let her kid fall in the water. Then she complained that the river is a hazard. I hear the boy was in, like, two feet of water. No danger at all."

Ellis had no words.

"Did you know about the fence?" the woman asked.

"No."

"Well, some of us are fighting it. You should come to the meetings. There's a flyer in the lobby of every building." When Ellis didn't respond, the woman said, "They have no right to ruin the river for us. Nature is important for good health. You probably know that if you were walking down there."

"Yes," Ellis said.

"The river and trees are important for those of us who have dogs." The woman patted the dog's head. "Mimi can't go out in the open. She needs privacy to do her business. She heads straight for the trees as soon as we get out. That's one of the reasons I rented here. To walk her by the river."

Ellis vaguely worried she would cry in front of the woman, but she was too hollow to produce tears.

"Speaking of which," the woman said, smiling, "she's gotta go." She let Mimi pull her toward the river.

Ellis quickly turned around. She didn't want her last look at the river and trees to be connected to this woman and her dog's bowel habits. But she supposed that had already happened.

She went back to the car and opened a bottle of pills.

9

The pill took effect as Ellis drove through her former hometown. She'd had to take something to function well enough to operate the car, just enough to deaden her awareness of the abyss she felt within herself. She believed she was safer driving with the drug than without.

She saw almost nothing around her, because she didn't care to see it. She aimed toward a phone store she'd seen on her way in. She would keep a charged phone in the car in case she needed a tow truck or had some other kind of emergency.

And maybe . . .

Maybe the ranger. She'd gotten the idea when she was leaving River Oaks Apartments. The hollowness had mostly erased her by then. She could hardly feel enough body parts to operate the car. And for some reason, she'd thought of the ranger and imagined him touching her. Not sexually. He hadn't looked at her that way. He'd looked at her . . . gently. That was how Ellis would describe the warmth she saw in his gaze. And if he could touch her that way—a soft hand on her hand, even an accidental brush against her body—she hoped she would feel her body again.

She knew all these feelings might be one sided. She didn't trust her ability to read a man these days. Maybe she'd seen only an absence of disapproval in the ranger's gaze. Since the abduction, she'd grown used to people looking at her critically.

She bought a phone and got out of town as fast as she could. The idea of calling Keith Gephardt stayed with her. She was surprised she wanted to ask a stranger to have a drink with her, but she couldn't think of a reason why she shouldn't. Her marriage had been over for much longer than two weeks. Even before she knew it. Calling a man for a drink wouldn't be that weird. It would hardly be a rebound when she hadn't been intimate with a man for more than a year. Just a drink. She sure needed one.

She waited until after sunset, but that happened early up north in the winter. She fueled the car and sat in the station lot drinking water, looking down at the ranger's card.

She took her new phone out of the box. Ellis Rosa Abbey had a new number. A new billing address. She'd even abandoned the Bauhammer name. It had never fit anyway.

She turned on the phone. It had no contacts. No call history. No photographs. Her past was buried far away in a river.

She could do whatever she wanted. She could call the ranger with the gentle look in his eyes, and she would not feel guilty about it.

She pressed his number into the phone. Just when she thought Keith wouldn't answer, he said, "Hello?"

She should have planned what to say.

"Hello?" he said again.

"So where can you get a decent drink around here?" she asked.

After a few seconds, he said, "Do I know you?"

"The odd camper."

Another pause. "I never said *you* were odd."

"But you were probably thinking it."

"Does the odd camper have a name?"

"Ellis."

"Is that a last name?"

"First."

"No last name?"

"Not until I know how you feel about having a drink with an odd camper."

"I've never done it, in all honesty. But I'm open to new experiences."

"My last name is Abbey."

"I think the nurse got your name backward when she put it on the certificate."

"I've heard that joke before," she said.

"Darn, and I thought it was good."

"You'll do better next time."

"So I gather the second grave didn't go well?" he said.

"It went about as badly as it could go."

"I'm trying to imagine that. Did zombies chase you out of the cemetery?"

"That's a pretty good metaphor for what happened."

"What happened?" he asked.

"I can't talk about it until I've had at least one stiff drink."

"Where are you?"

"Somewhere between where I last saw you and the second grave."

"That's real helpful, Ellis."

She liked him saying her name. "I can meet you anywhere."

"Okay, how about Pink Horses?"

"Pink Horses?"

"Yep."

"Please tell me you're not a weirdo who plays with My Little Pony toys."

"Why would that make me weird?"

"Maybe I'd better rethink my evening."

A soft laugh. "Pink Horses is a tavern. I swear. It's not in a town—sort of out in the cornfields. It might be hard to find, but I could text the directions to you."

"Okay. What time?"

"I'll meet you there at seven. Is that too early?"

"Not if they have food."

"They'll have something that's slightly like food."

"That'll do."

"All right, see you soon," he said.

A few minutes later, Keith texted directions to the tavern. It was farther than she thought. An hour away. But if she left right away, she'd be too early. She went to the gas station restroom to change clothes. She exchanged hiking pants for jeans and put on a new T-shirt. She wore the same flannel shirt on top. She didn't want to build up laundry too fast. Her hiking boots had dried, but she put on new socks.

She brushed her teeth and looked in the mirror. Her eyes were bright with nervous excitement. Maybe from the meds, too. She thought she looked better than usual, at least recently. She was glad she'd washed her hair that morning. It had dried well, in soft waves. She had packed no makeup when she left New York, so what the ranger had seen would be what he got.

Back at the car, Ellis looked up campgrounds near Pink Horses. She had to know where she would sleep, how long the drive was, how much she could drink. The campground where she'd met the ranger was forty minutes from the tavern. She didn't want to go back there. There was a small one on a fishing lake only ten miles from Pink Horses. The drive would be on one-lane roads that should be empty on a winter weeknight. Ideal.

She took the drive slow. Light snow was falling. Most of the route was on rural roads. Country houses glittering with Christmas lights lit the dark landscape like jewels. Every one of those houses added weight to her heart. She thought of River and Jasper. They had celebrated their fifth birthday without her. And now Viola was nine months old. Did the woman who had taken her celebrate Christmas? What would she give the baby?

Ellis shouldn't have let her thoughts go there. Any speculation about Viola's abductor inevitably led to visions of abuse. Ellis felt sick, almost had to pull over. She forced positive images to mind, imagined Viola crawling, giggling, pounding the keys of a baby piano like the one the twins had received for their second Christmas.

Tears dripped down her cheeks. Her wrenching need for her baby surprised her with its strength. She turned the radio loud to drown her thoughts.

By the time she arrived at the tavern, also strung with Christmas lights, she felt almost as hollow as she'd been when she left the river. She already needed another pill.

She looked at the old neon sign with two pale pink horses standing on their hind legs, the magenta words PINK HORSES between them. Why was she there? What did she think she was doing meeting a man in her condition? He would ask questions she couldn't answer. He would want to sleep with her, and she wasn't ready. She should leave.

A dark tavern. A drink. The first real food she'd eaten all day. A man who'd been kind enough to give her coffee and companionship when she needed it.

She realized she wanted to be with the man more than she wanted the drink. And that surprised her.

She smoothed her hair in the rearview mirror. Even inside the car, she heard the live country music. The parking lot was full, a sizable crowd for a weekday.

As she entered the tavern, a rich tang of booze wet her tongue. She looked around the dark room, billiard tables to her left, a long bar straight ahead, and a band of two men and a woman playing on a small stage to the right. Ellis scanned the wooden tables scattered throughout the room.

Keith Gephardt was seated facing the doorway. Watching her. He smiled when she found him. She was glad he'd chosen a seat far from the music. That meant he wanted to talk.

She walked over, unzipping her down coat.

"How's it going?" he asked.

"Okay."

He was dressed like her, in jeans, boots, and a light-blue flannel shirt over a white T-shirt. His short brown hair was neater than it had been that morning. But his dark eyes looked the same, warm and inviting.

She hung her coat on the chair next to him at the square table. When she sat down, she noticed the toy. A blue plastic My Little Pony next to his bottle of beer.

"No way!" she said.

He looked at the pony with her. "What? I don't go anywhere without her."

"You promised you weren't a weirdo."

"I did not."

She picked it up. It was old—dirty and scuffed.

He watched her, smiling, and took a sip of his beer.

"I haven't seen one of these for years," she said. "Where did you get it?"

"We bought it for my girlfriend's daughter at a yard sale." He added, "Ex-girlfriend."

"When did you break up?"

"Three months ago."

Well, he certainly wore his heart on his sleeve.

She placed the pony on the table. "Can I ask you something kind of personal?"

He lifted his brows.

"Did you say goodbye to her daughter when you broke up?"

"Of course I did. I'd been with her mother for almost two years."

"Do you still see her daughter?"

"I wanted to, but they moved away. They live in Missouri now."

"You should call her. Let her know you miss her."

"I don't think her mother and new boyfriend would be especially keen on that." He took a long drink of his beer. "You sure dive in deep right off the mark, don't you?"

She pointed to the pony. "You started it."

"It was meant as a joke."

"Was it?"

He leaned toward her. "Ellis Abbey, I think you need a drink. Those graves have made you much too serious."

"I think you're right."

He held up his hand to a passing waitress. "Please bring my friend anything she wants."

The woman smiled and winked at him, obviously knew him. "What would you like?" she asked Ellis.

"How about an old-fashioned? And may I see a menu please?"

"Sure thing."

Keith drank from his beer, appeared unfazed by the lag in their conversation. "You said you wouldn't tell me what happened at the grave until you'd had a drink, so I guess I'll have to wait."

"Are you always this impatient?"

He crossed his arms over his chest and sat back in his chair. "Patience is my virtue, as a matter of fact." He pretended to peer around the tavern while he waited.

"If you must know . . ."

He leaned toward her, elbows on the table.

"It was all gone."

"The grave?"

"There was no grave. It was a forest and river behind where I grew up. I'd put my mother's ashes there when I was thirteen. The whole place is now a bunch of apartment buildings." Saying it out loud to another person made the weight of it diminish.

He put his hand on hers, softly, just as she'd imagined he would. "I'm so sorry." "I guess I should have let you have the drink first."

"I've had a few hours to process that it's gone. It's still strange, though."

"When were you last there?"

"The day I scattered the ashes. I went to live with my grandfather in Youngstown that day. His was the first grave I visited."

His hand was still on hers, and he pressed down on it for a few more seconds before taking it off. "Are you going back to New York now?"

"I'm heading west."

"To where?"

"Wherever the wind blows me."

"Really? You'll be camping?"

She nodded.

"You don't have a job you have to get back to?"

"No."

"Family?"

"Nope."

"How long will you wander?"

"I don't know."

He sat back and stared at her.

"Odd?" she said.

"Brave, interesting . . . and yes, I guess it is considered odd for a woman to do that alone."

"What about for a man to do it alone?"

"Still interesting," he said.

"But not brave or odd?"

"Less so."

She nodded.

"No lecture on double standards?" he asked.

"No, you're right. I agree it's more dangerous for a woman to travel to isolated places than it is for a man. Women got the short end of the evolutionary stick when it comes to body strength. In most cases, a man can physically dominate a woman. And the anatomy of human genitalia makes the disadvantage even worse."

"Are these your usual topics when you first meet someone?"

"I'm sorry. It's my biologist background. I can't help it."

"You're a biologist?" he asked.

"I was supposed to be."

"What happened?"

"Life."

She didn't typically use that cliché, but the reply worked. He didn't pry.

Her drink and menu arrived, and he held up his beer for a toast. "To the most interesting odd camper I ever met."

She touched her glass to his bottle. "To the best My Little Pony weirdo I ever met."

He picked up the pony and said in its ear, "Don't be jealous, darling. You're still number one."

She liked his sense of humor. He reminded her of some of the biology students she and Dani had hung out with at Cornell.

The old-fashioned wasn't the best she'd tasted, but it had the essential ingredient: a big slug of bourbon. She was drinking it too fast. She had to put something in her stomach.

She ordered a salad and grilled cheese sandwich. He ordered a second beer, and she asked for another old-fashioned.

"I guess you needed that drink," he said.

More than he knew. She was feeling good, the pills and alcohol mixing well. And the park ranger was even better than she'd hoped. She was glad she wasn't drinking alone in her tent over at the campground.

"Normally I wouldn't ask this so soon," he said, "but since we've already discussed genitalia, I suppose we know each other well enough for a slow dance."

"We didn't exactly discuss it," she said.

He stood and extended his hand to her. "We can talk more about it while we dance. Come on—I like this song."

Ellis wasn't much for dancing, but she took his hand and went along. She'd asked him out because she wanted him to touch her, after all.

He held her close but didn't press into her. She liked the song, whatever it was. The bourbon was going strong to her head. She let herself relax into its mistiness and the music, movement, and him. He smelled good, very different from Jonah. She started to imagine what it would be like to make love to him.

As if he knew, he tucked her closer. When the song ended, she thought they might kiss. But it was too soon. He put his hand on her cheek and smiled at her.

Ellis returned to the table as drunk on the unaccustomed intimacy as the whiskey. She drank her new cocktail and ate her dinner. For the first time in months, eating didn't feel like something she was forcing on her body. She was almost hungry.

"Where did you study biology?" he asked.

"Cornell."

"How did you decide to go there?"

"It was the best of the schools that gave me a full scholarship."

"Wow, you must be a brain."

"The scholarship was more about economic hardship than academics. I grew up poor, lost my mother at a young age, and moved in with a grandfather who lived on a tiny pension."

"So you aren't at all smart?" he asked with a smile.

"I'm having a drink with a total stranger who carries around a plastic pony. How smart can I be?"

"I'm not a total stranger. We've met, and you've seen me in uniform where I work. You're smarter than you're letting on."

"What about the pony?"

He put his finger to his lips. "We shouldn't talk about the pony in her presence."

"Then let's talk about you. How does a person become a park ranger? Is that a specific program?"

"I have a degree in environmental science, but there are other ways to become a ranger."

"You knew from the start that's what you wanted to be?"

He nodded. "When I was a little kid, I wanted to be a cop—because my grandfather was a police chief. But I was happiest when I was running around the woods and creek of my parents' apple farm. I sort of split the difference and became a ranger."

"You grew up on an apple farm? That sounds idyllic."

"I guess it was."

"Where was that?"

He finished his beer. "A little town in Pennsylvania. Doubt you ever heard of it."

"Pennsylvania? Are you a Steelers fan?"

"Of course. Are you?"

"I had to be to live with my grandpa. His father was a die-hard fan from Pittsburgh."

"Now I see—that side of the family is where you got your smarts."

Ellis smiled at the joke but said no more about that side of her family. She wasn't sure about smarts, but they had gifted her with a predisposition toward addiction.

She finished her food. She wanted to order another drink, but she wondered what he'd think. And there was the matter of driving under the influence. He was sort of a law officer, wasn't he?

He put her dilemma on hold when he asked, "Would you like to dance again?"

She did because the band was playing another slow song.

They danced closer than the last time. Toward the end of the song, he tentatively nuzzled at her neck. She'd never felt anything so delicious.

She arched her neck to let him have more. When the song ended, he leaned in and kissed her. It was more intense than she'd thought it would be. The room, the people, the music, everything disappeared. Everything but him.

When they parted, he looked into her eyes. His irises were dark, his pupils like two black moons in eclipse.

"Would you like to come over to my place for some cognac?" she asked.

He smiled. "Your place? Where would that be?"

"I can't remember the name. Something to do with a lake. It's close. You can drink cognac while I put up the tent."

"I know the campground you're talking about. Wouldn't you rather come to my place?"

"No."

"It's snowing pretty hard out there."

"I know."

He kept staring into her eyes. "Why do I feel like a gorgeous witch is luring me into a dark wood?"

"Good, the spell is working." She took his hand and pulled him toward their table. "Follow at your own risk."

He followed. They paid their bill, put on coats, and went out into the snow.

"Are you sure you don't want to come to my place?" he said. "There's heat there. And electricity. And comfy furniture, flushing toilets—"

"French cognac?"

"I think I'm all out."

"Did you ever drink French cognac in the snowy woods at night?"

"Let me think . . ."

"I haven't either. Let's go."

"You follow me," he said. "I know the best campsite there."

She was glad she didn't have to bother with navigation. She followed him along snowy roads, her windshield wipers swatting at the falling snow. At the entrance to the campground, Keith got out of his car and paid for a campsite. He drove down a winding road and stopped at a wooded campsite that might have a view of the lake, but she couldn't see past the trees through the snow.

She started setting up her camp on autopilot. She lit two battery lanterns, found the tent pad despite the cover of snow, and laid out her insulated undercover. She emptied the tent from its bag on top. Keith tried to help, but Ellis could do it faster without explaining. She got the tent up fast and quickly outfitted it with blankets, pillows, sleeping bag, and other necessities.

She took two cups out of her cooking supply box and found the cognac buried in a box of food supplies. She'd been saving the expensive French cognac for a special occasion. She'd found Jonah's hidden stash of liqueurs when she was packing the few items she'd wanted from his house. He'd hidden it from her in their bedroom closet, and she'd felt no compunction about taking a few bottles.

She turned off one lantern and set the other inside the tent to dim its brightness. She gave Keith his cup of cognac. "What should we toast this time?" she asked.

"Gorgeous witches who lure men into the snowy woods at night?"

She held up her cup. "To gorgeous witches and their equally gorgeous prey."

He tapped his metal cup to hers.

In that setting, the strong, cold brandy tasted like a witch's brew, a magical mix of black-molasses night, falling-sugar snow, and a spice of stars hidden behind the storm.

"Good?" she asked.

"Very." He kissed her, and she tasted the sweetness again on his mouth.

They drank and kissed and drank and kissed until they'd emptied their cups.

"More?" she asked.

"I'd better not. The driving will be hazardous as is."

"You're leaving?"

Rather than answer, he smoothed her hair. It had turned to wet coils in the snow. "I love your hair. It's as wild as you are."

"I'm growing it."

"That will be beautiful. You're soaked. Aren't you cold?"

"Not yet. Are you?"

"No."

"Keith . . . ?"

"Yes?"

"You have to know—if we go in the tent, I'm still leaving tomorrow."

"I supposed that was the deal," he said with an air of wistfulness.

The snow, its muting of the woods, felt like words neither of them could say.

"Are you leaving?" she asked.

"I probably should."

"I understand."

He took her in his arms and held her against his chest. "How did you get like this?"

"Like what?"

"Like here but not here. Like this snow I can't touch without it melting in my hand."

"You become quite the poet when you drink, don't you?"

He held her out and looked into her eyes. "What happened to make you do this?"

"Do what?"

"Go off alone into forests in the middle of winter."

"Why do you think something had to have happened?"

"I saw it first thing this morning. You're sad. Deep down."

"Isn't everyone?"

"I don't know. Maybe."

The snow fell between them.

She kissed his cheek, cold, wet skin prickled with new beard. "I loved being with you tonight. It was more for me than you understand."

"I'm glad you called me."

She kissed him again, briefly, on the lips. "I'm going in the tent. I'm getting cold."

She walked away from him.

"Goodbye, Ellis."

When she unzipped the tent and slipped off her boots, she saw him vanishing into the snowy darkness. She sealed the door before he'd fully disappeared. She took off her clothes and put on thermal underwear, sweatpants, a fleece pullover, and wool socks. She would let her hair dry a little before she put on a hat. She slid into her insulated sleeping bag and turned off the lamp.

She wanted to sleep. Immediately. She didn't want to lie there wanting Keith, or thinking about the River Oaks Apartments, or seeing her phone with pictures of the kids in the river.

But that wasn't how it went for her anymore. Usually she had to take something to get to sleep. She felt around in the darkness for the pill bottle and water.

"Ellis?"

He was standing near the tent. Same as when he'd first called to her that morning.

"I don't care if I'll never see you again," he said. "I want to be with you. If that's what you want, too."

She unzipped the tent. "It's what I want," she said. "I'll even let you bring the pony."

10

Ellis pulled the pony out of her pocket. She set it on a boulder, framed by the snowcapped mountains. Ellis called it *Gep*. The day after she'd spent a snowy night with Keith Gephardt in her tent, she'd found it zipped into the pocket of her down coat. Keith had hidden it there before he left.

At first, the pony's name had been *Gephardt*, but that had become abridged, as had everything in her life as weeks and months went by. "What do you think, Gep?" she asked the pony. "We're at the top. Great view, isn't it?"

The pony gazed silently at the mountains. Ellis took out her water bottle and held it up in a toast. "To ten days of being sober," she said before she drank. "What do you think? Can I do it this time?"

The pony's smile looked more sardonic than supportive.

She hadn't succeeded the first time she tried to get sober, back when she was camping in the mountains of New Mexico. She'd nearly made it to two weeks of sobriety that time. She'd discovered ascents didn't work so well when she was drunk or zoned out on pills. That meant she had two choices: keep to her tent and look longingly at the mountains while she got stoned, or stay sober and climb. But even if she climbed, she'd return exhausted and usually drink a lot in her camp at night.

But this time she was determined. If she could get through this day without pills or alcohol, maybe she was finally strong enough to stay sober.

She said to the pony, "Guess what today is?"

Gep smiled.

"Today is the one-year anniversary of the day I left my baby in the forest."

His blue smile remained.

"Seriously. I put her down in a parking lot and drove away. I left her for some lunatic to find."

Two men and two women came up the trail. They looked at her oddly; maybe they'd heard her talking out loud. Ellis remembered the pony too late.

"I used to have one of those," said a woman with a bear-ear hat.

"That picture will be awesome," the other woman said. "Are you sending it to a little girl?"

"Yes," Ellis said. She took Gep off the rock and stuffed him in her pocket.

Now that the pony was out of the picture, the two couples started taking photos against the boulder. Ellis packed up her stuff and headed back down the mountain.

About a quarter of the way down the switchbacks, Ellis patted her pocket, and when she discovered the zipper open, she panicked for a few seconds. Gep was the one thing she owned that was irreplaceable. She reached in and felt the smooth mane. She zipped the pocket.

Ellis had slept with two men since Keith, and neither had been half as good as the ranger. She found that ironic. The partners she'd met on a trail and in a campground had been much more compatible with her. They wanted sex with minimal emotional connection. Keith was the reverse. He'd mainly wanted connection. He hadn't expected sex when they met in the tavern. He'd even walked away from it initially.

A raven was calling from the forest when she arrived at the campground. She still hated that sound. But another commotion distracted her. A group of six had put up three tents in the two sites next to hers. They were young and loud. Constant laughter and the smell of weed wafted into her camp.

She'd tented near much worse in campgrounds. Ellis might have even been with them, young and spirited, if her life had gone a different way. She mostly resented the noise because she wanted a quiet night on the anniversary of Viola's abduction.

She made a fire and heated a small dinner. A young guy from the adjacent camp walked past and waved at her. She raised her hand in greeting but made as little eye contact as possible.

Ellis sat on a log to eat. She stared into the fire, letting the shape of the flames steer her thoughts. Normally she'd sit by the fire and drink whiskey, but she tried not to think about that. And she tried not to think about where Viola was and what River and Jasper were doing on the other side of the country. They would start kindergarten in the fall. She knew they would do well. But River might have issues if his teacher was overly authoritarian. Ellis hoped Jonah would make sure that didn't happen. Mary Carol wouldn't be careful about that. Or was Irene more their mother now?

She felt like the growing dusk had leaked into her. An awful gloom she felt viscerally. Why had she let herself think about her children? She put down her bowl, unable to finish her food.

God, she needed a drink. But she'd hiked a trail for two days to make sure she couldn't get to her car easily. How could she have believed she'd get through this day without help?

She unzipped her left pocket and took out Gep.

He beamed at her.

"Your incessantly positive attitude makes me want to throw you into the fire," she told him.

She imagined the pony melting into an ooze of blue plastic in the orange flames. Sometimes she thought she should do it, be done with the bizarre addiction.

But there were worse addictions. She smoothed the pony's faded purple mane with her fingers. As Keith had done to her hair in the snow.

"Hey there," someone said.

Ellis looked up. It was the man who'd walked past her campsite earlier. She slid Gep into her pocket and zipped it closed.

"Want to share a joint?" he said.

"No, thanks," she said.

Her stomach plummeted when the man pulled a flask out of his pocket.

"Maybe a drink?"

She thought of what she'd said to River and Jasper. *I'll be in pretty places, getting better.*

But what did it matter what they thought when she'd never see them again? She needed it. Just one more night. To help her through this anniversary.

The man came over to the fire. He held his free hand down toward her, the other clasping the flask. "I'm Caleb."

"Ellis," she said, taking his hand.

"Ellis?"

"Yes."

"Want some?" he asked, holding out the flask.

"No," she said, surprising herself with how firmly she'd spoken.

"It's not drugged or anything." He opened the flask and took a swig, then pointed the open container at her.

"I said *no.*"

He heard the anger in her tone. *"Okaaay."* He slipped the flask into his pocket. "Want to join us next door? We're just talking and whatnot."

It was the *whatnot* that she didn't trust herself with.

"Thank you, but I'm tired," she said. "I'm going to bed soon."

He looked at the small tent she'd packed in. "You all by yourself?"

She'd been asked that question occasionally since she'd started camping and hiking alone in her college years. It always rattled her. She replied as she always did. "Why do you ask that?"

"Well, I saw this beautiful woman over here, and I was wondering if you were with someone. I assumed you were. But I haven't seen anyone. So here I am, making a total ass of myself. I'm sorry. I'll go."

He walked away.

She was afraid she was becoming her mother. A miserable person who poisoned people with her toxic moods.

"I didn't mean to be rude," she said.

He turned around.

"I'm having a bad night."

"Yeah?" he said. "Why?"

"Today is the anniversary of someone dying."

She had no idea why she'd phrased it like that. But it wasn't a lie. One year ago on this day, the person she'd been had died. Maybe her baby, too.

Caleb looked into her eyes. "Shit. Want to talk about it?"

"I can't."

He walked over and sat cross-legged next to the log. "Want to *not* talk about it?"

"That would be better. But nothing to drink. I'm trying to quit."

"Oh god. I'm an ass."

"You didn't know."

He stared at her, genuine concern in his eyes. He was attractive. Thick curls, dark eyes, sculpted face. Young.

"How long have you been in the park?" he asked.

"Two days. What about you?"

"This was our fourth day," he said. "Vacation?"

"No."

"So . . . you're on the road?" he asked.

"I guess so."

"I knew it. I saw a kindred spirit as soon as I set eyes on you. How long have you been wandering?"

"Since December."

"Where have you been?"

"Too many places to name," she said. "New York to New Mexico to California to here—and lots of states in between."

"Awesome. I've been wandering since I was nineteen."

"For how long?"

"Three years. I can't live any other way. None of us is meant to. You know that, right? Agriculture turned us into prisoners. We never wanted to grow crops and live in houses. We were nomads for millions of years."

He adjusted to face her. "You know that feeling you get when you live inside a house for too long? It doesn't matter if it's a little apartment or a house or a mansion. You're gonna feel it. Do you know what I'm talking about?"

She nodded. She had felt it.

"That's your genetic memories making you see, hear, smell, touch, and long for how we lived for hundreds of generations. Inside we're still a nomadic species. All people feel it, but most of them don't know what's making them want something that's always out of reach. They buy fancier cars and bigger houses, but it never makes them feel better. They just keep getting more depressed until they die."

He was more interesting than she'd thought he'd be. And doing a great job of distracting her from thinking about Viola.

He put his hand on her knee. "Hey, I'm sorry. I shouldn't be a downer when you're already down."

"It's all right," she said.

He took his hand off her knee and pulled a paperback out of his pocket. It was a battered copy of *Leaves of Grass* by Walt Whitman. "Do you know 'Song of the Open Road'?"

"A little."

"How about I read it to you? That poem always makes me feel better when things suck."

With his dark, melancholic eyes, Caleb was yet more intriguing. How could she say no to a lovely man reading poetry to her? And maybe more . . .

But Caleb looked like he might be a bit grimy beneath his layers of clothes.

"I'd love to hear you read," she told him. "But now that it's dark, I was going to take a quick bath in the stream. Do you want to come with me?"

He grinned. Ellis had apparently thrown a dry log into his hot spot. His eyes were ablaze. "Yeah, sure," he said. "I love a cold dip in a mountain river. Especially with a beautiful woman."

"And afterward, 'Open Road.'"

He clasped her hand in his. *"Forever alive, forever forward."*

Those words meant more to her than he knew. She had a feeling this night she'd been dreading wouldn't be so bad. Maybe it would even be good.

Caleb kept holding her hand as they walked toward the cascade. The rush of the water rose above all other sounds in the forest. For the first time in a year, Ellis felt like she was moving in the right direction.

PART TWO

DAUGHTER OF RAVEN

1

Mama would be home soon. Raven sensed it. But she couldn't guess what Mama's mood would be. Her temper changed as quickly as the spring weather recently, one day freezing cold, the next warm enough for bare feet.

Mama had left the house in one of her silent, stormy moods. She looked like big billows of dark clouds when she was like that. Before she left for her walk, she'd told Raven she had to do her work. *All of it.*

Raven finished the last math problem. 10 + 12 = 22. Easy. She set her lessons into neat piles in the order she had finished them: reading, science, social studies, and math.

She looked out the window at the rainy gray afternoon. Yes, Mama would be home soon. She didn't know what her mood would be, but she could try to guide it the way she wanted.

She put on rubber boots and a raincoat and walked into the woods. For a moment, she stopped and closed her eyes, picturing what she wanted as Mama had taught her. She imagined Mama coming home smiling. Happy. Talking instead of silent. When the picture was strong, she opened her eyes. She walked slowly, waiting for the earth to show her how to make what she wanted to happen.

That was how Mama had gotten her. She had wanted a baby, wanted one with all her heart and soul, so she asked the earth what she needed to do to bring her one. Mama was good at the Asking. She'd been doing it for many years. But a baby was a very big thing to ask for. Mama had to ask and ask and ask, until one day the earth gave her a dark-eyed daughter, exactly what she wanted. A raven delivered the baby to her. His spirit was Raven's father. That was why she was called Daughter of Raven.

Raven's gaze fell on a stick that looked like a squashed letter *M*. It was a sign. *M* for Mama. She picked up the stick and searched for more signs. She found a greenish stone. Green, Mama's favorite color. Then a tiny white feather. Mama loved birds.

When she saw the little flower pushing through the ground, she knew she had found her Asking place. Mama said she would know when she'd found it if she paid close attention to how her body felt. The right place to ask would make her feel suddenly bright inside, like a fire sparking into life.

Now she had to figure out the best way to ask for what she wanted. She would get better and better at doing that if she kept practicing. Again, she pictured what she wanted: Mama coming home happy.

Raven let the earth guide her Asking. She laid the *M* stick next to the flower. She sensed the feather had to go next. But it was stuck to her skin from the rain. She scraped it off her finger with the green stone, and she liked how it looked when it adhered to the stone's wet surface. She carefully laid stone and feather in a V-shaped space between the flower and the stick. She stayed squatted to study her Asking. It looked good. She felt it was right. Mama said she would know if she listened to her body.

She stood and walked back to the house.

Mama had returned from her walk. Her two braids dripped rain as she leaned over to take off her boots at the back door. When she saw Raven, she smiled, opened her arms, and said, "Come here, sweet Daughter."

2

Raven and Mama were frying venison strips when the alarms went off. The loud beeping that signaled a person coming down their private road always made Raven's heart pound. Mama said someday someone might try to take her away. Modern-day people didn't understand miracles of the earth anymore. They would steal Raven from Mama and make her live with people who didn't practice the ancient ways.

Mama hurried away to look at the video screens, and Raven ran to her hiding place behind a metal grate that looked like a heating duct. She crawled into the little room and pulled the metal door closed.

"Damn it!" Mama said when she looked at the video screens.

Raven's heart beat harder. Had the bad people come to take her?

Mama turned off the alarms. There was loud knocking on the front door, then the sound of Mama's footsteps coming toward the grating instead of going to the door. "Come out, Raven," she said. "It's your aunt."

Raven was relieved, but now she had to prepare for the arguing that always happened when Aunt Sondra visited. Raven hated it. But what she hated more was how Mama changed when her older sister was in their house. She never seemed as sure of herself with Aunt Sondra.

Raven crawled out of the hiding space and carefully closed the grating door tight. Her aunt must never know about the hiding place. She must never know her sister's child was the daughter of a raven's spirit. She was one of the people who didn't believe in the powers of the earth. People in the outer world had to believe Raven had come from her mother's body as most children did. That was why Raven must tell others that she had Mama's last name and was a girl called "Raven Lind."

"The doctor is with her," Mama said.

That meant more needles. Dr. Pat usually came with Aunt Sondra. She was a pediatrician, a person who studied children, Mama said. She always wanted to put medicine in Raven's arms with needles. Mama would argue, but Aunt Sondra and Dr. Pat kept at her until she gave in.

"You know the rules," Mama said before she opened the front door.

"Yes," Raven said.

Mama unbolted the three locks and opened the door.

"Hello, Audrey," Aunt Sondra said to Mama.

"Why have you come?" Mama said.

Aunt Sondra ignored her and pushed into the house with the doctor. She was a big woman with a soft body. Her face looked a little like Mama's, and she had the same creamy skin and pale hair. But she wore her hair short, and Mama usually wore hers in two long braids. Aunt Sondra's eyes were blue, but regular blue. Mama's were white-blue. Raven liked to imagine Mama's eyes had once been sky blue like her sister's, but her time in the spirit world had changed them to look more like starlight.

Aunt Sondra was carrying two paper bags with handles. The doctor had her black leather bag. That was where the needles were.

Aunt Sondra and the doctor looked over Raven the way they always did. As if they expected to find something terribly wrong with her. "How are you, Raven?" Aunt Sondra asked.

"I'm well," Raven said.

"You look well," Dr. Pat said, smiling. "You've grown tall since I last saw you."

"Today is a school day," Aunt Sondra said. "I'm surprised to see you home."

Mama's storm clouds were gathering. Raven wanted to get it all over with fast. She lifted the right sleeve of her shirt all the way up to her shoulder. She turned her bare arm to the doctor and said, "Put the needles in now. Mama and I want to finish cooking, and you have to go."

Mama made a little laugh and put her hand over her mouth.

"It's not funny," Aunt Sondra said. "Are you programming her to say things like that now?"

Mama's storm returned quickly. "My daughter speaks her own mind," she said.

"Why isn't she in school? Patricia gave her the immunizations with the understanding that she would go to school."

"There was no *understanding*," Mama said.

"Now she's missed both kindergarten and first grade," Aunt Sondra said. "She's two years behind children her age."

"Not true," Mama said. "My lessons are better than any school's."

"I study reading, writing, math, science, and social studies," Raven said.

Aunt Sondra didn't even look at Raven. "The importance of school is more than lessons. Patricia and I explained all this the last time we were here. She needs to play with other children. She needs socialization."

"We go to the library," Mama said. "She sees other children there."

"*Sees?* Does she have playdates with them?"

"Playdates!" Mama said with a laugh. "I don't recall I ever had one of those."

"I rest my case," Aunt Sondra said.

Raven didn't understand why Mama suddenly looked about to explode. "Leave my house! I want you to stop interfering with her!" she shouted.

Raven and Dr. Pat backed away from Mama's storm, but Aunt Sondra, as always, stood up to it without fear. "Stop interfering? What about the next time she has a high fever?"

Mama said nothing.

"*You* were the one who brought me into this child's life!" Aunt Sondra said, pointing at Raven. "I wouldn't even know she exists if you hadn't called me that day she was sick. Do you remember that, Audrey? Do you remember how you begged me to come?"

Mama wilted like a flower stuck in a jar without water.

"And just a year later, you called me because she couldn't stop vomiting. Do you know what it's like to get these calls? To think my niece might die because her mother is too stubborn to take her to a doctor? To have to drop everything and rush out here? Do you know how much I pay to fly Patricia here from Chicago?"

"I'm so sorry I've spent some of your millions," Mama said. "Or is it billions now?"

"Just because we have money doesn't mean we should throw it away."

"I'll pay for Patricia to come if it's such a hardship for you," Mama said.

"Why not take her to a doctor in this area?"

"I prefer my life to be separate from this community," Mama said.

"Why, when you live in it? If you can go to the library, you can take her to a pediatrician. You should have a doctor in town, too."

"I need no doctor," Mama said.

"You might one day. And you both should have a dentist. You're on well water without fluoride. She needs fluoride treatment or her teeth will rot."

Mama closed her eyes and put her hands on the sides of her head. She squeezed like she was trying to push out great pain. Usually she was about to have one of her bad moods when she did that. Raven knew it well. Aunt Sondra knew, too, because she looked worried.

"Audrey, I'm only trying to make sure she stays safe and well," she said in a soft voice. "I feel responsibility. She's my niece."

Mama didn't open her eyes or move her hands from her head.

Raven had to do something. Something that would make Mama happy. She said, "Aunt Sondra, I want to show you my lessons."

Mama had told her she should do that. She should show Aunt Sondra that she didn't need to go to school. That was why Raven and Mama had worked so hard on her lessons since her aunt started the arguments about school.

Her aunt said, "I would like to see your lessons. Let's look at them."

Raven knew why she was being nice all of a sudden. She was trying to stop Mama's bad mood, too. She led her aunt to her new desk that looked out a big window at fields and forest. She gathered her lessons from the shelves that had been delivered with her desk.

As Aunt Sondra took the lessons, Dr. Pat came into the room with Mama. Mama looked better.

"Ask her anything from those lessons," Mama said. "I guarantee she knows more than children in public school first grade."

Aunt Sondra sifted through Raven's work. "What's eleven plus ten?" she asked.

"Twenty-one," Raven said.

"What's three times three?"

Raven had no trouble visualizing three threes added together. "Nine," she replied.

"Impressive!" Dr. Pat said.

Aunt Sondra looked at more of Raven's lessons. "Your printing is very good," she said.

"Mama says my spelling is good, too," Raven said.

She nodded, scanning more of the papers. "What state do you live in?"

"Washington," Raven said. "And the capital of Washington is Olympia. The state south of Washington is Oregon. Its capital is Salem."

"Very good," Dr. Pat said.

Aunt Sondra studied the list of books Raven had read. "You've really read all these books?"

"I have. But those Dr. Seuss books are baby books. I can read harder ones."

Aunt Sondra smiled. She turned to some of Raven's science lessons. "It says here you studied evolution last week. Can you explain what that is to me?"

"Sondra . . . ," Dr. Pat said.

"What?"

"Even if she was told about it, explaining it would be too advanced for her age."

"I can," Raven said. "Evolution happens in a lot of years called . . ." What was the word? "Millennia?" she asked Mama.

Mama nodded.

"Plants and animals have something inside them called DNA," Raven continued, "and in the millennia, it keeps changing and making them better at staying alive. That's evolution. It's how we became people from amoebas since the Big Bang."

Aunt Sondra and Dr. Pat smiled. More importantly, Mama smiled. She was happy with Raven's answers.

Aunt Sondra put the stack of lessons on the desk. She squatted to be as tall as Raven and put her hand on her cheek. "You're very talented, Raven. I think you would like school. I hope you and your mother will consider it for next year."

Raven wished she hadn't said that. Mama was frowning again.

"I'm sorry I missed your seventh birthday," Aunt Sondra said. "May I hug you to wish you happy birthday?"

Raven moved into her arms and hugged her. She smelled like strong flower scents, very different from Mama.

"I have a gift for you. Would you like to open it?" Aunt Sondra asked.

Raven looked at Mama. She nodded to say it was all right.

They went back to where Aunt Sondra had set down purple and blue paper bags. Inside the blue bag was lots of crumpled purple paper. Beneath it was a book about planets and stars. There was a second book called *School Is Fun*. It looked like *My First Day of Kindergarten*, another baby book Aunt Sondra had given her.

"And you accuse me of programming her," Mama said.

The last thing in the blue bag was a little backpack with a blue, green, and yellow design of birds flying all over it.

"If you decide to go to school, you can carry your books and papers in here," Aunt Sondra said.

Mama crossed her arms over her chest and pressed her lips together.

Raven hoped there weren't more school things in the purple bag. She pulled the crumpled blue paper out. Beneath it was a pretty pair of tan boots that said UGG on them. And dark-blue leggings and a pale-blue sweater. When she unfolded the sweater, she saw it had a big black bird on the front.

"A raven," Aunt Sondra said. "I had that custom knitted for you."

Raven loved it, but she was afraid to say so until she knew if Mama liked it.

"It's beautiful," Mama said.

"It is," Raven said, hugging it against her chest. "Thank you, Aunt Sondra."

"You're very welcome. I went a little big because I didn't know what size you wear. I emailed your mother to ask, but she didn't answer."

"I don't use email anymore," Mama said.

"That's too bad," Aunt Sondra said. "I'd like to stay in contact with you and Raven."

Mama said nothing.

"I have a gift for you, too," Dr. Pat said. She opened her black doctor's bag and gave Raven a little wrapped box.

Raven took the paper off. Inside was a necklace made of colorful smooth stones.

"Lovely," Mama said.

"I like it," Raven said. "Thank you, Dr. Pat."

Mama smiled at her, happy with her politeness.

"Do I get needles now?" Raven asked when Dr. Pat took her stethoscope out of the bag.

"No, darling, you're up to date on your immunizations," she said.

She was relieved. Not because she cared so much about the needles. It didn't hurt too bad. But Mama always got upset about the medicine.

"I'm only going to give you a wellness exam," Dr. Pat said. "If that's okay with you and your mother." She looked at Mama.

"She's very well, as you can see," she said. "But go ahead, if you must."

Dr. Pat led Raven to the couch. Aunt Sondra wanted Mama to leave the room *to give the doctor and Raven a little privacy*. Mama walked to the far side of the room with her sister but refused to leave.

The doctor made Raven take off everything but her underpants. Raven hugged her arms around her bare chest. She was a little scared. She hoped the doctor would find her to be *very well*. Because Mama had said she was.

"She's a wonderful child," Aunt Sondra said in a low voice to Mama. "And she looks very healthy. Does she like to walk around the property with you?"

Mama kept her eyes on Raven as the doctor listened to her heart with the stethoscope. "Yes," she replied.

"Audrey . . . ," Aunt Sondra said in a quiet voice.

Raven strained to hear.

"You're doing a marvelous job with her schooling. I'm proud of you, but . . ."

Dr. Pat saw that Raven was listening and asked her if she liked playing outside. "Yes," Raven said, her full attention on the conversation across the room.

"Please don't teach her those things you do," Aunt Sondra said.

Mama turned to face her. "What things?"

"You know what," Aunt Sondra said, almost in a whisper. "The magic or whatever you call it."

"I never called it magic," Mama said.

"Your religion, your obsession—I don't know what it is or where you got these ideas, but please don't pull her into it. Living in this isolated way is going to be tough enough for her."

Dr. Pat talked, trying to keep her from hearing, but Raven ignored her. She used the sharp hearing of her father the raven to stay focused on what Mama was saying.

"What do you mean, *tough enough for her*?" Mama asked.

"You know what I mean! She won't fit in. You know how that feels! Don't you want her to feel comfortable in the world when she grows up?"

"I feel very comfortable in the world," Mama said. "I have since I stopped trying to please you and Father. Mother was the only one who understood. She let me be who I am."

"Will you let Raven be who she is?"

Raven's knee felt funny when Dr. Pat tapped it with the rubber hammer, but Raven kept her attention on her aunt and Mama.

"All parents guide their children," Mama said. "You did with Josh. You took him to Bible school and church. You educated him according to your views. You raised him to sit on the board of our father's corporation. How is my parental guidance any different?"

"I didn't *raise* my son to be part of our company," Aunt Sondra said. "He showed clear interest in the business from a young age."

"Are you certain you didn't pull him into your obsession with Father's business—your magic, your religion, or whatever it is you call it?"

Aunt Sondra stared at her with stormy eyes.

Raven smiled. Mama had won. This time, Aunt Sondra hadn't made her into that weak person Raven didn't recognize.

Mama walked over and helped Raven get dressed.

"She's healthy as can be," Dr. Pat said.

"Would you like lunch before you leave?" Mama asked the doctor. "It was nearly done cooking when you arrived."

"It smells delicious," Dr. Pat said.

"It's a deer," Raven said. "Mama and I cut it up ourselves."

Aunt Sondra grimaced. "You kill deer on your property?" she asked Mama.

"Tell the story, Raven," Mama said.

"It got hit by a car," Raven said.

Now both the doctor and her aunt looked upset. "You eat roadkill?" Aunt Sondra asked.

"It was still alive, and the person who hit it drove away," Raven said. "When she died, we brought her home in our truck. We took her out back, and Mama showed me how to cut her into pieces. A lot of her is still in our big freezer."

"Cutting up the deer didn't upset you?" Aunt Sondra asked.

"It was sad that she died young," Raven said, "but I didn't mind the cutting. It's better to use the meat than waste it. And Mama taught me all the parts of her body. She called it a biology lesson."

"How do you know how to butcher a deer?" Aunt Sondra asked Mama.

"I have many talents you know nothing about," Mama said. She gave Raven a secret look, and Raven returned it. Because only they knew Mama could ask the earth for a baby and get one.

"Would you like a venison sandwich before you leave?" Mama asked the two women.

"No, thank you," they said at almost the same time.

Mama showed them out the door. After she fastened all the locks, she knelt and took Raven's two long braids gently into her hands, as she sometimes did. "You've done well, Daughter of Raven," she said. "I'm very proud of you. After we eat, let's walk up the hill trail."

"Will we ask for something?"

"What do you want to ask?"

"For Aunt Sondra to never come back," Raven said.

Mama laughed and tugged her braids. "No, Daughter, we will not ask this of the earth. My sister truly cares about you, though she shouldn't interfere in your upbringing. You have to be careful what you ask for. What if you need her in the future?"

"Why would I need her?"

"If something happens to me, you'll need her help," Mama said in a serious voice.

"What would happen to you?"

"All things pass from this life into the life of the earth. You know this."

Raven's heart hurt just thinking about it. "Nothing will happen to you. And even if something did, I wouldn't need my aunt. I'd go to my father."

Mama smiled. "Oh, would you, now? You'd ask a great and mysterious spirit for help?"

"I would. And he would come, because I'm the best daughter he ever had."

"You certainly are," Mama said, hugging her tight.

3

Raven sat in the bean tent made of branches and looked around at her first garden. The once-brown patch was now green. To put seeds in soil and watch the plants grow was almost as miraculous as Mama asking the earth for a baby and getting one.

She flopped down on her belly and watched a beetle crawl up a leaf of lettuce. Ants scurried busily like people she saw in town. A white butterfly floated over the garden like a cloud.

"Raven," Mama called. "Come here."

Raven got up and met Mama as she came out of the woods from her walk. She had something in her hand. Mama uncurled her fingers, and there in her palm sat a naked baby bird with a few pinfeathers.

"Steller's jay," Mama said. "A raven killed all the babies but this one. It was on the ground beneath the nest."

"Will we feed it like we did with the baby robin?"

"You will," she said. "Because your kin made the bird lose her home and family, you will make amends."

"But won't my father be mad if I help it when his kin wanted to eat it?"

"I considered that before I helped it," she said. "But the raven stared at me as if to give me a message. I believe he wanted me to bring this bird to you. Caring for it by yourself will be like getting lessons from your kin. Ravens and jays are in the same family. Do you remember the name?"

"*Corvidae,*" Raven said.

She nodded. "Maybe the raven wants you to see what it's like to become a bird, to feel closer to your kin." She closed her fingers around the bird. "She needs to be kept warm until she grows feathers. She's been warmed by her nestlings and parents."

"I'll get the pouch." She ran inside to get the "nest" they had used for the robin, a fabric pouch with a foam bottom lined with pieces of soft flannel that could be removed for cleaning. She slung the strap over her neck, slipped on her hiking boots, and went back outside.

Mama gently settled the jay into the fabric pouch. Raven closed the drawstring over her, leaving it open a little. The jay's beady dark eye stared up at her through the opening. "She's scared of me. I think she knows I'm Daughter of Raven."

"Being afraid and staying still are her only hope of survival when she's in the presence of a predator. You'll have to win her trust and make her eat. Do you know what to look for?"

"Insects. Almost all birds feed them to their babies because they have lots of protein." She didn't know what protein was. She only knew it was something people and birds had to eat to live.

"What else will you need?" Mama asked.

"A beak."

"How will you get one?"

"I'll make it out of a stick."

"Do you have your knife?"

Raven pulled her folding knife from her pants pocket and carefully put the pouch inside her shirt, settling the bird against the warmth of her chest.

Mama patted her cheek. "Go to it, Little Mama. I won't see you until twilight. The bird's mother feeds her until the light fades. She has to take advantage of every bit of light she can."

Raven entered the forest with purpose. She must find food for her baby or it would die. She must keep her warm or she would die.

But first she needed a beak. She found a small, sturdy stick and whittled it into a rounded point. Then she rolled over a rotting dead branch. There was a centipede there. Maybe poisonous. She wouldn't feed it to her baby. She rolled over more logs and dug in the leaves, catching a fat cricket. She squeezed its life away. *Please forgive me for returning your spirit to the earth.*

She sat in the leaves and squished the soft part of the dead cricket onto the point of her stick. When she opened the pouch, the nestling scrunched in terror. "I'm your mama. Don't be afraid."

She remembered how they'd gotten the robin to eat the first few times. They had to coax the nestling to open its beak by gently pressing on the hinge at the side of the beak.

She pressed the stick with the cricket on the baby's beak. It wouldn't open. The cricket kept falling off the stick. She tried again and again. "I'm not giving up, baby," she said. "You have to eat."

The bird didn't understand her words. She tried the kissing sound Mama made to make baby birds open their beaks. But the baby was still too scared to eat.

When the bird at last opened her beak wide enough, she pushed the cricket a little way down her throat. The bird swallowed it. Raven smiled. She thought the baby looked surprised that she had been fed by a scary girl. She tucked the pouch nest back into her shirt and went in search of more insects.

She wandered over the land she'd been walking with Mama since before she could remember. The house Mama had built when Raven was a baby sat on ninety acres of woods and fields. There were forested hills they could climb, meadows, and a stream with salmon.

By the time Raven neared the stream, the jay had eaten five or six times. She wasn't yet begging with a wide-open beak, but she didn't fight the food as much. Raven used the kissing sound to tell her food was coming each time she fed her. Soon the baby would know this was the language of her new mama.

Laughter and voices drew Raven's attention away from her search for insects. She crept through the thick shrubs and ferns until she could see who was there. It was three boys, two older, one younger. They were walking in the stream, all wearing shorts and gym shoes. The older boy with pale skin and orangey hair had his shirt off.

"When did this happen?" the shirtless boy asked.

"He came to his first practice two days ago," the other older boy said.

"No way. Chris is a basketball and football guy."

"And really good at baseball. I finally talked him into it."

"What position will he play?"

"Probably third base. He's got a good arm."

"And he's awesome at batting," the younger boy said. "He hit two home runs during practice."

"Our best pitcher was scared to pitch to him," the dark-haired boy said.

The orange-haired boy broke into laughter.

Raven didn't understand anything they were saying. But she wished she did.

The boys had reached the deep pool in the stream. The two wearing T-shirts took them off and tossed them onto the bank.

They all went under the water and came up flinging their wet hair.

"Hoo, that feels good!" one of the older boys shouted.

"Good thing the werewolf died," the other older boy said.

"But may God rest his badass soul."

"We don't know for sure that the werewolf's dead," the younger boy said.

"Are you afraid?" said the orange-haired boy.

"No. I'm just saying we don't know for sure."

"You're scared!"

"Shut up."

The young boy didn't know the other boy had slipped under the water to grab his legs. He screamed because he hadn't been ready for it. The boy standing above the water laughed and shouted, "Werewolf's got you, Jackie!"

Jackie was pulled under the water, struggling with the older boy.

Raven didn't understand what was happening. She left her hiding place to help the young boy, but she didn't know how.

The two boys beneath the water popped to the surface, the older one laughing, the young one shouting, "Jerk!" He splashed the big boy. All three started splashing each other and laughing. The big boy didn't mean to hurt the smaller one, Raven realized.

The young boy called Jackie noticed Raven standing on the shore. He stared at her with wide eyes. Within a few seconds, the two older boys saw her. No one spoke for a long time.

"Hey," the older boy with tan skin and dark hair said to her.

She didn't know what a boy saying "hey" to her meant.

He waded toward her. "Sorry we're in your creek."

"Yeah, sorry," the orange-haired boy said. "We'll go."

Raven didn't want them to go. But the two older boys pulled on their shirts, staring nervously at her. The tall boy with orange hair had pretty blue eyes.

Jackie waded to the creek edge and put on his shirt. He was looking at her the same way the older boys were. She had to say something or they would leave.

"It's not my creek," she said.

"Oh," the dark-haired older boy said. "You aren't the girl who lives with the rich divorced lady?"

Was he talking about Mama? Raven didn't know what *divorced* meant. But she knew *rich* meant a lot of money, and she supposed Mama did have a lot. She'd figured that out the last time her aunt visited.

"I live here," Raven said, "but I don't *own* it. This creek owns itself."

The older boys grinned. "So, like, no one can own the earth and all that?" the orange-haired one asked.

She nodded.

"Her mom needs to meet your mom," the orange-haired boy said.

"Yeah," the other older boy said.

After another silence, he said, "We'd better get going."

"You can swim if you want."

None of the boys said anything. They didn't want to swim in front of her. She would have to leave for them to stay, but she didn't want to. For some reason, she liked to look at them. And she'd liked listening to them when they hadn't known she was there. She wished she hadn't come out of her hiding place.

But now she saw that they expected her to say things to them. Maybe if she did, they would stay. "I like to swim here, too," she said. "But today I was looking for insects."

"Insects?" the orange-haired boy said.

"I'm feeding a bird." She pulled the nest pouch out of her shirt. The boys drew closer as she opened the drawstring to reveal the baby jay.

"What kind?" the older dark-haired boy asked.

"Steller's jay," she said.

"You had it in your shirt to keep it warm?"

"Yes."

"Why did you take it out of its nest?" the orange-haired boy asked.

"A raven killed all the babies but this one."

"Damn ravens," he said.

She didn't like him cursing her father, but she couldn't say anything about that to outsiders. She had promised Mama.

Jackie reached a finger toward the nestling. When the bird opened its beak, he withdrew his hand quickly.

"That's the first time she did that!" Raven said. "She was asking you for food."

"She was?" Jackie said.

"We should give her an insect to show her that was good."

"Where do you find one?"

"Anywhere."

Jackie got out of the creek to help. Raven tucked the bird into her shirt and showed him the best places to look. The other two boys searched with them.

"Here's a moth," the orange-haired boy said. He brought it to Raven with its wings pinched in his fingers.

Raven took the bird out of her shirt and opened the pouch. She pulled her beak stick from her pocket. When she took the moth and softly crushed it, the boys winced. Then she plucked the moth's wings off and smashed its body onto her stick.

"Never saw a girl who'd do that," the orange-haired boy said.

Raven cupped the nest in one hand and brought the insect on the stick toward the bird's beak. The baby looked afraid of all the people standing around. Raven made the kissing noise with her lips. The bird opened its beak, and she quickly thrust it inside. It swallowed the moth and settled back into its nest.

"Cool," Jackie said. "I have a caterpillar." He held the brown insect out in his fingers.

"Do you want to feed her?"

"From my fingers?"

"She's not old enough for that yet."

"You do it," Jackie said, handing her the caterpillar.

The orange-haired boy laughed. "He doesn't want to squish it."

"Yeah? You do it," Jackie said.

"No, thank you," the orange-haired boy said.

Raven killed the caterpillar, put it on the stick, and gave it to Jackie. "Get ready," she said.

Jackie held the food close to the bird's beak as Raven made the kissing noise. The bird opened her beak slightly, but Jackie was too slow, and the caterpillar fell into the nest.

"Oh no," Jackie said.

"That happens sometimes," Raven said. She took the stick, got the bird to open, and pushed the caterpillar far enough down to swallow.

"Okay. I think I've seen enough squished bugs for one day," the orange-haired boy said.

The other older boy grinned.

"What's your name?" Jackie asked.

"Raven," she replied. Mama said she wasn't allowed to tell people her whole name because she must never speak about being the daughter of a raven spirit.

"Are you joking?" the dark-haired boy asked.

"No," she said.

"A bird raising a bird," the orange-haired boy said. "Makes complete sense," he said, grinning at the other older boy.

"I'm Jack," Jackie said.

"But we all call him Jackie," the dark-haired boy said, rubbing his hand in Jackie's wet hair.

Jackie swatted him away.

"I'm Huck, Jackie's brother," the dark-haired boy said. "And this is Reece."

"Nice to meet you," she said, as Mama had taught her.

Reece said, "I'd shake hands, but you have bug guts all over your fingers."

Raven smiled when they all laughed. Now she understood why Aunt Sondra said she should play with other children. It was fun.

"How old are you?" Jackie asked.

"Seven," she said.

"Really? I thought you were older," he said. "I'm eight."

Raven looked at Huck, wondering if she could ask how old he was. He seemed to understand. "Reece and I are ten," he said. "We're babysitting today."

"Shut up," Jackie said.

"We are. Mom said to take you for a walk."

"I go for walks by myself all the time."

"Your mom lets you walk out here alone?" Reece asked Raven.

"Yes."

"You're not afraid?"

"Of what?"

The boys exchanged glances.

"Doesn't your mother warn you about strangers and all that?" Huck said.

Mama certainly did. But Raven couldn't tell them that Mama made her land safe through her communication with the earth spirits. She said they watched over Daughter of Raven, and Raven knew it was true. She used to get scared when Mama left the real world to enter the spirit world, but the spirits had never let anything bad happen to her when Mama was away. If the boys were on Mama's land, the spirits must have guided them there for a good reason. That was why Raven hadn't been scared when she saw them. The only time Raven was afraid on Mama's land was when the house alarms went off.

"She should be afraid of the werewolf," Jackie said.

"What is that?" Raven asked.

"That dog that belonged to Hooper," Huck said.

"Hooper?"

"The guy who lives on the property next to yours," Reece said.

"His dog looked exactly like a wolf," Huck said. "It used to chase us when we tried to cross Hooper's property to come swim here. Jackie and I live on the other side of Hooper, but we don't own any of the creek."

"Nobody does. It owns itself," Reece said.

Raven smiled because she understood he was teasing her.

"Why aren't you at our school?" Jackie asked.

Raven had learned from *My First Day of Kindergarten* and *School Is Fun* that other children took lessons in a room with a teacher.

"I have my lessons at home," she said.

"Oh, one of *those*," Reece said.

"Reece . . . ," Huck said.

"What? She can take a joke. Can't you?"

Raven didn't know how to answer, so she just said, "Yes."

"Will you always do homeschool?" Huck asked.

"I don't know," she said.

"Don't you want to go to our school?" Jackie asked.

"I . . . do," she said.

The two words came out of nowhere. She didn't know why she'd said them. Mama wouldn't like it.

"Then you should go," Jackie said.

She didn't know what to say. She could never even mention school to Mama. It would make her angry the way her aunt did when she talked about it.

Huck looked in her eyes. "Your mom won't let you?"

Raven kept quiet.

"Our mom is the fifth-grade teacher," he said. "She could talk to your mom about it."

"Huck will be in our mom's class this fall," Jackie said.

"I will, too," Reece said, "and it's gonna be *sweeeet*!"

"It's gonna suck," Huck said. "She'll be harder on us than everyone else."

"Not on me," Reece said. "She loves me."

"Nope. You're like family. You're as doomed as I am."

"Crap," Reece said.

Raven liked the way they talked and laughed and made faces at each other. She didn't want them to leave. But her bird baby was restless in her nest. The jay was as eager for insects as Raven was for the boys to stay.

Huck said to Jackie, "Speaking of Mom, we'd better go. She wants us back for dinner early."

"What's she making?" Reece asked.

"Enchiladas."

"Can I stay over?" Reece asked.

"*Vegan* enchiladas," Huck said.

"I know," Reece said. "Your mom's cooking is awesome. I'll be lucky if my mom makes a frozen pizza."

Raven noticed the way Huck looked at Reece, as if he were sorry for him. "Yeah, stay over," he said. "My mom will want you to."

"Because she loves me," Reece said.

Jackie was staring at Raven. He had pretty eyes, big with many colors mixed in. Green, yellow, brown, maybe even some orange. But better than that was the happy way he looked at her. Raven thought that must be how a person looked at a friend, and she had never had a friend before.

"We have to leave," he said.

Raven could tell he didn't want to go. She felt the same. "Can I see you again?" she asked.

His eyes got brighter. "Yeah," he said.

"When?" she asked.

Jackie looked at his brother. Huck shrugged.

"You can swim anytime you want," she said. But she wondered how Mama would react if she saw the boys on her daily walks. The creek was one of her favorite places.

"We'll definitely come back," Jackie said. "Or maybe you could come over sometime. To our house."

Raven noticed Reece and Huck grinning at each other but didn't know what it meant. She was afraid to say she could go to Jackie's house. She had a feeling Mama wouldn't like that. But these boys didn't seem at all aware of her being the daughter of a raven spirit. As long as she kept it secret, why not go to their house?

Huck and Reece walked away. "Let's go, Jackie," Huck said.

Reece turned around and said, "Nice meeting you, Bird Girl."

"It was," Jackie said. "Gotta go. Bye."

"Bye," she said, mimicking his wave.

The boys stepped into the creek because the shores were too thick with shrubs for walking. She watched until they disappeared around the bend.

It was sad but also exciting—because everything they had said and done could not disappear with them.

4

Raven didn't tell Mama about the boys. She felt bad.

But she also felt good. She liked to think about the boys. Just imagining their faces made her happy.

She had gone to the big dictionary that night and looked up some of the words the boys had said. She got frustrated when she couldn't find *warewolf* or *veegin*. She figured out she was spelling *divorst* wrong when she found the word *divorce*. There were two meanings in the dictionary: *To end one's marriage with one's spouse* and *To make or keep separate.* Raven didn't understand the first meaning. She supposed the boys had meant the second meaning when they asked if she was the girl who lived with the rich, divorced lady. Mama kept herself and Raven separate from other people because of the secrets they knew about the earth.

But how had the boys known? It worried her a little.

The next morning, Mama woke Raven at first light. Because that was when mama birds fed their babies. Raven was glad to have an excuse to be away from the house and her lessons. As the day warmed and the baby jay's belly filled, Raven made her way toward the stream. She hoped the boys would swim again. By afternoon, the weather was hot enough.

But they didn't come that day. Or the next. When they hadn't returned on the third day, Raven decided she had to make a serious

Asking. She did it right there next to the stream. That had to be the best place to ask for what she wanted.

Beneath a cedar tree that overhung the water, she put four leaves of different colors in a flower pattern touching each other. Green, yellow, brown, and orange, all the colors in Jackie's eyes. Next to the flower "eye," she put an orange mushroom for Reece with his pretty hair. On the other side of Jackie's eye, she put a brown stone for Huck with his dark eyes and strong body.

She studied her Asking. It seemed to need something more. But what?

It needed her. Of course.

She took out her knife and cut some hair off the end of one braid. She sprinkled the hair over the three boys, bonding her to them. She felt good about it. Very good. She knew they would come back. Tomorrow or the next day.

Baby, as Raven now called her, was crying for food. She had fully accepted Raven as her mama.

As the sun sank behind the wooded hills, Raven made her way back home, searching for insects along the way.

"Look how your baby is growing!" Mama said when she got home. "You're feeding her well. You must be hungry, too."

She was. Mama gave her lunch to take with her when she was out feeding the bird, but it never seemed enough to fill her up.

Raven cleaned Baby's nest and put her on her warming pad for the night. Mama set a big plate of food on the table. Ham, baked potato, squash, and green beans. The delivery from the grocery store had come that day. Mama rarely went out to stores.

They sat across from each other at the table. "What did you see and learn today?" she asked.

"I learned a baby bird is always hungry," she said.

"You have a new appreciation for the work a bird must do. And imagine more than one in the nest."

"That would be so hard!" Raven said.

"What else did you see?"

"I saw a coyote. And a doe with a fawn. I saw many birds. I saw a raven and told him I'm taking good care of the baby he gave me."

Mama smiled and nodded.

"I found a white flower I never saw before. I saw a dead snake being eaten by ants. Oh, and in the morning, there was a spider's web that looked like it had little pieces of glass all over it. It was so pretty."

"Wonderful," Mama said.

Raven looked down at her plate. She felt bad about hiding her Asking from Mama. But she was afraid she would say she must never see the boys again. Raven couldn't let that happen.

Later, Mama tucked her into bed and kissed her cheek. "Good night, Daughter of Raven, my sweet miracle."

"Good night, Mama."

Raven was almost too excited to sleep, thinking about seeing the boys the next day.

But they didn't come. Her Asking was still there next to the stream.

The next day, she went straight to the stream to do all her insect searching. When the sun was high in the sky and Baby slept, Raven ate the lunch Mama had given her. Afterward, she lay down, put her hands under her head, and looked up at the sun shimmering through the cedar branches.

She sat up when someone said, "Hi, Raven."

Jackie and his brother were wading in the stream.

"How's the bird?" Jackie asked as he came closer.

"She's getting big." She held Baby out for him and Huck to see. That woke up Baby and made her beg for food.

"She has lots more feathers," Jackie said.

"She's good with taking the insects now. She thinks I'm her mama."

Huck was looking at Raven curiously. "Were you waiting for us?" he asked.

"Yes."

"For how many days?"

"Every day."

"I told you!" Jackie said.

"Where is Reece?" she asked.

"He's helping his mom today," Huck said.

Baby was calling for food again.

"Want me to help you find something to feed her?" Jackie asked.

"Yes."

Huck sat on the stream bank. "I'm not staying long, Jackie," he said.

His mood wasn't as nice as last time. But that was okay. She was used to that with Mama.

"He's kind of mad about coming here," Jackie whispered near Raven's ear as they walked.

"Why?"

"I don't know. I guess because Reece or one of his other friends isn't here. He kept saying you wouldn't be here, but I had a feeling you would be."

Raven smiled. Her Asking had made him feel that. She had thought of Jackie most when she did the Asking, so it made sense that he was the one who felt it strongly.

They fed Baby a crane fly, a few crickets, and a caterpillar. While the bird slept, they sat on a log. They could see Huck lying on his back next to the stream, but they were out of his hearing.

"How far from here is your house?" Jackie asked.

"It's far, but not *very* far."

"We can't see it from the road when we drive past your place."

He got quiet and twisted the bark off a stick. She had a feeling she was supposed to talk, but she didn't know what to say.

After a little while, he said, "Yesterday when we drove past your gate, I asked my mom if she'd ever seen your house. She said no, but she'd heard it was really nice." He looked at her. "I don't know how she knew that. Maybe the people who built it said that. People around here talk."

Raven had never thought about the people around there. Not until she met the boys.

"My mom said your mom tore down the old house that was here," he said. "You wouldn't remember that because you were a baby. You lived in a trailer she brought in while the house was built."

"What's a *trailer*?"

"A house you can move."

She tried to imagine that.

He threw down the stick he'd been peeling. "My parents are divorced like yours are," he said.

"I looked up that word in our dictionary," she said.

"Divorced?"

She nodded. "What do you mean by it?"

"You don't know? I thought your mom was divorced?"

She was afraid to say anything about Mama's divorce from the outside world.

"It means your mom and dad split up. They don't live with each other anymore. Didn't your mom tell you where your dad went?"

She couldn't say anything about that. She shook her head to say no.

"Do you ever see him?"

Even if she had permission to say, the question was impossible to answer. She saw ravens almost every day, but those birds were not her father. They were an *embodiment* of her father, Mama said. She still didn't understand that word.

He took her silence as a no. "I never see my dad either. He quit coming around when I was little. I don't even remember him."

An idea popped into her mind. Was it possible Jackie and Huck were born of earth spirits? Was that why they also lived in that place and had no father in their house?

"Do you know anything about your father?" she asked.

"No. My mom doesn't like to talk about him. Huck doesn't either."

"What does your father look like?"

He thought about that. "Like Huck, sort of."

Raven looked a little like her father. Dark eyes and hair. Her skin had taken some color from him, too, Mama said.

"How do you know what your father looks like?" she asked.

"From pictures. Didn't your mom keep any pictures of your dad?"

She shook her head.

"She must be really mad at him."

Raven supposed Jackie wasn't the son of an earth spirit if he had pictures of his father and Huck looked like him. But the idea had been nice. She wished she could talk to another person like her.

Jackie got off the log. "Do you want to see something cool?"

He'd used the word *cool* before, and she was pretty sure it didn't mean *cold*.

As they walked back to the stream, he said, "It's more funny than cool, I guess."

Huck stood as Jackie stepped into the stream. "Where are you going?"

"To show her the Wolfsbane," Jackie said. "Your boots will get wet," he told Raven. "You need shoes to walk in this stream. The rocks are killer on bare feet."

She knew that and didn't care if her boots got wet. They got soaked with dew every morning anyway. She wondered what the "wolfsbane" was.

Huck followed them into the creek. "What if she tells her mom?" he asked.

"She won't," Jackie said.

"It's on her property."

Jackie stopped walking and looked at Raven. "You won't tell your mom, will you?"

"No," she said.

"Did you tell her about us swimming in your creek?" Huck asked.

"No."

"You see?" Jackie said to his brother.

"So you didn't tell her about us at all?" Huck asked.

She shook her head.

"We didn't tell our mom either," Jackie said. "We didn't think she'd like that we go far and on other people's land."

Other children kept secrets from their mothers, too. She felt better about not telling Mama.

As they waded downstream, she saw why the boys walked in the water to get to the swimming hole. Both shores were thickets of blackberry thorns and shrubs that made land walking impossible. She had never walked so far downstream.

After a long stretch of shallow water rippling over rocks, then a deeper bend, Raven stopped when she saw the strange thing ahead. The boys grinned at her surprise.

In the middle of another wide, shallow riffle was a stack of objects topped by a small humanlike shape.

"It's better from the front," Jackie said.

She followed the boys to the other side of the thing Jackie had called "wolfsbane." Placed in the middle of the stream were two plastic milk crates, one blue, one red. On top was a boxy thing with broken glass in front. A TV, she guessed, because she'd seen them in pictures in books. Inside the broken TV was a deer skull with only one antler. On top of the TV was a rusty black microwave oven with a shattered glass door. And on top of that was a stone woman. She was carved to look like she was wearing a gown that draped over her hair down to her bare feet. She held her arms out with her palms up, but one arm was broken off at the elbow. The other shoulder had a piece missing. The woman used to be light gray, but now she was mostly green, covered in moss.

"Reece, Huck, and I made this last year," Jackie said. "To scare the werewolf away. Reece calls it the Wolfsbane because it's like that stuff in movies that scares away werewolves."

"Not *stuff,*" Huck said. "Wolfsbane is a plant."

Raven didn't understand any of what they were saying. She felt small in the presence of the stack that stood taller than Huck. The stone lady's green face was the part Raven couldn't stop looking at.

"The dog was chasing us down the stream," Jackie said. "We ran over there," he said, pointing into the woods, "and found a big pile of junk. There's an old car and we hid inside it. But the dog was gone by then."

Raven couldn't see the car or junk he was talking about.

"This is where Hooper's land ends and yours begins," he said. "We built this to be like a jinx to keep the dog away from where we like to swim."

"*Reece and I* built it," Huck corrected. "Because you were so scared and wanted to go home. We had to do something to keep you with us."

"I was not *so* scared," Jackie said.

"You were," Huck said, laughing. "You nearly peed your pants."

"Shut up!" Jackie said.

"It's okay," Huck said. "That dog would scare the pee out of anyone."

Raven looked more closely at the stone lady. Her eyes were looking downward, almost closed.

"Reece found the broken Madonna in the garbage," Jackie said. "That was how he got the idea to make the Wolfsbane. Because she would scare away evil spirits."

Raven pointed to the green woman. "This is called *Madonna?*"

Huck grinned. "You don't know who Madonna is?"

"No."

"She's the mother of Jesus. Don't tell me you don't know who Jesus is."

She shook her head.

"Oh my god!" he said.

"Ignore him," Jackie told Raven.

It was impossible to ignore. There were so many things she didn't understand. And she couldn't ask Mama because she dared not tell her about the boys.

"Do you like it?" Jackie asked.

She sized up the stack of objects, from crates to deer skull to the Madonna. She didn't like it and she didn't *not* like it. It was strange, maybe a little bit frightening.

"I think it's good to scare away something," she said.

"I know, right?" Jackie said. "We never saw the werewolf again since we built it. It totally worked!"

"I think the werewolf died," Huck said. "It's chased Reece and me for two years, and it suddenly disappeared."

"Because of the Wolfsbane," Jackie said.

It was a kind of Asking, Raven realized. She liked it more now that she knew what it was.

"I'm going home," Huck said.

Baby's soft begging sounds grew louder.

"You coming?" Huck asked.

"I'm gonna help her find bugs for the bird first," Jackie said.

"Don't stay too long," Huck said. "If Mom asks where you are, I'll say you're outside. But if she notices you're gone, it's your problem."

Jackie and Raven found insects and fed them to Baby. At first, they talked only a little. But she was afraid he would go away if she didn't say things. She asked him why he wasn't at school, and he said he was on summer vacation. He seemed surprised she didn't know about that.

"Your mom doesn't tell you much, does she?"

Mama told her about much more than he knew. A world he could not see. But Raven was beginning to realize she didn't know much of anything about Jackie's world.

They walked to the trash pile and looked at everything there. They found an old rocking horse and a bicycle with one wheel and two broken computers. There were many cans and bottles and some car tires. Jackie said the trash was on Mama's property but had probably been thrown there by Hooper or someone who lived on one of the two properties before. He said some things in the trash were old. Reece had said the TV they used for the Wolfsbane was *ancient*. The rusted car was from the 1950s, an *Invicta*, he called it. Jackie took her inside the car and showed her the dashboard. He kept saying everything about the car was *cool*.

After exploring the trash, they fed Baby more insects. They saw a kingfisher and tried to find its nest in the stream banks. That had been Raven's idea, and Jackie liked it.

They both knew he'd been at the stream for too long when the light turned a golden color.

"I'd better go," he said. "Huck is covering for me, but my mom might have noticed I'm gone."

"Will she be angry?" she asked.

"Worried," he said. "Doesn't your mom worry when you're gone for so long?"

"She likes me to be outside." She couldn't mention that Mama wanted her to feel close to her kin by learning how to feed a baby bird. Mama wouldn't expect her home until early evening when birds went to roost.

"My mom likes Huck and me to go outside, too," he said. "We aren't allowed to have phones or video games. Or watch a lot of TV. Are you?"

"No," she said. She didn't know what a video game was. There was no TV in her house, but Mama had a phone and computer she used to order things they needed. Raven wasn't allowed to even touch them.

"Do you want to meet again?" Jackie asked.

She got a bursting feeling in her chest and belly. Like sun shining inside her.

"Yes," she said.

"You can't wait for me every day," he said, smiling. "What if we meet at the Wolfsbane on Sunday around lunchtime?"

"Okay," she said.

"Don't forget," he said.

"I won't."

"Bye."

"Bye."

Watching him disappear around the bend of the stream hurt even more than the first time. She felt an aching kind of alone she'd never known before. When the sky turned gray, when it was time for mama birds to go to roost, she returned home. Mama was in a good mood again. She had been for many days in a row.

They ate dinner, and Mama asked the usual questions about what she'd seen and learned. After she told her, leaving out Jackie and Huck, she got brave enough to ask a question.

"Did you ever see a dog by the stream?" she asked.

The surprise she saw in Mama's eyes said she had. "Did you see a dog?"

"I did."

"Last summer?"

"Yes."

"I didn't realize you were going that far last year."

Raven wasn't, but she didn't say so.

Mama clasped Raven's hand on the table. "Have no worries," she said. "That dog won't frighten you again."

"Why not?" In her mind, Raven saw the TV deer spirit, microwave, and green Madonna scaring away the werewolf.

"It attacked me twice," Mama said. "I was afraid for my daughter. To keep her safe, I had to return the dog's spirit to the earth."

"How?" Raven asked.

"With a gun."

"When?"

"Late last summer."

Raven worked to hide her reaction. Except she wasn't sure how she felt about Mama killing the werewolf. If she hadn't, maybe the boys wouldn't have come to the swimming hole.

But Jackie believed his Wolfsbane Asking had made the werewolf go away. And that had made him happy. Raven decided she must never tell him what Mama had done. Because she wanted Jackie to always be happy.

5

Baby called to Raven and Jackie from up in a maple tree. Another Steller's jay heard and attacked her. Baby escaped, flying out of sight.

"Will she be okay?" Jackie asked. He was as worried about her as Raven was. Raven sometimes called him Baby's father, and that always made him smile.

"I hope she will be."

"Will the other birds ever get used to her?" he asked.

"I don't know."

Mama said normally a bird would have the protection of its parents' territory. But when Baby followed Raven around the land, she went through many birds' territories, and sometimes they attacked her. Seeing her chased and never accepted was sad. Even worse, she'd been attacked by a hawk once. Raven never stopped worrying about her. But Mama said that was part of being a mother.

Raven didn't have her raincoat, and the drizzle had soaked her clothes to the skin.

"Do you want to go to my house?" Jackie asked.

They had been meeting at the Wolfsbane for three weeks, but he'd never asked that before.

He looked up at the low gray clouds. "It's not going to stop."

"What about your mom?"

She had learned to use the word *mom* around him. She called Mama that when she was with him, too.

"My mom is really nice. She won't mind," he said.

"You said she would be mad about you coming here."

"We'll say we met closer to my house."

Raven didn't know what to say. She had never left her land when she wasn't with Mama. Would she be safe if she did? And what if Mama found out?

"Come on," he said. "We have a lot of games. Mouse Trap, Chutes and Ladders, Guess Who? Do you like any of those?"

As always, she didn't understand.

He had learned what her silences meant. "You never played those games?"

"No."

"I'll show you."

The rain came down harder. They were getting cold. She either went to his house with him or they each would go home alone.

She didn't want to leave him. "Okay," she said.

Jackie's smile was big. She followed him into the stream. Walking past the Wolfsbane, crossing onto Hooper's land, felt strange. She'd never done that before. She turned around and looked at Madonna. Her outstretched arms seemed to say, *Yes, go that way. Go. Go.*

"Will Baby follow us?" Jackie asked.

"I don't know."

They stayed in the rocky streambed through Hooper's land. The shores were still thick and brambly there. When the creek bent left, Jackie got onshore. They walked through a thicket of white-barked alder trees and followed a footpath into a field.

"That's my house over there," he said.

He pointed at a house on the other side of a wooden fence. It had a metal roof like Mama's, but it was smaller. Mama's house had natural logs on the outside; Jackie's looked like pale yellow planks of wood.

They climbed through the slats of the fence. Raven's stomach was a little bit sick. She hoped Jackie's mother wouldn't be angry. Raven would never bring someone home. There was no way to guess how Mama would react.

They crossed a field of short grass and entered the back door of the house as Raven did at hers. The door opened into a laundry room next to a kitchen. They took off their wet shoes and left them on a rug.

She heard boys laughing in the next room.

"Huck has friends over," Jackie said.

She thought he looked nervous and wondered why.

"Let's go in my room," he said.

He led her to a stairway, hurrying past Huck, Reece, and another boy watching TV in the living room, but the boys saw them.

"It's the bird girl!" Reece said.

"Where're you going so fast?" Huck asked.

Jackie stopped walking. "My room."

Reece and Huck grinned. The boy with dark, tight curls and brown skin was looking at Raven curiously.

"This is Raven," Huck told him. "This is Chris," he said to Raven.

She remembered the boys talking about someone called Chris the first day they'd met. "Nice to meet you, Chris," she said.

Chris only nodded a little. Raven wondered why his mother hadn't taught him what to say when he met a new person.

"Where's your bird?" Reece asked.

"Outside," she said.

"Really? It flies now?"

"Yes."

"Do you still feed it bugs?"

"Sometimes. Mostly I give her peanuts while she learns to find her own food." That was Mama's idea. She'd had unsalted peanuts in the shell delivered to the house.

"Come on," Jackie said to Raven, gesturing up the stairs.

"Jackie . . . ," a woman said. She had come into the living room with a laundry basket in her hands. She stared at Raven.

Raven felt like wings were fluttering inside her chest. She knew the woman was Jackie's mother. He looked like her.

"I didn't know you had a friend over," she said. She put the basket on a chair and walked over. Her face was nice to look at, like Jackie's. She had the same light-tan skin and dark-brown hair. She wore her hair in a ponytail and had on jeans and a blue buttoned shirt with the sleeves rolled to the elbows. Her eyes were green-brown when she came close.

"This is Raven," Jackie said.

"Welcome, Raven. I'm Jackie's mother, Ms. Taft."

"Nice to meet you, Ms. Taft," Raven said.

"And how did you get here?" she asked, smiling.

"She was walking in the woods," Jackie said. "We met out back."

Huck and Reece were grinning again. They knew Jackie was lying to his mother. Raven wondered why it was funny.

"So you live near here?" Jackie's mother asked.

"Yes," Raven said.

"She lives on the other side of Mr. Hooper," Jackie said.

"Does your mother know you're here?" she asked.

"She doesn't need to know," Raven said. "She likes me to go out and do new things."

"But maybe you should call and tell her where you are," Ms. Taft said.

"I can't," Raven said.

"Why not?"

"She doesn't use the phone except to order things."

"Do you know her number?"

Raven shook her head.

Ms. Taft looked at Jackie and raised her eyebrows a little.

"It's okay," Jackie said. "We just came in to get out of the rain for a minute."

"I see that," she said, looking at their clothes dripping puddles onto the floor.

Mama wouldn't like that on her wood floors. "I'll clean it up," Raven said. "Is there a towel in the kitchen?"

"Don't worry about that," Ms. Taft said. "I'll get you some dry clothes. Do you mind wearing something of Jackie's while I put yours in the dryer?"

Raven didn't want to take off her clothes in a strange house. But she was soaked, and anywhere she sat would get wet.

"I'll show you the bathroom," Ms. Taft said. "You can change there."

Raven dressed in gray sweatpants and a dark-blue T-shirt. The T-shirt was one she'd seen Jackie wear. It said MOUNT RAINIER NATIONAL PARK with a drawing of the mountain on it. She took out her braids and spread her hair into waves to help it dry. Jackie said he liked her hair like that.

Ms. Taft gave them hummus, avocado, and vegetable sandwiches. She told Raven they ate *vegan*, food with no animals in it. The hummus tasted strange, but Raven ate it so Ms. Taft would like her.

They went to Jackie's room upstairs after they ate. His room was smaller than hers but nice with its blue walls, ceiling stars, and pictures of things Jackie liked. There were dinosaurs, planets, and Star Wars movie characters. There were a few posters that said Seattle Seahawks, Jackie's favorite football team. Jackie closed the window blinds and turned off the lights to show her how the stars on the ceiling glowed like real stars at night.

Then he showed her how to play Chutes and Ladders. She liked it so much they played twice. They played Candy Land next. Then Mouse Trap, her favorite. Huck came in and asked if they wanted to play soccer. The rain had stopped, and the sun was coming out.

After she changed back into her clothes, she and Jackie went out to the mowed grass behind the house, and the boys explained soccer. They put Jackie and Raven on a team with Huck against Reece and Chris. It didn't work so well because there were supposed to be more people on each team and they had no goalies. Raven liked it, but she couldn't get the ball away from the boys. Jackie also rarely got it, but when he did, he'd pass the ball to her.

After soccer, the boys taught Raven how to play softball. In the second inning, when Raven was in the outfield, Baby flew down to her shoulder and begged for food. The boys gathered round and took turns feeding her peanuts. They said Baby was "cool" and "awesome." Huck and Chris started calling Raven "Bird Girl," same as Reece. Raven liked the attention, even if it made Baby nervous.

Ms. Taft had everyone come inside for dinner. Raven was having so much fun listening to the boys joke and tease she didn't notice the day—the best of her whole life—was ending.

After dessert, Jackie took Raven into the living room. He said, "Reece and Chris are sleeping over, and my mom says you can, too."

"Sleeping over?" Raven said.

Jackie was used to her not knowing things. He never looked surprised now.

"It just means you stay overnight. Like a long playdate."

Playdate. Raven remembered Aunt Sondra had said Raven should have playdates.

"It's really fun," he said. "We play games and watch a movie and stay up late."

Ms. Taft approached. "Would you like to sleep over?" she asked.

"I want to . . . ," Raven said. She couldn't remember ever wanting anything so much. But Mama would be upset if she didn't come home.

"Let's go ask your mother," Ms. Taft said. "I'll drive you over." She had car keys in her hand.

Raven couldn't let her talk to her mother. The alarms would go off, and Mama would get upset and probably mad when she found out Raven had gone to Jackie's house.

Ms. Taft saw Raven's worry. "I can't let you stay unless I ask your mother," she said. "I think I should meet her. She should know where you've been all day."

"I have to go home," Raven said.

"Okay. I'll drive you," she said.

"I'll walk," Raven said.

Jackie, Huck, Reece, and Chris stared at her.

"It's getting dark out," Ms. Taft said. "There's no way I can let you walk that far alone."

There's no way I can let you. That scared Raven. She looked at Jackie. She was afraid she would never see him again if she did what she had to.

"Will you come with me?" Ms. Taft said.

"No. I'm going home."

"Raven . . . honey, you can't—"

The front door was closest. She ran, flung it open, and hurried down the steps. She was halfway to the fence when Reece called out, "Hey! Cinderella! You forgot your boots!"

She ducked through the fence boards and kept running.

6

The next day, Raven went to the Wolfsbane and waited for Jackie for a long time. She wanted to cry when he didn't come. She had ruined everything. She remembered the looks on Ms. Taft's and the boys' faces just before she flew away. As if they were looking at an animal very different from them.

Baby stayed with her more than usual. She seemed to know Raven needed comfort.

Raven should have kept to her kin, the earth and the birds, rather than starting to want people. She felt like a bird around them. Always confused by what they did, always watching their every move, always ready to fly. Even Mama made her feel that way when she was in her moods.

She looked at the Wolfsbane, thinking of Jackie. He was the only person who didn't make her feel like she might need to fly away. She supposed it was the part of her that was a human being that made her like him.

But she wished she didn't. It hurt too much.

"Let's go find you an insect," Raven said to Baby.

She ran away from the Wolfsbane, pretending she was flying, and Baby flew with her.

When she got home, Mama was in a sad mood. Raven was almost more afraid of the sad moods than the angry ones. Mama was lying on the ground by the back door. Her eyes were open, staring up at the sky.

Raven knelt next to her. "I'm home, Mama," she said.

"I'm a bad mother," Mama said without looking at her. "I should have left you in the forest."

"You asked for me. I was yours. You were supposed to take me."

"I did ask for you." Tears pooled in her eyes, and when she closed the lids over them, they squeezed out like two tiny creeks that ran down her cheeks.

"You're a good mother," Raven said. She kissed her cheek. "I'm going to make dinner."

Mama was silent, her eyes closed. It scared Raven. Every time it happened, she was afraid Mama would never open her eyes again.

She went inside and heated leftover casserole in the microwave. When she returned to tell Mama dinner was ready, the sun was behind the trees and hills. "Mama, I'm going to help you get up, okay? You need to go inside."

She tried to lift Mama by her arm, but she wouldn't move. Raven went inside and put some casserole on a plate. She poured a glass of milk and ate sitting next to Mama in the growing darkness.

After she put the dinner things away, she tried to get Mama up again, but she wouldn't move. Raven got two pillows and a blanket. She lifted Mama's head, put a pillow beneath, and spread the blanket over her. She lay down under the blanket with her arm wrapped around Mama. A barred owl talked to Raven for a while, telling her everything would be okay.

She woke in darkness, wet with dew. She put her hand on Mama's cheek. Her skin was cold. "Mama, we have to go inside. Mama, Mama . . ."

She kept at her until finally Mama sat up. Raven took her arm to help her stand and walked her into the house. She led Mama to her bed, put a nightgown on her, and slipped socks on her feet. "I'll make you breakfast," Raven told her.

"No," Mama said, staring.

Raven always wondered what Mama saw when her eyes stared. It had something to do with the earth spirits. Raven was afraid the spirits would one day pull her too far into their world. They would want Mama more and more as she came to know them better.

Raven spent the day keeping Mama in the world of people. She talked to her, brought her water and food, made her go to the toilet. She did her lessons in Mama's bed, telling her about the work as she did it. She read her books.

A few times, Raven went outside to feed Baby. "Mama is with the spirits," Raven told her. "I can't be with you today."

Baby flew down from the tree and perched on the fence that protected the vegetable garden from rabbits and deer. "I wish you knew my way of talking," Raven said. "I would tell you to go to the Wolfsbane and see if Jackie is there. If he is, you could tell him I can't come today. I can't go there until Mama comes back."

Baby tilted her head and looked at Raven, her dark, shiny eyes serious, as if she understood. She opened her wings and lifted off the fence.

"Tell him I'm sorry," Raven called as the blue streak disappeared into the trees.

7

Mama spent almost two days in the world of the spirits. When she returned, she was sad and shaky. Coming back to the world of humans was always hard for her.

The next morning, Raven went to the Wolfsbane. Jackie wasn't there. Baby flew to a tree on Hooper's side of the stream and called to her. Raven thought she wanted her to go to Jackie's house. She walked farther downstream, past the Wolfsbane, saying to Baby, "I can't go there anymore. I ran away from his mother."

Baby kept calling to her.

"No," she said. She turned around and saw it right away, a blue piece of paper stuck onto the deer antler inside the "ancient" TV. The paper had writing on it. She pulled it off. Jackie's printing was bigger and more wobbly than hers. It said, *Meet me at noon Sunday.*

Baby landed on her shoulder.

"Is this why you flew over here? You wanted me to see this?"

Baby made a soft sound and fluttered her wings.

"Thank you for showing me." She gave the bird a peanut.

Raven wasn't sure what day it was. She hoped she hadn't missed Sunday while she was helping Mama. She crumpled the paper and hid it under a log as she walked home.

Mama was in the kitchen cooking. It was nice to see her doing that.

"Did you have a good walk?" Mama asked.

"I did." She couldn't say how wonderful it had been. Because Jackie had written her a note and wanted to see her again.

Raven went to the hanging calendar Mama made her mark every day to teach her about days, weeks, and months. "I forgot to mark my calendar," she said. "Do you know what day it is?"

"I've lost track. Let me see." She went into her office to look at her computer.

"Today is Saturday." She pointed to the day on the calendar.

Raven crossed off the days she'd missed. She wished she could fly like a bird into the next day and see Jackie right away.

She spent the rest of the day at home taking care of the garden and helping Mama do laundry and clean the house. She did lots of lessons to make sure Mama wouldn't make her stay home the next day. She went to bed thinking of Jackie and all the games he'd taught her to play. She looked at her wood ceiling and wished it had glowing stars.

The next day, she left the house before Mama returned from her morning walk with the spirits just in case she asked Raven to do more lessons or housework.

Raven waited for a long time, sitting in the stream pebbles next to the Wolfsbane. When the day grew warm, she took off her boots and put her feet in the water. Baby had taken food at the house that morning but hadn't yet appeared. Raven hoped she was okay.

She and Jackie saw each other at the same time as he came around the bend. He smiled. He was carrying her boots. She stood.

"Hi," he said. "You got my letter?"

"Yes."

"Here are your boots." He looked at the boots she'd taken off. "I guess you didn't need them."

"I have lots of boots." Mama bought her many to make sure she always had dry ones for walking.

He placed the boots next to the other pair. "My mom was afraid you'd need them. She tried to go to your house to give them to you, but there's no way to get in the gate."

Only Mama and Aunt Sondra knew the numbers to make the gate open from the outside.

"What did your mom say when you came home without your shoes?" he asked.

"I told her I lost them when I took them off by the stream." And that had helped her explain why she'd come home late that night. She'd said she was looking for her boots.

"She wasn't mad?"

"No."

"My mom said those are expensive hiking boots."

Raven didn't know what that meant. Mama ordered things and they came to the gate in boxes.

Jackie looked around. "Where's Baby?"

"I don't know."

Raven felt his nervousness. He'd never been like that with her.

"I'm sorry I ran away," she said.

"It's okay."

"Is your mother mad at me?"

"No. Not at all." He picked up a stone and looked at it. "She's more like worried."

"Why?"

He looked up from the stone. "About you. And your mom and everything."

Her mom and *everything*. What did he mean? Had his mother figured out that Raven was the daughter of an earth spirit? The boys never acted like they knew, but maybe a grown-up could see something Raven should have hidden.

"My mom didn't understand why you don't want her to meet your mom."

"My mom doesn't like to meet people."

"Why not?"

She had no answer. Not one she could tell him.

"Reece's dad is dead, and his mom drinks a lot. That's why he kind of lives at our house."

Raven didn't know what *drinks a lot* meant.

"My mom would understand if something like that is happening with your mom," he said.

Ms. Taft wouldn't understand anything about Mama. They almost lived in different worlds.

He held out the stone in his hand. "The white lines on this look like an *R*. For *Raven*."

She took the rock. It did have an *R* on it. She handed it back to him, but he said, "Keep it."

The stone was surely a message from earth spirits. But Raven didn't know what they were saying. She slid the rock into her shorts pocket.

"So . . . my mom wants me to ask you to come over," he said.

"She knows you came here?"

"Not exactly *here*," he said. "She said to invite you over if I see you again. I've been looking for you to tell you."

She felt like two very different birds were inside her. One was happy about going to Jackie's house, swooping around, making her stomach feel funny. The other felt like her heart had dived down into brambles to hide from a predator. Raven was afraid Ms. Taft would try to see Mama again. If Mama found out she'd been keeping Jackie a secret from her, she might close her eyes and never open them.

As if he knew her thoughts, he said, "My mom said she doesn't have to talk to your mom. She just wants to know you're okay."

"I am okay."

"I know. But come over and let my mom see. She's worried about you."

Raven didn't like Ms. Taft being worried about her. Mama was right about the outsiders. They didn't understand anything. They ignored what was important and made trouble about things that didn't matter.

"Okay," she said.

"You'll come to my house?"

"Yes." She would go there and show Ms. Taft she was not a person to worry about. She was Daughter of Raven. Her father was a powerful earth spirit. Her mother walked in a spirit world few knew how to enter. Even if they knew, they would be too scared to go there.

She put on the wet boots and left the pair Jackie had brought on pebbles near the Wolfsbane. When they started walking in the creek, Baby swooped down and landed on her shoulder.

"There you are. Where have you been?"

Jackie petted his finger on Baby's back, and she asked for food. Raven gave him a peanut to feed her, and she flew away.

"Reece is over," Jackie said. "He's been asking about you, too."

"Why?"

"He likes you."

"Why?"

He shot a smile at her as they walked. "I don't know. Everyone likes you. My mom says you have *a powerful presence*. I'm not sure what that means, but she likes you."

Raven didn't know what Ms. Taft meant, either, but the word *powerful* worried her. Possibly Ms. Taft saw some of her spirit side. Raven would have to make sure she acted like a regular girl around her. Maybe she should show her how many school lessons she knew.

They splashed through deeper water in silence. When they got to the alder trees, Raven asked, "Why did you say Reece's mother *drinks a lot*? What does she drink?"

"She's an alcoholic, Reece said."

"What's that?"

"A person who drinks too much beer and whiskey and things like that. She takes drugs, too."

The only drugs Raven knew of were the white pills Mama gave her for fevers. "Why does that make Reece have to stay at your house?"

"Because his mom is wasted a lot of the time. She doesn't take good care of him."

"Wasted?"

"Drunk. High. Haven't you ever seen people like that?"

"No."

He was quiet for a little while. "I guess my mom doesn't need to worry about your mom being like that."

Raven didn't understand any of what he was saying, but she wouldn't ask more. Jackie's house came into view. She had to act like a regular girl who knew all the things other children knew.

8

Huck threw a short pass to Raven. She caught the foam football and ran for the end zone. She was near the line, but when Reece leaped and tagged her, he lost his balance and fell on top of her. Chris had been close behind, and he fell on Reece and Raven. It hurt a little, but she liked feeling the weight of them. And their earth and sweat smell. And them asking if she was okay, and laughing, and saying how tough she was.

Ms. Taft jogged over from her garden. "Are you all right, Raven?"

"She's fine!" Reece said, pulling Raven to her feet.

"It's supposed to be *touch* football, Reece."

"It was an accident."

Ms. Taft gave him a look as she brushed grass and dirt off Raven.

"I'm okay," Raven said. "I don't care about being tackled."

All the boys laughed or smiled. There were seven of them, the most that had ever been at the Taft house at one time. Jackie had invited two boys, and Huck had three friends over. It was a sleepover party, *A Funeral for Summer*, as Reece called it, because school started in a few days.

"Awesome catch," Huck said. He held up his hand, and Raven slapped him five.

"Penalty for Rexes," Jackie said. "Half the distance to the goal line."

The Dacs, short for the Pterodactyls—named for Bird Girl—scored, but the T-Rex team still won the game.

They went inside for dinner. They made their own tacos and burritos from the many bowls of food Ms. Taft set out. At first Raven was surprised to see ground meat, but Jackie told her it was made from plants. Raven had gotten used to the vegan way of eating and even liked it.

The boys turned on a movie about people who could make magic with sticks called wands. The best part was sitting squished on the couch between Jackie and Chris, all the other boys close, joking and teasing, sometimes burping and farting. Raven could burp as loud as any of them when she drank a soda.

"Raven . . . ," Ms. Taft said. "It's getting dark."

Raven had dreaded that moment all day. The party really was a funeral. The most wonderful of all summers had died. Her friends would go to school, and she wouldn't get to see them whenever she wanted.

Even Ms. Taft wouldn't be home now. She was a teacher who had to go to school all day. Jackie and Huck went to after-school care until she was done with her work. Jackie said they didn't get home until dark in winter. That meant Raven wouldn't see them at all on school days. Ms. Taft didn't allow her to walk to or from her house in the dark. That was her one big rule.

When Raven got off the couch, one of the new boys said, "Aren't you sleeping over?"

"No," she said.

"Why not?" he asked.

Reece said, "Her carriage and horses turn into a pumpkin and mice if she doesn't go before dark." He'd said things like that since the day she ran away without her boots. When the sun sank below the trees, he'd say, "Better get going, Cinderella," or "Your carriage is waiting, Cindy."

"Actually, she's a vampire, and it's time for her to feed," Huck said.

"I thought she was a werewolf?" Chris said.

They were making jokes so she wouldn't have to explain to the new boys why she was leaving early. Raven loved them all so much. She didn't want to go. She didn't want school to start.

Jackie stood. "I'll walk you to the fence."

He usually did, but Ms. Taft said, "No. I will. Stay and watch the movie."

The strong way she said it made Jackie say, "Okay," and sit down.

"Bye," Raven said.

All the boys said goodbye.

The sun was already behind the trees, and the clouds were pretty shades of pink and purple.

"Does your mother ask where you've been when you're here?" Ms. Taft asked as they walked to the fence.

Raven didn't know how to answer. Mama had gotten used to Raven being gone all day during the weeks she was feeding Baby, and that had made going to Jackie's house without her knowing easy. One day after Baby learned to feed herself, Mama said, "You are much more at ease alone in the woods since you raised the jay. You must enjoy your time alone with your kin."

"Yes," Raven said. Her stomach felt like a hard knot of wood. Because she hadn't been alone many of those times she was away from Mama's house.

Mama hadn't noticed the flush of guilt Raven felt. She'd beamed, put her hand on Raven's cheek. "I came to know the joys of being alone with the earth when I was about your age. I'm delighted to see you bonding with the spirits. Raising the bird was an important lesson for you."

Ms. Taft stopped waiting for an answer. Like Jackie, she had learned not to press Raven with questions about Mama. "Have you thought about what we talked about last time?" she asked. "About school?"

"I think about it a lot," Raven said.

"Have you talked to your mother?"

"No."

She stopped walking and faced Raven. "I spoke with the principal at the school. Remember I told you that's the person who makes decisions?"

Raven nodded.

"I've told her about you—how advanced your homeschooling has been—and she says she would be willing to let you into second grade. You'd only have to take a few easy tests to prove you can do second-grade work."

"Would I be with Jackie?"

"He's a year older, going into third grade. You would be with children your age in second grade."

"Would I see him?"

"You would see him on the playground. And Huck, Reece, and Chris, too." She smiled. "There aren't many girls your age who can keep up with a pack of older boys like you did today. I'm confident the playground will be easy for you. All of school will be."

Raven wanted to go. She wanted the playground. She even wanted the hard reading and math and tests the boys talked about. She wanted to show everyone she was smart.

"I could talk to your mother about it," Ms. Taft said.

Raven wasn't worried she would force a meeting anymore. She'd let Raven come over all summer without talking to Mama. But it couldn't happen. Just getting in the gate would be a problem. And the alarms. And Mama's surprise when she found out Ms. Taft was Raven's friend. She sometimes thought Ms. Taft knew her better than Mama did. That hurt and felt good at the same time.

"Okay, I can see you don't want me to talk to her," Ms. Taft said. "But please try yourself."

When Raven remained quiet, she said, "I know you want this, Raven. You're young, but you have a right to ask for what you want."

Ask for what you want. Raven knew what she would do. She would do the Asking. She would ask the earth spirits to help her. If Mama could ask for a baby and get one, couldn't her daughter ask for school and get it?

"It's getting dark. You'd better go," Ms. Taft said.

She walked Raven the rest of the way to the fence. Inside the house, the boys burst into laughter. Raven looked at the golden light in the windows of the little yellow house. She wondered what funny thing had been said and who'd said it. Probably Reece. He could always make people laugh.

"Someday you'll have a sleepover," Ms. Taft said.

Raven saw no way that could happen.

Ms. Taft took her in her arms and held her. She did that sometimes since they had learned they could trust each other. Raven held her tight, breathing in the last sweet smells of her and the house for the day. "Ms. Taft . . ."

"Yes?"

"Sometimes I wish I lived here."

Ms. Taft held Raven out in her arms. Tears colored with pink sky wet her eyes. "It's okay to wish that. Sometimes I wish you did, too."

Raven's chest hurt. Like it was pressing too hard on her heart. She slipped through the fence boards and ran. She was far away when she realized she'd forgotten to say goodbye.

9

Jackie and Huck couldn't play. The day after the party, they went to the doctor and shopped for school clothes and supplies. The next day, they had to go to school with their mom while she set up her classroom.

Raven cooked and cleaned with Mama. They discussed her lessons and took walks as they always did. Mama didn't seem to notice that Raven was staying home more in recent days. Even when she was in the same room with Raven, part of her lived in the spirit world. Raven felt more alone than she used to when Mama was away with the spirits. She hadn't known anything was missing from those solitary hours until she met the boys. Their absence was a hollow kind of hurting. It made Raven more certain about making an Asking to go to school.

During her walks with Mama, Raven questioned her to make sure there wasn't more to be learned about how to do an Asking. Mama said she must feel a very strong conviction and confidence in what she wanted. Raven knew she would have no problem with that. She wanted to go to school with the boys and Ms. Taft more than anything.

Mama said once she knew with all her soul what she wanted, the most important part of an Asking was a deep connection to the earth's energy. She told Raven she certainly had that. Mama had started bringing Raven outdoors when she was a little baby. She had put rocks in her tiny fists and let her taste their elemental power. She had carried her up mountains to let her breathe in the scents of the many spirits that lived there. She had rested her on the ground and let tree spirits sing her into sleep.

"Other people put their babies in little prisons called cribs and playpens," Mama had told her. "They keep them locked inside their houses. Your crib and playpen were woods, creeks, and fields. Your one cradle was my arms—but only until you could walk. When you were strong, I set you free."

"I went into the woods alone when I was a baby?" Raven asked.

"No, Daughter. You needed many lessons before you could be left alone. I guided you in the ways of the earth, teaching you what was dangerous and what was good. But while I gave you those lessons, I mostly let you wander. I would test you every day to make sure you knew how to return home."

"When did I first go out alone?"

"Just before you turned six," she said. "Don't you remember that day?"

"The day I left early in the morning when you were asleep?"

"Yes," she said, smiling. "Do you remember what you brought to me when you returned home?"

"A raccoon skull."

She nodded. "The earth spirits were speaking to me through that gift. They said Daughter of Raven was ready to wander like a bold and clever raccoon."

Mama still had that skull. It was on the bone table. That was where they kept the skulls, bones, teeth, carapaces, and shells she used to teach Raven about animals.

The second day after the party at Jackie's house, Raven made her first Asking for school. She did it on the shore of the creek where she'd first met Jackie, Huck, and Reece. Her Asking for the boys to return had been there, and it had been answered very well.

The next day, Raven did another Asking. She made it close to the house to be near Mama while she cooked lunch, hoping its nearness might influence her with more strength. She put all of her wanting into the Asking. Jackie and the boys started school the next day. She would have to talk to Mama that night.

Fortunately, Mama was in a good mood that day. Raven helped her harvest vegetables from the garden and cook them for supper. But she could hardly eat because her stomach was quivery.

When they were almost done eating, she said, "Mama . . . ?"

Mama saw she was afraid. Her star-colored eyes seemed to look straight into Raven's heart.

"What do you want to say, Daughter of Raven?"

Already she sounded almost angry. As if she knew it all before Raven had said it.

Raven thought of Ms. Taft saying, "You're young, but you have a right to ask for what you want."

"I want to go to school," Raven said.

Mama's eyes looked like they did when Aunt Sondra talked about school. "You already go to school," she said.

"I want to go where the other children go to school."

"Why would you want this? Are my lessons not enough?"

"They're good lessons! I know more than most kids my age."

Mama jumped to her feet. "Who told you that? Who have you been talking to?"

Raven froze, unable to speak. Mama's eyes. They looked so cold, more like ice than starlight.

"Who have you been talking to?" Mama shouted.

"I haven't—"

"Don't lie to me! I have never heard you say that word *kids* before! Where did you hear it?"

Raven thought of Jackie. She would not let Mama keep her from him.

139

She stood. "I met a boy."

"A boy! Where?"

"He came to swim at the big pool in the creek."

"When was this?"

"I don't know. When Baby was in her nest."

"Was the boy with another boy?"

"Two others."

"Did one have red hair?"

"Yes."

"I saw them there last summer," Mama said. "I let them be because they have as much right to earth's gifts as we do. You should have let them be as well. I've told you this!"

"You never told me I can't talk to people. You only said not to talk about earth spirits and my father."

"And you didn't?"

"I know not to, Mama!"

"How long did you speak to them? Why would they tell you to go to school?"

"I made friends with them. That's why they want me to go to their school."

Mama stepped closer, her eyes so cold Raven could feel their chill. "Friendship doesn't happen in one meeting."

"It did happen in one meeting. I wanted to see them again. I wanted it so bad, I did an Asking."

Her eyes went wide. "An Asking!"

"Yes, and I used my hair. The most powerful tool. And it worked. I bonded them to me."

Mama's mouth hung open.

Her surprise made Raven feel strong. "I go to their house," she said. "I made friends with their mother. She's a teacher at the school. She told me I'm far in my lessons. She said I can go to second grade."

The storm in Mama's eyes was as bad as Raven had ever seen.

"You went to their house and spoke to their mother?" she shouted. "This is reckless! She might have stolen you and made you live with terrible people!"

"She doesn't know anything about the spirits. None of them does! Like you said!"

"Yes, and you'll become like them! You'll want nothing but TVs and video games! They'll undo everything I've taught you!"

"They won't! I'm good at what you taught me. I work hard at it. Yesterday and today I did Askings!"

"For what did you ask twice?"

"To go to school."

"To influence me to let you go to school?"

"Yes."

"You would use my spiritual knowledge against me?" she shouted. Raven's heart pounded so hard, it made her body shudder. She wanted to run away from Mama's fury. But she thought of Jackie and tried to be strong.

"Mama . . . you said I should practice. You said when I knew with all my soul what I wanted, I could make an Asking."

"You're a child who doesn't know what her soul wants!" she shouted. "But even worse, you've been lying to me all these days! I saw something was different with you, but I thought it was maturity. And all this time it was these stupid boys!"

"They aren't stupid! They're smart and they're nice!"

"Get away from me!" she shouted. "I want you out of my sight!"

She had never said that. Not in the worst of her moods. Tears seemed to squeeze out of Raven's heart all the way up to her eyes.

"I said go!" Mama screamed.

Raven ran out of the house. Toward the stream. She had good moonlight to see by.

She stopped running when her feet stung from pounding over stones and sticks. She had only socks on. She walked to the stream and sat on the bank with her knees under her chin.

She didn't understand how two Askings she'd made with all her soul could have gone so bad. Mama hadn't been at all giving. Not the tiniest bit. It made no sense. She was the daughter of a powerful earth spirit. Why hadn't he helped her?

She got up and walked to the place where she'd made her first Asking to go to school. Moonlight glowed upon her careful arrangement of stones, flowers, and leaves. She kicked and made it all scatter.

She stepped into the creek and walked downstream. The water was cold, made her feet numb. When she came to the Wolfsbane, she walked to its front side. The moon shined on it. The deer skull in the TV shined brightest because it was white, and the black holes of its eye sockets were a little scary in the moonlight. Raven thought maybe the deer spirit was mad at her for using Mama's spiritual knowledge against her.

She looked at Madonna's face, but it was almost too dark with moss to see. Raven took off one of her wet socks and gently scrubbed at the moss on the lady's face until she could see it. When she was done, Madonna's face glowed pale gray. It had creek water shining on it like tears. She looked as sad as Raven felt.

"I only wanted to go to school like everyone else," Raven told her. "I thought Mama would see that if I told her about the Askings. She would know I wanted school as much as she wanted a baby."

Madonna had nothing to say.

The creek was the only spirit in the forest that spoke to what Raven had said. Its trickle sounded like it always did, in a hurry to go where it was going. It didn't seem mad at her, but it didn't comfort her either. Creek water moved too fast to much care about anything it passed.

A dog barked far away in the direction of Jackie's house. Raven thought of the werewolf. Since she'd gotten to know the boys, she'd learned a werewolf was a person who turned into a wolf on nights of the full moon. It was only a made-up story, the boys said. But if they believed it wasn't real, why had they built the Wolfsbane to scare away the werewolf?

The dog kept barking. Raven wanted her bed. She was cold. The warmth of summer had gone away with the boys.

She looked toward home. Mama had told her to go from her sight. Raven couldn't go back or even be seen.

She walked toward Jackie's house. When she got to the fence between Hooper and Taft land, she sat in the tall grass. She stayed on Hooper's side, looking through the fence at the glowing windows of Jackie's house.

She woke shaking with chills. She couldn't stop her jaw from bouncing her teeth together. They rattled like a woodpecker drumming on wood.

Jackie's house was dark. Only the front porch light was on. Raven imagined Jackie asleep in his bed with the fake stars shining over him. She imagined getting under his blanket and feeling how warm he was. She imagined him saying, "It's okay, Raven. Everything will be okay."

She slid through the fence rails. She was so cold, she could hardly think what to do. She only could go to Jackie.

The moon shined down on his little yellow house like it was a pretty drawing in a book. She walked quietly to the back door. It was locked. She went to the rooster statue where they hid the key and found it underneath. Her hand was shaking so much, she could hardly get the key in the lock.

The heat in the house felt good. Raven crept toward the stairs, trying not to creak the old wood floors. Ms. Taft slept in the big bedroom downstairs. Jackie and Huck were in the small rooms upstairs. Raven made it to the stairs without making any noise, but the steps squeaked a few times as she went up.

Jackie's door was open, and a little light was on in the bathroom he shared with Huck. She went in Jackie's room and softly closed the door behind her.

"Jackie," she whispered, touching his arm.

"What?" he said in a sleepy voice.

"I'm cold," she said.

He sat up and looked at her. "Raven?"

"Shh!"

"What are you doing here?"

"I asked my mother if I could go to school."

"What happened?"

"She got mad. She said to get out of her sight."

He stared at her, his face white in the moonlight.

"I'm so cold. Can I come under the blanket?"

"You've been outside all night?"

"Yes."

"We need to tell my mom!"

"No! She'll take me home! There will be a big fight!"

"Raven—"

"Please don't tell her! I only want to get warm for a little while."

He moved back in the bed and held up the covers. She took off her soaked socks and lay down with her back to him. He dropped the covers over her. It felt so good.

"You're wet," he said.

"From the creek and grass."

"Are you shaking?"

"Yes."

He put his arm around her. "Is that better?"

"Yes."

They didn't say anything for a long time. Her shaking stopped.

"Why aren't your stars shining?" she asked.

"They absorb light and lose it after a while at night."

144

"Why?"

"I don't know."

She was glad real stars didn't lose their light.

"What will we say in the morning?" he asked.

"I'll leave before your mom sees me."

"We should tell her."

"No."

The soft whir of heat blowing into the room made her sleepy.

"I guess you finally got your sleepover," he said.

"I wanted it to be fun," she said, almost crying.

He pulled her in tighter. "Well, it's nice . . . that you're here."

"Is it?"

"Yeah. I always wanted you to stay over."

She would never be able to again. She would have to be like the stars on his ceiling, absorb the glowy feeling for as long as it lasted. After that, everything would go dark. Probably forever.

She fell asleep before she got to absorb enough of being with Jackie in his room at night. She woke to the smell of coffee and the sound of Ms. Taft clinking dishes downstairs. The sun was already making the sky gray.

She climbed out of the bed and looked down the stairs. She was trapped. Ms. Taft would see her if she tried to leave. She went back to Jackie's room and closed the door, sitting on his beanbag chair, watching him sleep. She put on her socks, now mostly dry.

The stairs creaked. Ms. Taft was coming. Raven ran into the closet and closed the door.

She heard Ms. Taft in Huck's room saying, "Time to get up, Huck. First day of school. You have a really great teacher this year."

Huck made a sleepy, groaning sound. He acted like he didn't want his mother to be his teacher, but Raven had figured out that he and Reece were glad about it. Raven would give anything to have lessons with Ms. Taft.

Next Ms. Taft came in Jackie's room. "Time to get up, Jackie. First day of school, sweetheart."

Jackie must have gotten out of bed fast because she said, "Wow, you're bright eyed and bushy tailed this morning. Do you know what you'll wear?"

"Yes," he said.

When Raven heard the door close, she peeked out of the closet. Jackie stared at her with wide eyes.

"I forgot to get up," she said. "Will your mom come upstairs again?"

"Not unless Huck doesn't get out of bed."

"Go wake him up."

"He's probably awake. He usually gets up faster than I do."

The door opened too quickly for Raven to hide. "Who are you talking to?" Huck said, bursting in. He gaped at Raven.

"Shh! Close the door!" Jackie said.

Huck closed it behind him. "Why are you here?" he whispered.

"I was cold," she said.

"Her mom made her leave her house last night," Jackie said. "She was mad because Raven asked to go to school."

"Oh my god," Huck said. "Did she hit you or anything?"

Raven shook her head.

"Don't tell Mom," Jackie said.

"If she finds out, she'll probably call the police," Huck said.

"The police!" Jackie said.

"Yeah. It's illegal to treat your kid like that."

Raven's stomach felt sick, and her legs were wobbly.

Huck saw how scared she was. "I won't tell her," he said. He looked out the door to make sure his mother was downstairs. "Stay up here while we have breakfast and leave after we go. Use the back door and make sure you lock it behind you. The key is under the rooster."

"Can I get dressed in your room?" Jackie asked.

Huck smiled. "Yeah."

Jackie got his clothes and backpack and left the room. Raven sat in the closet in case Ms. Taft came back. After the boys had been downstairs for a while, Huck came back and whispered, "Raven!"

She peeked around the door.

He held out a bowl. "Here's something to eat."

It was oatmeal with strawberries and sweet soy milk.

"Clean the bowl before you leave or she might get suspicious," he said.

"Okay."

"Are you going home when you leave?"

"I don't know."

"Don't run away or anything," he said. "My mom will help."

Raven knew she would, but her help could only make everything worse.

"Let's go, Huck!" Ms. Taft called up the stairs.

"Bye," he said.

"Bye."

When she heard their car pull away, she sat down to eat the oatmeal. But being in the house without them was too sad. She had to leave that terrible silence. She flushed most of the oatmeal down the toilet, washed the bowl, and put it in the cupboard. Then she left and locked the door, placing the key under the rooster.

She walked toward her house because she was cold and there was nowhere else to go. The morning was gray and chilly. The leaves were starting to turn colors. The spirits of the earth were telling her that everything was changing.

She sloshed in her stocking feet through the stream, stopping at the Wolfsbane. Madonna looked very different without the moss on her face in daylight. A pale, round face surrounded in green. As if last night's bright moon had turned her into a moon-faced forest spirit.

Please, Moon Madonna, don't let Mama send me away again. I don't know where to go.

10

Her steps slowed as she neared the house. She didn't know how long Mama wanted her to stay out of sight. Maybe forever.

She peered through the trees and saw Mama sitting on the porch steps. Mama with her sharp sight spotted her seconds later. "Raven, come to me," she said, standing up. "Don't be afraid."

Raven walked out of the trees. She was surprised when Mama almost ran and pulled her into her arms. "Oh, my miracle. My dear Daughter of Raven! I was so worried!"

When at last she let Raven go, she had tears on her pale cheeks.

"Why didn't you come home?" she asked.

"You told me to go from your sight."

"I only meant in that moment. When I was angry."

"You aren't anymore?"

"I'm very disappointed in you. For lying. For going to those people's house and keeping it from me." She lifted Raven's chin with her fingers. "What do you have to say?"

"I'm sorry, Mama."

"Good. Now, let's go inside. We have much to discuss."

Inside, Mama had her change into clean clothes. She told Raven to sit on the couch in the living room, and she stood in front of the stone fireplace.

"Tell me why you want to go to school. Is it the lessons or those boys you met?"

Raven dared not lie again. "The boys."

"I thought so," she said in a bitter voice. "You will find, Daughter, that gangs of children at a school are not something to want. They will see you're different, and they will hurt you."

"They would never hurt me."

"Perhaps not them, but there are those who would. And once you go to that place, you're trapped. You will be the raven's child caught in a cage. You'll feel like a bird beating against glass in your desperation to get out. The freedom of your present life, the trees and grass you see out the school windows, will be taunting misery."

"You'll let me go?"

Mama sighed and didn't say anything for a while.

"School started today," Raven said.

"I know."

That surprised Raven.

Mama paced back and forth in front of the fireplace. She stopped and said, "I've decided I should trust the instincts of my Daughter of Raven. As I've said, you will one day be more skilled at communing with earth spirits than I am. Because you're half-spirit yourself. You were a gift from that world, and I must listen to what you and they want."

She stepped closer, her white-blue star eyes wet. "The spirits punished me last night by taking you into their fold. Your absence was terrible. I was afraid they would never give you back."

Guilt made Raven's cheeks burn. She had been with Jackie, not with the spirits. But the bad feeling went away when she realized the spirits had sent her there. They had made her cold and wet. They had sent her to his house to get warm.

Mama said, "I've been asking the spirits for help with a problem that has come up since you turned five. I believe your kinship with the spirits connects to my search for answers. Your three Askings—the one that bonded you with the boys and the two that expressed your strong desire for school—have shown me how I must respond to this problem."

"What problem?" Raven asked.

"When you came into being, you didn't have a birth certificate—proof of your birth in the human world. The outer world didn't know of your existence. But my sister and Dr. Pat insisted your birth had to be recorded or there could be trouble. I saw the wisdom in that and let the doctor record your birth."

"I thought we must never speak of the miracle to anyone."

"We must not. But not having a certificate might have brought worse suspicion. The information I gave for the certificate is a false version of your birth. It says your father is an unknown person. It has times and dates that aren't true."

"Are you in trouble for making it up? Is that the problem?"

"The problem is you're now known to the outer world. It was inevitable. I couldn't hide you forever. Once a child is known in this country, she must be schooled. And the government oversees the schooling even if a parent wants to do it at home. In recent months, my sister has sent me many warnings about this. She mailed government papers to me. They say I have to be qualified enough to teach you. I have to have a planned program. They will come here and stick their noses in my house and my teaching. They may say I'm not capable of being your teacher."

"You're a good teacher!"

"They go by their own rules, Daughter. Out there is an ugly machine that wants to control everyone, and now its lens is focused on you. They will make you be schooled their way, file papers for everything you do, pay taxes to the government. Buying this property and building this house was a nightmare of government machinery you can't imagine."

She couldn't imagine. She didn't want to. She wanted only to think about going to school. Was Mama really going to let her?

"Am I going to school today?"

"Not today. But you will. I can't have the government snooping around here. I think the recent events are a warning. When the spirits took you last night, they were showing me what could happen if you don't go to school. You must go and pretend to be a human child to protect both of us."

Raven was too excited to sit. She got off the couch. "When will I go? Tomorrow?"

"You are very eager despite my warnings. You want school so badly?"

"Yes!"

She had a strange look in her eyes. "Sit down, Raven. I have more to say."

Raven sat and folded her hands in her lap.

"I have made two decisions along with allowing you to go to school. The spirits have guided me in these judgments."

Raven knew by the sharp look in her eyes that she wouldn't like the decisions.

"First, I have decided we will spend summers away from here from now on."

Raven's chest felt hollow. "Where will we go?"

"My parents owned a large ranch in Montana. When they died, they left it to my sister and me. Sondra took the big house, and I have the cabin. The cabin sits far from the house in beautiful country. It's next to a stream and looks out on mountains."

She sat next to Raven and took one of her hands in hers. "I promise Daughter of Raven will be happy there. My mother started taking me to the cabin when I was a few years older than you. Living in the big city of Chicago made me feel sick most of the time. But I would get better at the cabin. My mother took me there every summer, and we went any time I got sick. I learned how to speak with earth spirits in that place."

Raven doubted she would love Montana as much as she had loved her summer with the boys.

Mama let go of Raven's hand. "The second decision has to do with a promise you will make. Will you do that?"

"What promise?"

"You will never again set foot on the land of the teacher and those boys."

Tears stung her eyes. "Mama . . . why?"

"I will not have them influencing you, distracting you from your kinship with the earth spirits. I will not have that teacher woman digging around in our lives. No doubt she's already asked questions about me."

Ms. Taft had asked questions. Mostly she had wanted to know if Mama hurt her.

"Has she?" Mama demanded.

Raven nodded, tears spilling over her cheeks.

"I knew it," Mama said in an angry voice. "You're too young to understand why this is dangerous for you. If you go too far into your bond with those people, you'll think you can trust them. You'll tell them about your father."

"I won't!"

"I have talked to the spirits, and they have verified this danger. You will go there no longer. And when you see those boys at school, you will tell them I don't want them on my property ever again. Tell them I have a gun."

Raven's tears fell faster.

Mama wiped them away with her fingers. "You'll see them every day at school. That will have to be enough."

Could it be enough? Raven thought of the boys piled around her on the couch, the games, the joking and laughter. But Raven would have seen them only on weekends now that school had started. If Raven went to school, she would see the boys and Ms. Taft five days a week.

"Do you want to start school tomorrow?" Mama asked.

"Yes."

"I'll call the school now. But first, tell me you'll never go to that house again. Do you promise?"

Raven felt tricked by her spirit kin. She would get what she had asked of them with all her soul. She would go to school. But what she would lose might make her wish she had never asked.

"Raven, speak your promise aloud," Mama said in an angry voice.

"I promise I won't go to the boys' house."

"Not one foot on their land."

"Not one foot."

Mama stood. "The spirits will be watching you, Daughter of Raven. They will tell me if you break this promise."

In that moment, Raven hated her father. If she went outside and saw a raven spying on her, she would want to throw a stone at it.

Just thinking that scared her more than anything ever had.

PART THREE

DAUGHTER OF THE WILD WOOD

1

Leaving the western mountains was like leaving home. For a year and a half, Ellis had stood on their peaks, drunk water straight from their rushing rivers, bathed in waterfalls, meditated in meadows aflame with alpine flowers, spent hours and hours watching the mountains' marmots, pikas, moose, elk, bears, jays, dippers, and hummingbirds. The western mountains were like rooms in a familiar house.

But she didn't want a home.

> Allons! we must not stop here,
> However sweet these laid-up stores, however con-
> venient this
> dwelling, we cannot remain here . . .

The words always brought her back to the night Caleb introduced her to the "Song of the Open Road." He had read in her lamplit tent after they bathed in the mountain river, after they made love, at first numb and dripping ice water but soon streaming with sweat and in need of another rinse, washing in Whitman's words instead.

She'd found a used paperback of *Leaves of Grass* in a Montana bookshop a month after the night with Caleb. It had the same cover as his copy. She often read the poems as she fell asleep in her tent. A better way to self-soothe than whiskey.

She turned onto a new highway. For two weeks, she'd been gradually moving eastward, camping along the way. She had to leave the west, at least for a while. She didn't want to get too used to any one place. "Forever alive, forever forward," as Caleb had quoted.

She was eager to see the woodlands of her childhood and college years. A conversation with hikers she'd met in Colorado had given her the idea to hike the Appalachian Mountains during spring bloom. Spring beauty, woodland phlox, trillium, lady's slipper, bluebell. She hadn't seen eastern wildflowers for a long time. For almost two years, since the day Viola was abducted.

But she wouldn't think about that. She was about to cross the Mississippi River. She saw the bridge ahead.

She had her foot on the brake. She didn't know why. She wanted to turn the car around. Go back west. All the ghosts were still there, waiting for her on the other side of the Mississippi.

She felt them coming closer as the bridge neared. The sweet smell of a baby cuddled in a towel after a bath. Jasper climbing into her lap to sleep. The softness of the boys' hair. The weight of Viola's body as she nursed. The two freckles next to River's nose. "Heckle and Jeckle, my favorite freckles," Ellis used to say, dabbing her finger on each.

No, she wouldn't let a trajectory, the simple act of heading east, do this to her. She was better. So much better. She'd been sober for three months, the longest she'd ever maintained sobriety. She was strong from climbing mountains. She could go east if she wanted. Nothing would stop her.

"Check out this bridge," she said to Gep. "Pretty cool, isn't it?"

The blue pony had been riding on her dashboard since last summer. Ellis had worried she might lose him every time she packed camp. She'd stuck him to the dashboard with little pieces of duct tape under each hoof. Exposure to the sun was fading his blue plastic, but nothing could erase his tireless smile.

Ellis took a deep breath as she arrived on the eastern side of the river.

"These are your old stomping grounds," she told the pony.

Gep's smile suggested he felt better about that than she did.

She was talking to the pony too much. Like she used to before she got better. She needed rest. She'd been up at dawn, hiked for four hours, and been on the road longer than expected because of a traffic jam. She was heading for a campground in a nearby national forest. It had a stream where she could bathe.

She found it at twilight, relieved to see it was empty. Navigating the winding gravel roads to find it was difficult, and people rarely camped on weekdays in cold weather. She'd been worried turkey hunters might be there. She didn't mistrust hunters per se, but she avoided men with weapons and alcohol when she was in an isolated campground. She'd gotten a bad feeling a few times in the past.

She put up the smaller of her two tents and went to bed with a book. Reading at night had replaced drinking. She couldn't sleep unless she read at least a few pages. If she was too tired to get into a book, she read poetry.

She'd been asleep for several hours when she was awakened by the slams of car doors. A man swore about how cold it was. "Go get a room at the Hilton," another man said.

She looked outside. The men, probably hunters, were only a few campsites down from hers.

The noise gradually abated, and she went back to sleep. She woke as the sun came up, ate, then put her bathing supplies in her backpack and headed to the trail.

Billows of clouds in every shade of gray hung low over the forest. The forest stream was beautiful with the stone bluffs rising over it. Its rocky pools were clear and deep. When she was far from camp, she bathed with vegetable soap so she didn't harm the water ecosystem. She cleaned and changed into fresh clothes with practiced quickness. Then she washed her soiled clothes and put them in a plastic bag that she stuffed into her backpack.

She rubbed leave-in detangler into her hair and sat on a rock to pick the knots out. Her unruly curls were long past her shoulders now. Her hair hadn't been that long for years. Since Zane used to call her Lion Queen and chase her around growling. Since Mick used to say he'd seen a bird fly out of it.

Ellis had cut off her hair in the fall of her senior year at Cornell. She thought it would make her look more professional. More adult. But what she'd seen when she looked at her shorn head in the salon mirror was a man. She'd been insecure about her small breasts and lack of curves since high school, and the short hair made her feel more lacking. She'd cried when she got back to her dorm. Dani had insisted she looked great, said her eyes and cheekbones were all *WOW* without her hair hiding them.

Maybe the haircut had changed her life, possibly brought her to this very rock in this forest, because the next day, Dani had dragged Ellis to a Halloween party to try to cheer her up. The party she'd nearly refused to attend was where she'd met Jonah.

Ellis was dressed as a cloud, a costume she'd made in a half hour by gluing pillow stuffing to a short white dress Dani was giving to Goodwill. Jonah was Zeus in toga, sandals, and beard, a costume from a rental store. Every time he was near her, he'd poke his plastic lightning bolt into her cloud billows. "I'm trying to make thunder," he said.

"This symbolism is a bit obvious, isn't it?" she said.

"No, explain what you mean," he said, grinning.

The third time he poked her, she stole his lightning bolt and stuck it into the fluff on her chest. He said it looked so good on her, he'd let her keep it. He reclaimed it later that night, when they were both drunk. They talked for a while, and he kissed her.

The kiss was a surprise. She looked ridiculous in her costume, not at all sexy. She'd hidden her lack of breasts beneath the cloud, only exposed the full length of her legs—her best feature, she thought.

After two months with Jonah, when he told her he'd fallen in love with her, she started cutting her hair regularly. She wore fitted clothes that showed off her slender figure, a shape that had captured a smart, attractive law student.

But everything about her figure changed soon after. Only eight months into their relationship, her breasts swelled, and new curves emerged all over. By then, she was four months pregnant and had been married for a month. They took the oaths at a courthouse with only their best friends as witnesses. The senator and his wife had refused Jonah's invitation.

Ellis put the comb in her backpack and climbed off the rock. She had to move to generate some heat. She climbed a bluff and looked down over the ravine. The trees were just beginning to leaf out. The chartreuse hue of early spring in the eastern forest brought to mind her Wild Wood. But she didn't dwell there. *Forever forward*, she told herself.

She followed the trail back to camp but froze as she neared her tent. Her pulse skipped, then rushed with a suddenness that made her light-headed. There were two men in her camp. One was keeping watch as the other broke into her car.

The man keeping watch saw her at almost the same moment she saw him. She turned and ran, no time to contemplate if she should. She looked backward as she tore into the forest, sickened when she saw both men chasing her. Why would they chase her and not run away when she'd seen them trying to burglarize her car?

Maybe she shouldn't have run. Maybe they thought she had something valuable in her backpack. A camera. Binoculars.

She did have binoculars, but they could have them. The backpack was slowing her down anyway. She pulled it off and let it fall behind her as she ran. She had her hunting knife on her, as always, but it was in its sheath, attached to the belt of her hiking pants. She took it out of its case and hid it in her pocket. But the sheath would give it away. She popped the snap on the case and let it fall.

Seconds later, one of the men grabbed her. His momentum knocked her facedown onto the ground, his body sprawling over hers. He moved off quickly, replacing his weight with his boot on the small of her back. The gesture said everything she feared. She was afraid she was going to vomit.

"Got her," he said breathlessly.

"She's fast," the other man said, walking over.

Ellis had to stand. She appeared too vulnerable on the ground. She forced strength into her quivering body, rolled out from under the boot, and jumped to her feet. The men didn't try to stop her.

She faced them. They were in their late twenties, both fairly big. The taller one, with a short, dark beard and brown eyes, had a beer gut. He was still breathing hard and holding her backpack. The other, the one who'd put his boot on her back, had a face prickly with a day or two of red-blond beard growth. He was fitter than the other man, and his blue-gray eyes made her stomach reel again. Something about how he looked at her. As if her capture excited him.

"Now, why were you running?" he asked, scratching his fingers in his cropped hair to feign puzzlement.

"You know why. I saw what you were doing."

He grinned. "What was I doing?"

"Breaking into my car. Take it. Take everything. Even the car. The keys are in the backpack."

"Take everything?" He cast a look at the other man.

She wanted to cry, but she couldn't show her weakness. She pressed her arm against her side. The knife was still in her pocket.

"Let's just go our own ways, okay?" she said. "I have no phone on me. I can't call the police." She half turned to walk away. "I'll go. Take the car."

The strawberry blond grabbed her arm.

She shrugged him off. Again, only because he allowed it. "Come on. Just let me go," she said.

"I can't let a woman go off alone into the woods," he said. "That wouldn't be right. You should know it's not safe to be in a place like this all alone."

It was worse than she thought. She forced a show of confidence through her dizzying terror.

"I'm not alone," she said. "I'm a biologist doing research here, and some of my colleagues are meeting me soon. You should go before they arrive."

"Uh-oh, her *colleagues* are coming," he said to his friend.

The bearded man grinned.

"I think you're lying to me," the blond told Ellis. "Why would a biologist be sleeping all alone in the cold woods?"

"Biologists who study forest species sleep in the woods in all seasons."

"What *species* do you study?"

"Hickory trees," she said, because there was one just behind him.

"What about them do you study?"

She tried to give him a look that didn't betray the quaking mess she was inside. "I've had enough of this," she said as boldly as she could. She moved to walk around him, but he blocked her with his body.

"I said I wanted to hear more about the hickory trees," he said. "Biology always was my favorite subject."

His friend snickered, and when the blond looked at him and grinned, Ellis slid her hand into her pocket. She felt the handle of the knife.

The blond rubbed his hand down the front of his jeans. "I got a damn hickory tree down here just looking at you, girl. You're the prettiest biologist I ever saw."

He slanted his eyes at his grinning friend. Ellis could tell a signal had passed between them. She gripped the knife handle. She had to stay calm, be smart, but her brain was a frenetic rush of adrenaline screaming for her to run.

"How about we take a moment to study a few trees?" the red-blond said.

The men lunged at her. Ellis thrust the knife at the blond's chest. He ducked and grabbed her arm. She punched him with her other arm and kicked at his groin. The bearded man jerked her away from the blond by her left arm. Something cracked in her wrist, but she felt no pain. She screamed and kicked and fought wildly.

But it ended as it always did. As it had for thousands of years. They had her trapped on the ground. The blond straddled her legs. The bearded man had her arms pinned over her head. Blood seeped fast out of one of her nostrils. Her lips tasted salty, were already swelling, and her right cheek throbbed.

The blond held up her antler-handle knife, making a show of studying it. "This is a nice hunting knife. An old one." He looked into her eyes. "Do you know how to use this? Do you hunt?"

She looked away from his face.

"I'll take that as a no," he said. "You shouldn't be playing around with weapons you don't know how to use." After a long pause, he said, "How about I give you a lesson?"

She closed her eyes. She wouldn't watch. She couldn't.

"I know all about what's inside bodies. Deer, possums, people. I know where you can put a knife so it hurts bad but doesn't kill. I don't want you dead when we do this. But you have to pay for the stupidity of pulling a knife on a man who knows how to use it."

He pushed up her shirt, baring her stomach, and jerked down the waist of her pants. He swirled the knife point on her left side.

She squeezed her eyes tight. She thought she'd die of fear. Was it possible? She wanted to. Or at least lose consciousness.

"Right here," he said. "I can poke it here and miss all the vitals. It will only hurt. I promise. You won't die."

"Hey," the bearded man said, "you're not really going to—"

The blade stabbed into her. Hot. It felt hot. She screamed.

"Jesus Christ!" the bearded man said.

The blond laughed. "Don't barf. At least not on her. I don't want to deal with that when I'm on her."

Ellis heard them, but their words didn't register. She felt like she was in a dark room. A little room that had no air. Pain replaced the air, and she couldn't breathe pain. She was dying. He'd said she wouldn't die, but she had to be dying.

"Let her go," the blond said.

She felt the weight of both men lift from her. Her hands now free, she instinctively reached for the knife handle protruding from her abdomen.

The blond grabbed her hands. "No, it stays. If you try to take it out, I'll find a new spot for it. Just stay still and it won't hurt as much."

He was right. It didn't hurt as much when she didn't move.

But he was taking off her boots. And her pants.

He wasn't going to do that.

He will not. Through the pain, her mind suddenly became clear. This time she had to plan better. She would have one chance. Just one. She had to do it at the perfect moment.

"You all right down there?" he asked. He was standing over her, unbuckling his belt.

She sobbed. She had to make him think she'd given up. But she was watching his every move, getting ready.

His pants were open, pulled partway down. He was going to leave them on while he did it. That might be better. Tie up his legs.

"Stay still so I don't knock the blade handle," he warned.

She readied herself. One chance. Just one. She whimpered like a wounded puppy, but inside she calculated how to rip out his throat.

She was right. Leaving his pants on had been a mistake. He had to put his full weight on his hands to balance. Ellis ripped the knife out and jerked it upward into his chest. Or his belly. She had no idea where it went, but she'd shoved as hard as she could, and she was strong from climbing mountains and hauling water. The knife sank deep.

She hardly heard his screams, she was so desperate to get out from under him. She shoved him, and he fell over on his side, staring wide eyed at the knife sticking out of the right side of his stomach. Her knife. The hunting knife had been passed from her great-grandfather to her grandfather to her.

Ellis stumbled to her feet and yanked the knife out of him. He wailed.

"I know how to use a hunting knife!" she screamed. "I know how to use it!"

The bearded man threw his fist into her face. Then another. Her left cheek and her right eye exploded. She saw red like splattering blood and white sparks and fell to the ground.

The blond was gasping, blood oozing down his belly. "Dean, help me!" he cried. "Get me in the truck!"

Ellis got up and ran. Into the trees. Deeper and deeper.

She didn't stop until she hit a log. She fell over it and lay in the dead leaves, breathing hard. Just breathing.

The birds told her when to get up. They were twittering above her. Titmice and chickadees. They knew the sudden violence of predators in the forest. But when the threat was gone, they could fly again.

She risked stirring the leaves. When she stood, she felt her injuries. Sharp pain in her left side. Her left wrist sprained, possibly broken. Her eye already swelling closed. Her cheeks, nose, and mouth were throbbing and caked with blood. Her bare legs and feet were cold and torn up from running through branches and thorns.

She realized what was in her right hand. The bloody knife. She gripped it in case they were still there.

It took a minute to get her bearings. She had run down the hill. Now she had to go back up. It was tough. More difficult than when she'd climbed her first mountain. But she did it. Step by step.

When she got to the top, she stood quietly, knife in hand, listening for the men. She thought she saw the campground in the distance, a break in the trees. When she arrived at the campsites, the truck that had pulled in the night before was gone. She backtracked until she found her pack, boots, and pants. The sheath to her knife.

She dressed and walked to her camp, her hand pressed on the oozing cut in her side. She had to stop the bleeding. She pulled her medical supply box out of the back of the SUV and poured alcohol over the cut. Stifled a scream. When her skin dried, she smeared the gash with antibiotic cream, pressed on gauze pads, and taped it with duct tape. To be sure it held, she wrapped a strip of tape completely around her waist, then washed three ibuprofen tablets down with water.

Ellis sat on the ground, eyes closed, waiting for the medication to take effect. She tried to think what to do. She didn't have health insurance. But if anyone found out about the knife wound, they would make her go to a hospital. The doctors would ask questions. She'd stabbed a man, possibly killed him. The police would get involved. Her history dug up. They'd link her to Jonah and Senator Bauhammer. The boys would find out.

It would be like the day Viola was abducted all over again.

And, of course, the doctors would give her pain medication. She didn't want that. She couldn't risk her sobriety. But they would make her. Maybe even knock her out with an IV to fix the cut. And when she woke, Jonah would be standing in her hospital room. His eyes would have that same look. Like a mirror reflecting what he saw. A bad mother. A screwup. Trailer trash.

She didn't have to go to a hospital. The man who'd stabbed her said he knew the right place. He'd said she wouldn't die. If she kept the cut clean, it would heal.

She'd have to hope her wrist was sprained, not broken. She could move it a little. It would be okay. Everything would be okay. She needed only a safe place to rest for a few days. Not a campground. She'd go to a motel, where she could take a shower and sleep in a bed.

When the ibuprofen blunted the pain, she packed camp. But bending and lifting made her feel like her insides were coming out. She had to move slowly and carefully. Once the tent was down, she used water and rags to wash the blood and dirt off her face. She zipped her coat over her bloody shirt and pants.

She got in the car and started the motor.

Gep was smiling on the dashboard. Everything would be okay.

2

She couldn't stop seeing the dead deer.

Zane, and another chef everyone called Rocky, had brought it over to show her mother when Ellis was eight. Zane had never been hunting before, and Rocky wasn't the best with a gun either. That was how the deer had gotten *gut shot*, as Zane said.

While the men and Ellis's mother joked about what a mess they'd made of killing the deer, Ellis had stared at the dead animal slumped in the back of Rocky's pickup. The buck with big antlers was one of the most beautiful things Ellis had ever seen. She'd glimpsed deer in the Wild Wood but never up close like that. The stag's eyes were open, his tongue hanging out. Ellis remembered the bloody hole in the side of his belly. She had wanted to cry, thinking how bad that would hurt, but she knew her mother would tease her if she did. She kept quiet and cried inside.

Ellis held the stab wound in her side and staggered out of bed. She barely made it to the bathroom in time. After she emptied her stomach, she lay on the floor next to the toilet. The cold tile felt good on her feverish skin.

She shouldn't have thought of the gut-shot deer. That was what made her vomit. But the fever delirium was making her see and think all kinds of things she didn't want to.

She awoke on the tile, quaking with chills, and managed to drag herself up. She put a trash can next to the bed so she wouldn't have to run to the bathroom the next time. She took more ibuprofen, drank more water. Fell into restless sleep.

She woke on fire. Why wasn't the fever reducer keeping her temperature down? Maybe the fever had to do with her wrist. It was swollen to double its normal size and throbbed right through the large dose of ibuprofen. The stab wound hurt even worse. She pulled back the covers and lifted her T-shirt. She peeled back the duct tape and gauze. The wound was purple and rimmed in red. It looked bad.

She needed help. Someone she trusted.

She got out of bed, walked with teetering steps to her car parked in front of her motel room door. Just seeing Gep's happy face made her feel better. She ripped him off the tape sticking him to her car dashboard, got herself back to the motel room, and cuddled him under the covers. "Do you think I should call Keith?" she asked him.

She couldn't see him, but she knew he was smiling.

Gep was right. Keith would help her. He'd bring her antibiotics.

She took her phone off the bed stand and opened the messages. There was one conversation from two winters ago. First the directions to Pink Horses, then four one-sided texts:

December 28: How's it going? I hope you got out of the Midwest before that big storm. Let me know how you are. (This is Keith BTW)

January 10: Where are you? Seeing great stuff?

January 24: Hi, Ellis. Could you just send one word so I know you're okay?

February 2: One word. Or maybe just randomly type letters.

February 2, a minute later: Give the pony my regards.

She hovered her finger over the buttons. The only personal call she'd ever made from the phone was to him. She pressed her finger down. The ringing in her ear felt more like a fever hallucination than a real sound.

He picked up on the third ring. "Ellis?"

"You remember me?"

"Of course I do."

She started crying.

"What's wrong?" he said. "Tell me. Please stop crying and talk to me. What's going on? Do you need help?"

"Yes. Yes," she sobbed.

"Where are you?"

"Sweet Dreams Motel. Room 133."

"Where is that? What town?"

"I don't know."

"What state?"

"I'm near you. I think I was trying to get to you after it happened . . . but I was afraid, and I stopped here and now I can't leave."

"I don't understand. What happened? Why are you afraid?"

"I need antibiotics. Will you bring me some?"

"Are you sick?"

"Yes." She started crying again.

"You'll be okay. I'm coming. If I can find the motel, I'll be there as fast as I can."

"Really?"

"Yes. Wait a second. Let me look it up on my computer."

She waited. She was afraid it was all a fevered delusion. Had he said he was coming?

"I found it," he said. "On Long Lake Road?"

"I don't know. Yes, I think so. Are you really coming?"

"Of course I am."

"Will you bring antibiotics?"

After a pause he said, "Yes, I will."

"Keith?"

"What?"

"Promise me you won't call the police."

"What happened? Why would you say that?"

171

The alarm in his voice scared her. "Promise or you can't come!"

"Okay, I promise. Hold on tight. Don't go anywhere."

"I won't."

"I'm already walking out the door. I'm on my way."

The phone went silent. Ellis stared at it until the screen went black.

She held Gep against her chest and tried to sleep. A few minutes later, she threw up in the trash can, then fell back asleep.

Brown leaves madly spinning. She ran and ran through a forest. Someone was screaming. Screaming in her ears.

Pounding. Pounding. It stopped for a while. Then started again.

"We're coming in," someone said.

Ellis opened her eyes.

The ceiling light flashed on, and Keith rushed over. Everything was too bright. Glowing light shined off him, and she had to squint to look at him. There was another man who stayed by the door.

"Ellis!" Keith said when he saw her face. "This man says you were in a car accident. Is that true?"

She had lied to the desk clerk when she checked into the motel. She was afraid he might call the police when he saw how battered she was.

"You're burning up!" he said.

"I . . . know." It was so hard to talk. "Do you have medicine?"

"This isn't from a car accident! Who did this?"

Keith pulled off the covers to examine her. He saw Gep clutched in her hand and stared at the pony for a few seconds.

"Who hurt you?"

"I don't know."

"Why do you have tape on your stomach?"

She tried to pull her T-shirt over the bandage.

"Let me see. Please." He gently lifted her shirt and peeled back the duct tape and gauze. "Oh my god," he whispered. "That's a knife wound. It's infected. You have to get to a hospital fast."

"No!" she said with a sudden surge of vigor. "You promised!"

"I never promised not to save your life!"

"No police!"

She had stabbed someone. The police would ask a hundred questions. She could already see their judgmental looks when they found out she'd gone alone to an isolated campground. She couldn't bear more of what she'd been through when she left Viola.

Keith scooped her into his arms. "Where's your wallet?" he asked. "Ellis, where is your wallet?"

"Backpack," she said.

"Would you please bring that backpack?" he said to the motel clerk. "And don't remove anything from this room. Keep her checked in."

"Got it," the young man said.

Keith sat her on the back seat of his car and wrapped his coat around her. When he pulled her hand in the sleeve, she had to let go of Gep. "Will you put him in my backpack?"

"Him?" he said, smiling. "I can't believe you still have it."

"He's good luck."

His expression said the pony's luck didn't appear to be working.

"This has nothing to do with him."

"Who does it have to do with? Tell me who did this to you."

"Why? How will that change it?"

"This person deserves to be brought to justice!"

"I did that."

"What do you mean?"

She sank into the seat, curled up tight and shivering.

3

She had a broken wrist and cracked nose. The knife wound was infected but required no surgical repair. The doctor said it was a deep slice that had just missed her ovary and bowel. He said Ellis was very lucky.

Almost everything Ellis hadn't wanted happened. She had expensive treatments with no health insurance to pay for them. She was given an IV and pain medication that made her loopy.

But she prevented them from contacting next of kin. She told them she had no family, and they let that stand. Jonah, the boys, and the senator and his wife would never know about her latest screwup.

An hour after she'd been admitted to the emergency room, two police officers arrived.

"So you're saying you don't remember anything about getting stabbed?" one of the men asked. "Where you were, what the attacker looked like—nothing at all?"

Ellis felt the burning pain of the knife in her side. Saw the man with red-blond hair standing over her. The fierce arousal in his blue eyes as he unzipped his jeans.

She tried to hold back the stinging tears.

"You know him, don't you?" the other officer said. "Is he your boyfriend, a family member?"

"No!" she said.

"If you know he's not an acquaintance, you must remember the attack," the officer said.

She shouldn't have answered. But she was so tired. So sick.

She felt Keith's look of concern almost physically. He knew she was lying because of what she'd said in his car.

Ellis imagined telling them everything. The blond attacker was probably dead. His friend would have buried him where no one could find him, and by now he could be anywhere. The men would be forever vanished while Ellis suffered for their crimes. Just like when Viola was abducted.

It would all be her fault again. Hadn't people told her for years that a woman shouldn't camp alone?

She couldn't hold back. She wept in gasping sobs.

"She needs to rest," Keith said to the policemen. "Let's talk outside."

He drew the officers out of her room, and Ellis never saw them again.

She insisted on leaving the hospital after less than a day. They didn't fight her when they learned she had no health insurance. But she was in no shape to drive. She had to depend on Keith.

He set her up in the back seat of the car with blankets and pillows. She was so groggy, it took her a few minutes to realize it was her SUV.

"Where's your car?" she asked.

"Don't worry. It's safe. And I got all your stuff from the motel."

"Where are we going?"

"Home."

"Yours?"

"You should rest," he said. "The doctor said you should sleep as much as you want for the next several days. He said that's all you'll want to do."

It was all she wanted to do.

"Go to sleep," he said. "It'll be dark soon, and this is a long drive."

"How long?"

"You're safe, Ellis. Everything is okay."

She slept. And slept and slept. She woke in darkness needing a bathroom. He helped her into a McDonald's restroom, then made her take a pain pill.

After he fueled the car, she asked, "How far are we from your house?"

"A ways still. Go back to sleep."

The pain medication helped. She didn't care how good it felt. She wanted to be dead to everything that had happened in the campground.

It was still dark out the second time she needed a bathroom. She was confused about how long she'd been in the car. "Why is it taking so long?" she asked.

"We had to take a little detour," he said. "How's the pain?"

"Coming back."

"You'd better take another pill with your antibiotic."

She took the pill. Much too willingly. She was getting used to the feeling again.

When the sun came up, she was still in the car.

"Why is it morning?" she asked.

"That's what usually happens after night," he said.

"Seriously. What are we doing? We've been in the car for too long."

"It's been good rest for you."

Had he been driving around all night to let her sleep? Ellis sometimes did that with the boys. When they fell asleep in the car, she kept driving. She didn't want to wake them, and she always needed the quiet time. She never had to do that with Viola. Viola was a sound sleeper, even when taken out of the car. Ellis wondered if she still was.

They were in a town somewhere. She noticed that the car kept stopping.

Ellis watched a palm tree stream past the window. And another. How could palm trees grow in Ohio? She sat up.

"Almost there," he said.

"Where are we?"

"Don't you recognize it?" He looked at her in the rearview mirror.

She peered around. Palm trees. Signs with alligators. Everything was "Gator" this and "Gator" that. It wasn't early spring. It looked like summer.

A truck that said GAINESVILLE'S #1 FLORIST drove past.

"What are you doing?" she said.

"Taking you home."

"This isn't my home!"

"We're almost there."

"Stop saying that! Stop the car! Stop!"

"We're nearly at your house. We'll talk there."

She couldn't believe it. She had trusted him. Fully. And he had done this to her. He had put her in her car, drugged her, lied to her, and driven her to damn Florida.

He pulled the car into the driveway of a pastel-blue cinderblock house with fake white shutters. Ellis recognized the address. It was the one she had given to the bank, Dani's address.

The last time Ellis and Dani were together, Dani was trying to put her back together after she lost Viola. Ellis couldn't face her like this. Not again. A friend shouldn't have to deal with screwups this big.

Keith parked the car and turned off the motor.

"How could you do this to me?" Ellis said.

He twisted around to look at her. "I assume you know this house?"

"I've never seen it before! I don't live here!"

He looked alarmed. "I hope you're joking."

"I'm not!"

"Shit!" he said. He pushed his hands through his hair.

She saw how exhausted he was. He had dark circles under his eyes and at least two days' stubble on his face.

"I need to stretch my legs," he said. He got out, slamming the door hard.

She clambered out of the soft bed he'd made for her and got out.

He was standing in the driveway, staring at the house. He turned to her. "This is the address on your driver's license. It's what you gave the hospital. And to make sure, the cops and I verified it from your car's plate."

"How dare you do that!"

"There was a crime! You were beaten and stabbed. They needed to make sure there wasn't more."

"More what?"

"More anything!" He strode up to her. "You have no family. No job. No health insurance. And for some reason I can't fathom, you live in campgrounds. But you can't do that right now. You're too sick. I knew you'd be too stubborn to see that, but I can't take you to my house. I live with someone now. I had no choice but to bring you here. I thought there would be someone who could help you."

She was too sick to fight the tears. She turned away, trying to hide them, but he took her into his arms. His scent was strong from the long car drive, but he smelled good. Like the night they'd made love in her tent.

"Don't cry," he crooned. "We'll figure out what to do."

"Who are you with now?"

He held her out in his arms, smiling. "Don't tell me that's why you're crying?"

"No. It's good. But won't she be angry you're with me all this time?"

"She's away—spending the weekend with her parents in Michigan. But I've told her I had to help a friend. She knows I'm here with you."

"She's lucky to have you." She wiped the wrist that wasn't in a cast across her running nose. "I'm sorry I'm being like this after everything you've done."

"It's okay." He looked at the house. "Is there anyone here you know?"

"A friend. She and I roomed together for three years at Cornell."

"Maybe she can help? She must know you use her address."

"Yes."

"Why? Why do you do that when you've never been here?"

She didn't answer.

"Why didn't you report the assault as soon as it happened? Why did you nearly die in a motel room rather than get help? I don't understand any of this."

"Neither do I."

She truly didn't. She'd felt like one of her paper notes in the river ever since she'd found out she was pregnant with twins. She'd let the current take her wherever it threw her.

"I don't feel good." She walked to the grass and sank down.

Keith crouched and put his hand on her forehead. "Your fever is spiking."

The front door of the house opened, and a young man stepped onto the small cement porch. "Do you guys need help?" he asked. He must have been watching them from the window.

"Is Dani here?" Ellis asked.

"Yeah. Who should I say is asking?"

"Ellis."

The man disappeared. Seconds later, Dani burst through the door, apparently straight from bed. She was barefoot, wearing loose shorts and a T-shirt, and her shoulder-length black hair was tousled.

"Ellis! What happened to you? Oh my god!"

Ellis stood with Keith's help.

"I ran into a little trouble," Ellis said.

"A little! Can I hug you? I don't want to hurt you."

Ellis opened her arms.

Dani held her softly. She smelled of things Ellis had forgotten. Floral shampoo, Dove soap, laundry detergent, food cooked over a stove.

"I've been so worried about you," Dani said into her ear. "That day you called . . . it scared me. And then Jonah called . . ."

Ellis pushed out of her embrace. "When did he call?"

Dani glanced at Keith. "Last July."

"What did he say?"

"He wanted to know if I knew where you were. I told him I didn't."

Dani was eyeing Keith, clearly wanting to know who he was.

"Dani, this is Keith Gephardt," Ellis said. "Keith, this is Danielle Yoon."

"Just Dani," she said, holding out her hand. "Nice to meet you."

Dani glanced at Ellis, waiting for more explanation.

"Keith was nice enough to drive me here," Ellis said.

Ellis detected a bit of amusement in Keith's eyes.

"He's a friend," Ellis said. "And now we have to figure out how he's getting back to Ohio."

"I'll drive a rental back," he said. "I'll take a cab to the nearest rental place."

"I can take you," Dani said.

"That's not necessary," he said.

"Maybe not," she said, "but Sunday is laundry and cleaning day, and I'm the roommate who will make any excuse to get out of it."

"You've been on the road all night," Ellis said to him. "You need to rest first."

"I do," he admitted.

"We have a spare room you can use," Dani said. "One of my roommates moved in with her boyfriend, but her bed is still here. I can put on clean sheets."

"Give the bed to Ellis," he said. "If you have a couch I can sleep on for a few hours, that will be fine."

"Good. Now I have a reason not to vacuum the living room," Dani said. "Are you guys hungry?"

Ellis shook her head, and Keith's silence probably meant he was.

"Do you eat bacon and eggs?" she asked him.

"I do. But I don't want to be a bother."

"You can bother as much as you want. You brought Ellis." She wrapped her arm around Ellis's shoulders and kissed her cheek. "Come inside. Ellis can put a clothespin on her nose while I cook the bacon."

Keith asked for a bathroom, and Dani sent him to the nearest, warning, "I take no responsibility for the state of this bathroom. It's Brad's."

Brad walked out of the kitchen eating a bowl of cereal. "He doesn't care, Dani. He's a dude." He held out his hand to Keith and introduced himself. He tried not to stare at Ellis's bruised face when he shook her hand.

"You should see the other guy," Ellis said.

"I hope you deep-sixed him," Brad said.

Keith cast a shrewd look at Ellis before he entered the bathroom.

"Can I talk to you for a minute?" Ellis asked Dani.

Dani took her to her bedroom and closed the door. "Did a man really do that to you?"

"The official story is I don't remember," Ellis said.

"What are you talking about?"

"Nothing." Ellis lowered her voice. "Do me a favor. Don't say anything else about my family in front of Keith."

Her eyes went wide. "You're sleeping with him and he doesn't know you were married and have kids?"

"I'm not sleeping with him. I hardly know him. That's why I don't want him involved."

"You hardly know him, but he drove you here from Ohio?"

"He's a nice guy."

"Ellis, what's going on? What is all this secrecy—Jonah calling around looking for you, you showing up bruised with this guy you supposedly don't know? Are you in trouble with the police?"

"I'm not. All my trouble is my own."

"Will you stop with this cryptic crap? We're friends! We used to tell each other everything!"

She was wrong about that. She had no idea how much Ellis had withheld. Dani knew she'd been raised by her grandfather in Youngstown, but Ellis never talked about the trailer park, her mother being an addict and dying of an overdose, or that she didn't know who her father was. She didn't want any of that known to her college friends. Jonah was the only one she'd told, and she'd sworn him to secrecy. His parents had found out only because the senator had a private investigator look into her, her gift for getting pregnant with their son's twins.

"Promise me you won't tell Keith about Viola or anything else," Ellis said.

"What does it matter if you hardly know him?"

"Would you want people to know you left your baby in a forest and abandoned your sons?"

She looked about to cry. "Ellis . . ."

"Promise you won't tell him anything!"

"Okay, I promise."

"I need to lie down. My fever is going up."

"Why do you have a fever?"

Ellis saw no reason to mention the knife wound. It would only upset her.

"I don't know," she lied. "Maybe something to do with my broken wrist."

Before Dani could ask more, Ellis opened the door and went to the kitchen. Keith and Brad were talking about Brad's research on sea turtle conservation.

"Are you a biologist?" Dani asked Keith.

"A park ranger," he said.

"I guess that explains how you know Ellis. She loves camping."

"She sure does."

Dani looked about to ask him more, but she glanced at Ellis and kept silent.

Ellis knew Dani wouldn't pry into their relationship. And she wouldn't say anything to Keith about Viola or her sons. Dani was the kind of person who would take a friend's secrets to her grave. She could be trusted with Keith while Ellis slept. And if Keith revealed the knife wound or what had happened at the motel, so be it. She had to leave the kitchen before she fell over.

"If I'm asleep when you're ready to go, wake me up," she said to Keith.

When she closed her eyes, the recurring scene enveloped her. Two monsters. Chasing her and pinning her like a calf to be branded. *You should know it's not safe to be in a place like this all alone.* The blade point swirling over the soft skin on her stomach. *I know where you can put a knife so it hurts bad but doesn't kill.*

She put the pillow over her face and pressed hard, trying to smother away the memory.

She woke to the sound of a light knock. She was groggy, must have been asleep for hours. "Yes?" she said.

Keith sat on the side of the bed. He had a glass of water and her pills in his hands. "It's past time for all three," he said, holding out the antibiotic, ibuprofen, and pain medication. She was reminded of when Jonah had pushed the first sedative into her mouth.

"No more pain pills," she said.

"Why suffer the pain if it helps?"

"Just get it out of here."

He studied her eyes. "Are you recovering? From pill addiction?"

She didn't answer.

"I thought I saw that the night we were together. You looked high on more than the drinks."

She didn't deny it.

"Are you doing better with it?"

"I was. Until . . ."

He put down the water and pills and rested his palm on her cheek. "I'm sorry."

A sob erupted from her. Then another and another. As if her body were trying to eject a poison.

He gathered her in his arms. He'd showered and changed clothes. He smelled like Dani's Dove soap. "You need to talk about it," he said. "Stop holding it in or it'll fester like that knife wound."

Ellis cried harder.

He tucked her into his chest and rocked. He rocked her like Zane had sometimes.

She understood that he'd come to say goodbye. She shouldn't keep him when he had a long drive ahead.

She pulled away and wiped her face. "Is Dani going to drive you to the rental agency?"

"Yes. I have a car reserved."

"I guess you'd better go."

"Will you do something for me?" he asked.

"What?"

"Let me know how you are. Answer my texts."

"I don't like texting."

"One word. Just send one word. Will you promise to answer me?"

"Okay." She couldn't say no after all he'd done for her.

"Good. But can we do three words?"

"You can't change the conditions."

"We can't say enough with one word. If we're both allowed three, I can say, 'How are you?' And you can say, 'I'm doing great.' If you're on the road, I can ask, 'Where are you?' And you can say, 'I'm in Saskatchewan.'"

She laughed through her stuffy nose. "This all sounds very boring."

"It's not. I really want to know how you are."

"My rule is no multiple texts. That would break the three-word limit."

"Okay. No more than six words exchanged within twenty-four hours."

"How long will we do this?"

"I don't know. Let's see how it goes."

"And what will your girlfriend do when she sees you texting me?"

"Let me worry about that," he said.

"If it worries you, we shouldn't do it."

"I hope you talk this much when you text."

"I'll only have three words."

He kissed her cheek. "Goodbye, Ellis." He got up and left the room abruptly, without making her take the medication.

She didn't even have a chance to say goodbye. Like with Zane. And her mother. Viola.

The odds weren't in favor of her seeing him again.

4

Dani followed her out to the car. "Please reconsider," she said. "It's only been a week. You need more time to recover."

"I'm recovered," Ellis said. "I feel fine."

"Physically, you're better. But that doesn't mean you're recovered. You still can't even talk about it."

"Why do you say that?"

"Because you haven't told me anything! Why did someone beat you up? Who was it? Did the police catch him?"

"Why would you need to know any of that? Why would you even want to?"

"Because I care! I'm your friend. I can help you."

"I'm okay. I just need to get back to how everything was."

"What, living in campgrounds by yourself?"

"Yes. I need the mountains. I'm going up to the Appalachians."

"Ellis . . ."

"What?"

"You have to stop running away from what happened to Viola. You need to go back to your boys."

"I need to get on the road." Ellis gave her a hug that Dani didn't reciprocate. "Thank you for letting me stay."

"You can keep staying. We need a third roommate."

"And what would I do here?" Ellis asked.

"Go back to school. If you can't get into a UF grad program right away, you could get a job first."

"Why do you assume grad school is what I want?"

"Because you said it was!"

"People change, Dani. I don't intend this to be mean, but you don't really know me now. And I don't know you. I've been married, a mother of three, and divorced all while you've been in grad school."

"So what? Have your dreams really changed so much?"

Ellis wouldn't tell her the truth. She didn't have dreams anymore. She had no idea what she wanted in her future. It had become a big blank. She didn't know why or if that would change someday. Maybe she'd be like Caleb and wander all her life.

"I'd better go," she said. "Thank you. And tell Brad thanks, too."

Dani finally hugged her when she realized Ellis wasn't going to stay. She had tears in her eyes.

"Come on! Why are you crying?"

"I'm afraid for you. I'm afraid I'll never see you again."

"Why would you think that?"

"Because no one knew where you were for a year and a half, and when you finally appeared, you looked like you'd nearly been killed!"

"Remember, if Jonah calls, don't tell him any of that. Don't say I was here. You promised."

"Is that really all you care about right now?"

"Bye, Dani."

Ellis drove away, leaving Dani on the lawn with her arms crossed. She wanted to put Florida behind her. Not that she'd hated her week in Gainesville. Dani and Brad had been welcoming, the city was a decent but typical college town, and the warm weather had been a nice change. But everything about Gainesville, Florida, reminded her of the reason she was there. And she wanted to forget that.

She had a long drive ahead to the Georgia campground. She looked at the clock. She shouldn't have let Dani slow her down. She wouldn't get there until twilight. Or past, if she ran into bad traffic.

That didn't matter. She'd set up her tent in the dark often enough.

Ellis took a deep breath. And another. She didn't understand the peculiar feeling in her head. Like it was full of humming bees. She felt dizzy. She shifted the car out of cruise control. A semitruck sidled up to her in the right lane. Too close. It was too close. She slowed down more, clenching the steering wheel with both hands.

Her lips were numb. Her whole face was. She took another deep breath but couldn't get it all the way into her lungs. She tried again, but it seemed like her chest couldn't expand wide enough. She needed more air.

She must be having a bad reaction to her antibiotic. She'd taken her last dose a few hours earlier. The huge truck on the right roared past her. Then a car, the driver staring at her. Everyone was going around her. She felt sick. She was going to pass out.

So many people zooming past. She couldn't get over to the right. She braked even more. She was going only about thirty-five. What was she doing? That was dangerous on a big highway. She wanted to cry, but she was too frightened to risk giving in to emotion.

When a gap finally opened, she pulled into the right lane, pressed the brake, and steered onto the highway shoulder.

Shaking, sweating. She'd been certain she was going to die. But she couldn't understand why. She finally started to sob.

Her SUV rocked as vehicles sped past. They were coming too close. Her breaths weren't enough again. What was wrong with her? It had to be anaphylaxis from the medicine. She picked up her phone and typed in Dani's number.

"Hello?" Dani said.

"Dani . . . there's something wrong with me. I can't breathe. It's the medicine. I'm going to pass out!"

"Ellis! Should I call 911?"

"No. I don't know for sure what's wrong. Can you come? Can you come here?"

"Where are you?"

"On 75. Not far from the entrance ramp from your house. On the shoulder."

"I'm coming. I'm coming as fast as I can! I need to hang up but try to stay calm."

Ellis turned off the car. She slid the seat back from the steering wheel and lowered the backrest. She curled on her side, facing away from the traffic. She closed her eyes and concentrated on breathing.

She didn't lose consciousness and she didn't get worse. Now she understood what was wrong. She was having a panic attack. She'd had mild ones in the past but never like this, never so bad she'd thought she would die.

The revelation was devastating. It meant something she knew deep down but didn't want to believe. She was too scared to go camping alone. The one tool she had, the thing that could save her, was ruined forever.

She was crying when Dani arrived at the passenger side of the car, knocking frantically on the window. "Open up! Ellis, unlock the car!"

Ellis sat up and released the lock. Dani jumped into the passenger seat and closed the door against the sound of traffic. "How are you? Are you sure I shouldn't call 911?"

"I'm having a panic attack. A really bad one."

"Ellis!" She held Ellis in her arms over the console. "Are you feeling better now?"

"Yes. Well, no. Because I think I know why."

"Why?"

"When it started, I was thinking about arriving at the campground at night."

Dani looked into her eyes. "Is that where you were attacked by that man? In a campground at night?"

"It was two men. During the day. But the campground was completely empty because it was a weekday and it's cold up there."

Dani took Ellis's hand. "Why did they beat you?"

"You know why."

"Oh no. No . . ." Tears pooled in her eyes.

"They didn't do it," Ellis said.

Her eyes went wide. "You fought them off?"

"I stabbed one of them. Bad. The other had to take him to get help."

"Oh my god!"

"I think he may have died."

"You don't know? The police didn't tell you?"

"I never told the police."

"What? Why not?"

Ellis put her hands over her face. "Dani . . . there's so much you don't know." She moved her hands away and looked into Dani's eyes. "Even since we were close at school."

"I know," she said.

"I'm sorry. It's not you. It's hard for me to get close to people."

"I know that, too." She squeezed Ellis's hand. "I've always admired you. You're so strong about everything. But now I see I shouldn't have admired that." She made her familiar wry half smile. "I should have tried to help you not be strong, to let your guard down sometimes."

"You did try. I saw that. But I couldn't." Tears burned her eyes. "I'm messed up, Dani. I have been for a really long time."

Dani wrapped her arms around her again. "I love you, Ellis. Please trust me. Come back to the house and we'll talk, okay?"

Ellis looked out the windshield at the three lanes of cars traveling at high speed. "I'm afraid."

"To go on the highway?"

"Yes."

"We can leave one of the cars here."

"No," she said, remembering the two men breaking into her car.

"How about we both turn on our flashers and go slow in the right lane? The next exit isn't that far. Just follow me. Can you do that? Just look at me and nothing else?"

"I'll try."

"You can do it. Think of all those mountains you climbed. Pretend the highway is a mountain and you just need to get to the top."

5

Ellis heard her phone ping on her way to work. If it wasn't spam, it had to be Keith. He was the only person she texted. Even Dani knew not to.

She pulled her car into the employee lot. She'd heard from Keith yesterday. He always initiated contact, but he rarely texted more than once a month. She supposed he didn't want to risk Ellis giving up on what little communication they had.

Their six-word exchanges had become a sort of joke between them since his first text more than a year and a half before. They each delivered three words, never one or two, and he never broke the one-text-per-day limit, even when one of her answers elicited a response. Like the time he asked, How's it going? and she replied, Got a job. He'd waited until the next day to ask, What's the job? She replied, A plant nursery.

Ellis looked at her phone, and her chest tightened. I'm getting married.

She stared at the three words. Keith Gephardt getting married. Yesterday he had asked, How are you? and she'd answered, I'm doing great, because all weekend she'd been keyed up about a house a real estate agent had shown her on Friday. She was going back to look at it after work.

The news was difficult to process. When she imagined Keith, she didn't associate him with another woman. She saw him at their table at Pink Horses grinning at her, looking into her eyes after they slow danced. She saw him drinking cognac in the snow. Laughing as he lifted off her layers of clothes inside the tent.

He was probably waiting for an answer.

Ellis typed three words: How great! Congratulations! She pressed "Send."

He couldn't answer. That was their limit for the day.

But maybe the game was over. Maybe that was why he'd told her. He was trying to let her know they had to stop.

Ellis still had five minutes until she was supposed to be inside the nursery.

I'm happy for you, Keith, but we should stop doing this now, she wrote.

Hey, you broke the rules!

So he hadn't expected to stop.

We're breaking bigger rules if we keep texting.

He didn't answer for a minute.

I guess you're right.

Have a good life. I mean that.

You too. And so do I.

She stared at their last words until the phone went black and her face reflected back at her. Like when she'd put her phone beneath the rock in the river. That was the day she'd met the park ranger.

She threw the phone into her backpack and got out of the car. She had a lot to do. She was making mixed planters to show off the pansies, snapdragons, and other fall annuals. And later, a big shipment of camellias was coming in. Gardening was a year-round hobby in north-central Florida.

She had time to make only one planter. The garden shop was busy for a Monday morning. She helped a customer select ten shrubs to make a privacy barrier and loaded them into her pickup. She discussed different kinds of bamboo with another customer. A woman using a cane asked for help pulling her cart around the lot as she selected annuals.

At noon, she took time to eat lunch because the shipment would arrive soon. She sat in her usual place at the picnic bench beneath a huge live oak behind the garden shop building. Ellis loved it back there. There was a small trickling pond—one of four the owners had built to display water plants—and the space was bordered with blooming azaleas in the spring and camellias in the autumn and winter. The large shrubs provided complete privacy because they were planted thirty years before by Ruth and Anne, the two sisters who owned Southern Roots Garden Shop and Nursery.

Ruth entered the employee garden while Ellis was eating the second half of her sandwich.

"Is the truck here?" Ellis asked.

"Not yet." The white-haired woman limped to the other side of the bench and sat down. "I have some news. We have a buyer."

Ellis set down the sandwich.

"Yeah, I know," Ruth said.

"When would it change over?" Ellis asked.

"Not sure. But before it's final, I'll ask you once more: Are you sure you don't want to find a partner and buy it?"

"I can't. I think I'm going to buy that place out in the country. There's no way I could afford both."

"This is the place you looked at last Friday?"

Ellis nodded. "Twenty-eight acres with an old house and barn."

"Sounds expensive."

"The house is a shack and a fair portion is wetland."

"And you still want to buy it?"

"It's gorgeous. Huge live oaks, old pastures with wildflowers, and even a cattail marsh. You should see it."

Ruth smiled.

"I'm hoping I can get the price down. The seller is the granddaughter of the former owners. She lives in LA, and she's been trying to sell it for four years."

"Be careful. A property that's been on the market that long must have problems."

"I know what the main problem is. The house is basically unlivable."

Ruth looked alarmed. "And you'd still buy it?"

"I need somewhere to live. Both my roommates are finishing their doctorates and leaving soon. I don't want to live in town anyway."

"But where would you live if the house is that bad?"

"It's livable enough for me. I'm used to camping."

"Are you sure the house is worth fixing?"

"I'm going to bring Max out there after work today and see what she thinks."

"That makes me feel better," Ruth said. "She'll tell you straight."

"If she thinks it can work, I'm going to ask her if she wants to hire on to do some of the labor."

"Great idea!" Ruth said. "Anne and I have been worried about her. If the new owners won't let her stay on here, I don't know where she'd get a job. She's been with us for twelve years."

"She could get a job anywhere. She's a brilliant carpenter."

"I know, but why do you think she works here instead of with a contractor? No one would hire her. The communication situation was seen as a problem."

"Well, their loss."

"It is. I bet she'd love fixing up a house."

Ellis hadn't intended to talk to Ruth about her idea yet, but it burst out before she could stop herself. "Do you think she'd have any interest in running a plant business?"

"There's no way she can buy this place. She and her father are barely holding on."

"I didn't mean Southern Roots," Ellis said. "I'm thinking . . ."

It was all so unlikely. But it was a goal. A dream. The first she'd had in years.

"I'm thinking of starting a native plant nursery on the property."

"Ellis!" was all Ruth could say.

"You've seen how everyone comes in here asking for natives. They're growing in popularity."

"But our bread and butter is the nonnatives."

"I know. But gardeners are becoming more ecologically conscious. Even the big landscape companies are doing natives."

"You'd be out in the country. Who would drive that far to buy plants?"

"People who really want native plants. I've seen them. I've talked to them. I think this area is ripe for natives."

Ruth grinned. "Damn, I wish you could buy this place. You haven't been here two years and look at you! You could easily take over."

"Thanks to you and Anne. You've been great teachers. How is Anne doing?"

"Not good. They say she needs another surgery."

"I'm so sorry," Ellis said.

Ruth nodded and patted Ellis's hand. "I like this idea you have. I'll help you with it as much as I can. I want you to quit work early today and show that house to Maxine."

"What if it gets busy?"

"This is more important."

Three hours later, Ellis left in her SUV, Max following in her old pickup. The property was rural but only about thirty minutes from Gainesville. The old cattle gate at the entrance was open when they arrived. The real estate agent was already there.

Ellis drove slowly down the winding gravel road that led to the house. Her reaction was as intense as it had been on Friday. As she drove under the huge moss-draped oaks, cabbage palms, and loblolly pines, she felt giddy with need for the place. It was wild like Wild Wood, like the mountain forests she'd camped in, yet wholly different. Nowhere she'd lived looked like Florida's forests. There were no memories here. None. Not even ravens. There were only crows, including a new kind she'd never seen—the fish crow that said "carr" instead of "caaw."

Ellis pulled up to the old house with its wide porch and tin roof. She could so easily imagine herself living there. And she already knew the name of her business. Wild Wood Natives. She would allow that one memory from her past. Nothing but those two words.

Even Keith would be banished from this place. How appropriate that their texts ended today. Ellis would erase the conversation. She would delete his number. And very soon, she would forget him because she would be starting a new life.

Ellis greeted the real estate agent on the front porch, being careful of the rotting boards beneath her feet. Max ignored the agent, immediately sizing up the house. She shot Ellis an amused look, an expression that seemed to say, "Seriously? You want to buy this piece of crap?"

Ellis shrugged.

Maxine smiled, shaking her head, and walked into the house.

The agent followed the sturdy middle-aged woman into the kitchen. "I hear you're a carpenter?" she said.

"She can't hear you," Ellis said. "She's deaf. But yes, she's a carpenter. She does all the building repairs at the nursery where we work. Last year, she built a new pavilion for the shade plants. It's really beautiful."

"I've seen it," the agent said. "I buy all my plants at Southern Roots. I've seen her working there but never knew she was deaf."

Many nursery customers thought Max was either very rude or had a mental problem. When they asked questions, she'd ignore them rather than signal that she couldn't hear them. Ellis liked that about her, her refusal to explain herself. She had lost most of her hearing and was badly scarred in an accident that killed her mother and nearly took her life when she was a teenager. She never talked about what happened or her reasons for refusing to learn sign language. Her father had taught her his plumbing, electrical, and carpentry knowledge, hoping the skills would provide her with a livelihood. But few employers other than Ruth and Anne had been willing to adjust to Max's code of silence.

Max spent an hour looking at the house. She delved into every closet and cabinet, beneath every sink. She took her ladder off her truck and walked all over the tin roof. She climbed into the attic and crawled around in the dirt beneath the house. She looked at the water pump and the septic hill. Then she spent another half hour inspecting the barn.

The real estate agent was getting impatient. Ellis lifted her eyebrows at Max to ask what she thought.

Max took her notepad and pencil out of her pocket. *I like it,* she wrote. *Really cool Old Florida style. Roof and barn in pretty good shape.*

Ellis nodded.

But needs LOTS of work, Max wrote.

Ellis took the pencil and paper and wrote, *I know. But I can barely afford it as is. And I love the acreage that goes with it. Is the house fixable?*

Max looked thoughtfully at the house, then wrote, *Would be sad if it was torn down. It is beautiful.*

Ellis agreed, but she needed more advice than that. She let the question remain in her eyes.

Max looked around at the mossy live oaks and palms, the two huge swamp chestnut oaks rising up from behind the house. She took a few steps toward the porch, her gaze distant, as if she were seeing what the house could become. She wrote, *It can be fixed. But will take a long time.*

Ellis took the paper and wrote, *Any chance you'd want to work on it? I'd pay the going rate.*

A sudden brightness appeared in Max's eyes. She liked the idea. *And after that—maybe help with the native plant nursery I want to open here?*

Max's eyes lit up even brighter. She'd been despondent since Ruth and Anne had decided to sell Southern Roots. The nursery and Ruth and Anne were like her home and family.

Ellis flipped to another page in her notepad. *Wild Wood Natives, created by Ellis Abbey and Maxine Kidd.*

Max frowned, grabbed the pencil, and drew a big X over the words.

Ellis felt awful. She'd presumed too much.

Max flipped to the next page in the notebook. *Don't let the agent see how eager you are! I hope you haven't told her these plans?*

Ellis shook her head.

Good. Keep quiet. Say I said it's worth 80K less than they're asking.

Ellis took the pencil. *80K! It's already been reduced.*

Max shook her head and tapped her finger on her words.

Ellis wrote, *If I buy, are you interested?*

Max stared at the old house, a little smile on her lips, and that was answer enough.

6

Ellis lightly touched Max's boot to let her know dinner was ready. Max withdrew from under the sink and eagerly took the sandwich Ellis handed to her. They ate seated cross-legged on the sandy floor planks. When she finished, Max leaned her head toward the sink and nodded to indicate that she was almost done.

"Wow, running water in the kitchen," Ellis said. "That will be luxurious."

Max smiled.

Ellis had learned she could lip-read many words, or at least understand the gist of much of what she said. Ellis nodded to the front door, code for quitting time. Max shook her head and held up a finger to say, *One more minute.* They both still had jobs at Southern Roots but tried to cram as much renovation as possible into their evenings and days off.

Ellis walked to the front porch to watch the sunset through the trees. Max had fixed the porch boards when Ellis took over the house two weeks earlier. Ellis sat in one of two rocking chairs Dani and Brad had given her as a housewarming gift.

Above her, one of the pair of barred owls called, "Whoo-a!" Its mate returned a call from down the hill. Ellis had a feeling they had nested in a sizable hollow in one of the chestnut oaks behind the house, close to the screened porch. Ellis had laid her queen mattress on the floor out there. She liked to listen to the owls, tree frogs, and katydids as she fell asleep.

She wondered where Quercus was. Usually he sat on the porch with her in the evening.

Ellis had adopted Quercus from animal control. She told the woman at the shelter to take her to a big dog that had been there for a long time. As soon as Ellis set eyes on the Newfoundland mix, she knew he was the one. Few people wanted a dog that size, and at age four or more, he'd already lived out half the expected years for a large breed.

Quercus was barking at something up by the road. Maybe the lady with the horse who occasionally trotted by.

Ellis stood when the dog's barking got closer and more intense. Someone was on her property. The usual panic crushed down on her. It always felt the same. Her chest was tight, and she could swear the scar from the stab wound ached.

She reminded herself that Max was there, and she carried a gun in her truck. Ellis jogged up the hill to see what was going on. When she was halfway to the fence, Quercus quit barking. A few more steps and Ellis saw the dog. He was standing over a man lying on his back on the ground. Quercus appeared to be licking the man's face.

"Quercus!" Ellis called.

The dog looked at her for a few seconds, wagging his fluffy tail, then returned his attention to the man.

Ellis approached slowly. "This is private property," she called to the man.

"I could use some help here, Ellis," the man said. "I'm drowning."

"Keith?"

"Yes, Keith. Soon to be ex-Keith . . ."

Ellis hurried over. "Quercus, come!" she said, pulling on the dog's collar.

"Quercus. Good name," Keith said from beneath the dog. "I feel like there's an oak tree on my chest."

Ellis lifted the dog off him, and Keith got to his feet. But as soon as she let go of the dog's collar, Quercus nearly knocked him over again.

"No! No!" Ellis said.

"Quercus, *sit*!" Keith said in a firm voice.

The dog sat and stared up at him, tongue lolling out of his grin.

"How did you do that?" she said.

"Firm tone. He has to know you mean it."

"Well, that's not good if someone with bad intentions knows how to use it."

He looked at her as he petted the dog's head. "I figured that was why you had him."

His comment irritated her. Since she'd bought the property, she'd been getting the same warnings she used to get when she camped alone. It brought back fears she'd worked hard to conquer.

"How did you get in?" she asked.

"The gate was locked, so I climbed the fence. Dani gave me your address—but failed to provide the tiny detail of this behemoth guarding your property."

Behemoth. How could she be angry at a man who used such a great word? *Was* she angry about him suddenly showing up in her front yard? And why had he come? She truly couldn't sort out how she felt about Keith Gephardt being there.

"You went to my old house?"

"Yes, and I couldn't call to ask if I could come over because, according to Dani, you never turn on your phone."

"Not never. Only when I have to."

"Which is nearly never."

That was true. Since she'd stopped communicating with him, she had no reason to leave her phone on. It was off except when she had to make a call.

"This is a big surprise," she said.

He studied her eyes. "A bad surprise?"

"Just a surprise."

She saw that had hurt.

"Should I leave?" he asked.

"Of course not. Come down to the house."

"Talk about surprises. I could hardly believe it when Dani said you'd bought a place."

"Why?"

"You know why. You're the wandering queen."

"People change."

His sympathetic look irked her. Because he knew what had changed her. Dani often looked at her like that, too.

Just as the house came into view, Keith stopped walking. "Can I tell you something?"

She stopped and faced him. "What?"

"You didn't kill that guy."

"What guy?"

"You don't have to hide it from me. I haven't told anyone." When she didn't respond, he said, "I know you stabbed one of two men who attacked you."

"How do you know?"

"I'm a park ranger. I know cops. I did some research."

How she felt about that confused her as much as his sudden appearance.

"He and the other guy showed up at an ER. They said he'd been mugged. He very nearly died. He needed emergency abdominal surgery."

"Why are you telling me this?"

"To give you peace of mind. And closure. You might also want to know he's in jail now."

"Oh god. Did he attack another woman?"

"He stole a car and robbed a store at gunpoint. It wasn't his first offense. He got twenty years."

Someone could have died in the robbery. Ellis had felt guilty about that—the possibility that her failure to report the crime might lead to another person's death. Or rape.

"The other guy is dead," Keith said.

"What happened?"

"Not sure. A fight that went wrong, from what I can tell."

"Why did you look them up if you weren't going to report the crime? Why do you care so much?"

An odd look surfaced in his dark eyes. "You should know why."

"What should I know?"

"It's that spell you put on me back at Pink Horses. Do you remember?"

She remembered.

"It won't rub off no matter how hard I try. I came here to ask you to take it off."

"Does what's-her-name know you're here?"

His lips curled slightly. "No. Chloe knows nothing of my whereabouts since I broke off our engagement."

Ellis tried to conceal how that news made her feel—mostly from herself. "Why did you end it?"

"Aren't you listening?"

"Oh—the spell?"

"Yes, the spell."

"You drove all the way to Florida to ask a witch to take a spell off you?"

"A gorgeous witch."

"Just so you know, flattery gets you nowhere with a witch."

"What does? I can't handle this much longer. Please remove it."

She saw by the look in his eyes that it was no joke. The park ranger had fallen for her. But how could she pretend not to have known that? He'd come rushing to her aid from miles away in the middle of the night. He'd spent a whole day driving her to Florida. He'd texted all those months when he was living with another woman.

"Hey . . . Ellis . . . there's someone pointing a gun at us."

She followed his sight line. It was Max.

"She's pointing it at you, actually," Ellis said.

"I assume you know her?"

"That's Maxine."

"Any chance you could get her to lower the gun? Confronting my mortality twice in five minutes is a bit much."

Ellis motioned downward. Max lowered the gun but held it at her side and kept her eyes fixed on Keith.

He looked at Ellis. "Are you with someone now? Is she . . . ?"

"She's not my girlfriend."

He stared at Max again.

"She and I are renovating the house—that shack behind her. She's teaching me some carpentry skills."

"How's that going? She seems a little intense . . ."

"It's going okay." She put her hand on his cheek to turn his attention away from Max and her gun. "Can we get back to the spell?"

"Yeah, definitely. Will you help me with that?"

She kept her hand on his face, and he leaned into it. His face felt good, familiar. As if they had parted only months ago.

"Before I help you with it, you need to know about me. I'm not a good witch."

He smiled.

"Seriously. I'm a bad witch. You have to be okay with that."

"Bad like you might turn me into a toad?"

"Bad that I regret and don't ever talk about."

He looked uneasy.

"Agreed?"

"You're doing it again. Like you did that night when you invited me into the woods. I had no idea what I was getting into."

"Caveat emptor," she said.

"What does that mean again?"

"Let the buyer beware."

"Damn, you are the most mysterious woman I've ever met."

She stroked his cheek. "Do you like that?"

"Apparently, I do. I can't stop thinking about you. You've wrecked me."

She gestured for him to follow her. "Come on."

"Where?"

"To help you with the spell."

"In the shack?"

"In the shack."

"That's a seriously witchy-looking house." He gazed around the twilit acres as they walked. "And these giant trees with the moss hanging down. This place suits you, Ellis."

"I call it the Wild Wood."

Max was getting in her truck to go home. She'd seen Ellis touch Keith's cheek, now knew she could leave them alone together. She smiled when Ellis waved from the front door. Quercus flopped down on the porch, panting heavily from the heat.

In the bare living room, Keith immediately spotted Gep on the fireplace mantel. The blue pony was one of Ellis's very few belongings.

He took Gep off the mantel. "This is why I'm here, you know."

"I thought you were here to be freed from a spell."

"I am. But I decided to risk entering the witch's realm because of this pony. When I saw you'd kept it, I supposed there had to be a reason."

"I told you why. He's a good luck charm."

"Why would a powerful witch need a good luck charm?"

"I use whatever presents itself to make my magic."

"If I take it back, will the spell be removed?"

She took the pony from his hand and returned it to the mantel. "I'll divulge no secrets."

Outside, one of the barred owls called, "Whoo-a!"

Keith smiled, looking out the window at the forest. "Is the owl your familiar?"

"There's a pair that might have a nest hole out back. Come see."

She led him to the screened porch. "Their nest might be that hollow in the big chestnut oak over there. I sleep out here so I can be close to the owls and all the other night sounds. You should hear when the flocks of black-bellied ducks fly over at night."

He looked at her mattress, a lamp, and several bags of clothing on the floor. "So you're basically camping in the woods again."

"But with a toilet, shower, and kitchen close by. And a fan." She pulled the chain to turn on the overhead fan.

"How very civilized. But no air-conditioning?"

"It's broken, and I can't afford a new system yet. For now, I just don't wear clothes."

He grinned. "Really?"

"No one can see this house. And if someone tries, Quercus would put a quick end to their peeping. He hears anything that moves out there."

"So I noticed."

Even in the dim twilight, she could see how much the heat and humidity were making him sweat. He was dressed for October weather in Ohio, in khaki pants, long-sleeve button-down shirt, T-shirt, and closed shoes. She was barefoot, wearing shorts and a tank top with nothing under. When Max was around, she had to wear clothes, but she wore as few as possible in the muggy weather that wouldn't abate until closer to December.

"Speaking of clothes, you need to shed a few," she said.

He lifted his brows. "Do I?"

"You look hot." She gestured toward the mattress on the floor. "Have a seat. That's my couch, dining room chair, reading recliner, and bed. Take your pick."

"Do I have to say which I chose?"

"It'll be your secret."

He sat down. She sat next to him while he took off his shoes and socks. She slid off his shirt and T-shirt. "Better?"

"Much. Are we starting the spell removal?"

She stroked her hand on his chest. "You know, you're much too trusting."

"Am I?"

"Here you are in a witch's lair at night, and you assume I'm going to remove that spell?"

"You aren't?"

She rose up on her knees and almost but didn't quite kiss his lips. "Maybe I'm going to make it stronger instead."

"That would be bad," he said, taking her in his arms.

"I told you I am."

He pulled her down to the mattress, holding her against his chest. "Bad witches like to be on top, if I remember correctly."

"You have a good memory."

"It's been painfully good."

"I can fix that." She stripped off her tank top.

"I feel better already. Your magic is strong."

"You have no idea. Ready for more?"

"Why ask when your spell has me in unconditional surrender?"

"I seem to remember you have some pretty strong magic of your own."

"You knew?" he asked.

"I knew. That was no toy pony you hid in my pocket." She pinned him beneath the weight of her body. "May the best magic win."

PART FOUR

Daughter of Raven

1

Raven stood a foot away from the wooden fence. She was always careful when she went to the boundary. She made sure her feet didn't touch a piece of grass that leaned over onto Jackie's land.

Jackie's family was busy, hurrying in and out of the house. None of them noticed her standing at the fence. They were packing their car for a long camping trip. To Colorado—Rocky Mountain National Park—Jackie's mother had told Raven on the last day of school.

Raven watched Jackie's new father, Mr. Danner, arrange things in the back of the SUV. He'd been Raven's gym teacher for three years, starting when Raven was in third grade. He and Ms. Taft fell in love right away and married the summer after Jackie finished elementary school.

Jackie came out of the house and gave something to Mr. Danner that made him laugh and pat Jackie on the shoulder. Raven was glad Jackie and Huck had a nice man like Mr. Danner for a father. And Ms. Taft was very happy. Her name was Ms. Danner now—because she hadn't wanted to keep her ex-husband's name, Jackie said. Jackie called himself *Jack Danner*. He had told his friends to call him *Jack* since fifth grade, but his family still called him *Jackie*. Raven did, too. He was a lot bigger now, but he would always be *Jackie* to her.

Raven stepped closer to the fence when Reece came out of the house with Huck. He must have slept over, and the Danners would take him home as they left town.

Reece immediately noticed her. He said something to Huck, and both boys jogged across the lawn toward her.

"Checking out the greener grass on the other side of the fence?" Reece said.

"I guess so," she said.

Huck looked sad and angry, as he always did when anything about the fence was mentioned. Reece, of course, had made it into a joke since the day she'd told them she couldn't put one foot on the other side.

"When do you leave for Montana?" Huck asked.

"Tomorrow," she said.

"Why is everyone going to see more of this nature shit?" Reece said, gesturing at the fields and trees. "If I could get out of here, I'd go to New York City."

"I'll go with," Huck said.

Reece held up his hand for a high five. "Road trip. First one of us who gets a car."

Huck slapped his hand and looked over his shoulder. "Speaking of trips, I have to get more stuff into the car before Jackie takes up all the space that's left."

"Hair products?" Reece said.

Huck snorted. "Yeah, and clothes."

"Jackie is into hair and fashion these days. He was quite the stud of sixth grade," Reece said to Raven.

Raven hardly knew anything about Jackie now. She saw him only briefly on the rare occasions his mother brought him to the elementary school.

"I gotta go," Huck said. "Have a good summer."

"You too," she said.

Reece stayed when Huck jogged back to the house. He leaned his arms on the top board of the old wood fence. "You know this is ridiculous, right?"

"What is?" she asked, though she knew.

"This fence thing. Just come over here. Say hi to Jackie."

"I made a promise. You know that."

"You were seven when Maleficent made that decree. You're old enough to know it's bullshit now."

"Stop calling her that."

He sighed and ducked through the opening in the fence. He sat in the long grass, and she settled next to him.

"How's it going with her?"

"Okay."

He looked in her eyes. "You can tell me the truth, you know. I live with my own version of Maleficent."

"There's nothing to say."

"There are volumes to say, I bet."

She watched a grasshopper climb up a grass stem. If she were still seven, she'd think it might be one of Mama's spies. She didn't worry about that so much anymore. But she wouldn't be surprised if Mama were watching her from the trees.

Reece wrapped his arm around her. "Please don't let her make you crazy. I know how it feels to battle that."

The weight of his arm felt so good. She had missed that. He'd sometimes hugged one arm around her when they were on the school bus. Or out on the playground. He didn't care if the other boys teased him.

She leaned into him and breathed in his new grown-up scent.

He hugged her tighter. "I'm always here for you, Bird Girl. Remember that. Anytime."

"I know." She smiled. "Do you remember my first day on the playground?"

"That was your second day."

"Those kids never called me Bird Girl again."

"Of course they didn't. *Bird Girl* is mine. Trademarked. Legally punishable by my fists if anyone else uses it."

That was pretty much what he'd said to the kids who'd taunted her after hearing Reece use the pet name. Reece and Huck quickly put an end to the teasing. They and all their friends—and Jackie—had been loyal protectors while she was getting used to the bizarre world of elementary school.

They sat quietly watching Mr. Danner pack the car.

"I still haven't gotten used to Danner being their dad," Reece said.

"I know. Why couldn't everything stay the same?"

"Same as what?"

She didn't answer because she knew what she'd said was stupid.

"You mean the summer we met you?"

When she didn't reply, he hugged his arm tighter around her shoulders and tried to look at her down-turned face. "That is what you meant, isn't it? The last thing you and I should want is for time to stand still. We need to get away from this place—from our mothers."

She couldn't even imagine that kind of future.

"Aren't you excited about middle school next year?" he asked. "You'll have Jackie to talk to again."

"I wish you and Huck were going to be there."

"You wish we'd flunked?"

She smiled. "No. I just wish you were there."

"If only to be with you, I wish I was, too."

"Do you want to go to high school?" she asked.

"Yeah. One step closer to getting out of this damn place." He pulled his arm off her. "So what's this place like in Montana? Is it nice like your house here?"

"How do you know my house here is nice?"

"People talk."

She remembered Jackie saying that when she first met him.

"The cabin in Montana isn't anything like the house here," she said. "It's tiny and doesn't have running water."

"Really?"

"We use an outhouse and get water from a pump out front."

"My god. No wonder you hate it."

"I never said I hated it."

"No, but you have a look of gloom at the end of every school year."

"It's really beautiful there. The mountains are right outside."

"I bet it's lonely," he said.

It was. But she wouldn't say anything bad about the Montana cabin. Mama loved it there.

"Well, look who's coming," Reece said. "The boy with the awesomest hair."

Huck had probably told Jackie that Raven was there. She could see how he'd been *quite the stud of sixth grade*. He was beautiful. But of course, she'd always thought that.

Raven stood but made sure to keep her feet away from the grass at the boundary.

"Hey, Raven," Jackie said.

"Hi," she said. "Ready for your trip?"

"Yeah. We're about to leave. If Huck would stop loading stuff into the car."

Raven and Reece shot each other a smile.

"What?" Jackie said.

"Nothing," Reece said. "Your hair looks nice today, Jacko."

"Shut up," Jackie said.

"So much for my random act of kindness for the day," Reece said, and even Jackie smiled.

"My mom told me about Baby," Jackie said. "She said you think she might have died."

"I know she died," Raven said. "She stopped coming for peanuts three months ago."

"Maybe she flew somewhere else."

"She always came to me. Even after we returned from Montana every year."

She couldn't hold back her tears. Or come to terms with never seeing Baby again. The thought of her getting plucked and eaten alive by a hawk haunted her. Raven had seen it happen often enough to imagine it in horrific detail.

Reece took her in his arms. "Good job, Jackie."

"What? I just found out yesterday."

"You didn't have to bring it up." Reece hugged her tighter.

"Jeez, Reece."

"What?" Reece said.

"Nothing. You'd better come. We're leaving. Bye, Raven."

She pulled away from Reece's embrace and wiped away the tears. "Bye, Jackie. Have fun."

"I will." He cast an odd look at Reece and jogged toward the house.

"That's hilarious," Reece said.

"What is?"

"He's jealous."

"Of what?"

Reece grinned. "You know what."

Raven stared at Jackie's tall figure, wishing it to be true.

"Oh my god. You too?"

"What?"

"Now I wish I was still in middle school."

"Why?"

"I want to see this thing play out."

"You'd better go," she said. "Mr. Danner is looking over here."

"Is Jackie looking?" he asked.

"Yes."

He took her in his arms and gave her a very long goodbye kiss on her cheek.

2

Kids in high school thought a lot about sex. And talked a lot about it. And smirked and joked about it. And speculated about who was doing it with whom. Raven didn't understand all the intrigue. She supposed that was because she was Daughter of Raven. In a raven's world, acts of procreation were straightforward survival. If an organism failed to pass its genetics to the next generation before it died, its genes would be forever lost to the earth. Reproduction was a serious business out in the fields, forests, and rivers.

As she'd gotten older, she'd sometimes questioned the truth of her parentage. She'd not met one person who practiced Mama's ancient earth arts—though, of course, she wouldn't know how to find them when they were also hiding their true nature. But Raven couldn't doubt her origins for long when she keenly sensed her differences from other people. At school, away from the comfort of Mama's fields and forests, she felt distant from the teenagers and her teachers. She could actually feel her raven spirit perched apart from them, watching them with wariness and growing cynicism, which must come from a convergence of her raven and human souls.

She suspected many students viewed her with equal suspicion. She had felt their scrutiny since her first week in elementary school. The children had been curious, even envious, of her group of defensive boys, and that in itself made Raven stand out too much. Jackie's mother had been as protective, probably had told the other teachers about Raven's background. Raven knew some of the teachers paid extra attention to her because they felt sorry for her: the homeschooled girl who wasn't allowed to use computers, phones, or TVs at home and who could use the internet for schoolwork only if absolutely necessary. Mama had been adamant about that when she brought Raven to the office to register her for second grade. Raven had felt odd and pitied by the principal and office workers within minutes of entering the school.

Raven ate her lunch and tried to ignore that the hushed chatter at the table was about her. Or more accurately, about Chris. Lately he sat with her and talked to her more. Raven could tell many at the lunch table were watching everything they did.

Being a freshman was a large part of the interest. Chris was a senior. Huck, Reece, and Jackie didn't think a senior should hit on a freshman. Specifically, they didn't think Chris should hit on her. They thought she was too naive for high school boys.

She was grateful that they *had her back*, as kids said, but she resented that they still saw her as an innocent who'd been raised by a crazy mother. That perception bothered her more and more. She wanted the boys to treat her like they treated their other friends.

When Raven finished her sandwich, Chris leaned close and whispered, "Happy birthday." He put a cupcake he'd been hiding in front of her. "Sorry it got a little squished."

Raven hid her surprise. She'd forgotten that March twelfth was the day Mama had put on her birth certificate. She and Mama always celebrated her birthday at the time of the spring equinox.

The cupcake caused a stir among the lunch group.

"You better have brought one for everyone," Reece said to Chris.

"It's her birthday," Chris said.

Everyone at the table said, "Happy birthday, Raven!"

Jackie mumbled something about being sorry he'd forgotten. His mother had been the first to acknowledge the date. When Raven was in second grade, Ms. Taft had looked up her birthday in the school records. She'd given her birthday treats to hand out to her class at lunch—an important ritual in elementary school. That was how everyone found out about her fake birthday.

"How could you possibly remember that?" Huck asked Chris.

"Easy. My birthday is on the twelfth, too," Chris said.

"Today?" someone at the table asked.

"August. I hope you like chocolate cake?" he asked Raven.

"I love it."

She didn't want to eat the cupcake with them all watching, but she did for Chris's sake.

"Want some?" she asked him.

"Maybe a bite." He bit it next to where she had and handed it back to her.

That caused a lot of raised eyebrows, and Chris cast a challenging look. Raven liked that. Joining his rebellion, she dabbed a smear of chocolate from the side of his mouth with her paper napkin.

Reece fanned his T-shirt. "Does it feel hot in here or is it me?" he said.

Several at the table snickered.

"It's hot," Chris said, looking at Raven.

"Let's go," Jackie said to Raven. "Bell's about to ring."

He always walked her to math class because his was in the same hall.

When Jackie stood, Sadie, his girlfriend since December, made a show of kissing him goodbye. Raven found all the posturing amusing. It was like when she watched marmot colonies in the mountains of Montana.

Jackie was quiet as they walked out of the lunchroom. When they neared their classrooms, he asked, "Do you like Chris?"

"Of course I like Chris."

"As a friend?"

"You know he's my friend."

"You know what I mean," he said.

"Why are you asking me this?"

"Because . . . I just want to make sure you know what you're doing. Chris is a lot more experienced than you are."

"Are you saying you don't trust him?"

"No. He's a nice guy."

She stopped walking and faced him. "Then what's the problem?"

He searched her eyes, as if trying to read her feelings for Chris. "There is no problem," he said. "I'll see you on the bus."

"You aren't driving home with Huck?"

"He has baseball practice."

Raven sat at her desk and opened her backpack. She ran her fingers over the old copy of *Great Expectations* she'd picked up from the library on her way to lunch. She couldn't start it on the bus because Jackie would want to talk to her. And that would make Sadie jealous and she'd start babbling to get his attention. It happened every time Jackie rode the bus. She liked to be with Jackie, but she almost wished he wasn't going to be on the bus.

Raven had started reading library books on the bus in fifth grade, the first year she rode alone because her friends had moved up to middle school. She relished immersing herself in novels, especially in love stories, and she still hid her library books from Mama. Her mother said reading love stories was a silly waste of time. But she had to be wrong about that. *Romeo and Juliet* and *Pride and Prejudice* were love stories, and she had studied them in English class. From novels, Raven had learned things about people and their relationships she couldn't have found out from Mama or the earth spirits.

Chris was waiting for her in front of the doors to the buses. And thanks to everything she'd learned from novels, Raven knew why he was there. She perceived that he liked her as more than a friend, and now he'd decided to do something about it. That was always a good part in a love story. She wondered if he'd try to kiss her. Her heart beat fast.

"Hey," Chris said.

"Hey," she said.

"I was wondering if you'd want to drive with me instead of take the bus," he said. "We could stop at Bear's and get something to eat for your birthday. I'm buying."

"You already gave me a gift."

"That was nothing."

"It was nice."

"Then let me be nicer."

"Chris . . . you know how it is. At my house."

A familiar glint of resentment lit his eyes. Chris, Jackie, Huck, and Reece were the only four people Raven had told about her promise to never set foot on the Taft property. She'd told them mostly to warn them not to come on her property—because her mother had made the comment about her gun. That was long ago, but it still enraged the boys.

"Are you worried about the driveway cameras?" Chris asked.

She nodded.

"I'll drop you off where the cameras can't see. I'll get you back around the same time as usual. That's a long bus ride."

Even if he did, the cameras would record the bus going past her driveway without letting her off. Raven didn't know if Mama looked at those videos. If she did, if she found out Raven had come home with a boy, Raven couldn't predict how she would respond.

"Don't you ever want to say *screw it* to all that?" Chris said.

She'd never had a reason to, but now maybe she did.

"Just try it," he said. "You said she never hits you. What's the worst that could happen?"

Mama's anger was what would happen. It had terrified her more than anything when she was little. But she wasn't little anymore. She was old enough that a beautiful senior boy might want to kiss her.

"Okay," she said.

"Okay? Really?"

She nodded. She liked how happy he looked.

They were a few steps out the door when Jackie caught up to her. "Aren't you taking the bus?"

"Chris is driving me home," she said.

"What about your mom?"

It was as if they saw double when they looked at her: Raven plus the shadow of her mother. She was so tired of not being just Raven to them.

"I guess my mom will have to deal with it," she said.

Jackie looked stunned. Chris grinned.

"See you tomorrow," she said to Jackie.

"The rebel emerges!" Chris said. "I like it!"

His car was parked in the senior lot. Many of the seniors stared at them. Some said hello to Chris, and a few greeted Raven.

It made her feel different. Less of an outcast. And maybe prettier than she usually saw herself. Chris was popular, a football player.

She was suddenly aware of what she was wearing. She was glad she'd worn her favorite jeans, sweater, and boots. Raven had endeavored to look like her peers since she'd started school, and to that same end, Mama let her order almost any clothes she wanted.

"Bear's?" Chris asked when he started driving.

"I hear the milkshakes are good," she said.

"They're awesome. Cookies and cream is my favorite."

"I'll get that," she said.

"Have you ever been there?" he asked.

"Yeah, all the time. It's my mom's favorite junk food."

He laughed, realizing she was joking. He glanced at her as he drove. "You're different today."

Good, he'd noticed. She leaned back in the seat and looked at scenery she didn't usually get to see.

When they pulled into the lot at Bear's Burgers, she saw more students from their high school. They were staring.

"Crap, it's crowded today," Chris said. "Do you want to eat here or do drive-through? We could go somewhere quieter to eat our food."

"Let's do that," she said. She wasn't keen on having her every move watched.

At the little window, he ordered two milkshakes. Raven watched everything that happened. She'd never been to a drive-through window. Mama packed food to eat in the truck when they drove to Montana every summer.

He handed her one of the milkshakes. "Good?" he asked as she sipped.

"Really good. Where are we going?"

"You'll see. Birthday surprise."

She looked at more of the town as they drove. She'd rarely seen it, and mostly long ago. Mama had taken her to the library a few times because Aunt Sondra had said Raven needed schooling and socialization. But when Raven went to school, Mama stopped doing that.

Chris drove out of town. But not far down the highway, he turned into a rutted dirt road. A very old sign said STARLITE DRIVE-IN THEATER. He pulled into an open field with rusted metal posts sticking out of the ground. He parked in the middle of the field facing a big dilapidated blank rectangle. "I think they're showing something good today," he said, turning off the car.

"What is that?"

"A movie screen. This used to be a drive-in theater."

She knew what a movie theater was, but she'd never known about going to movies outside. None of her books had mentioned that.

Raven looked around the field scattered with trash. She didn't feel the presence of earth spirits there. Perhaps they had left.

"I would have brought you somewhere nicer," he said, "but we don't have enough time to go farther."

"This is okay," she said. She liked that earth spirits weren't there to spy on her and tell Mama what she was doing.

"Are you too cold from the milkshake to eat outside?" he asked. "I have a blanket we can sit on."

"I'd rather be outside," she said.

"I thought you would."

He took a blanket from the trunk. He spread it some distance from the car, and they sat facing the screen drinking their milkshakes. "So what are we watching?"

She looked at the crumbling white screen. "Nothing."

"Come on, use your imagination. What kind of movie is it? Sci-fi? Horror?"

She wasn't used to playing games like that, but she wanted to. "Love story," she said.

"Really? You got me to watch a love story? You must be persuasive."

"I am."

"Are you enjoying it?"

"It's the best movie I ever saw," she said.

He grinned. The funniest part was that her statement was true. She preferred the blank screen to the movies she and the boys had watched that summer long ago. When they turned on a movie, they mostly stopped talking and stared at the TV. She'd rather have played games or talked and joked with them.

Chris held up his milkshake for a toast. "Happy fifteen," he said as they tapped cups. He kept his dark eyes on hers. "Can I confess something?" he asked.

"Okay."

"Starlite is a famous make-out place."

"Is it?" She didn't know what else to say.

"That's not why I brought you. It was just close, and I knew no one would be here. People come here at night mostly."

He kept looking at her. Something other than the cold drink and chilly air made her feel quivery. She set down her drink and wrapped her arms around her body.

"You're cold." He moved closer and asked, "Is this okay?" as he circled his arm around her.

She thought of Reece, who often did that. And the night Jackie had taken her under his covers and made her chills go away.

"I was telling the truth when I said I didn't bring you here to make out," he said. "But would a kiss be okay?"

She couldn't believe it was going to happen. But she didn't know how to do it. She was too scared to answer.

He moved closer to face her. "Have you ever kissed anyone on those trips you take to Montana?"

She shook her head.

"You've probably never kissed anyone, then? I know you haven't gone out with anyone around here."

He smiled when she didn't answer. "I guess you haven't." He looked at her lips. "I want to be your first kiss. More than anything."

"You . . . do?" She felt peculiar. Her body was as light as air. Almost like flying. As if she had become the half of her that was a feathered spirit.

He looked in her eyes. "Can I give you a birthday kiss?"

"Yes," she said.

He put his lips on hers.

At first it was strange to be touching lips. Only Mama had ever done that. But the way he did it was different. It lasted longer. And he held his mouth a little open. He tasted like cookies and cream.

He moved back and looked in her eyes again. His irises were like black glass. "Like it?"

"Yes."

He took her face in his warm hands. "You're so beautiful. Do you even know that?"

She hadn't known, but now she believed she was.

He kissed her again. A stronger, longer kiss. It was easier than she'd imagined. Her body felt good, like when she was reading about lovers kissing in a book. Except much better because it was really happening. To her.

After the kiss, they held each other. It felt so good, but too soon he took his arms down. "I guess I'd better get you home," he said. "I hope you don't get in trouble."

She realized she had to go right away. Probably the bus would pass her house soon. Jackie's house was the stop after hers. She imagined him looking out the window at her gate and road as he passed. She wondered what he would be thinking, if he might be a little jealous.

They folded the blanket and put it in the car. Raven took a last look at the peculiar site of her first kiss.

"Does your mother watch the cameras for when you arrive?"

"I don't know."

"Let's hope she doesn't." He looked at her as he drove. "If it works out okay with her, do you want to go out again?"

"Yes," she said, though she couldn't imagine how it would happen again.

As they approached her house, she had him stop far enough from the gate that the cameras couldn't catch her getting out of the car. They kissed before she got out. "Good luck," he said. "See you tomorrow."

He drove past the gate rather than turn around. It would have been better if he hadn't passed the gate before she appeared in the cameras, but it was too late to fix that.

She pressed the code into the pad to open the gate and walked the winding lane to the log house. Once behind the protection of the gate, she usually felt like her true self, Daughter of Raven. But after being with Chris, she felt different. An exciting, happy kind of different.

Mama didn't answer when she knocked. She was out with the earth spirits. That happened fairly often. Raven turned off the alarms she'd triggered.

The silence of the house comforted her. Mama didn't know she was late.

Raven would make something special for dinner. Today was her birthday in the human world. Today she had been kissed. She felt more human than usual, as if the raven inside her was sleeping.

3

Raven and Chris became a *thing*, as the kids at school said. They sat together in the lunchroom, and Raven risked letting him drive her home again. They went for a walk in a park. Another day they went to a Mexican restaurant because it was raining. When Mama still hadn't said anything, they went out a fourth time, returning to the Starlite Drive-In with milkshakes.

Reece took her aside at school to warn her, same as Jackie had. He said Chris had a lot more experience than she did. She asked if he trusted Chris, the same question she'd asked Jackie.

"It's not so much whether I trust him," Reece said. "It's more about if I can trust you." He saw she was angry and said, "You know you've lived . . . in a different way than most kids. Your normal isn't the same as his normal. You know what I mean?"

She saw no reason to reply. He was stating the obvious.

"He's been with girls, and you've never been with a guy."

"So what? There has to be a first time for everyone."

"I know. But he might assume things and go too quickly. You'll think you have to . . ."

"I'm not stupid, Reece!"

"I know, I know. I'm sorry. I'm just worried about you. Chris is— he's been kind of obsessed with you. You should know that."

"Obsessed?"

"Yeah. For a long time. Didn't you see it?"

"No."

"Well, we all did. He knew we thought he was too old for you, so you know what he did? He waited for your birthday to ask you out. You turned fifteen—which sounds a lot older than fourteen—and he won't be eighteen until August. So numbers-wise, you're only two years apart. How ridiculous is that? He actually thought that made a difference."

"It's not ridiculous."

"He planned it out."

"Why is that so bad?"

"Because it shows he's kind of nuts about you."

"Would I want to be with a boy who isn't *nuts* about me?" She thought of Jackie. Of all the boys she knew, he was the one she'd wanted to give her a first kiss, but he certainly wasn't nuts about her.

"Just go slow, okay?" Reece said.

"Okay."

He held up his hand. "Still friends, Bird Girl?"

"Of course." She slapped his hand.

Reece's speech had the opposite effect from what he'd wanted. She now trusted Chris more. The next time they went out after school, he took her to an abandoned house he thought was cool. They made out a lot in there. She let him touch her under her shirt.

Spring break came, and they had to stop seeing each other for a week. Raven missed the excitement of going out with Chris. Her life with Mama felt dull in comparison. She would replay her best moments with Chris, but for some reason that often made her think about Jackie. It bothered her a little that she couldn't stop her thoughts about Jackie from intruding into those reveries.

The following Monday at lunch, Chris whispered, "I missed you."

"Me too," she said.

"Did your mom say anything about the videos over spring break?"

"No."

"She must not look at the cameras."

Raven had come to the same conclusion. The five times she'd been with Chris after school, the videos would have shown that she didn't take the bus home. But Mama hadn't said anything, even those times she was home when Raven arrived later than usual.

"Let's go out today," Chris said.

"Okay."

"Where do you want to go?"

She noticed Jackie staring at her from across the lunch table. "I liked the old house," she whispered.

"Yeah?"

"I liked it a lot."

They returned to the abandoned house after school. The afternoon was cool and rainy. Chris spread the blanket on the wood floor, and they used his sweatshirt and coat for a pillow. He lay on top of her as he kissed her. He put his hand in her shirt and pushed his pelvis down on her. She knew he wanted to have sex. And the more he touched her, the more she wanted to. But sex education made her think she shouldn't. She might make a baby or get AIDS.

That day, she got home later than ever. Mama was waiting for her. She smiled in a strange way as Raven came in the door. Raven's heart beat fast. She knew that look. It meant her mother was about to do something she probably wouldn't like.

"Good day at school?" Mama asked.

"Yes."

"How is biology going?"

"Good," Raven said, hanging her coat on the peg.

"Is it mostly human biology right now?"

"No. We're doing dissections."

"Have you learned about reproductive isolation yet?"

Raven couldn't recall learning that phrase.

"It means unlike species can't produce offspring," Mama said. "For example, a dog can't make babies with a cat."

"I don't think we learned about that yet."

Mama nodded and turned back to something she had cooking on the stove.

During dinner, they didn't talk much. Raven was nervous. Mama stared at her more than usual. Maybe she was perceptive enough to feel what Raven had been doing in the abandoned house. Maybe she could even smell Chris on her.

When Raven got up to clear the dishes, Mama said, "Sit, Daughter."

She sat.

"Do you like this boy?"

Raven tried to keep her panic from showing. "What boy?"

Mama had a wry smile. "The boy who drove you home today and five other days."

Raven didn't know what to say. Her mother's casualness confused her.

"What is his name?"

"Chris. Chris Williams."

"Are you having sex with him?"

"No!"

"Have you kissed him?"

She wanted to cry. Talking about it with Mama would ruin it.

"I suppose you have," Mama said.

Raven looked down at her empty plate.

"I'm not angry," Mama said. "It's a natural part of growing up. Raven or human, the urge to create new life will be an undeniable force."

"That's not why I'm with him."

"It is, but social conventions make you say otherwise. In the time when humans were one with other creatures of the earth, a girl your age would already have a baby. She would likely become pregnant shortly after she bled."

"I'm not going to get pregnant," Raven said.

"I know," Mama said. "That's why we're having this discussion. I want you to feel relaxed with this boy. Have sex with him if you wish. Your body can't make a baby with him."

Raven was too shocked to respond.

"Reproductive isolation," Mama said. "You and Chris are two unlike species. There can be no baby."

"I bleed every month."

"That doesn't matter. His sperm can't impregnate the daughter of an earth spirit. It's impossible. Look it up in biology books."

Look it up in biology books? What would she find about earth spirits having sex with humans in a biology text?

"It's a very natural urge for your age," Mama said. "Don't let this repressive society ruin your joy."

"Are you sure?" Raven asked.

"I'm sure," Mama said. "And it's too bad. I'd love to have another baby in the house. I've been asking for one for many years."

"You've asked for another baby?"

She nodded. "I suppose one was miracle enough for the spirits." She leaned across the table. "But you should ask, Daughter. I'd think your request would be granted. I'd like you to perform an Asking right away. Tonight."

"You want me to ask for a baby?"

"Yes, tonight and every day. Until we receive a child."

"I'm in school. How can I have a baby?"

"I'll take care of the baby." She stood. "Go and do the Asking. I'll clean the dishes."

"I have homework."

"The homework can wait a little while."

Mama brought her coat. Raven put on her boots.

Before she walked out the door, Mama said, "You may go with Chris Williams as much as you like. I won't interfere. I want you to explore the natural pleasures of your human side."

4

Raven didn't ask for a baby. She didn't want one, and Mama had said she should want something with all her heart and soul when she did an Asking. If Mama felt that way, she could ask for a baby all she wanted.

During her walk in the forest, she pondered why Mama would suddenly allow her to date a boy when she'd been so against her friendships years ago. And she wondered about reproductive isolation. It was all very strange.

Strange but good. Why question the freedom that was now hers for the taking?

The next day, Raven told Chris her mother knew about their relationship. She told him she was okay with it, and they could be together as much as they liked. Chris said to celebrate, they should go on a real date. On Friday night, they went out for dinner and a movie.

Mama was curious about the date when she arrived home. Again, she asked if she and Chris had sex. Raven replied that she had not. She tried not to be angry about Mama's prying. She reminded herself that Mama was very different from other people. Her fascination with Raven's attraction to Chris must come from her deep connection to the earth's natural cycles of reproduction.

On Monday, Chris asked Raven over to his house to do their homework. Both his parents worked, and his older brother was in college, which meant they had the place to themselves.

He showed her around his house, which was small and neat. Then he took her hand and led her to his bedroom. The room was similar to Jackie's and Huck's but with more sports posters and trophies. Raven sat at his desk to do math problems while he rested on the bed to read an English book he had to finish.

Raven had hardly started when Chris got up, closed the door, and locked it. "Get over here, beautiful," he said, pulling her to the bed.

They kissed and tussled. Raven liked tickling and play fighting with him almost as much as kissing. It reminded her of her summer with the boys. He always let her win their mock battles. Raven sat up on top of him and looked down at his face. He liked when she did that.

"Remember that first day we met?" he said. "We were playing softball, and your bird flew down and landed on your shoulder. I had no idea what was going on. I thought you were some kind of magic girl."

She smiled and traced her finger around his navel.

"Reece used to call you Cinderella, but to me you were more like the witches and wizards in stories. I swear I wouldn't have been surprised if you'd turned into a bird and flown into the forest with that bird you raised."

He had seen her true being—her raven spirit. She was afraid to respond.

Abruptly but gently, he laid her down on the bed. Leaning over her, he said, "I'm in love with you, Magic Girl. Do you know that?"

In love. Those were big words. She knew that from the books she'd read. Those words and what he'd said about her being a bird had her unable to speak.

"I want to make love to you," he said. "Really make love."

"Now?"

"Yes. If you're ready."

234

Was she ready? One part of her wanted to; another didn't. It must be her human and spirit sides in conflict.

"Not to ruin the moment, but I have condoms," he said.

He seemed to interpret her silence as willingness. He lifted off her shirt. He'd never done that before. She liked the way he stared at her chest and pink lace bra. She had ordered the bra and matching panties with him in mind. Mama had let her buy pretty underwear after she found out Raven had a boyfriend.

He put his hands and lips on her chest. "Raven, I want you. You're so beautiful."

His voice and eyes were different. What a strange power her body had over him. Or was it her spirit side?

He unfastened her jeans and slid them down. He touched her in places he never had before. She touched him, too. She did want to make love.

And yet, half of her remained infuriatingly detached. Like a raven perched on a distant branch. It couldn't feel what she did.

Chris stopped touching her. He leaned over and looked into her eyes. "Are you okay?"

She wasn't okay. She didn't know why, but she wanted to fly away. She wished she could. Just lift away from that bed and disappear into the sky.

"Are you afraid?" he asked.

"Yes." She was afraid. But of what she wasn't sure.

"Afraid it will hurt?" he asked. "I'll go slow."

The urge to fly away grew stronger. What was her spirit side trying to tell her?

She slid out from under him and put on her shirt.

"I'm sorry," he said.

"Why?"

"I think I pressured you."

"It's okay."

He handed her jeans to her and put on his shirt.

"Do you still want to do homework?" he asked.

"I'm not in the mood. Would you take me home?"

"Sure."

He had driven about halfway to her house when he asked, "Is everything okay with us?"

"Yes. I just wasn't ready."

"Some people are all fired up to do it at thirteen. Some wait till they're out of high school. It's all good." He looked at her, smiling. "But I can tell you'll want to do it soon."

He seemed to speak from experience. Both Jackie and Reece had said that about him.

"Have you done it before?" she asked.

"Yes," he said.

"A lot?"

"Come on. You're not supposed to ask that."

She wondered why.

He parked in the usual place, away from the driveway cameras. They kissed, and everything felt all right again.

He said, "This may not be the right time to ask, but do you want to go to prom with me?"

Senior prom was a big deal at school. Of course he would ask her. He'd said he was in love with her.

"That sounds fun," she said.

"Are you sure your mother will let you? We'll be out all night. And you have to get a dress and everything."

"I think she will."

"Great. Let me know what color your dress is so I can match my tux."

"Okay," she said, though she wasn't certain what it all meant.

Mama was in the house when she arrived.

"Did you go out with Chris today?"

"Yes," Raven said. "He asked me to go to the senior prom."

"What was your answer?"

"I said yes. But I need a dress."

"And shoes. We can find all that online."

"He said we'll be out all night."

Mama smoothed her hair. "Of course you will, pretty girl. And I bet this won't be your only prom. You'll be asked every year."

The drastic change in Mama unsettled Raven. Or was it the thought of being out all night with a big group of teenagers? She usually felt exhausted from trying to fit in at the end of a school day, and that was only seven hours. How would her raven spirit handle a whole night? She thought of the way she'd felt in Chris's bed, the urgent desire to fly away. She almost wished Mama had said she couldn't go to the prom.

5

Raven lay awake for a long time thinking about what had happened with Chris and why she was uncertain about staying out all night with him. Her raven spirit must be making her feel afraid.

She shouldn't let it. She had the right to feel human with men. Mama said she should experience that joy.

The next morning, she wore a sweater Chris liked. She couldn't wait to tell him she'd ordered three prom dresses; she was going to see which one she liked best.

The bus was quieter than usual. Jackie's girlfriend, Sadie, got on, and she looked like she'd been crying. She went straight to Raven. "Have you heard?" she asked.

Raven shook her head.

"Jackie's dad died in a car accident last night."

"Mr. Danner . . . died?"

"Yes," Sadie said, her voice breaking.

She and some of the other girls started crying. They'd had Mr. Danner for gym class in elementary school as well. Raven wanted to cry with them. She wanted to cry for Jackie and Huck and their mother. But she couldn't. Again, her raven side wouldn't let her. It just sat on its branch apart from her sadness.

Everyone at school was talking about Mr. Danner. Jackie and Huck weren't there. The lunch group was quiet, even Reece, but some talked in quiet voices about the car accident. They said Mr. Danner was in a head-on collision after someone swerved into his lane on a highway. He was coming home from the grocery store.

Chris was very quiet. He didn't invite Raven over. She didn't want to go anyway. Everything felt too sad.

That evening, as the sun set, Raven walked to the fence on Hooper's land, keeping her distance from the edge. She sat in the grass and stared at the lit windows of Jackie's little yellow house. Finally, the raven let her cry. She cried until dark and walked home in moonlight.

Jackie and Huck didn't come back to school all week. Chris invited Raven to drive with him to the memorial service and funeral. They were having it on Saturday because so many people wanted to say goodbye to Mr. Danner.

Chris had been to Jackie's house, and he said that Jackie, Huck, and their mother were heartbroken. He used that word, *heartbroken*. It hurt Raven's heart just to hear it. She did Askings on Wednesday, Thursday, and Friday, imploring the earth spirits to please heal the broken hearts of the three people she loved. She made the last Asking in front of the Madonna Wolfsbane, using only two materials, the strongest: stones and her hair. She asked the spirits to give Jackie the strength of her own spirit to help him heal. She asked Madonna, too, because she might understand Jackie's world better than the spirits did.

The memorial service in the church was so crowded that people stood in the aisles. The raven in Raven was nervous among all the people in the enclosed space. Chris and Reece took her to a seat near the front of the church. Jackie, Huck, and their mother were seated in front of them. After the minister spoke words for the people of his religion, many went to the microphone and told funny or sweet stories about Mr. Danner.

Jackie cried a lot, and Raven asked the earth spirits to help him. Mama might have said she couldn't do that in a church, because the followers of the Christian spirits were in opposition to the earth spirits. But Raven chose to believe that powerful beings were compassionate no matter who believed in them.

Jackie and Huck were two of six pallbearers. Raven's heart about stopped at the beauty of them in their dark suits and white gloves, carrying the casket.

The minister said more words at the grave site. Mr. Danner, he said, was going to heaven. Raven wondered if people went to whatever afterlife they believed in. She and Mama would become earth spirits when they died. If Jackie went to heaven, would she see him again after they died? Did the spirits of heaven commune with those of Earth?

Raven brought a wild bouquet to put on the grave. It was mostly evergreens and dried herbs and grasses because the weather was still cold. After the ceremony, Jackie came to her and said, "Thank you for the flowers. And for being here."

He looked different. His face was pale and purplish beneath the eyes. She keenly felt his pain, and she knew why. She had asked the earth spirits to give him part of her own spirit to help him heal. His heavy spirit was crushing her own, his grief too strong for the piece she had given him. She had to give more.

She pressed her hand on his heart. "I give you more strength of my spirit," she whispered.

"What?" he said.

"I love you, Jackie," she said.

When she stepped back, she felt a rush of darkness, like a storm that comes on suddenly. The teenagers who heard what she'd said to Jackie were frowning at her. Even Reece looked upset. Worst of all, Jackie was looking at her as if he didn't know her.

Should she not have mentioned spirits in front of Christians? But she had only said she was giving him the strength of her spirit. She'd said nothing directly of earth spirits.

Sadie took Jackie's hand, keeping her hard stare on Raven. Chris looked at Raven with similar outrage. Suddenly Raven understood. They were angry because she had said "I love you." The words had come as naturally as breathing. She refused to feel guilty. She had spoken with all her heart and soul. It had been an unusual kind of Asking, and Askings were pure, above the pettiness of human teenagers.

Jackie's mother saw Raven's trouble. She took Raven's hand and said, "How are you, sweetheart? I haven't seen you for so long. I've missed you."

"I've missed you, too," Raven said, letting Ms. Danner guide her away from the grave. "I'm sorry about Mr. Danner."

"Thank you," she said, patting Raven's hand.

When they arrived at the parked cars, Chris said, "Let's go," in a gruff voice.

Chris brooded in silence as he drove out of the cemetery.

"What was that?" he finally said.

"What?"

"The hand on the heart. The *I love you.*"

She refused to explain herself.

"Tell me the truth," he said. "Are you in love with him?"

Of course she loved Jackie. She had since she was seven.

Chris looked at her as he drove. "You know Reece says you are. And vice versa. He's joked about that for years."

"Reece jokes about everything," she said.

"I know. That's what I thought. But I saw the way you were with him. Everyone did."

"I was trying to help him."

"It was pretty embarrassing, Raven. We're going out. Everyone assumes we are."

"Does that mean I can't be myself?"

"It means you don't publicly display affection with other men."

"He's heartbroken. He needs help."

"Oh my god. Seriously? I think you used the funeral as an excuse to go at him."

She could remember only one time in her life when she had felt as she did in this moment. The day Mama had told her she could never again set foot on Jackie's land. That day she had cursed the raven spirit that made her.

Now she could curse only Chris and the other teenagers. They were shallow and didn't understand her spirit world. She wanted nothing more than to be out of his presence.

"Where are we?" she said. "Why aren't you taking me home?"

"We're invited to the lunch at the restaurant. I told you that."

"Take me home."

"Goddamn it, Raven!"

"Take me home!"

He swerved the car, making the tires squeal. He drove recklessly, frightening her, but she said nothing. She was already opening the car door before he'd fully stopped on her road near her gate.

"Come back here!" he shouted.

"Why? So you can insult me some more? Go away!"

He drove slowly alongside her. "I get it. This is why you can't get physical with me. It's because of him. Right? Is that it?"

"I said go!"

He stopped at the gate as she pressed the code. "Are we going to prom?"

"No!" she shouted.

He jumped out of the car and followed her inside the gate. The first alarm was going off inside the house. If Mama was looking at the video screens, she would see that he was on the road to their house. That was absolutely forbidden.

"You can't be in here!" she said.

"I don't care about that bullshit," he said.

"Get out!"

"I only want to talk about this."

"I don't. I've seen how you are. Now I know I don't want to be with you."

"Are you kidding?" he said. "Five minutes and I'm out?"

"Yes. Now go. I'm closing the gate."

"So close the goddamn gate!" he said.

She looked behind her, afraid she'd see Mama coming.

"Raven . . ." He ran his hand over his hair. "It's just . . . what I said the other day was true. I'm, like, in love with you. It just made me kind of crazy to see how you looked at him. And in front of everyone."

"I can see it made you crazy," she said. "That's why I can't be with you anymore."

He stepped toward her. "Let's just talk about it."

"What could we talk about that hasn't already been said? You accused me of using Mr. Danner's death to influence Jackie. You said I'm not allowed to say *I love you* to Jackie when he most needs to feel love."

"So you do love him?"

She walked down the road fast, hoping he'd go back to his car, but he followed her. He jogged to catch up and blocked her.

"What are you doing?" she said.

He grabbed her arm. "Come back to the car."

"You need to go."

"Just come back to the car, damn it!"

"Get your hands off her!" Mama called out. She was hurrying down the road, her rifle pointed at him. As she got closer, she said, "I do believe my daughter asked you to leave."

He backed up. "You're crazy, old lady, you know that?"

Raven's mother cocked the gun. "I am. And you never know what a crazy old lady will do." She walked toward him. "You're on my land, and my signs clearly say trespassing isn't allowed."

He left, muttering curses. Raven closed the gate, and Chris pulled away with a screech of tires.

Mama lowered the gun. "What a child he is."

"I know," Raven said. "I just found that out."

Mama held the gun on one arm, wrapped her other around Raven's back as they walked to the house. "What drew you to such a boy?" she asked.

"I don't know. Maybe only that he liked me. My raven spirit always kept its distance when I was with him. It seemed afraid of him for some reason."

"He wanted to possess you, put you in a cage," Mama said.

He did, Raven realized. Her raven side had been trying to tell her that from the start.

"The prom dresses arrived while you were gone."

"Let's go find two big pairs of scissors," Raven said.

6

Raven turned off her alarm, buried herself beneath the duvet, and went back to sleep.

Mama woke her hours later, her hand on Raven's forehead to check for fever. "Are you unwell?" she asked.

"Not really."

"Since second grade, you've missed only two days of school. What happened?"

"I don't want to talk about it."

Mama's pale eyes glittered with resentment. "I know what happened. That boy—Chris Williams—has caused trouble for you, hasn't he?"

Raven looked away from her eyes.

"I should have shot his balls off," she muttered.

"Mama!"

"What has he done?"

"He's telling people only his side of the story. And he told them about you coming at him with the gun."

Mama grinned.

"It's not funny. They're all treating me different."

"Well, you are different. You're a miracle. Keep that in mind and hold your head high."

Glendy Vanderah

Miracle or not, she hated going to school now. Reece was the only one who wasn't aloof with her. Chris was bitter, didn't even sit at their lunch table. And Jackie and Huck were like different people. But that had nothing to do with her. Their father's death had changed them. They were serious all the time, and when they laughed at a joke, Raven saw they were pretending.

School had become seven hours of bleakness. She remembered Mama's warnings about school when she was younger: *You will be the raven's child caught in a cage. You'll feel like a bird beating against glass in your desperation to get out.*

"I don't want to go back," Raven said.

"In this state, you have to go until your eighteenth birthday. You may quit then if you like."

"I'd nearly be done with high school by then," Raven said.

Mama shrugged.

Raven sat up in the bed. "Am I going to college?"

"Why would you? You can learn anything a college teaches from books." She stood. "Let's eat and spend the day outdoors. The spirits will do you good."

Raven doubted that. Their ninety acres sometimes felt as much a prison as school did.

"Let's ask the spirits for a baby together," Mama said. "We haven't tried that yet. Having a baby in the house is what we both need." She caressed Raven's cheek. "I know you can't imagine the joy of it yet. You'll understand when it happens."

Mama's talk of having a baby always unsettled her. Raven didn't crave it, and that felt like betrayal when Mama wanted it so badly. To ask for a baby with Mama would be as difficult as school. Her heart and soul were in neither.

◆ ◆ ◆

For the remainder of the school year, she mostly kept to herself. She found quiet places to eat away from everyone. Reece sometimes hunted her down and made her go back to the lunch table. She went without a fight, mostly because she liked to see Jackie. He was gradually recovering. And as he did, he was attentive to Raven when they were together. He didn't seem to care anymore that it made Sadie angry. Raven wondered if her Asking had bonded him too much to her. It made her feel a little guilty.

In June, Huck and Reece graduated. Huck would study environmental engineering at the University of Washington in autumn. Reece was working to earn money for college and helping his mother. As always, Raven's life with the boys was changing too fast. She couldn't imagine school without Reece the next year. But she was glad her freshman year was over. For the first time, she wanted to go to Montana for the summer.

Summers in the tiny cabin had been the same for seven years. The eighth year, their life there changed in a bad way, like everything else recently. Mama had trouble climbing the mountain trails she'd been trekking since she was a girl. She breathed hard and had to slow down. But when Raven asked, she insisted she was fine.

By the end of summer, Mama admitted she felt different. But she refused to see a doctor or talk to Aunt Sondra about it. She said the earth spirits would heal her. Raven performed many Askings, begging the spirits to heal whatever was wrong with Mama's heart. She knew it was the heart because Mama sometimes put her hand on her chest. In her Askings, Raven used anything she could find that was shaped like a human heart—a stone, a leaf, a bit of mollusk shell. And she asked with all her heart and soul.

But Mama was still sick when they returned to Washington. She was getting caught in the spirit world more often, the bad spells where Raven had to feed her and dress her like she was a baby. As Mama withdrew more and more into the spirit world, Raven felt as if her spirit were retreating with her.

She wished she didn't have to go to school. She wanted to keep watch on Mama. She wanted to go to the woods and fields to ask her kin for help. But every day she got on the bus because Mama said she had to.

She sat at the lunch table with Jackie and his friends. Since Chris Williams and his poison had left, they treated her well again. What had happened at the funeral seemed forgotten. But Raven didn't pay much attention to them. Usually she read a book to distract her from thinking about Mama.

What would she do if Mama went to the spirit world? How would she live? Maybe the bad people of Mama's warnings would find her when she no longer had the protection of Mama's powerful spirit.

Raven forced herself to focus on her book. The roar of her frantic thoughts and the chaotic lunchroom receded as she read the words.

"What are you reading?"

She looked up at Jackie. His multicolored eyes were beautiful. Sometimes she could hardly look into them. In a way, Jackie was a disease of the heart, an actual pain that made her want to press her hand on her chest the way Mama did.

She showed him the cover of the book.

"*One Hundred Years of Solitude,*" he said. "Sounds like your life."

It was the kind of joke Reece would have made. But Jackie couldn't sustain the humor. He immediately looked regretful.

"I'm sorry. I shouldn't have said that," he said.

"Why not? It was funny."

He glanced at the others at the table to make sure they weren't listening. "Are you okay?"

"Yes," she said.

He whispered, "No one cares about that stuff Chris said last spring. It's over."

"I know."

"Then why are you always so quiet now?"

She wished she could tell him. She wanted to feel the way she had the night she'd sneaked into his house. The warmth of his body beneath his blanket. His arm around her.

"Raven?"

"It's nothing."

His look said he didn't believe her.

After school, he found her before she got on the bus. "Let me drive you home," he said.

It was almost a command. His father's death had changed him. He wouldn't have been so bold last year. Maybe it was simply maturity. And the absence of a girlfriend. Over the summer, he'd broken up with Sadie.

"It should be okay, right?" he said. "Your mom let you drive home with Chris last year."

"You've probably heard what happened the last time he drove me home."

"Yeah, the gun."

"Are you sure you're up for that?"

He looked worried. "Do you think she'll—"

"I'm joking. Let's go."

He'd taken over the old car Huck used to drive. Raven was aware of the students in the parking lot watching her get in his car, but she didn't waste her thoughts on them. She now knew the consequences of caring about "hive mind," as Reece called it. She wouldn't get stung again.

"So how've you been?" he asked. "I never get a chance to talk to you alone these days."

"We haven't really talked alone since I was seven and you were eight."

"I guess not," he said.

"How's your mom?" she asked.

"She's better. But she hides her sadness well."

"What about you?"

"I really miss him, but I'm better than I was." He glanced at her as he drove. "I asked how you are. Why don't you tell me what's going on?"

"I told you—"

"I've known you for a long time. There's something wrong."

"I can't talk about it."

"Why not? Your mother told you not to?"

"If she did, why would I talk about it?"

"I know. She told you never to set foot on our land again, and you never did. You take your promises to her too seriously."

"What is this? Are you the new Reece?"

"My hair's the wrong color."

"I miss him," she said.

"I know. He hardly ever stops by now that Huck's gone."

"At least you see him sometimes. And Huck is close enough to visit."

"Yeah, but the house feels really weird with just my mom and me." He added, "I guess you're used to that."

She was used to that. What would she do if Mama went to the spirit world? She looked out the window to hide her tears. When she thought he wouldn't notice, she quickly wiped her hand over her face.

"Are you crying?"

"No."

"Raven . . ."

"Could we just not talk for a while?"

That was how the rest of the drive was. Both of them quiet, her absorbing as much Jackie light as she could store up until the ride was over. She wondered if he still had the plastic stars on his bedroom ceiling.

He stopped the car in front of the gate, not hiding from the cameras.

"Do you want to ride with me again?" he asked. "It gets you home faster than the bus."

She would arrive earlier to check on Mama. "I'd like to drive with you," she said.

"Okay, good." He looked out the front windshield in the direction of his house, about a mile down the country road. "I'd offer to take you to school in the morning, but I'd have no way to let you know when I'm not going to school. You'd miss the bus."

He had already missed two days of school, and it was early in the semester. When he came back each time, he'd said he was sick.

"Sometimes I just can't go," he said.

Raven remembered the day she'd been too depressed to go to school.

"Because you're too sad to go?" she asked.

He looked away from her. "Something like that. Over the summer, I had a few panic attacks. I see a psychologist sometimes."

She'd heard other kids talk about panic attacks. "Is it bad when it happens?"

He nodded. "It took me a while before I could drive. Because my dad . . ."

"I can see how that would happen," she said.

"I like having someone in the car. It helps."

"I'll ride with you anytime you want," she said.

He looked anxious. "I asked you today because I wanted to talk to you. I didn't ask just because of that."

"I know."

He looked out the window at her driveway. "Is your mom watching us? Is this okay?"

"It's okay, but I'd better go."

"I'll see you tomorrow." He waited until she was inside the gate before he drove away.

After that day, they rode home together three or four times a week. Sometimes he went out with friends instead, but he wasn't interested in any particular girl as far as Raven could tell.

At first when they drove together, he'd ask if she wanted to stop for food at Bear's or another drive-through. She always said no. Mama was getting sicker and acting stranger. Raven had to be at home as much as possible.

He knew something was wrong but stopped asking about it. They talked about their classes, or he would tell her something happening in the news or about a movie he liked. She would describe whatever book she was reading. Sometimes they said very little. She didn't worry about being quiet with him anymore. In fact, she found their silences comforting. She sensed he felt that way, too.

The second day after Thanksgiving break from school, Raven found Mama on the floor when she woke up. Her eyes stared, but she was breathing. She had entered the spirit world.

Mama had lost a lot of weight, but Raven still had to use all her strength to raise her to her feet and support her until she got her into bed. She pulled the covers over her. "Mama . . . are you okay? Do you want me to make your tea?"

Mama stared as if she weren't there. She had entered the spirit world many times since Raven was little, but this time Raven was afraid her body was too weak to come back. She decided she wouldn't go to school.

She propped Mama up and held cooled tea to her lips. "Drink, Mama. This is your favorite. It has licorice in it."

She was relieved when Mama sipped at the tea and gradually focused her eyes on her.

"Daughter . . . ," she said.

"Yes, Mama?"

"The spirits won't heal me. I don't understand . . . I don't understand . . ." Tears dripped from her pale eyes.

"It's time to see a doctor," Raven said. "Let's call Aunt Sondra and have her bring Dr. Pat. Tell me her phone number and how to get in your phone. I'll call right now."

"No!" Her former will gleamed in her eyes. "You will promise me no doctors! Promise me now!"

Raven thought of what Jackie had said. *You take your promises to her too seriously.*

Mama saw she didn't want to promise. "This is my body and spirit, Daughter," she said with surprising vehemence. "I will not have anyone fiddling with it! I will not be attached to their machines and needles. I will not let them do what they did to my mother!"

"What did they do?"

"They took all dignity and fight out of her. She wanted to die on our land in Montana, and they wouldn't let her."

Mama's face blurred in tears. "Are you saying you think you're going to die?"

Mama held her hand. Her skin was cold. "I'm fighting this thing, Raven. I'm still speaking to the spirits. If you take me to one of those hospitals, I will surely die as my mother did. Promise me no doctors. Not ever."

"But what if—"

"Promise!"

"I promise, Mama." Tears dripped down her cheeks.

"Daughter . . . I'm comfortable with going to the spirits. They've been good to me. They gave me you. And it's for you that I need to stay in this world. Surely the spirits see that. You aren't ready to be on your own yet."

"I know. I'm so scared."

Mama squeezed her hand. "Don't be afraid. I'm here. I'll keep you safe."

For how long? If the spirits hadn't yet helped her, would they ever?

Mama's eyes started losing focus again. But she seemed to look at something behind Raven. Raven turned around but saw nothing. It must be a spirit Mama could see. But earth spirits were unlikely to come inside a house. They would feel trapped there.

"I have to keep her safe," Mama whispered to the spirit. "Let me keep her safe." After a silence, she said anxiously, "I did no wrong! She was given to me. Don't punish me! I did nothing wrong!"

Raven clasped her hand. "No one will punish you, Mama."

Mama turned her eyes toward her but seemed to look through her. "They might be punishing me. I'm not sure. I don't remember what I did . . . how I got you. They might be angry about what I did. That might be why I'm sick."

"What do you mean? They gave me to you."

"Yes . . . they gave you to me. A perfect baby. A miracle." She clutched Raven's hand so hard it hurt. "Don't ever let that man say you're his! He's bad! He kills the earth spirits! He's like my father with his corporations and his chemicals poisoning the land! You were never meant to be his!"

"Who? What man?"

"That senator. Bauhammer!" Mama pressed her hand to her forehead. "He's dead. I remember now. He can never come here. He can't take you."

Raven didn't understand what she was talking about with the senator. But Mama often confused memories when she was halfway between the material and spiritual worlds. Raven could easily see how that would happen.

Mama's body suddenly went slack, and her eyes closed. Raven frantically pressed her hand on Mama's heart. She couldn't feel it beating. She laid her head on her chest, listening.

She heard it. The heart beating. Mama hadn't died. Yet she looked so pale and lifeless.

When she was certain Mama would continue breathing, Raven left to make breakfast. And later lunch, then dinner. By nightfall, Mama hadn't woken to eat. Raven slept in her bed, her arm tucked around Mama to feel her warmth.

Raven had never missed school because of Mama's shifts into the spirit world. The times it happened on a school day, she had trusted Mama's health enough to leave her. Mama would stay in the spirit world for a day, sometimes two. This shift had started on Tuesday, and Raven was still at home taking care of her on Thursday. She had missed three days of classes, but she was too panicked about Mama to care.

She was trying to spoon broth into Mama's mouth when the alarm went off. Someone was coming down the driveway. Probably a deer or a coyote. That had happened before. Yet her heart still throbbed as fast as it had when she was a little girl.

But maybe it was her aunt. She was the only person who knew the code—so she could get in when she visited with Dr. Pat.

Raven put down the soup and ran to the video cameras. The second alarm joined the first, which meant whoever or whatever was in the driveway was getting closer. There were three warnings in total.

She stared at the third video camera. A man. She leaned closer to the grainy image. It was Jackie, walking fast.

She flung open the front door. People were absolutely forbidden anywhere near her house. The rule was so ingrained that she ran in a panic without putting on shoes. She hardly felt the cold or the driveway stones bruising her feet.

She met Jackie at the place where the last alarm triggered. Now three sounded inside the house. She should have turned them off. But she doubted Mama was aware enough to be upset.

"Jackie!" she said breathlessly.

He had stopped walking about ten yards from her. "Did you see me coming on the cameras?"

"Yes."

He stared at the house, now visible around a bend. "What's that sound?"

She had left the door open. Each of the three alarms made a different sound to tell them the location of the intruder. There were two others in back that turned on after they went to bed.

She didn't even try to explain.

"You jumped the fence?" she asked.

"Yes. I'm sorry, but I've been really worried. You've never missed three days of school. I just wanted to know you were okay."

"I'm okay."

He stared at the house. "Are those alarms?"

"Yes."

"Not fire alarms, I hope?"

"No."

He walked closer, studying her face. She probably looked bad. "Are you sick?"

"I'm fine."

"Then why—"

"My mother is sick."

Normally she wouldn't give out any information about her mother. But she thought it might make him leave faster.

"Does she have the flu? It's going around school."

"Yes, it's the flu," she said. "You shouldn't get near us."

The way he looked at her, he might know she was lying.

"I'll open the gate so you can get out," she said.

They had taken only about five steps away from the house when Raven's mother weakly cried, "Who are you? Where do you think you're going with her?"

They turned around. Raven's heart about stopped at the sight of Mama stumbling down the steps in a nightgown, the pistol she kept in her bedside drawer aimed at Jackie.

"You will not take her!" Mama said as she staggered toward them. "You have no right to her! Give her back, or I swear I'll shoot!"

Raven jumped in front of Jackie with her arms stretched out. "Mama, stop! He's a friend! He's a friend from school!"

"No, he's tricking you!" Mama said. "Don't go with him! I know who he is! He's from New York! I recognize him!"

"Mama, please! He lives down the road. He's not from New York."

Mama nearly fell, and as she tried to right herself, Raven was terrified the gun would go off.

"His name is Jack Danner," she said. "I went to his father's funeral. Do you remember that? His mother teaches at the school I used to go to."

Mama steadied herself, swaying, and stared at Jackie. Her white-blonde hair was in wild disarray, and her face was pale and gaunt. The light of the setting sun illuminated her bony body through the thin fabric of her nightgown. She looked like a human ghost in stories.

Raven walked slowly toward her. "Let me take the gun."

"I heard the alarms," she said softly. "I woke up. I didn't know where you were."

"I know. That must have been confusing." She carefully released the gun from Mama's grip and set its safety switch.

She turned to Jackie, frozen in the same spot. "My mother has a high fever. I'm sorry."

"It's okay," he said.

"Why are you on my land?" Raven's mother asked. She looked and sounded much more herself. She had fully departed the spirit world.

"I was worried about Raven. She's missed three days of school."

"If you go to school, I assume you know what the words *no trespassing* mean."

"Yes, I do. I'm very sorry, Ms. Lind."

Mama continued to stare imperiously.

"Mama, he said he's sorry," Raven said. "It's cold, and you're sick. You should go inside."

"I am not sick," Mama said.

"Please go inside. I'll let him out."

She crooked a finger at Jackie. "Don't you ever come back here."

"I won't," he said.

Raven felt like she could breathe again when Mama turned toward the house. She and Jackie walked to the outer road in silence. She still had the gun, held down at her side. She pressed the code into the pad to open the gate.

"Can she hear us?" he asked, looking at the nearest camera.

"No."

He started to say something but stopped himself. Instead, he wrapped his arms around Raven and held her. He had never done that. She couldn't hug him back because she had the gun in her hand. She supposed it was mostly a pity hug, but it still felt good.

He let her go and said, "I hope you come back to school soon. I miss you." He got in his car and drove away as the gate closed.

As bad as the last ten minutes had been, Raven was elated that Mama had come back to the human world. Jackie had made it happen. Maybe the spirits had guided him into trespassing on their land. If there was one thing that could pull Mama out of the spirit world, it was a perceived threat to her daughter.

The alarms were off when she returned to the house.

"Is he your new boyfriend?" Mama asked.

"He's a friend."

She smiled slyly. "I saw him embrace you."

"Why were you watching us?" Raven asked.

She took Raven's face in her thin hands. "Because you are my treasure. I will watch over you in this life and also in the next."

7

The last bell signaled winter vacation. The halls were loud with celebration.

Every year Raven wondered what it would be like to live in that world, to have all those fun events to look forward to. Throughout the day, she heard talk about what presents people were getting, and family visiting, ski and beach vacations, and what people were giving their boyfriends or girlfriends.

She had nothing to look forward to. Days away from school were no joy. At first it was nice to have a rest from studying. Then the monotony set in. And this year would be more difficult because Mama was sick. Rather than escape the constant worries for a few hours, they would be there all day and every day.

And there would be no Jackie. For almost two weeks.

She met him at his car. "You look less than merry," he said as he started the engine.

"I don't like winter break."

"Don't you like sleeping in?"

"That's overrated."

"What about Santa?"

"Santa has never stopped at my house."

"You don't get anything?"

"My aunt will send me a gift."

"Nothing at all from your mother?"

"No."

He pulled into a line of cars waiting to get out of the school parking lot. "I know something that will make you like winter break."

"What?"

"A little Christmas party at my house with our old crew: Reece, Huck, my mom, and me. This Friday."

"Reece is coming?"

He smiled. "I knew that would do it. He's sleeping over. We're having dinner around six."

Why was he tormenting her by telling her this?

"Come on! Don't say you can't. Your mom let you go all over the place with Chris last spring."

"That was Chris. This is—"

"I know, the forbidden land. Not one foot, *etcetera*."

"It's not funny. I really want to come."

"So come. I'll pick you up. I'll be at your gate at quarter to six."

"I haven't asked her yet."

"We have to preplan because you don't have a phone."

"I don't need a ride," she said.

"That's a long walk. And the stream will be too cold for wading. Just let me pick you up."

"You know I can't agree right now."

He went silent. The quiet in the car didn't have its usual companionable ease. Raven kept her face turned away, looking out the side window at the snow-dusted woods and fields.

He parked in front of her gate. She lifted her backpack off the floor.

"Will you ask about the party?"

"I have to see how she is."

"Is she . . . ?"

"Is she *what*?"

"Is she always like she was that day?"

He hadn't mentioned anything about that day. And she was certain he hadn't told anyone about Mama threatening him with a gun—as Chris had.

"She was unwell," she said. She opened the door to prevent further discussion of her mother.

"Please at least ask her," he said.

She stepped out of the car. "I don't understand why you'd do this when you've known the situation all these years. It's kind of mean, Jackie."

"Mean! Huck and I wanted you and Reece to do something fun for Christmas. His mother doesn't do anything for the holidays either. How is that mean?"

"Does Reece know it's a pity party?"

"Oh my god, are you serious?"

"Does he?"

"You know what? He does know we've invited him over all these years to give him a break from his mother. And he's okay with that because he gets it. He knows we really care about him. And he really cares about us. If you see something wrong in that, I'm sorry." He leaned over the passenger seat and pulled the door closed.

She backed away as he put the car into gear and drove away. Her feet felt almost too heavy to walk.

Mama wasn't in the house. Lately she'd been going out every day. Probably asking the spirits to heal her.

Raven made dinner. When Mama got home, she was out of breath and holding her chest. She was quiet and barely ate anything. Raven didn't ask about the party. She dared not risk getting her angry and overexcited.

The next few days, Raven spent many hours walking the land. She did Askings, not to go to the party but to heal Mama. She thought a lot about Jackie and wished she hadn't called his invitation a *pity party*.

She was the one who was mean. Whatever was poisoning Mama was seeping into her.

On Friday, the day of the party, Raven decided to ask Mama. She wanted to see Jackie. She wanted his little yellow house and Reece and Huck and Ms. Danner. She wanted to go back to the best summer ever.

Mama woke in a worrisome mood, muttering to spirits Raven couldn't see. She sometimes did that before she collapsed, before she entered the world of spirits. Raven had to wait to ask about the party.

But Mama left the house, still whispering. Raven stayed home to wait for her. She wanted to catch Mama when she returned, hopefully in a good mood from being with the earth spirits.

While she read a book assigned for English class, snow started to come down fast in the late afternoon. She was worried for Mama in the cold and slippery snow. She made soup so she would have something warm to eat.

At least two inches of snow had fallen when Mama returned. She was out of breath as always, pale, and sweating despite the cold. But she wasn't whispering anymore.

"I have hot beef and barley soup ready for you," Raven said. "I'll put bread in the oven."

"No bread," Mama said. "I'll just have the soup."

Raven put one bowl of soup on the table. She wouldn't eat because Jackie said they'd have dinner at the party.

"Aren't you having any?" Mama asked.

"I had some while I made it. I'm not hungry."

Mama's hand shook slightly as she brought spoons of soup to her mouth.

"The snow is pretty, isn't it?" Raven asked.

"Yes." She looked at Raven with gleaming eyes. "I saw a spirit I've never seen before. It looked like my mother made of white swirls. She was calling to me."

A cold lump of snow seemed to fall into Raven's stomach. "You never told me your mother's earth spirit is here. Why has she come to this land?"

The fervent shine in Mama's eyes diminished. "I don't know if it was her. Maybe it was a dream. I think I was sleeping. No, but . . . no. I don't remember."

Mama pushed back her chair and stood shakily. "I need to rest. Please don't disturb me." She went to her room and closed the door.

Raven put the soup away and cleaned the kitchen. She dusted the furniture with a cloth, though she'd done that two days before. She kept looking out the windows at the snow. It called to her, too. But not as a dead person. It was very much alive, inviting her to go outside.

She put on her boots and coat and wrote a note for Mama: *I'm out walking in the snow. I'll be home later.* She put the note in the usual place on the refrigerator with a magnet.

Darkness was coming fast with the snow. She found a flashlight and her warmest hat and gloves.

She crunched through the snow in the direction of the stream. She hadn't yet decided if she would go to Jackie's party. The invitation of the snow might be enough for her. She had never walked in heavy snow in the dark before. The crystalline flakes looked like falling stars in the golden beam of her flashlight.

It took a long time to get to the stream. She dawdled in the falling stars, and twice the white darkness tricked her into going the wrong way.

She shined her flashlight on the trickling stream. Its depth would swamp her boots. Her feet would be soaked, cold, and heavy. She either stepped into the water and went straight to Jackie's house, breaking her promise, or she walked away.

The burbling water was telling her to go downstream, toward Jackie. But that was what water always did. It went where it wanted without thought of consequences.

But what were the consequences? She could think of none. Mama had been exhausted. She would sleep for a long time. If she woke, she would see the note and appreciate that her daughter wanted to walk in the snow. Anyway, she was much too sick to come looking for her.

Raven stepped into the water, and her boots filled. Her feet hurt, then went numb. She walked as fast as she could. She shined her light on the Wolfsbane. All those years, and it was still there keeping the werewolf away.

She hurried onto dry land, through the alder trees, across the field. She saw the fence ahead. Beyond it, the little yellow house with golden windows was a sweet dream in the falling snow.

She walked to the fence. She couldn't tell if her boots were touching grass that leaned over the boundary. Snow covered everything. She leaned down and slid through the fence boards. She walked a few steps and turned around, shining her light on the fence and her new footprints in the snow. How easy it was.

She jogged the rest of the way to the house, laughing when she tripped over something and fell on her stomach. She ran to the front door and pressed the doorbell, her breath coming out in fast white clouds.

"I'll get it!" Reece called from inside.

The door opened. "I don't believe it!" Reece said. "You breached the fence magic!"

"I did."

"And you survived in one piece!"

"I think I lost my toes. I can't feel them."

"Get over here, you damn crazy Bird Girl!" He grabbed her in his arms and swung her in a circle.

Jackie hugged her, then Huck and Ms. Danner. They peeled off her hat and coat, even helped her pull off her boots.

The house smelled delicious, like apples, spices, evergreen, and woodsmoke from the blaze in the hearth. Raven wouldn't let Ms.

Danner take her to get dry clothes until she looked at the fir tree with its tinsel, lights, and shiny ornaments. How strange it made her feel, to see that poor dying tree inside a human house, even as its glittering beauty lit up her heart.

"We started doing Christmas trees when my mom got married," Jackie said. "My dad loved them."

"I'm still not keen on it," Ms. Danner said, "but the boys wanted to continue the ritual."

"Go put on dry clothes," Reece said. "We were just getting ready to eat."

"And you don't mess with Reece when he's hungry," Huck said.

"Unless you're Bird Girl," Reece said, rubbing his fingers in her hair.

After Raven changed, Ms. Danner poured her a cup of hot spiced cider. At Reece's request, dinner was vegan tacos and burritos, same as the last meal Raven had at their house.

After dessert, Reece stuck a third cookie in his mouth and shrugged on his coat.

"Where are you going?" Ms. Danner asked.

"Snow softball," he said through the cookie.

"It's a tradition," Huck said.

A tradition Raven wanted to be a part of. She grabbed her coat and boots. Reece turned on a floodlight that lit up the falling snow and backyard.

Softball quickly devolved into a snowball fight. First it was a free-for-all, then Jackie and Raven versus Huck and Reece. Next came the snow rubbing. In the hair, in the face. It hurt, but Raven didn't care. She was having the best time. Reece started shoving snow inside everyone's coats, so Raven, Jackie, and Huck ganged up and pulled him down into the snow. "Puppy pile!" Raven yelled, and they all flopped on top of him. That had been one of her favorite games with the boys when she was young.

While they were on the ground, Raven pushed a snowball down Jackie's back.

"You're going to pay for that!" he said.

She ran across the yard laughing. He tackled her, and she screamed at the shocking cold when he retaliated. She rolled over and tried to rub snow in his face, but he pinned her arms. They were breathing hard, their faces close. The warm, wet smell of him was intoxicating.

"Are we doing puppy pile, Jackie?" Reece called.

"No," Jackie called back.

Reece and Huck broke into laughter.

"If you need any tips, we'll be inside," Reece called.

They went in the house, tittering. The floodlight turned off.

The sudden darkness was startling. But the touch of Jackie's lips on hers wasn't. She knew they were going to kiss.

"Is this okay?" he asked.

"If it wasn't, you'd know," she said.

"I'd have a fat lip."

"Worse."

He still had her arms pinned.

"I want to try this." She rolled on top of him, pinned his arms, and kissed him.

"Which did you like better?" he asked.

"This."

"I think I do, too. But I need more to be sure."

She obliged.

"I'm sorry I said you were mean," she said.

"I knew you were only frustrated."

He sat up and wrapped his arms around her. "It's weird how easy this is," he said.

"I know. But maybe not that weird."

He held her out in his arms and looked at her. The lights in the house projected enough glow that she could see his shadowed features and a little shine in his eyes. He was smiling.

"You aren't surprised at all?" he asked.

"I've wanted to kiss you since I was seven, I think."

"I think I have, too."

She kissed him again. He was right. Being with him was so easy. As easy as breaching the fence magic had been.

He pulled off his gloves and combed snow out of her hair with his fingers. "I finally get to touch your hair."

"You like my hair?"

"I love your hair. It's always reminded me of shiny black raven feathers—because of your name, obviously."

Chris had seen through to her raven side, too. Maybe the closeness of spirit made it happen. But she hadn't felt a hundredth the soul bond to Chris as she did with Jackie.

"Want to go inside?" he asked.

"I could stay out here all night."

He smiled, stroking his hands on her hair. "I bet you could. That's how I always see you: out here. Even at school. You're like a piece of the forest that comes inside for a little while."

"I feel like that at school a lot of the time." She kissed his lips lightly. "I went there for you, you know. And for Reece and Huck."

"I know. We all knew. You paid too heavy a price. That's why we've been so pissed off about it all these years. And really guilty."

"Why guilty?"

"Huck said it best. He said we lured you to school, and it was like a trap. The door closed, and we could only see you there, like visiting you in a cage. You lost all your freedom because of us."

"Let's not talk about that. I'm here now."

"Does she know?"

"No. She's asleep."

"When are you going back?"

"I don't want to talk about that either. I want you to kiss me."

He touched his lips to hers and said, "I will. As much as I can until you go."

They stayed outside for only a few more minutes. They were soaked and getting cold. As they entered the back door, Jackie said, "Reece's jokes about this will be endless."

"I don't care."

"Neither do I."

Ms. Danner came to the door as they slid off their boots and coats. "I figured you'd be as wet as Huck and Reece were. I put dry clothes in the half bath for you, Raven."

"Thank you," she said. "I'm sorry we're creating so much laundry. I could put a load in the washer for you."

"That's sweet of you, but you go have fun. When do you have to be home?"

"No set time."

Ms. Danner frowned. "Does your mother know you're here?"

Raven shook her head.

"She must be frantic by now!"

"She's asleep. And if she wakes up, I left a note saying I was on a walk."

"At night in a snowstorm?"

"That's what she and I always do."

"What is?"

"Go outside."

She looked at Jackie. "This worries me. Drive her home soon, okay?"

He nodded. But when his mother wasn't looking, his mischievous glance at Raven said *soon* wasn't what he had in mind.

Raven and Jackie met in the living room after they changed. Huck and Reece were watching a movie. The living room was pretty with no lights but candles and the colored bulbs on the Christmas tree.

"Get lost in the storm?" Huck asked.

"Yep," Jackie said.

"I hope you had your moral compass with you, young man," Reece said in a teacher voice.

Jackie pulled Raven next to him on the L-shaped couch. "Where's Mom?" he asked Huck.

"Reading in her room."

Jackie unfolded a soft blanket and spread it over Raven and him. He moved close, nestling her in his arms.

"Whoa, what's this?" Reece said. "Do you two move fast or what?"

"Not really," Huck said. "They've already slept together."

Reece pretended to choke on a piece of popcorn. "And you didn't tell me?"

"I was told I couldn't," Huck said, looking at Jackie.

"And yet, you just did," Jackie said.

"When was this?" Reece asked.

"A while back," Jackie said.

Reece looked at Raven. "Aren't you going to defend your honor?"

"I don't have to. I was seven years old."

"I know for a fact that Cinderella always left long before midnight that summer," he said.

"She snuck into Jackie's bed in the middle of the night," Huck said.

"You little minx!" Reece said to Raven.

They all laughed.

"But really, did you?" he asked Raven.

"I really did. My mother was angry with me, and I ran away."

"And you crawled into bed with him?"

"She did," Jackie said, hugging her tighter. "She was freezing cold and wet."

"That was because I fell asleep in Hooper's field."

"You never told me that," he said.

"I was too busy shivering," she said.

"This is some story," Reece said. "Can I have rights to it when I become a famous author?"

"We'll think about it," Jackie said.

"Are you still writing?" Raven asked Reece.

"I write when I'm not dead tired from working, and driving back and forth, and doing laundry, and making sure my mom eats more than whiskey every day. Which means, no, I'm basically not writing."

"That sucks," Jackie said.

"I know, and I suffer well, don't I?" Reece said.

"Admirably," Huck said. "Are we watching this movie or what?"

"Rewind it to where we were when the love pups came in," Reece said.

She and Jackie didn't stay long. After a few minutes, he whispered, "Want to go to my room?"

She nodded.

"Tell Mom you're doing homework?" Huck asked when they headed for the stairs.

"Yeah, I'm sure she'll believe that," Jackie said.

"Don't study too hard," Reece said, and he and Huck sniggered.

Jackie turned on the light and closed the door. He'd repainted, a stormy blue-gray replacing the pastel blue. The bed was bigger, making the room feel smaller. On his desk and dresser were photographs of him with his father and family, many from their camping trips. The only decorations on the walls were a mirror over his dresser and a corkboard covered with photographs of friends and other memorabilia that dated back to elementary school. Raven was in a few of the photographs from school events. Scattered over the board were stickers from places he'd visited—Mount Rainier, Yellowstone, Grand Canyon—and conservation messages: THINK GREEN, PLANT POWER, RECYCLE. Jackie said he was going to study conservation biology in college.

"You still have the stars," she said, looking up at the white ceiling with plastic stars.

"I wanted them gone when I started middle school, but they tore the plaster when we pulled a few off. We decided to leave them on rather than redo the ceiling."

"I like them."

"Then I'm glad they're still here." He took her in his arms. "What do you want to do?"

"We could play Chutes and Ladders."

"I don't think we have that game anymore."

"Candy Land?"

He grinned. "That sounds like code for something else."

"It does. Let's play." She lifted the bottom of his sweatshirt up his chest.

"You really do move fast."

"I only want to look."

"Yeah? Can't wait till it's my turn."

She studied his bare chest. She thought of the day she'd first met him, when he, Huck, and Reece swam in the deep pool in the creek. His tanned body had been smooth and soft. Now he had some hair on his chest, and his shape was that of a man, contoured with beautiful bulges of muscle.

He was as easy about her looking at him as he'd been about kissing her. Maybe because he'd been with other girls. "What do you think?" he asked, holding his arms out.

"Remember Huck used to say you were Jolly in Candy Land? You're King Kandy now."

"I guess I'll take that as a compliment?"

"You should." She ran her fingers along the line of man fuzz below his navel. "When did you get this?"

He made a soft laugh. "I don't remember exactly."

"It's nice."

"You keep touching me there and it'll be way too nice." He removed her hand and pressed her close to kiss her. "Is it my turn now?"

"You're going to take off my sweater?"

"I'd love to check out the Gumdrop Mountains. But if my mother comes up here, she'll freak."

"Will she come up?"

"I don't know."

"I want to see the stars."

She turned off the overhead light. A constellation of stars glowed greenish white above them. She lay on her back to look at them. "I always wanted to see these stars again."

He stretched out next to her. "Only the stars?"

"And you."

He leaned over and kissed her. "Will we be able to see each other during the vacation?"

"I want to."

"I know. We have to figure out a way."

She imagined asking Mama if she could go out with him. If he were anyone but the boy who lived in the house she'd forbidden, it would be much easier. But maybe Mama didn't care about that now. She didn't have the energy to care about much.

Jackie stroked his fingers on her face. "Raven . . . ?"

"Yes?"

"Will you tell me what's going on? I know something's been wrong since you came back from Montana."

"My mother is sick."

"Physically?"

"Yes. Her heart."

All the forbidden words spilled out. She didn't know why.

"I think she's going to die, Jackie."

"Raven, I'm so sorry. Did a doctor say that?"

"She won't go to a doctor."

"She has to! Maybe they can do surgery."

"She won't. I've tried."

"Why won't she?"

"I think because of her mother. She died in a hospital, and my mother said she died without dignity."

"But maybe they could fix what's wrong and she wouldn't die."

"I know. I tried . . . she made me promise . . ." The weight of it broke through. All the ache poured out in her sobs.

Jackie held her. "I'm sorry. I'm so sorry," he said.

"Where will I go if she dies? What will I do?"

"It'll be okay. Maybe she won't die."

"She's getting worse and worse."

"You said you have an aunt. Can she help?"

"I'm not allowed to tell her."

"Maybe you should break that promise."

"I can't! My aunt will put her in a hospital. They'll attach her to machines. She doesn't want that. She has a right to be in control of what happens to her body, doesn't she?"

"I don't know. She's put you in an impossible situation."

Raven cried harder.

Someone tapped on the door.

"Jackie?" Ms. Danner said. "What's going on? Why is Raven crying?"

"Crap," Jackie whispered. He pulled on his sweatshirt and turned on the desk lamp before opening the door.

His mother surveyed Raven wiping her tears. "I don't want to pry, but I'm obviously concerned."

"Raven told me something . . . ," he said.

Raven shook her head. Ms. Danner saw.

"It's private," he said.

"I understand," she said. "I came up to say Raven should go home. I heard her crying . . . I didn't mean to eavesdrop."

"It's okay," Raven said.

"Can I help in any way?" she asked.

"No. Thank you," Raven said.

"Honey, I'm worried that your mother doesn't know where you are in this storm. I really think you should go home."

"Okay," Raven said.

Ms. Danner took Raven in her arms. "We're always here for you, Raven. Anything you need, please ask."

Raven hugged her, thought of that night long ago when she'd told her she wished she lived at her house. Saying it had made her feel terribly guilty, and she'd had to run away. In a way, she still felt like that same little girl running across Hooper's field.

Huck and Reece saw that Raven had been crying, curbing the expected jokes about what they'd been doing upstairs. They both hugged Raven goodbye. "Are you okay?" Reece whispered in her ear.

"Yes."

"Liar, pants on fire," he whispered, and she sniffed a stuffy-nosed laugh.

Outside, the snow had accumulated to about six inches.

"Don't take me to the gate," Raven told Jackie as he started the car.

"Where will I take you?"

"I'll show you. Before the gate."

"Why?"

"I'll climb the fence. The alarms will wake her up if I walk down the driveway."

He looked at her, and she could tell he wanted her to explain about the alarms.

"We'd better go. And make sure you turn around in the road—don't go past my driveway."

He drove slowly on the one-lane road so Raven could look for a good place to climb the fence. She had him stop at a place where there wasn't too much brush.

"This will be a pretty long walk," he said.

"That's okay."

He got out to say goodbye, and they kissed in a flutter of snow lit by the headlight beams.

"When will I see you?" he asked.

"I don't know."

"You can't say that. I have no way to contact you. We have to make a plan now."

"I'm going to ask her if I can start seeing you. But I can't predict what her answer will be."

"Let's just say we'll meet right here day after tomorrow. What's a good time for you?"

"I'll tell her you want to take me out for dinner."

"I do want to take you out for dinner," he said.

"What time?"

"Five thirty," he said.

"But don't count on it."

He kissed her. "I'm going to count on it. Every minute. Let me give you a boost over the fence."

"I don't need a boost."

"I was hoping to grab your butt."

"All right, I need a boost."

8

Mama didn't know she'd left the house.

Raven was too keyed up to sleep. She lit a fire in the hearth and curled up with blankets and a pillow next to the dancing flames. Everything that had happened with Jackie played over and over in her thoughts. Was she really with him? Finally?

She woke at dawn next to the cooled fire. Mama was standing in front of the big living room windows that looked out at a field outlined by two clusters of trees. The storm had cleared, and she was transfixed by the snow-cloaked landscape.

Raven walked to her side. "I went out in the storm last night. It was so beautiful."

"I wish I was well enough to walk in snow all day as I used to," she said.

"I'll walk with you, if you want."

"I don't need help, Daughter," she said. "But let's walk after breakfast."

Walking in the snow and crisp air invigorated Mama. She almost seemed well. Raven decided to ask her about the date with Jackie while she was in a good mood.

"Remember that boy who came onto our property?"

"Yes, I remember Jack Danner, the one who drives you home from school most days."

She still reviewed the driveway videos.

"May I go on a date with him tomorrow? He asked me to dinner."

"Dinner!" Mama said. "I'd thought you and he would be far beyond that by now."

"What do you mean?"

"You've been with him for months. I assumed you two were having sex."

"How could we be having sex? You've seen what time he drops me off. We come straight here from school."

"You haven't had sex with him?"

"No. This will be our first date. If you let me go."

"He was more polite than the other boy. Do you like him?"

"I like him a lot."

"He lives down the road, doesn't he?"

"Yes."

"His mother was the one who interfered in your schooling."

"That was a long time ago. And she didn't interfere. She only said I was smart and should go to school. Of course a schoolteacher is going to say that."

Mama paced silently. Raven was afraid the conversation about Jackie's mother had ruined her chances.

Mama stopped walking and faced her. Already she was short of breath. "Yes, go with him. But enough of the inane dining and dating rituals. Just let your creature side free and enjoy physical pleasure with him. That's what he wants more than some silly dinner, too."

Raven snorted. "I bet you're the only mother in my high school who tells her daughter to have sex rather than go on a date."

"You're different, Raven. Human mating games won't appeal to your wild raven side."

"That's not true. Ravens engage in many rituals before they copulate. They do sky swooping together and dances and preening. They make those soft little sounds like love words. And I've seen males bring females gifts of food. That's the equivalent of me going out to dinner with Jackie."

Mama burst into laughter that ended with coughing.

"You have me, Daughter. I think this boy has very much captured your raven soul."

She was afraid to say how much he had. Mama might get jealous, as she had when she found out about her visits to Jackie and his house.

"Go on your date, then," Mama said. "And preen and dance and whatever you and your raven spirit like."

They began walking again.

As Raven let herself get excited about her date the next day, she realized Mama's peculiar endorsement of sex gave her an advantage to ask for something more.

"If we do want to do it, we would need a place to go," she said. "May I go to his house afterward if he invites me?"

"Aha, you do want to sleep with him," Mama said.

"I might want to."

"Well, don't bring him here."

"I know. What about his house?"

"His mother would allow that?"

"We could sneak." She felt awful even saying that. But getting Mama's permission to go to Jackie's house was well worth the lying and guilt.

Again, Mama laughed and coughed.

"Yes?" Raven pushed.

"Yes, go to his house." Mama grinned at her. "You've always liked to sneak around. You have more than a little of the raven's roguish spirit in you."

"When do I sneak?"

"That summer when you were little. And with Chris Williams." She looked into Raven's eyes. "And last night."

She was afraid to say anything. And that made Mama laugh again. She hadn't seen Mama this jovial for many weeks, even months.

"Yes, I've figured it out," Mama said. "I know you were gone for many hours last night. And now you ask for this date. You met him during the storm, didn't you?"

"I did."

"That must have been fun," she said.

Raven sensed envy in her tone. "It was."

Still chuckling, she patted Raven's arm. "My dear Daughter of Raven, go and have your fun while you're young. Your papa would want you to."

How easy it had been. Like how it had been with Jackie the night before. And what a relief that Mama was glad about it. Maybe her father's spirit was influencing the situation. Her father, after all, had led her to Jackie. The raven had left one nestling jay alive and had given it to Mama to give to her. Baby had brought Raven to Jackie at the stream that day, and Raven had felt something deep inside from the moment she looked into Jackie's hazel eyes. Perhaps a premonition.

The next day, Raven met Jackie on the road at five thirty. He was as stunned as she had been when she told him Mama's reaction.

Raven had the best winter vacation of her life. She went to Jackie's house on Christmas Day and opened presents. New Year's Eve was a party at one of Huck's friend's houses. Raven had her first drinks that night, but Reece made her stop when she got too giggly. She didn't mind. She knew he didn't like drinking because his mother was an alcoholic. Jackie was tipsy, too, and they danced and joked around.

When school started, everyone knew they were a couple and started inviting them out. They went to movies, parties, and restaurants. Mama gave her a credit card to pay for everything. There were jokes about

"Rich Raven" and her credit card. Raven learned how to act like Jackie in those situations. She just teased them back.

But shadowing the fun was a vast, creeping darkness. Mama was getting sicker. And she wouldn't let Raven take care of her. "I don't want you to see me like this," she would say. "Go out with Jack. Seize the joy of youth." Raven protested, but Mama would get angry and become sicker from being upset. Raven had to do what she wanted and leave.

When Raven got home late on Valentine's Day, she found Mama on the floor. She wasn't in the spirit world; she was very sick. Raven wanted to call an ambulance, but Mama wouldn't let her. She reminded her of her promise. So Raven sat by Mama's bed for the rest of the night, watching every ragged breath. She didn't go to school the next day. She missed another day the next week and two days at the end of February.

One cold March morning, Mama woke her earlier than usual. She sat on her bed and caressed her face. "I love you, Daughter of Raven," she said. "You are my miracle. You have been the best sixteen years of my life."

"I'm not sixteen yet," Raven said sleepily.

"You began as a beautiful dream long before you came to me. It's been sixteen years and more."

"You're feeling better today?"

"Yes. Very well. Are you going out with Jack after school?"

"I don't know."

"I want you to. Stay out and have fun. Now that I'm old, I see that I should have done that when I was your age. I was always too serious. I'm glad you have your father's lively spirit and not mine."

"I have both. I love your spirit."

Tears grew like dewdrops in Mama's pale eyes. She put her hand on Raven's cheek. "You will have my spirit with you always, dear one. You need only look at the beauty of the earth, and I'll be there."

Raven didn't like the sound of that. She sat up and held Mama's hands. "I need only look at you right here in front of me. You're getting better. I know you are."

"I am," she said. "I talked to the spirits. They will give me what I need. Now get up and go to school. And then have fun with Jack."

All day, Raven couldn't stop thinking about Mama. After school, Jackie wanted to meet some of their friends at Bear's. Raven went, because Mama said she should, but she only wanted to go home. While she drank her Coke at an outdoor table, a raven perched in a tree over the parking lot. It stayed there, calling and calling. A terrible, sickening gloom fell over her. She was afraid she might vomit.

"I need to go home," she whispered in Jackie's ear.

"What's wrong?"

"I feel sick."

He led her to the car. "Those greasy fries got you probably," he said as he pulled out of the lot.

She could still hear the raven's croaking call. She felt like she was in an eerie dream, as if remembering a nightmare from when she was very little.

"Are you okay?" he asked.

"I need to get home. Hurry."

She said goodbye but didn't kiss him. She opened the gate and ran down the driveway. She unlocked the front door and turned off the alarms she'd triggered. If Mama hadn't turned them off, she wasn't home. Or she was too sick.

Raven strode quickly through the house. Mama wasn't there. A white piece of paper on the refrigerator caught her eye:

Raven, Remember what we talked about this morning. I'll be out for a while. You will see me soon. I love you. Mama

She was so relieved she nearly cried. Mama had felt well enough to go out and do an Asking. She would be home soon.

But twilight came, and Mama still wasn't home. Fortunately, the temperature wasn't dangerously cold. And Mama often came home late.

But that was many months ago, when Mama was still healthy.

By nine o'clock, Raven was certain something was wrong. She took a flashlight outside and searched around the house in widening circles. The temperature had dropped. If Mama was unconscious out there, she was in serious trouble. Raven walked for many hours before giving up and going home.

Exhaustion put her to sleep quickly, but she slept only a few hours. She got up at dawn and began searching more carefully. She would miss school, but she didn't care. Why had she thought school was so important when she was a little girl? Why had she spent all those days away from the person who mattered most? All she wanted was Mama. She would give up school if only she could find her alive. She would even give up Jackie if the spirits said she must to bring Mama back.

But she saw no signs from spirits and no trace of Mama. She searched until dark and stumbled into the cabin weak with exhaustion and hunger. She had to force herself to eat before falling into bed.

At dawn, she returned to her search. This time, she brought a sandwich to keep up her energy. She looked in all of Mama's favorite places on their ninety acres, calling, "Mama! Mama! Mama!"

Even when she didn't say it aloud, her name was a constant supplication in her mind. *Mama. Mama. Mama. I need you, Mama! Please come back!*

As the sun sank low, she searched near the stream and swimming hole for a second time. Mama loved that place. She carefully scoured the weeds and brambles. She waded into the stream and looked into thickets on either side. When she got to the junk pile, she searched it thoroughly, even inside the old Invicta. She doubted Mama had ever gone there—she would have seen it as a blight on the earth—but Raven was desperate. In two and a half days, she'd covered the entire property and found no sign of Mama.

Darkness slowly swallowed her. Utterly spent, she plopped into the stream in front of the Wolfsbane. She looked up at the strange tower of objects, resenting that it was still there and Mama wasn't.

"You didn't scare away the werewolf," she said to the Madonna. "Mama made the boys and me safe. Mama killed the werewolf. You never did anything!"

She dropped her head between her muddy knees and wept.

There was no moon or stars to guide her, and she was too tired to go home. She didn't want to be in the house without Mama anyway. Maybe she would lie down in the creek stones and let the spirits take her. That surely was what Mama had done. She had gone to the spirit world. That was why there was no trace of her on their land.

Of course she had. Mama had a deep understanding of the earth few ever attained. She was powerful. She had brought a baby, body and all, out of the spirit world. And now she had finally discovered how to bring her body there.

Raven thought of her last conversation with Mama.

You are my miracle. You have been the best sixteen years of my life.

You will have my spirit with you always, dear one. You need only look at the beauty of the earth, and I'll be there.

She had been saying goodbye. Raven understood that now.

When she'd said, "I talked to the spirits. They will give me what I need," she meant she'd figured out how to go to their world. That was why she'd looked so bright and happy. Raven understood why she wanted to go. Living in her sick body in the human world had been agony for Mama. And she hated for Raven to see her like that.

The note she'd left in the kitchen. Those were Mama's last words for her: *I'll be out for a while. You will see me soon. I love you. Mama.*

Raven wondered what she'd meant. Why would she say she was coming back if it wasn't true? She must have been certain she would return. Maybe she knew it would take some time to heal and find her way back. That was why she'd said she would be *out for a while*.

Her heart pounded. Mama was coming back. That was why she hadn't said goodbye, why she hadn't left instructions for how to take care of the house without her.

Raven stood, and her head swam with dizziness. She'd barely eaten during the relentless searching. The darkness would make navigating home difficult. One side of her wanted to lie down and become one with Mama's world. Her other side, her human side, wanted Jackie.

Her need for him rose up in her like the spirits of every hungry animal in that forest. His house was closer than hers, but getting there without stars or moon would be difficult. She would almost have to feel her way.

She could do it. If she were blind, she would know how to find that sweet little house.

By the time she arrived at the fence, she was bruised and scraped and covered in mud. She stopped on the Hooper side of the fence and looked to the guiding light of the house windows.

What would she tell them? She couldn't explain. Not even to Jackie.

She ducked through the fence, staggered to the front door, and rang the bell. Ms. Danner answered. "Raven!" she said. "Come in!"

Jackie and his mother stared at her.

"What happened to you?" Jackie asked.

"I got lost. I was walking and forgot to bring a flashlight. There's no moon or stars tonight."

He knew she was lying. She saw it in his eyes.

Ms. Danner frowned, too. "Let's get you some dry clothes," she said.

Raven followed. She stumbled on a chair and nearly fell, but Jackie caught her.

She took a stack of Jackie's clothes into the bathroom, and when she looked in the mirror, she understood why they were alarmed by her appearance. Her hair was tangled with leaves and vines. Her face was smeared with dirt, one cheek scratched by a blackberry vine. Her clothes were wet and filthy.

She turned on the faucet and gulped water with her cupped hand. Then she rubbed the water over her face. She hardly had enough energy to change into the clean clothes. Jackie's soft, soap-scented sweats were like a warm embrace.

"Are you hungry?" Ms. Danner asked.

"A little," she said. She had to eat, though she had no appetite.

Ms. Danner rewarmed a plate of food from their dinner.

"Can you stay awhile?" Jackie asked.

"Yes."

"Come upstairs."

He would ask what was wrong. She had to make sure she didn't cry as she had in December.

Jackie closed his door. Raven sat on the side of the bed next to his homework.

"I've been so worried about you!" he said. "You ran off the other day and missed two days of school. You missed your birthday yesterday."

March twelfth, her fake birthday. That meant it was Friday.

"Why are you home doing homework on a Friday night?" she asked.

"Why would you ask me that?" he said in an angry voice. "You know why. Because I haven't heard from you for two days. Do you really think I'd want to go out without you tonight? I almost went over there today."

"But you were afraid of the gun."

"Of course I was! I thought your mother was going to kill me that day!"

Tears were coming. She couldn't let them. She curled onto her side on the bed and closed her eyes.

"What's going on? Did she kick you out of the house again?"

"No," she said, keeping her eyes closed.

"Then why do you look like you've been living in the woods for the last two days? And I'd swear you've lost a lot of weight."

"Stop. I'm tired. I just want quiet."

"My mom is going to ask me what's going on. She knows that's why I brought you up here."

"I was lost."

"As if I'd believe you, of all people, could get lost on your land. You told me you've been trusted to wander alone since you were six."

Raven bit the inside of her bottom lip to feel pain that would stop the tears.

Jackie sat on the bed next to her. He stroked his fingers through her hair. "I'm sorry I sound angry. I'm not. I've been worried."

She dared not speak or she'd cry.

"Happy birthday," he said. "I have a present for you. Do you want to open it?"

"Not now," she managed.

He sighed. "I don't know why you don't trust me enough to tell me what's going on." His fingers stopped stroking her hair. "Raven . . . did your mother . . . did she . . . pass?"

Yes, she had *passed* as some people said. She had passed from one world to another. And if she couldn't find her way back, Raven would never see her again.

She would find her way. She'd said she would.

"Did she?" he asked.

She kept her eyes closed. "No."

"Is she really sick?"

"She's getting better."

"If that's true, why did you leave Bear's and run away from me?"

"I forgot to do something my mother asked."

It hurt to lie to him, but she had to. At sixteen, she probably wasn't allowed to live alone. Police would take her away from her land. Mama wouldn't be able to find her when she returned.

"Would you turn off the light?" she asked. "I want to rest a little."

He turned off the desk lamp and tugged the comforter out from under her. He got in the bed behind her, pulled the cover over them, and wrapped his arm around her.

"Whatever's going on, I'm glad you're here," he said.

"Me too," she said.

He hugged her tighter.

She pushed away all thought. She only let herself feel his warmth and hear the soft rhythm of his breathing. She fell asleep without once looking up at the plastic stars.

9

The lying got easier. And taking care of the house by herself wasn't difficult. She conserved propane by rarely using heat. She wore layers of clothing and turned on the furnace only if she was afraid the pipes might freeze. She was careful not to use the food in the big freezer. She often ate out with Jackie after school, and a few times she had him take her to the grocery store to get perishables. The credit card Mama had given her continued working.

She went to school every day, did her homework, got good grades. She went out with Jackie and their friends as often as she had before. She made sure there was no reason to suspect anything in her life had changed.

At the beginning of spring break, the water stopped working inside the house. Something was wrong with the well pump. That had happened before, but Raven couldn't remember what repair was needed. She knew how to do many repairs—clogged sink pipes, jammed kitchen disposal, leaky toilet tanks—but this was beyond what she knew.

Though she knew which plumber Mama used, she wasn't sure if he fixed wells. And she had no phone now that Mama wasn't there. Mama believed phones were strictly utilitarian devices. She had used hers only to order groceries or call repair services. Her phone was always locked, and Raven didn't know the code.

She would have to ask Jackie to call the plumber. He was coming to the gate with Huck and Reece to pick her up for lunch. Huck's spring break from the university coincided with their high school break, and Reece had his day off from work.

She dressed without a shower. She made tea and brushed her teeth with emergency bottled water Mama kept in the pantry.

She thought about how she would explain needing Jackie's phone as she walked down to the gate.

The boys arrived a little late. Reece hung out his window as the car slowed. "Need a ride, babe?" he asked.

Raven messed his hair with her fingers.

"Hey, I worked on that for an hour!"

She sat in back with Jackie. As Huck started down the road, she asked, "Do any of you know who to call when a well pump isn't working?"

"What's wrong with it?" Reece asked.

"I don't know. All I know is I had no water to take a shower."

"Is *that* what I smell?" Huck said.

"I thought we'd driven over a steaming sewer," Reece said.

Jackie kissed her cheek. "You smell great."

"Doesn't your mom know who to call?" Reece asked.

"She's not here."

They all shot surprised stares her way.

"Where is she?" Jackie asked.

"She went to be with my aunt for a little while."

"Where is that?"

"Chicago."

"She left you here alone?" Reece said.

"I'm old enough."

The car went silent. Jackie looked in her eyes, his gaze searching. He'd promised he wouldn't tell anyone her mother was sick. And with

Huck and Reece there, he couldn't ask how her mother had gone on a trip when she was so ill.

"Did you tell her the pump is broken?" Reece asked.

"I can't. She's getting medical treatment."

Jackie couldn't hold in his question. "She went to a doctor?"

"I finally convinced her. She called my aunt, and my aunt knew of a good doctor in Chicago."

"What's wrong with her?" Huck asked.

"We're still not sure. She's getting tests."

"That's great!" Jackie said.

"I know," she said.

"Why didn't you go with her?" Reece asked.

"Because of school. She left before spring break."

"You've been living alone?" Jackie said. "Why didn't you tell me?"

"You know why. My mother doesn't like me to talk about our personal matters."

She was proud of the story. It was believable. But lying to the people she loved hurt.

She told herself it wasn't such a bad lie. Mama *was* getting healed. Raven had to believe she was. With all her heart and soul. That was the only way she could bear the pain of Mama's absence.

"Turn around," Reece said to Huck.

"Why?"

"Because I'm going to look at the pump."

"You know about wells?" Raven asked.

"Reece knows how to fix anything," Jackie said.

"Except my mother," Reece said.

Raven understood him so much better now. The pain of watching your only parent struggle with illness when you were powerless to help.

Huck turned the car around. "Will it be okay for us to go on your property?" he asked. "Won't your mother be angry when she comes back and sees that on video?"

"I think it will be okay," she said.

She pressed the code to open the gate, and Huck pulled the car through.

"I don't believe this. I've entered the Forbidden Kingdom," Reece said.

The log house came into view.

"What an awesome house!" Reece said. "Can we see inside?"

She unlocked the door and let them in. She'd turned off the alarms when she left.

How strange it was to watch them walk through her house, eagerly examining the private spaces of her sheltered life. She worked hard to hide how difficult the collision of her two worlds felt.

"I love this room!" Reece said. He was in the living room, looking out the big windows to the woods, fields, and distant mountains. That was Raven's favorite room, too. It had log beams and columns, a fieldstone hearth, wood floors covered with rugs, and a soft couch and chairs. The library attached via sliding glass-paned doors.

Jackie and Huck were in the library, poring over the many science books and field guides.

Reece joined them, stopping to look at the skulls on the bone table. "Are these the shrunken heads of the last guys who trespassed into the Forbidden Kingdom?"

"That's right, so watch your step," Raven said.

Huck held up the beaver skull. "This is what you'll look like when Raven's done with you," he told Reece.

"Quite an improvement," Jackie said.

"Really?" Reece said, sticking out his front teeth. "I thought I pretty much looked like that now."

Raven was starting to feel more comfortable with them in her house. Their playful banter filled the terrible emptiness that had haunted her since Mama went away.

An idea popped to mind. Reece's birthday was in two days. When he got off work, the four of them would meet at Jackie's house.

"I'll make a deal with you," she said to Reece. "If you can fix the water pump, we'll have your birthday party here."

"Nice!" he said. "Start a group invite," he said to Huck. "We'll call it 'Raven's Rave for Reece.'"

"Good name," Huck said. He pulled his phone out of his pocket.

"No!" Raven said, grabbing at the phone.

"They're joking," Jackie said.

"They better be. I've seen how those parties get."

"Let's look at the pump and get this party started," Reece said.

Raven took him outside. In minutes, he figured out what was wrong using just a few tools from the house. He said the switch was out, an easy repair.

"The part is cheap, and I won't charge you too much for labor," Reece said. "Just a birthday dinner in the log house of my dreams."

"What's your favorite dinner?" she asked.

He looked at Huck and Jackie apologetically. "Prime rib."

Jackie and Huck groaned.

"I like prime rib, too," Raven said.

"Great. We'll send the vegans out to pasture, and we'll feast."

"Do you like baked potato?" Raven asked.

"Love it," Reece said. "Butter *and* sour cream. Salad for the vegetable. Bleu cheese dressing. Cheesecake for dessert."

"Wow," Huck said. "Do you plan to live much past your nineteenth birthday?"

"A day or two," Reece said.

"You can drive me to the grocery store," Raven told Jackie. "We'll plan vegan dishes for you and Huck."

"You *can* cook, right?" Huck asked her.

"Of course I can cook."

"The fancy kitchen makes that obvious," Reece said. "We'll have to alter our image of her. I'll no longer imagine her toasting squirrel on a stick over a fire."

"I can do that, too," she said.

The boys laughed.

"It's a good survival skill," Raven said.

"Let's do a non-survivalist menu, okay?" Reece said.

Preparing the party menu made her happier than she'd been in weeks. The cooking did, too.

On the evening of the party, Raven unlocked the gate. It was strange and a little frightening to leave it open and walk away. Jackie and Huck arrived first. Ms. Danner sent candles with a little decorated vegan cake that said, *Happy Birthday, Reece.* Huck brought a speaker to play music, and Jackie had a bag with presents for Reece.

Reece arrived at about six. He had a long drive from work, and he'd gone home to shower first. He walked in the front door holding up a bottle of champagne and announced, "Happy birthday to me." The alcohol was unexpected; Reece still rarely drank.

"How'd you get that?" Huck asked.

"My mom, of course," he said.

He also had a paper bag but wouldn't show them what was in it. "It's my birthday entertainment," he said.

"Fireworks?" Jackie guessed.

"Nope."

"Music?" Raven asked.

"No."

"Ferret that rides a little bicycle?" Huck asked.

"Getting warm," Reece said.

Raven was excited about the dinner. "How do you like your meat cooked?" she asked Reece.

"Mooing," he said.

"Disgusting," Jackie said.

Raven had them sit in the living room next to the fire while she cooked. She loved hearing their music, voices, and laughter in her house. Not once had she visualized friends entering her house. She wondered what Mama would think of her party. One of the last things she'd told Raven was to have fun while she was young. Perhaps Mama's spirit was still with her in some form. Maybe she had broken the water pump switch so all of this would happen.

"Okay, Jackie, let's see how your better half cooks," Reece said when dinner was ready.

They were impressed by the jars of evergreens, berry branches, and grasses on the table. Huck popped the cork on the champagne and poured four glasses. He toasted Reece: "Happy birthday to the best ass I've ever known."

"My ass thanks you," Reece said, popping up and baring his butt for a second. "Did you see the sideways smile?"

They all laughed, and Jackie said, "I've lost my appetite."

After dinner, they put candles on the cake and sang "Happy Birthday." Raven thought she saw a glaze of tears in Reece's sky-blue eyes, but after the song, he said, "Can we try that again in key? You guys sounded like a bunch of cats in heat."

Reece was stunned when he saw that Raven had made the cheesecake from scratch rather than buy one ready-made.

"Of course I baked it," she said. "And I have blackberry preserves I made with my mother to put on top."

"Oh my god, will you marry me?" he said.

She was glad for the joke, because thinking about the preserves she'd made with Mama nearly made her cry.

They moved to the living room, where Reece opened two gag gifts from Jackie and Huck, then two real ones. Raven gave him a necklace she'd made, a small tan stone with a hole in its middle. She'd tied it to a deerskin lace made from the deer Raven and Mama had butchered when she was young.

"A stone with a doorway is rare," she said. "It can carry great power if you use it right."

"It's beautiful," Reece said. He put the cord over his head. "I feel something happening already."

"Good," Raven said. "Use it well."

"With great stone power comes great responsibility!" he said in a deep, theatrical voice.

"Shut up and let the ferret out of the bag," Huck said, handing him his mystery bag.

"Right," Reece said. He withdrew a stack of games.

They were games for adults, and every bit as fun as the ones they'd played when they were little. She nearly peed her pants from laughing a few times.

Around ten o'clock, Reece and Huck asked Raven and Jackie if they wanted to hang out with some friends who were in town from college. Raven was relieved when Jackie said he'd rather stay at the house with her. She wanted some alone time with him.

Reece kissed her on the cheek. "Thank you. Best birthday ever."

"Too bad about all those dishes we left," Huck said, shrugging on his coat. "Better get on that, Jackie."

"Yeah, right away," Jackie said.

"I suggest an apron with nothing beneath," Reece said.

"But you've done enough, Raven," Huck said. "You can watch."

"From behind," Reece added.

"We appreciate the suggestions," Jackie said, giving Reece a little push toward the door.

As soon as Reece's old car rumbled down the driveway, Jackie took her in his arms. A long, delicious kiss.

"Do you mind if I turn down the heat?" she asked.

He pulled her closer. "Turn it down?" he said, smiling.

"The thermostat. I'm trying to conserve propane while my mother is away."

"Didn't she leave you enough money?"

"I have to budget," she said.

"Sure, turn it down," he said. "We'll figure out how to stay warm."

She turned the thermostat down and led him to her bedroom.

"You kept it," Jackie said. He was holding the black rock with the white *R* for Raven, the one he'd given to her when they were little.

"Best gift ever," she said.

He smiled, watching her pull the comforter off the bed. "Why are you taking it off? That bed looked pretty comfy."

"I'll show you how I liked to sleep when my mother lit a fire. Get a pillow."

They brought the blankets and pillows to the living room. She fashioned the duvet into a bed next to the fire. "My mother said I started curling up on the warm hearthstones like a puppy when I was a toddler. When I got older, I'd make a bed like this."

She put more wood on the fire and turned out the house lights.

"Are you going to seduce me?" he asked.

"Of course I am."

"Good."

They stretched out on the folded duvet and pulled a blanket over themselves. They lay on their sides facing the fire, Jackie curled around her from behind.

"That was a great party," he said. "I haven't seen Reece that happy for a while."

"I know. It was like the old Reece again."

"He couldn't wait to get out of school, but now that he has, he's miserable. He hates his job, and he spends most of his free time taking care of his mother."

They watched the bark on one of the new logs catch fire.

"It's strange to be in your house," he said.

"It is for me, too."

"Do you have any idea when your mother will come back?"

"No."

"Do you talk to her much?"

"Not that often." She turned around and kissed him to silence his questions.

Being in a house without parental scrutiny was new for them. They had often made out in Jackie's bedroom or in the woods behind his house, but they couldn't explore each other as they wanted in those places. On Valentine's Day, in Jackie's car, they had talked about sex but decided they didn't want their first time to be in a car. That night, Jackie had told her he'd never done it. He said she was the only girl he'd ever wanted to be with that way.

The freedom of being alone changed everything. Jackie took off her shirt and pants. She took off his. They had only their underwear between them. She felt the soft duvet beneath her, his warm skin on hers, and the fire's heat dancing around them.

Jackie leaned over her, his dark hair falling onto his forehead. How beautiful he was, his hazel eyes flashing with reflected flames.

"Do you want to?" he asked.

"Yes," she said.

"Me too. But I have to go out to my car."

"To get a condom?"

"There are still some in the glove box from Huck."

"You don't need that."

He looked stunned. "You're on birth control?"

"My body can't make a baby."

"Why not?"

After a few seconds of thought, she said, "Because I was born different."

"Raven, I'm so sorry!"

He truly was. She saw it in his eyes. She wished she could tell him the truth, that she might have a baby one day when she asked for one with all her heart and soul.

"I don't mind," she said. "It's no big deal."

She'd spoiled the mood. He now looked at her more with concern and sympathy than desire.

"Does it change how you think of me?" she asked.

He put his hand on her cheek, his gaze softened. "No. Not at all. I love you the same."

"It makes things a lot easier, doesn't it?"

"Definitely."

She sat up and slid off her bra.

He refocused on the topic at hand. He guided her down and kissed her. "Who gets to be on top?" he asked.

"Both of us," she said.

"Is that physically possible?"

"You didn't think we'd only do it once, did you?"

10

Mama was right about the creature joy of sex. It was like lapping icy water straight from a Montana mountain stream when she was thirsty. It was a kind of satiation in the most beautiful of ways.

But making love with Jackie was much more than simple gratification. Because of what she felt for him. With Chris, her raven side had stood apart. With Jackie, she and her spiritual side were one. Her raven fully trusted Jackie's gentle soul. And her human side, of course, loved him body and soul.

They wished spring break would never end. They spent as much time together as they could. Ms. Danner knew Raven's mother was away, but she didn't know how many hours Jackie was in Raven's home and walking the acreage with her. She wouldn't have allowed it. She'd barely agreed to the unsupervised party for Reece.

Sunday, the last day of vacation, was warm and sunny with a delicious taste of spring in the air. Jackie came over at noon after he did a few chores for his mother. They made a picnic lunch and headed for the stream. Jackie wanted to make love there, at the place where they had met.

"You're quite the romantic," she said when he suggested it.

"I am, but don't tell anyone," he said.

When they arrived at the stream, Raven spread out a blanket. "This is exactly where I was standing when we first saw each other."

They ate lunch. They made love. They lay wrapped together watching clouds billow.

"The anniversary of my dad's accident is next week," he said. "Maybe you could come over that day."

"Of course," she said. "What would you like to do?"

"We need to be with my mom. Huck will be at school, and I think three will feel less lonely than two. Will that be okay?"

"Yes, of course." She swept his hair off his forehead and kissed him there.

"One year since I last talked to him. Sometimes it seems longer, sometimes like the accident just happened yesterday."

"Everyone loved him. He was a good man."

Jackie leaned over her, tears in his eyes. "Do you remember at the burial, what you said?"

She remembered very well.

"You put your hand on my heart and said something like, 'I give you the strength of my spirit.' You said you loved me."

"Were you upset?"

"What? No! That was bullshit how everyone got angry with you! It made me realize how empty most of my relationships were. You were the only person other than my mom who ever made me feel better."

He looked as serious as she'd ever seen him. "I changed because of what you did. I broke up with Sadie because she kept bad-mouthing you. And I quit hanging out with anyone who treated you like that. I realized that day that you were the only girl I wanted to be with."

"You did?"

"Didn't you see how much more attention I gave you? But you were so different when you came back from Montana. I didn't think I'd ever get to be with you."

"I didn't either."

He took her in his arms. The creek murmured senselessly in its hurry. The wind rushed through the cedars. But she and Jackie held tight.

She tried lifting his mood as they walked home. She kissed him. She stuck weeds in his hair and made him laugh. When the house came into view, she yelled, "Beat you to the stairs," a game they'd played at his house when they were little.

"No fair! I have the cooler," he said as she sprinted ahead.

She was carrying two blankets. It was an even race.

She got to the back stairs first and ran in the house. "I won!"

"You had a head start," he said breathlessly.

She tossed the blankets in the laundry room and took the cooler from him. She brought it into the kitchen, startled when a figure rose from a chair at the table. A white-haired, pale-skinned woman.

Not Mama returned from the spirit world. It was Aunt Sondra.

"Raven . . . ," her aunt said. "I was worried. I found the gate open and the house unlocked."

Raven had been too preoccupied with Jackie to lock up.

Aunt Sondra walked toward Jackie with her hand extended. "I'm Sondra Lind Young, Raven's aunt."

"Jack Danner," he said nervously as he shook her hand.

"Nice to meet you, Jack," she said.

Jackie believed Raven's mother was with her aunt in Chicago getting medical treatment. Sondra's appearance without her mother could signal only one outcome to him, confirmed by his expression of sorrow.

Her aunt said, "We need to talk, Raven."

Jackie looked at Raven. "Do you want me to leave?"

"You probably should," Aunt Sondra said.

You probably should. That meant bad news. Her aunt was holding a large manila envelope. It was addressed to her aunt in Mama's handwriting.

"I want you to go," Raven said to her aunt.

"Raven . . ."

"Go!" Tears burned like fire in her eyes, then dripped like ice down her cheeks.

Jackie took her in his arms and held her against his chest.

"How long has your mother been missing?" Aunt Sondra asked in a quiet voice.

Raven cried into Jackie's shirt.

When Raven didn't answer, her aunt said, "Jack, do you know?"

"Raven told me she was with you. In Chicago."

Raven pulled away from Jackie. "She's coming back! You're too blind to understand!"

Tears glossed her aunt's eyes. "You know she isn't. She sent me her last will and testament."

"I don't care what she sent you," Raven said. "She's coming back!"

"She told her lawyer to send this envelope to me on a certain date. I think she waited to have it sent—until she carried out what she wanted to do. But I was on a trip with my husband when it arrived. I didn't find it until I returned home last night."

Jackie stared at Raven. Now he knew she'd been lying to him.

But she hadn't been. Not really. Mama was coming back.

"Please tell me what happened," Aunt Sondra said. "She's my sister. I need to know."

Jackie took her arms and looked into her eyes. "Is that what happened the night you came to my house all wet and dirty? Did she die?"

"No. I don't know. I don't know!" she cried.

"You haven't found her body?" Aunt Sondra said.

"I looked. I looked everywhere. But I didn't find her. That's why I know she's coming back. She wouldn't have left without saying goodbye if she wasn't coming back!"

She felt her lunch rise up her throat. She ran to the bathroom, barely making it in time. Jackie wiped her face with a wet towel. "It's okay," he said. "Everything will be okay."

Jackie and her aunt helped her to the couch, sitting on either side of her. Her aunt said, "Raven, I'm so, so sorry. But please explain what happened. Do you think it was suicide?"

"She didn't kill herself," Raven said. "She would never leave me that way."

"She was sick," Jackie said. "Possibly something to do with her heart. Since last year. She made Raven promise she wouldn't tell you or get a doctor."

Aunt Sondra clasped her hand on her forehead. "Audrey! Why? Why would you do that?"

"You know why," Raven said. She glanced at Jackie, afraid to say too much. "She was trying to work things out."

"With whom? Those damn earth sprites?"

"Don't call them that! She knew what she was doing!"

"Raven—"

"You can't make me leave here! She wants me to wait for her!"

Her aunt sighed. She opened the envelope and pulled out a hand-written letter. "I don't know if she meant for you to see this, but I think you'd better read it."

Raven didn't want to, but her aunt thrust it into her hand. Jackie got up and stood near the window to give her privacy.

Sondra, Mama had written in unsteady script. *In this envelope is my last will and testament, all documented by my attorney. I leave everything I own to my dear daughter, Raven. I want her to keep and stay in the house in Washington until she comes of age to live there alone. I know you will find a way to make this possible. If you can't be her guardian until she turns eighteen, please find a trustworthy person to watch over her. This person will be paid from what Raven has inherited.*

She didn't want to read more. Why was Mama saying these things? Maybe the letter was only a backup plan if she had trouble finding her way back from the spirit world.

The next paragraph read, *If Raven has children, they will inherit all that Raven owns. If she is currently pregnant, you will not try to take this child from her. I'm adamant about this, Sondra. Though she's considered "underage" in this society, she is fully capable of raising a child in the ways she and I prefer to live. Here again, I know you and your attorneys will know how to get her and the child proper care and legal guardianship until she comes of age.*

If she is currently pregnant? Why would Mama say that when she was certain Raven's body couldn't make a baby?

Raven suddenly understood. She had never confessed to Mama that she wasn't asking for a baby as Mama had requested of her many months ago. She must have thought the earth spirits would give Raven a baby soon, and of course she would have to pretend a baby that came from the spirit world had come from her daughter's body.

The letter continued. *My final request will be difficult for you, Sondra, but you must understand this is my decision and mine alone. Our mother wanted her death to take place in the Montana mountains. She wanted to draw her last breath there and be left as she was for the earth to recycle. Instead, you and Father forced her into a hospital and made her die drugged and attached to machines. You buried her in a New York grave next to her parents, though you knew she had not once in her life asked for that. I have never forgiven you for that crime. It is a deep wound in me that never healed.*

It was also a warning to me. In recent months, I prepared my final resting place on my Washington land. I have carefully chosen, excavated, and sanctified this burial ground according to my spiritual practices. In the event my attorney passed this letter to you, I have been resting there, by my own hand, for a week or more. You must not try to find me.

"No!" Raven cried.

"I'm sorry," her aunt said.

Raven kept reading through a blur of tears. *My daughter must never view my deceased body. I want her to see me in my true state, in that land she and I know and love well. We will remain on that land together. Tell her nothing has changed. I am there with her always and forever.*

The letter was signed Audrey E. Lind.

"I'm very sorry," her aunt again said as Raven let the letter go limp in her hand.

"You aren't sorry." Raven threw the letter at her aunt. "My mother did *not* want me to read that letter. That's clear from what she wrote at the end! You were wrong to show it to me! Why have you never honored her wishes? Why did you do that to her mother? I want nothing to do with you! I want you to leave my house!"

Her aunt rose from the couch. "I had to show it to you. You refused to believe she isn't coming back."

Raven still believed she might come back. Mama had sent the letter to state her wishes in case she couldn't find her way back to Raven. She knew she had to be clear in what she wanted because of the wrong her sister had done to her mother.

"Raven . . . ," Jackie said. "Do you want me to leave?"

His eyes reflected deep grief. The approaching anniversary of his father's death was magnified by everything he'd witnessed in the last fifteen minutes. And now he knew Raven had been lying to him.

She went to him, and he enclosed her in his arms. "I'm sorry I lied to you," she whispered.

"It's okay. I understand why you did."

He didn't, really, but she was grateful for his forgiveness.

"Why did Audrey mention a child?" her aunt asked.

Raven spun out of Jackie's arms. "That's none of your business!"

"Apparently it is if she put it in a letter addressed to me." She looked at Jackie and back to her. "Is it true?"

"No!"

"Well, that's a relief." She picked up the letter and put it back in the envelope. "I've talked to her attorney. Everything is in order. She's left you the entirety of her estate—which is substantial."

"I don't need anyone to be my guardian," Raven said, "but if that's the only way I can stay here, I'm willing to comply. Please go now. I want to be alone."

Her aunt drew in a big breath, then expelled it. Raven knew what that meant. She was preparing for a fight, as she often had done with Mama.

"It's not that easy, Raven. Your mother can't just disappear like this. There will be many questions. Police will have to be involved."

"You will leave her alone!" Raven shouted.

"How can I? I need a death certificate for you to inherit. How could your mother have overlooked that problem?"

"You know the ways of that world. You'll figure it out."

"My god, you sound just like her."

"Just go!" Raven said.

"I will not! My sister has given me the responsibility to fix this mess she's left, as she has all her life. And so I will."

"My mother would help," Jackie said. "I'm sure she'd agree to become Raven's guardian. She could live with us if she's not allowed to live here."

Ms. Danner. It was perfect!

"That's what I want," Raven said to her aunt. "Ms. Danner lives right down the road."

Her aunt nodded. "What about your father?"

"What about him?"

Her aunt looked at her curiously. "He needs to be told what happened. Do you know who he is?"

"No."

"No hint of who he is all these years?"

Raven shook her head. She didn't like the way her aunt was looking into her eyes, as if she knew she was lying.

Aunt Sondra came closer. "When you were a baby, Audrey once asked me to come help when you had a high fever. It was the first time I'd seen you. I hadn't even known she was pregnant." She looked at Jackie for a few seconds. "She had one of her episodes while I was there—you know what I mean by that?"

"Yes," Raven said.

"She said something very strange to me. About who your father is."

Raven's heart thudded. She could easily see Mama talking about her father the raven when she was immersed in the spirit world. She sometimes lost control of her thoughts when she was halfway between the human and spirit worlds.

"Did she tell you that? About the raven?" her aunt asked.

Raven tried to hide her panic. If her aunt found out what Raven believed about her father, she would put Raven in a place for people with mind sickness. Mama had said Aunt Sondra and their father had tried to put her in one of those places—because she practiced earth arts they didn't understand. From the time Raven could remember, Mama had forbidden her to speak of her father being a spirit. She had warned of the dire consequences over and over. Raven was terrified she would be taken from her home if she told anyone the truth. Her aunt would say she was sick and couldn't take care of herself.

She had to say something her aunt would believe. She remembered a man Mama had mentioned recently. "My mother told me my father was someone she didn't want me to know. A bad man. A senator."

"A senator!" Aunt Sondra said. "I very much doubt that, Raven!"

What was that name her mother had said the day she was halfway in the spirit world? If Raven said it, her aunt might believe she'd been told about her human father. The senator was somehow associated with Mama's father—her aunt would believe her sister had known him. And the man would pose no threat to Raven because Mama had said he was dead.

"Bonhammer, I think was the name," Raven said.

"Bauhammer? Senator Bauhammer?" her aunt said.

"Yes. That's him."

Aunt Sondra looked too stunned to speak.

"He's dead. I have no father," Raven said.

"I know he's dead. My father—your grandfather—went to his funeral."

Raven was relieved to hear her verify that.

"He was a married man, Raven," Aunt Sondra said. "And much older than your mother."

"What does that matter?"

"My sister would never have—"

Aunt Sondra abruptly went silent. She looked strange. Inexplicably horrified.

"What's wrong?" Raven said.

"Oh my god," Aunt Sondra whispered. She took out her phone and typed something into it. As she scrolled her finger on the screen, Raven and Jackie looked at each other. He was as confused by her aunt's actions as Raven was.

Her aunt stopped scrolling and stared at her phone. She pressed her hand to her mouth.

"What?" Raven said. "What are you reading?"

"Oh god . . . Audrey. What have you done?" Tears spilled from her eyes. The most brazen person Raven had ever known was crying.

"Why are you crying?"

She held the phone out so Raven could see. There was a news article.

Granddaughter of Senator Bauhammer Abducted. Search Widens Beyond New York.

"This happened sixteen years ago. She took you, Raven."

"You're wrong! That has nothing to do with me!"

Her aunt typed into her phone again and scrolled some more. She whispered, "Dear god." She gave the phone to Raven. "Does that woman look familiar?"

The caption on the photograph said the woman was Ellis Bauhammer.

Raven stared at the woman's face. It was almost like looking in a mirror.

PART FIVE

Daughter of the Miraculous Universe

1

RAVEN

The limousine stopped at a gray stone building with shiny gold letters that said, YORK, BAUHAMMER & SCHIFF LLP. The driver opened the door. "I don't know how long we'll be inside," Raven's aunt told him.

"I'll stay close," he said.

Raven followed her aunt into the building. They entered a tiny room that made Raven nervous, her first time inside an elevator.

"Sondra Lind Young to see Mr. Bauhammer," Aunt Sondra said to the receptionist behind a desk. The woman showed them to a wooden door down the hall. The nameplate said, JONAH M. BAUHAMMER III, ESQ. The receptionist knocked lightly before she opened it. "Mrs. Lind Young is here."

"Send her in," a man inside said.

Aunt Sondra went ahead of Raven. The man was standing next to a big desk. He had wisps of white in his thick, dark hair, and he looked a tiny bit like Jackie might look when he grew up, except with blue eyes. He was wearing a gray suit, white shirt, and purple patterned tie. Behind him, tall windows looked out at the sky and city buildings.

"Thank you for seeing me on short notice," Aunt Sondra said, extending her hand. "My father met your father on several occasions. He spoke well of him."

The man shook her hand, glanced at Raven, then looked back at her more closely.

Aunt Sondra stepped away to observe his response.

The man kept staring, and Raven's heart beat like a trapped bird was trying to fly out of her chest.

Aunt Sondra sighed. "I thought so."

"You thought what? Who is this?" the man asked.

"Does she look familiar?"

"She looks like . . ." He gazed at Raven, didn't finish the sentence.

"Your ex-wife?"

Ex? Raven didn't know they were divorced. She'd been told almost nothing. And she hadn't asked. She didn't want to know anything about these people. She only wanted to go back to her house and Jackie and school.

"Who is she?" the man demanded.

"I think she may be your daughter."

Again, the man stared at her.

"Obviously we'll have to do a paternity test."

"Viola . . . ," the man said. He stepped toward her.

She backed away. If he thought he would hug her, he was very much mistaken.

"My name is Raven," she said.

"Raven?" the man said.

"She's been called that since she was a baby," Aunt Sondra said.

"Where did you find her? Have you gone to the police?"

"I wanted to talk to you before police got involved. I'd like to do the genetic testing first. If she's your daughter, I'm hoping we can keep this as quiet as possible. She's already badly traumatized. She had no idea she'd been abducted. She's been living out in Washington."

"Washington! Do you know who took her?"

"The woman she believes to be her mother is dead."

"She *is* my mother!" Raven said.

"You see?" Aunt Sondra said to the man. "We need to keep this from becoming a media spectacle so she can come to terms with it in a quiet atmosphere."

Raven didn't like the way she talked about her as if she were a child who didn't understand anything.

"But who took her?" the man asked. "Was it the woman who raised her?"

Aunt Sondra looked down for a few seconds. When she lifted her head, she said, "I'm very sorry to say, my sister, who had mental problems all her life, probably took her."

"She doesn't have mental problems!" Raven shouted.

"Please lower your voice," her aunt said.

"I want to go home!"

The man raised his palm to his forehead and whispered, "My god."

"Yes, it's going to be a difficult situation," Aunt Sondra said. "That's why I'm speaking to you privately. I hope we can agree on a plan that will protect her. And, I admit, I'd like to keep my company as uninvolved as possible."

The man turned a critical look on her.

"I'm sure you'd rather not dig up this mess again," Aunt Sondra said. "It can only bring negative attention to your family and law firm."

"How so?" the man said sharply. "I was the one who had a child abducted."

"Do you want your boys and mother dragged through it all again?"

"That can't be avoided."

"It can be minimized. You're an attorney for celebrities. You must have your ways."

The man looked angry again.

"My sister left everything she owns to Raven—significant assets and investments, including two large properties. I'm willing to let the inheritance stand without contest even if she isn't my niece."

"Are you bribing me to keep this quiet?"

"I'm being pragmatic. It's in everyone's interest to make this transition as smooth as possible."

"Your sister has to be held accountable for what she did."

"My sister is dead."

"Are you sure?"

"That's another problem."

"What is?"

"I'm certain she's dead—I have her last will and testament—but I have no body. I believe she ended her life somewhere on her acreage in Washington, and we haven't yet located her body. I'd have to get police and cadaver dogs in there."

"You will not!" Raven shouted. "You read her last wishes. She wants to be left alone! And you're wrong about it being suicide!"

A white-haired man opened the door and looked in. "Is everything all right, Jonah?"

"Yes, thank you," he said.

When the door closed, Aunt Sondra said, "I'm trying to minimize the stress of this situation, mainly for Raven. I hope you and I can work this out together. If you'd like to involve her mother, that's up to you."

"She's not my mother," Raven said.

"Ellis and I have no contact anymore," he said.

"Why don't we do a paternity test and go from there?" Aunt Sondra said.

The man walked to his desk and nearly fell backward into the chair.

"Finally sinking in?" Aunt Sondra said.

He didn't answer. He just kept his gaze fixed on Raven.

"Tell me where you prefer to have her sample taken. Do you know a lab that has a fast turnaround?"

"Yes." He wrote something on a piece of paper and handed it to her.

She gave him a card with her cell phone number and wrote the name of their hotel on the back. "Call me anytime."

He nodded. He kept looking at Raven like she was a strange kind of animal.

She knew he wasn't her father. She felt no connection whatsoever to him and his ugly city. So what if Raven looked like his ex-wife? Lots of people looked like other people; kids at school called that having a doppelgänger. But Raven was still scared Sondra and Jonah would never let her go home. Everything Mama had warned her about was happening.

They returned to the limousine. Raven was afraid about the test, but all the woman did was rub a Q-tip inside her cheek.

"What should we do for the next few days while we wait?" her aunt asked. "We're close to New York City. Would you like to go there?"

Raven remembered Reece saying he wanted to go there, but she hated everything she'd seen so far.

"We can do anything you want," Aunt Sondra said.

"I want to go home," she said. "I can't miss this much school."

"I've talked to your school. Everything will be fine."

Raven went to bed at the hotel, though it was the middle of the day. She wouldn't get up when her aunt tried to make her. Most of the day, her aunt talked on her phone, telling people at her company what to do. Sometimes she spoke in a quieter voice to someone, probably her husband or son.

The following day went the same, Raven in bed, her aunt on the phone. Raven couldn't eat. Her aunt had all kinds of food delivered, but Raven never wanted to eat again. She wanted Mama not to be dead. She wanted to be in Jackie's arms.

The next day, Aunt Sondra sat on her bed. "Raven, please look at me. I have news."

Raven's empty stomach squirmed. All those fears and doubts that had spun relentlessly in her mind for a week. Would they turn out to be real?

"Raven . . ."

Raven didn't move. "I don't want your news."

"I know you don't. Of course you don't." She put her palm on Raven's back. "The test results are in. Jonah Bauhammer is your father."

Muted city noise filled the room. Raven's tears soaked the pillow fast.

"Please, let's talk about this," her aunt said.

"There's nothing to talk about. He's not my father."

"Half your DNA comes from Jonah Bauhammer," her aunt said. "And I know you understand about DNA. You told me about it when you were just seven years old."

Raven hadn't really understood about DNA until she was in middle school. That was when she'd once asked Mama if she had half raven DNA in her cells. The question had angered Mama. Raven was a miracle, Mama said, and who knew what differences lay inside her? That was why she had been kept away from doctors other than Dr. Pat. To probe the mystery of her being could be dangerous for her. For both of them.

Raven had asked no more about her DNA. She had only been curious about what might be unusual about her body—because she certainly knew she was different from other people—even Mama. She had felt the two sides of her spirit from the time she was a tiny child.

But now the test said Jonah was her father. She felt like the news was the cascading effect of a gale uprooting trees in the woods. One tree falls and knocks over a second tree, and that one pulls down another. If Jonah was her father, Mama must have stolen her from him and his wife. And that led to the worst blow of all: Mama had lied to her about everything. *Everything.*

It hurt too much to believe. She curled up tight and cried.

Aunt Sondra sighed, pressed her hand more firmly against Raven's back. "I'm sorry, Raven. But we can't deny the science of a DNA test."

Raven wished she could just run away. From Aunt Sondra, from the hotel and city, from everything that had happened since the day Mama sat on her bed and said she'd been the best sixteen years of her life.

She didn't want Mama to be a bad person. She wanted to be Mama's miracle. She wanted to be the child of a powerful earth spirit.

She felt eviscerated of all spirit, both raven and human. She couldn't even cry anymore. She lay still beneath the blankets, wishing her body to depart with her spirit.

A few hours later, her aunt returned to her room. "You have to get up," she said. "A detective needs to talk to you. We're meeting your father there. Afterward, he wants you to have dinner at his house with the rest of the family."

"Don't call him my father," Raven said into her pillow.

"Okay, we'll call him Jonah. Please get up, Raven."

"No."

"You can get through this. You're strong. You've excelled at school, made friends, and grown into a fine young woman—despite every-thing . . ."

Raven sat up. "Despite what?"

Her aunt looked sad and tired. "I know what it's like to live with her. The episodes. Speaking to spirits. Her disappearances into the woods. It had to be frightening for you."

"It wasn't."

"Please at least meet your family. See if you like them."

"If I don't like them, can Ms. Danner be my guardian?"

"I suppose that's a possibility."

"It is?"

"Please shower and get dressed."

Raven was dizzy from lying in bed and not eating for two days, but the thought of Jackie's mother being her guardian gave her new strength. She did everything her aunt asked, even drank a glass of green slush that was supposed to give her energy.

A limousine took them to see the detective. Jonah was already there. Two detectives, a man and a woman, wanted to talk to Raven alone. They asked a lot of questions about Mama. Raven could tell they hated her. The green drink still felt thick and cold inside her stomach, and she was afraid she would vomit. When they asked what she knew about Audrey Lind's death, Raven started crying and couldn't stop.

They took her back to her aunt and Jonah. But they immediately brought Sondra into the room, leaving Raven alone with Jonah.

"I hear you lived in a log house out in the country," he said. "That must have been great."

"I *live* in a log house," she said. "I own it, and I'm going back as soon as I can."

A few minutes later, he spoke again. "Your brothers are excited to see you. Their names are River and Jasper. They're twins, a little more than four years older than you."

Raven looked away to let him know she had no interest in his sons. Jonah didn't say more.

Aunt Sondra returned looking almost as upset as Raven felt when she came out of the room. She asked Raven, "Do you want me to come with you to Jonah's house, or do you prefer to go alone?"

"I want you to come."

"I think that's better, too."

Aunt Sondra asked the limousine driver to follow Jonah's car. The drive was long. To the "suburbs," Jonah had said.

Jonah's house was big with lots of mowed lawn around it. There were a few trees and bushes that were trimmed to look like shapes from a geometry book. As they walked to the front door, Jonah looked tense, just like Raven felt.

Two young men and an elderly woman were waiting inside the door. The men looked like their father, one more so than the other. That one had blue eyes. His name was Jasper. The other, River, had more blue-gray eyes, and his skin was a little tanner like Raven's.

The elderly woman was very thin, her blue gaze as sharp as a hunting hawk's. Her hair was brown streaked with gold, obviously dyed. Her face unsettled Raven because it looked too smooth for her age. She'd probably had surgery to make it look like that. Jonah introduced her to Raven as her grandmother, Gram Bauhammer. Aunt Sondra called her Mary Carol and shook her hand as if she'd met her before.

"This is Raven, as she prefers to be called," Jonah said.

River smirked. Raven immediately disliked him and his mocking expression.

"Nonsense," Gram Bauhammer said, coming toward Raven with open arms. "She's our dear Viola come back to us. She'll soon get used to her name."

Raven backed away from her. "If you call me Viola, I won't answer."

River snorted. Jasper looked amused, too, but hid it better.

"And I haven't come back to you," Raven said. "I'm only visiting. I'm going to live in Washington at my house."

Aunt Sondra said, "Raven—"

"Let's not discuss this now," Jonah interrupted. "I'd like to show Raven around."

Jonah took Raven all through the house. Jasper joined while the others sat in the living room.

Upstairs, Jonah took her in a room with a huge TV on the wall. "This was the nursery. First for the boys, then for you."

"It used to be light blue," Jasper said, "with birds and wildflowers on the walls. And clouds on the ceiling. Our mother painted them."

Raven couldn't imagine she'd ever been in that room. Or in the house at all. She didn't like its style. It felt too sterile and fancy, very unlike the natural-wood spaces of her log home. And the views out the windows were of lawns, houses, and a road. She wouldn't want to live in a home that didn't look upon woods and fields.

They went back to the living room, and Raven sat on the couch with her aunt. The others faced them.

"Your aunt tells me you do very well in school," Jonah said, trying to fill the awkward silence.

"I won't if I don't get back to my classes soon," Raven said.

Again, both boys smiled, River's grin more open than his brother's.

"We'll work that out," Aunt Sondra said. "Don't worry about it."

"What year are you in?" Jasper asked.

"Sophomore," she said.

"What's your favorite subject?"

Did he really care, or was it filler talk?

"I like English and biology," she said.

He nodded. "I go to Cornell, where our mom and dad met. I'm premed majoring in biology."

Raven had nothing to say, and the uneasy silence returned.

"I guess it's my turn," River said. "I'm a community college dropout majoring in . . ." He winked at Raven and held up his glass as if to toast.

"River!" his father said crossly.

"What?"

"You know what."

"This is a special occasion that requires a drink. I mean, how often do you meet your long-lost abducted sister?"

He was drunk. Raven was quite sure he was stoned on pot or pills, too. She'd seen that look at her school often enough.

"Do you attend church?" Gram Bauhammer asked Raven.

Raven shook her head.

"Did the woman who took you—"

"Audrey followed no particular faith," Aunt Sondra interjected.

"I remember that about your parents," Gram Bauhammer said. "They abandoned their faith, and that led to their divorce."

Aunt Sondra looked livid about her apparent criticism of her parents, but she kept her composure. "Not true," she said. "It was only my mother who left our church."

"She dabbled in Eastern religions, didn't she? That had to be confusing for you and your sister."

"Not for me," Aunt Sondra said, "but it might have been for Audrey."

"That explains everything," River said. "No wonder she abducted someone else's baby."

"I was not *abducted*," Raven said.

He looked both amused and angry. "You weren't hers, she took you, and she ran away with you. I think that's officially called *abduction*."

"I *was* hers," Raven said.

River drained his glass. "You have a bad case of Stockholm there, sis."

"I'm very sorry," Jonah said to Aunt Sondra and Raven. "My son is having some problems."

River rose out of his seat with a stagger. "I am. My glass seems to have gone dry."

"Jasper . . . ," Jonah said, nodding at River.

Jasper took his brother's arm.

"And away we go," River said as his brother led him out of the room.

"I believe dinner is ready," Jonah said. "Please come into the dining room."

Two women wearing uniforms came out of the kitchen to serve them. Beef tenderloin, mashed potatoes, and green beans. Gram Bauhammer said a prayer, most of it gratitude to her god for "returning Viola to the love and guidance of her true family."

Raven wanted to throw her plate of food at the woman.

River and Jasper came back. "I apologize for my rude behavior," River said to Raven.

He and his brother sat across from her and Aunt Sondra. Jasper was brought a completely different dinner. From what Raven could tell, he was vegan. He even looked a little like Jackie. Raven looked down at her food to stop her urge to cry.

Jonah and Jasper attempted to keep a conversation going. They mostly talked about what Jasper was doing at college. Gram Bauhammer inserted her strong opinions throughout. She told Aunt Sondra, "River would be in school with his brother if they didn't give scholarships to people who have no right to be in an Ivy League school."

"I have no right or desire to be at Cornell," River said. "You'll remember, I didn't apply."

"Only because you knew they would give preference to all those—"

"Mom, please keep those opinions to yourself," Jonah said sharply.

Gram Bauhammer cast a sour look at her son but said no more.

Raven had no stomach for the food or the strange family seated around her. She ate just enough to be polite and kept quiet.

As dessert was served, Jonah asked, "Raven, is there anything you'd like to ask us?"

She wanted to ask them why they were forcing themselves on her. She wanted to ask if she could leave and never see them again. But she was curious about one topic all but Jasper had avoided: the woman who looked like her, the one who had painted birds and flowers on the nursery walls. "I would like to know about Ellis," she said.

"Also known as *your mother*," River muttered.

"We've been out of contact with her for a long time," Jonah said.

"Since not long after you were abducted," River said pointedly. He stared at her, expecting her to challenge the word *abducted*.

She had no interest in playing games with the drunken attention-seeker. "Where does she live?" she asked.

Jonah looked uncomfortable. "I don't know."

River snickered, and his father aimed a dark look at him.

Their exchange implied that Jonah did know. She wondered why he'd lie.

Raven was relieved when the dinner ended. She whispered to her aunt that she wanted to leave. Sondra drew in a deep breath, then slowly exhaled, that familiar sign of an impending fight. "Come sit with us in the living room," her aunt said.

Raven went but refused to sit.

"The situation is this . . . ," her aunt said. "I have to get back to my work and family in Chicago, and you have nowhere to live but here. At least for the time being."

"I have a house in Washington! I'm not staying here!"

"You don't own that house yet. It belongs to my sister until I can prove she's deceased."

"Ms. Danner will be my guardian. I'll live at her house."

"Neither she nor a judge would agree to that when you have a legal guardian. Your father is here for you, Raven. He's here to help and guide you."

Raven looked at Jonah. His smile came off too weak to inspire confidence.

"This is your family," her aunt said. "You need time to get to know them."

Raven had a desperate feeling she knew well, her raven spirit wanting to fly away. But then she remembered she had no raven spirit. She felt as she had in the hotel bed, cold and sick and empty.

"Jonah has talked to a psychologist who will help you get accustomed to your new home," Aunt Sondra said.

"You're leaving me here?" Raven said. "You lied to me at the hotel?"

"You have a family that's been missing you for sixteen years, and you have nowhere else to go. This is a reality I can't change."

"I'm never going back to Washington?"

"You'll go back, but I don't know when. I'll have anything you want sent over. I promise the movers will be careful with your belongings."

She didn't want to cry in front of them, but she couldn't hold it back. "This is why she didn't like you, isn't it? You lied to her and bullied her and never did what she wanted. No wonder she didn't trust you!"

She saw guilt glaze her aunt's eyes.

"I bet you're lying about leaving her body where she wanted it. I bet you already had police look for it!"

"I haven't," her aunt said.

"Not yet. But you'll do it when you go back there. You'll leave me here and ignore everything she asked in her letter. She wanted me to live there. With her spirit. She wanted me to have a guardian and stay on that land."

Her aunt looked at Jonah, pleading for help.

"Raven," he said, "what Audrey Lind wanted for you is based on a lie. She took you from us. All these years, you were supposed to be here."

"I'm glad I wasn't!" Raven said. "Who would want to live in this family?"

"Ha!" River said, holding up his glass to toast her.

Everyone ignored him.

"I'm sorry you don't like it here," Jonah said. "That's completely understandable when you're used to another way of living. But I can tell you're a strong person who will get through this rough time. Your aunt knows that, too. The psychologist you'll see is very good. What you've been through is her specialty."

"*What I've been through?* What I've been through is *my life*. You're trying to take away my whole life!"

He and Aunt Sondra had no reply. Raven could see by the grim looks on their faces that they would not allow her to return to Washington. But she couldn't live with these odd people in this ugly house in the suburbs.

She turned to River. "Where is Ellis?"

He glanced at his father but said nothing.

"I know you know where she is. Tell me."

Jonah said, "When she left, she made me sign a legal document that said I wouldn't try to find her or contact her."

"Why?" Raven asked.

"Because she was a very disturbed person," Gram Bauhammer said. "She left you in a parking lot—that was why you were stolen. Has anyone told you that yet? Then she left her sons and never spoke to them again. Believe me when I say you want nothing to do with that woman."

Jasper and River looked upset by her harsh words.

"Ellis Rosa Abbey lives in Florida," River said abruptly. "She owns a business called Wild Wood Natives."

"How do you know that?" Jonah asked.

"Well, Dad, it's this thing called the internet." He laughed at his father's fury. "What, are you pissed that I found out for free? How much did you spend on private detectives to find her?"

"You knew where Mom was and never told me?" Jasper said.

"Dude, internet," River said.

"I didn't know her name to look her up," Jasper said.

"And why is that?" River said. "Why didn't we even know her name? Why did I have to dig through Dad's papers in secret to find it? What bullshit is that?"

"She specified that she didn't want contact," Jonah said. "I was honoring her wishes."

"But you knew?" Jasper asked his father. "Even those times I asked?"

Jonah looked haggard. "I didn't at first. She completely disappeared for a long time. As River says, I had a private detective try to find her. Because I was afraid for her. You may not remember how she was when she left . . ."

"I do, and good riddance," Gram Bauhammer muttered.

"Enough, Mom!" Jonah said. He said to Jasper, "When she bought property and started a business, she showed up in public records again."

Raven didn't like the constant tension and anger she felt in these people. She couldn't live with them. And she had no interest in being with Aunt Sondra, who had caused so much pain in Mama's life. Her only hope for an acceptable living situation was Ellis. A slim hope but better than none.

"I want to talk to Ellis," Raven said.

"I can't contact her to arrange that," Jonah said. "Though I'm bound by my agreement to leave her alone, I've tried in recent years. I have a financial matter to discuss with her. But she has no email and doesn't answer calls to the phone listed for her business. I tried sending something through the mail and never heard back."

"How can she run a business without answering calls?" River asked.

"She must filter the calls, only answer the numbers she knows."

"She'd lose customers if she did that," River said.

"Your mother has never followed the usual rules of society."

Raven was intrigued by this woman who'd divorced her family and society as Mama had. "Do you know her address?" she asked.

"There's a business address for the plant nursery," Jonah said.

"Then we can go there," Raven said to her aunt.

"This doesn't sound promising," her aunt said. "She clearly wants no contact with her family."

"I don't care. I'm going."

"And you expect me to take you?"

"If you don't, I'll get there on my own. I'm not staying here."

"I'll drive you down there," River said.

"You will not!" his father said.

Raven sensed River had only been trying to stir trouble, but Aunt Sondra glanced at him uneasily. "I'll take you," she said. "But only if you promise to stay with your family after you've met her."

Another promise that felt like being trapped in a cage. Just like Mama. Maybe she had learned to force promises on people from her elder sister.

"Do you promise?" Aunt Sondra said.

"I promise."

2

ELLIS

Ellis helped Tom load the last of the potted Fakahatchee grasses into his truck. She stood back and surveyed the thicket of native plants in the dark cavern of the truck interior. She would send many more trees, shrubs, grasses, and wildflowers with Tom and his landscaping crew in coming months. The plants were going to a new upscale subdivision, the largest order Wild Wood Natives had ever filled.

"Thanks for the help," Tom said.

"Of course," Ellis said.

"Damn, it's hot," he said. "More like August than April." He lifted the bottom of his T-shirt to wipe his face, exposing his muscular stomach and chest.

Ellis turned away, filled a cup from his big thermos of cold water. She gulped the water so fast, it ran down her chin onto her sweaty T-shirt.

"I like a woman who knows how to drink."

"Seems I don't," she said, wiping her chin.

He gestured at something behind her. "The ranger has perfect timing."

Keith was walking over from the house, still in his uniform. Quercus III plodded behind him, tongue hanging.

"I came over to help," Keith said.

"Too late," Tom said. "Ellis does the work of two of my crew in half the time."

Keith wrapped his arm around her waist and kissed her.

Tom closed the truck and pulled out.

"Truthfully, I came over to kick his butt out of here," Keith said, watching the truck turn out of the nursery.

Ellis snorted.

"Don't say I'm imagining it. His flirting is too obvious."

He wasn't imagining it. But Ellis knew how to handle Tom.

"He's a friendly guy," she said.

"Too friendly." Keith pulled her tight against his body. "And I can see why. You look damn sexy when you're covered in dirt and sweat."

She pressed harder against him. "I think you should come home from work early more often."

"Do we have time?"

"There's always time."

She led him into the nearest trees, slid down her shorts and panties, and leaned her chest against a big live oak.

"Jesus, Ellis. How do you still do this to me?"

"Do what?"

She heard him quickly unbuckling his belt behind her. "You know what, Witch."

She smiled. Even after all these years, he still sometimes called her *Witch*.

Quercus paced around them barking, as if he thought their love-making was a game.

"Remind me to lock the dog in the house next time we do this," Keith said afterward.

"That might ruin the spontaneity," she said.

They walked hand in hand to the house. Inside, Keith gave her a few pieces of mail. There was a card from Dani. More pictures of her baby.

Keith picked up the photos. "Wow, she's adorable, isn't she?"

"Yes," Ellis said.

He put the photos on the refrigerator with the other babies and kids. There were a lot of them now, his nephew and two nieces at all ages, years of Christmas card photos of friends' children, and ten months of Dani's baby. Ellis would rather have a clean refrigerator, but she wouldn't make a big deal out of it; he enjoyed the ritual.

While she showered, Keith changed into shorts and a T-shirt.

They put Quercus in the house and locked the door.

They sat in the old SUV they were trading for a new full-size pickup. She hoped the old car made it to the dealer. Keith had kept it running far beyond the usual mileage, but now it was definitely in its last throes.

"Excited?" he asked.

"You know I'm not one to get excited about cars."

"It's difficult to get rid of it, isn't it?"

She ran her hands over the faded, sticky steering wheel. "Yeah, it's been all over the mountains with me."

"And your husband gave it to you. That must matter."

"It was part of the divorce settlement. Not exactly sentimental circumstances." She started the motor and drove down the lane to avoid the conversation.

Keith had left the gate open when he came in. They'd gotten lazy about that because Quercus III didn't roam like his predecessors. As they arrived at the gate, a car was turning into the lane.

"Probably someone who doesn't know the nursery hours," Ellis said.

She rolled down her window. The woman in the driver's seat opened hers.

"The nursery is only open to the public Wednesday through Saturday," Ellis told the woman.

"We're not here for the nursery," the woman said. "Are you Ellis Abbey?"

"Yes."

"We've come to talk to you."

Ellis could see someone in the passenger seat. A young woman.

"We were just leaving," Ellis said.

"I'd appreciate it if you'd see us. We've come a long way."

Her license plate was from New Jersey. But that didn't mean anything. It was probably a rental.

"Weird," Keith said.

"Yeah. They better not be selling something."

She turned around and parked next to the house. She and Keith stood in the gravel driveway and watched the woman park. Both doors opened. The older woman had fair skin and hair and was well dressed. Ellis didn't recognize her. She now realized that the younger woman was a teenager. She was slim with long, wavy dark hair and tan skin. Her dark eyes were intent on her and Keith.

She looked familiar . . .

No, what she was thinking was impossible. It was a coincidence. Jonah would have told her if her daughter had been found. He knew where Ellis lived. He'd tried to contact her about a life insurance policy a few years ago, but she'd ignored him.

The woman and girl stood in front of Ellis. Why were they staring at her like that?

"I like your house," the girl said. "And these woods. Is that moss on the trees?"

"It's called Spanish moss, but it's not a moss. It's a bromeliad, if you know what that is."

"We have lots of moss on the trees where I live."

"Where is that?" Ellis asked.

"Washington."

"The moss is beautiful out there. I've seen it."

The older woman extended her hand to Ellis. "I'm Sondra Lind Young."

Ellis shook her hand. She looked at the girl, waiting to be introduced.

"This is Raven Lind," Sondra said. "She's . . . perhaps we should go inside to talk."

"Why would we need to do that?" Ellis asked.

"Because I used to be Viola," the teen said.

Ellis felt like she'd stepped into a blaze. Her face was that hot.

Raven. They must have gotten that detail from Jonah. He was the only one who knew about the raven calling the day Viola was taken.

"This is disgusting," Ellis said to Sondra.

She looked stunned.

"Why would you do this?" Ellis demanded.

"Do what?"

"Try to pass her off as my daughter. What are you after?"

"She is your daughter," she said. "It's been proven with genetic testing. We've come here from Jonah's home in New York."

Ellis had the same hollow feeling she'd had the day she stared at the empty ground where she'd last seen her baby. As if most of her body and soul had vanished with the child. Now the portal had opened again, thrusting her grown child back into her world. But there was so much Ellis had lost that could never come back.

Sondra took out her phone. "Would you like to talk to Jonah to verify? I'll call him right now."

The girl's face was her own, just younger. Ellis even saw a similar ache in her gaze. What had she been through all these years?

"Don't call him," Ellis said. "I see it. She's Viola."

The girl defiantly lifted her chin. "I want to be called Raven. I've been called that since I was a baby."

"Who named you that?"

"My sister did," Sondra said. "I'm sorry to say she was the one who took your daughter."

The raven. She had named the child after that damn raven. It had to be where she got the name. Ellis was afraid she would faint. "Where is she? Where is your sister? Do the police have her?"

"She's dead," Sondra said.

"Ellis . . ."

She turned around and saw Keith. How had she forgotten he was there? And talk about wounded gazes.

"What is this? You have a daughter?"

"I . . . yes. She was kidnapped. Sixteen years ago."

"How could you not have told me this?"

"I can't explain . . ." She looked at the girl. At her daughter. "Not now."

"I'll leave, then," he said in a shaky voice. "You obviously need time alone with her."

He went inside and emerged with the keys to his car.

Ellis followed him to his car. "I'm so sorry," she said quietly.

"*Sorry* seems inadequate, Ellis." He opened the car door.

She would never see him again. She was certain of it. She'd expected it to happen long ago.

"Before you leave . . . I want to tell you the rest. When she was a baby, I left her in a parking lot. I was upset because . . . well, it doesn't matter why. I forgot her and drove away. By the time I remembered, she was gone."

"Were you stoned?"

"That didn't start until after it happened. Her abduction was why it happened."

"Jesus, Ellis, this is a hell of a lot to have kept from me."

Tears burned. "It's worse."

"How can it be worse?"

"I have two boys. I walked away from them. I don't know why. I don't know what was wrong with me. And then I couldn't fix it. Or tell you. I'm just not right. I never have been. I always thought you'd figure that out and leave. I didn't see the point of telling you when you'd leave soon anyway."

"You have three children?"

She nodded, wiping her hands down her cheeks.

"All this time . . . this is why you wouldn't have a baby with me?"

"Yes."

"Why you refused to marry me?"

The tears fell faster.

"I moved in with you ten years ago, Ellis. Ten years. And we've been together longer than that."

"I tried to warn you that first night you came here."

"I was supposed to see all of this in those jokes you made that night? Caveat emptor?"

"That wasn't a joke."

"I'm the only joke in all of this. How could I have trusted you?"

"I'm sorry."

"Don't you see how ridiculous it is for you to say that? I've wasted years on your lies!"

He got in the car and slammed the door. He drove away and disappeared into the trees.

Gravel crunched behind her. Her daughter and Sondra. Ellis wasn't sure how much they'd heard.

"I'm sorry," Sondra said.

I'm sorry. Keith was right. What stupid words those were. The woman's sister had wrecked her whole life, and that was all she could say?

Ellis looked at her daughter. "Do you live with Jonah now?"

"I want to live with you."

"Is she serious?" Ellis asked Sondra.

"She refuses to live with her father. She didn't like it there."

333

"Please let me live with you," her daughter said.

"You have to go to your father's."

Again, the willful tilt of her head. "I won't."

"Did you hear any of that conversation? I left you in a parking lot and drove away."

"I know," she said.

"I left my boys."

"I know."

"You don't want to be with me. I have no ability to be a mother."

"I don't want a mother. I have one."

Ellis was glad her heart had been ripped out long ago. Those words would have done her in if she still had any maternal urges left.

"I thought the woman who raised you was dead?"

An odd look surfaced in her eyes. "She's still with me in spirit."

Sondra reacted with an uneasy stare at the girl.

"I only want to live here for a while," the girl said. "When they let me go back to my house, I'll leave."

Ellis looked to Sondra for an explanation.

"My sister left the Washington house to her," Sondra said. "But it won't be legally hers until many issues are settled. And Jonah, as her legal guardian, doesn't want her living alone out there at sixteen."

"She can inherit the house when she isn't related to your sister?"

"I could contest it, but I won't. My sister tore apart many lives. I saw that at Jonah's, and I see it here. I know the estate my sister left to your daughter can't repair your lives, but it's a start."

The girl opened the rear door of the rental car. She slung a backpack over her shoulder and pulled out a large suitcase.

"You've got to be kidding," Ellis said.

"She has nowhere else to go," Sondra said.

"What about school?"

"I talked to her school. They know the situation, and they'll let her finish this semester remotely. She may be able to finish all of high school that way."

Ellis gestured toward the woods around her. "Look at how isolated this place is. A teenager won't want to live here."

Sondra smiled slightly. "This one will. And this is the ideal place to be if her reappearance triggers a media frenzy."

"Do you expect that?"

"I don't know what to expect. Jonah and I plan to keep it as quiet as possible."

"Do the police know yet?"

"Raven, Jonah, and I have spoken to detectives in New York."

"Can I see inside the house?" the girl asked.

"Why don't we all go inside?" Sondra said to Ellis. "I'm sure you have many questions."

Two questions came to mind: *How can you possibly do this, Ellis? How will you not damage this girl more than she already is?*

3

RAVEN

Ellis Abbey was better than Raven had hoped. She didn't want her at her house. That had been clear enough. But that was okay because Raven didn't want to be there either.

But she liked the house made of wood, the forest around it, and the huge trees laden with long, swaying hair. She was greatly relieved when the ancient trees stirred the kind of earth kinship she'd known in Mama's woods. She'd sensed no presence of earth spirits at Jonah's house or anywhere else since she'd left Washington. She had begun to worry that she'd never feel their presence again. Maybe Mama had been as wrong about the ancient earth arts as she'd been about how Raven had come to her. But the land around Ellis's house was definitely a place of spirits. Raven had felt them even before she got out of the car.

They followed a flat-stone walkway to a big, open porch. There were two wooden rocking chairs that looked out at the trees.

When Ellis opened the door, a huge dog came out and barked at Raven and her aunt.

"Quiet, Quercus!" Ellis said. "He's friendly. Are you okay with dogs?"

Raven couldn't answer. The only dog she'd ever known—or not known—was the werewolf.

The dog licked her hand. "Quercus is a good name for him," she said.

"You know what it means?" Ellis asked.

"Yes, the genus of oaks."

Ellis seemed surprised that she knew.

Raven was happy to see the house had wood walls and floors, same as her log home. And the furnishings were simple and few, as Mama liked. The house was smaller, but it felt good. There was even a stone fireplace in the living room.

Ellis showed Raven and her aunt around. There was a guest room, where Ellis put Raven's suitcase. The patterned quilt and wood bed with posts were beautiful. Aunt Sondra said, "I love the country feel of this house. The antique furniture is a perfect complement."

"Most of the furniture was more trash than *antique* when I found it," Ellis said. "My business partner is a carpenter who can work magic with any junk I haul home."

Raven loved the screened porch at the back of the house. It looked down a hill at a garden—all native plants, Ellis said—and beyond it were more woods and fields.

"Are those fields out there part of your property?" she asked Ellis.

"Yes. Those are old pastures I've seeded with native wildflowers and grasses. And beyond that is bottomland forest with more big oaks and a marsh."

"How many acres do you own?" Aunt Sondra asked.

"Twenty-eight. About five acres of that is used for the nursery."

"This place is perfect for you," Aunt Sondra said to Raven.

Only Mama's land in Washington could be perfect for her. But the Florida land would be all right until she was allowed to go home.

"Did you live in a rural area in Washington?" Ellis asked.

"We live on ninety acres of woods and fields," Raven said.

"It's beautiful," Aunt Sondra said.

Ellis had a cold look in her eyes. "Isolated, I suppose?"

Aunt Sondra nodded.

"Did she take the baby straight there from New York?"

"I assume so. She bought the acreage around that time. She lived in a trailer on the property while the house was built."

"Weren't you at all suspicious that she suddenly had a baby?"

Aunt Sondra said, "Raven, why don't you go unpack your clothes while I talk to Ellis?"

Raven almost refused to let them talk about Mama behind her back. But she also wanted to know what they'd say. She pretended to leave the screened porch but stayed around the corner, where she could hear them.

"I live in Chicago," her aunt said. "I didn't see my sister very often. I assume she'd been visiting our mother's grave the day she took the baby. That cemetery is very near the woods where you left the baby."

Silence.

"I'm sorry. I shouldn't have worded it that way," Aunt Sondra said.

"Why not? It's true," Ellis said stiffly.

"I didn't find out she had a baby until Raven was about seven months old. Audrey called me in a panic because the baby had a high fever. I flew out with a doctor to help."

"She was afraid to take the kidnapped baby to a doctor. That should have made you suspicious."

"No, that fear was typical for her. At a young age, she developed phobias about doctors. Our father sent her to physicians to help her with her mental illness. Those irrational fears became extreme after our mother died. Audrey was very close to her and traumatized by her death. She believed the doctors, medicines, and hospital killed her mother."

"Didn't you think it was strange that she had no birth certificate or evidence of a father?"

"Again, that fit Audrey's life. She was a loner who preferred wilderness to society. One day when we met—she was thirty-two, I think—she told me she was trying to get pregnant. She was suddenly obsessed with having a child."

"Was she in a relationship?"

"No. From what I could tell, she was randomly meeting men and trying to get pregnant. I was concerned about that, but more so because I didn't know if she could competently care for a child. When I found out about the baby, she told me the father was a man whose name she didn't know. She said she'd birthed the baby alone in a forest. That was why there was no birth certificate."

"The school took her without one?"

"I asked the doctor who gave Raven her immunizations and wellness exams to create one for her."

"You and this doctor went there often?"

"Once or twice a year."

"And you never saw anything unusual?"

"I admit I did the first time I went there. The house was protected with video cameras, alarms, and locks. But as I said, Audrey had other irrational fears, so that didn't seem too unusual for her. And these days, lots of people monitor their properties with video cameras."

"But if you visited only once or twice a year, you didn't really know what was going on."

"I knew how it was to live with my sister. She'd had emotional problems from a young age. So yes, I was worried. I did everything I could to normalize Raven's life. After she turned five, I pressured Audrey for years until she finally gave up on homeschooling and let Raven enter second grade. That was important. The socialization of public school did wonders for Raven."

After a long silence, Raven was about to leave for the guest room when Ellis said, "All these years, I've been tortured by the thought of someone hurting her."

"The doctor and I never saw any hint of abuse. I wouldn't say her childhood was normal, but I can assure you, she was loved."

Raven pressed her hand over her mouth to hold in a sob. No matter what bad things everyone said about Mama, she had certainly loved her. And Raven loved her back.

She sensed the conversation was over and hurried to the guest room, wiping at tears. She brought out stacks of folded clothes and laid them on the bed. She opened the closet and found a hanger for her favorite sweater.

"I doubt you'll need that anytime soon," Aunt Sondra said from the doorway. "It's already summer here."

"I guess so," she said.

"Raven, I need to leave," her aunt said, coming into the room. "You have my number, and Ellis has a phone. Call if you need anything."

Raven stayed silent. Because she and Jonah were withholding everything she *needed*.

"We'll work out what you want sent from the house later. First we should see how things go here."

Raven looked out at the trees to stop herself from crying again.

"It will get better."

It wouldn't until she went home. She wanted Jackie so badly her chest hurt.

Her aunt hugged her. Raven returned the embrace, though she was angry.

"I feel better about you being here than with your father," Sondra said. "Your grandmother is mean-spirited, and Jonah has completely lost control of River. That wouldn't be a favorable environment for healing."

Ellis came to the door.

"I'm going to buy a ticket and drive back to Orlando," Aunt Sondra said.

"You're leaving already?"

"I have to. There's a situation that's come up at my company."

Ellis glanced at Raven. Raven sensed she felt the same way she did. She didn't want to be left alone with her.

Aunt Sondra booked a flight and left in a hurry.

Raven closed herself in the guest bedroom, unpacked the rest of her clothes, and slid the suitcase under the bed. She held the rock with an *R* in her palm. Today was the anniversary of Jackie's father's death. And she wasn't there to help him. Even worse, Raven's absence made the anniversary more troubling for him.

She squeezed the rock into her palm and curled around it on the bed. She felt like she had no heart inside her but that cold little stone Jackie had given her.

When she woke, the room was gray with twilight. The house was dark except for the glow of one lamp in the living room.

Ellis wasn't inside. Raven looked out the front windows and saw her sitting in one of the rocking chairs, staring out at the trees. Quercus was sprawled at her feet. Beyond the trees, the sky was pink, red, and orange.

Ellis didn't say anything when Raven sat in the chair next to her. Raven liked that Ellis knew how to be quiet. Like Mama. And Jackie.

The sky turned lavender, then a sad and indescribable color that ended the day.

"That man who was here . . . ," Raven said.

"His name is Keith Gephardt."

"Will he come back?"

After a few seconds, Ellis said, "I don't know."

Because of Raven, he had left. And because Raven had once belonged to Ellis, she was far from Jackie. They were even.

As all traces of daylight vanished, lamp glow emanating through the windows took over.

"The mosquitoes are getting bad," Ellis said. "We'd better go inside."

She turned on a porch light as they went into the house. For Keith probably.

"I made dinner," Ellis said. "It's warm on the stove."

Raven followed her into the kitchen.

Though Raven hadn't asked for food, Ellis dished out two plates and set them on the table. It was some kind of casserole with greens and a bean salad.

"I'm vegan," Ellis said. "I hope that's okay for you."

"A friend of mine is vegan," Raven said. She sat down and ate, thinking about Jackie. He would be happy she was in a vegan house.

Raven had little appetite, but she ate most of the food and told Ellis it was good. She helped wash and dry the dishes. Ellis had a dishwasher but washed the few dishes by hand. That was what Mama usually did, too.

After the last dish was put away, Ellis leaned against a counter and faced Raven. "So . . . I have a problem we need to talk about," she said.

"What problem?"

"Your name."

Raven prepared for battle.

Ellis looked into her eyes. "I know. It's the only name you've known. But I can't call you that."

"Why not? I call you *Ellis*."

"The day you were abducted . . ." Ellis paused and looked out the dark window for a few seconds. Maybe to stop herself from crying. She looked at Raven. "When something traumatic happens, you remember all these weird little details. And those details become bad associations—forever, as it turns out in my case. And one of the bad associations I have from that day is a raven. There was one calling over and over when I left you in the forest."

A shock seemed to zing all over Raven's body.

"I almost felt like . . . this will sound crazy, but later I felt like the raven had distracted me with all that noise. I blamed it a little bit for what happened." After a pause, she said, "I guess it was some kind of self-preservation. I was sick with guilt, and I needed to put some of the blame on someone or something other than myself."

Mama had told the truth about a raven giving a baby to her! The raven spirit had known Ellis and Jonah weren't the right parents for the baby they called *Viola*. It had distracted Ellis and given her to Mama. Raven wanted to cry with relief.

"I still hate the sound of ravens," Ellis said. "But I don't have to hear them now. Ravens don't live in Florida."

Too bad. Raven would miss them. Especially now that she knew a raven spirit truly had given her to Mama. Mama had thought the baby was born of the spirit world, but of course she would think that when a raven called and showed her a baby all alone in the forest. Raven could still think of the raven spirit as her father.

"Do you understand the problem?" Ellis asked.

"Yes."

"Can you think of a solution?"

"You mean call me something else?"

"You could let me call you *Viola*. If you knew *Quercus* is the oak genus, maybe you know that *Viola* is the genus of—"

"Violets. I knew that since I was a little girl. My mother and I picked violets to eat every spring."

Ellis recoiled a little when she said *my mother*. "Then maybe she'd like the idea that you're named for the genus of that flower."

"She might have liked that, but she would want me to keep the name she gave me."

Ellis's gaze hardened. "She had no right to rename another person's baby."

"I wasn't yours anymore when she named me. I was hers. I was given to her."

"What do you mean *given*? She stole you from me!"

343

"Not *stole*. You left me all alone, and she found me. She dreamed of having a baby for a long time. And there I was. That was no accident. There must have been a reason."

"How dare you say that!" Ellis shouted. "Do you have any idea how much pain this woman you call *Mother* has caused me and my family? You have to deal with the reality that you were abducted. What she did was wrong. She'd still be in jail now if they'd caught her."

"But she wasn't caught. Why was that?"

Ellis trembled. "What, you think some divine intervention helped her escape with you?"

"I think there must have been a reason."

"What reason?"

Raven couldn't say she believed earth spirits had helped her. That was a forbidden topic.

"Did she tell you why she named you *Raven*?"

"Yes."

"What did she say?"

Everyone now knew Raven hadn't been born of Audrey Lind's body. She could tell Ellis the truth. "She told me she heard a raven calling to her in a forest. When she went to see what it wanted, there I was, a baby girl with raven eyes and hair—exactly what she wanted. She named me for the raven that brought us together."

"Oh my god," Ellis whispered. "You've known all along she didn't give birth to you? You never told anyone?"

"What did it matter that I didn't come from her body? I was born to be with her."

"You were born to be with me!" Ellis shouted. "And with your father and brothers!"

"No, I met them. And that horrible grandmother. I was never meant to be with them. Or in that ugly house. My spirit would have gotten sick and maybe died if I lived with them. I think that's why you left, too."

Ellis stared at her openmouthed.

"If you like a pretty place like this, that house and those people were killing your spirit. You weren't meant to be there either. But I'm sorry I had to be taken away from you for you to see that."

Ellis held on to the counter and slid down to the floor. Raven must have hit on the truth.

"Are you for real? Am I imagining this?" Ellis said.

Raven smiled for the first time in many days. "I'm real." She sat on the wood planks next to Ellis. She took her hand in both of hers. "I never meant to make you sad. I didn't want to come here either. But I'm glad I got to meet the person who gave birth to me."

"I can't do this," Ellis said. "You have to go live with your father."

"I told you. I can't live there."

"Then go back to Washington."

"Can you make them let me?"

"No. I have no say in that."

Raven looked down at their entwined hands. Raven's skin was a little lighter tan than hers. "Can I please live here for a while? Maybe you could just call me *R* instead of *Raven*."

"It's about so much more than your name. It's just . . . you need more than I can give you."

"I don't need anything. Please let me stay here if I can't go home."

Tears dripped out of Ellis's eyes. "I mean it. I can't be here for you."

"That's okay," Raven said. "I'm used to that."

4

ELLIS

Over ninety degrees as the sun was setting. On June first. She would have to water the pots that didn't get irrigation again. When she walked over to the nursery, she saw Max. She'd just finished watering.

Max made two familiar gestures, a flying motion and a signal that indicated a question. The flying sign was her way of saying *Raven*. She wanted to know where Raven was. Usually she helped water with a second hose.

Ellis gestured that she didn't know. Max nodded as she coiled the hose. Ellis knew her well enough to see she was disappointed. Max and Raven had been drawn to each other almost from the moment they met. Max didn't usually go for buddy stuff, but she was more aware of Raven when she was in her presence than she was of anyone, even Ellis.

Ellis continued the conversation with signs she and Max had perfected over the years. She told her she'd finished the bookkeeping and everything looked good. She said Tom would be coming for another load of plants in three days and asked how the remodeling of her house was going.

Max said the work was going well and told Ellis to say hello to Raven.

When Ellis returned to the house, Raven wasn't there. She was as independent as Ellis had been when she wandered the Wild Wood behind the trailer park. But Ellis was a little worried; she hadn't seen Raven since breakfast.

She called Quercus. He leaped up, tail wagging, immediately sensing they were going for a walk. They went east. The land gently sloped from the house on the wooded hill, through old pastures, a wet meadow and bottomland forest, and finally to a marsh at the far end of the property. The marsh had increased in size and depth from heavy rains. When they arrived at the water's edge, Quercus trotted to something white and sniffed it.

Raven's T-shirt, and underneath it her hiking pants and shoes.

Ellis stared out at the silent marsh water. Had she drowned herself? The abyss, the moment she had discovered her baby was taken, was swallowing her whole again. Why had they trusted her with the girl? Had Ellis not proven she couldn't be a mother?

A splash.

"Raven?" Ellis called out.

Insects thrummed. Distant cranes cried.

"Raven! Are you there?" she shouted.

Raven rose out of the deeper water and looked at Ellis.

"I've told you not to go in this water!" Ellis said.

"No you didn't. You said Quercus isn't allowed."

"I told you I train all my dogs not to go in there because of alligators. Come out of there now!"

"You said alligators like to eat dogs."

"They eat people sometimes, too."

Raven treaded water and kept staring.

"Please come out. Dusk is when alligators become active."

Raven breaststroked toward her and stood where the water became shallow. She was wearing only a bra and panties. Ellis was startled by how bony she was. She'd already been slim when she arrived, and she'd lost more weight than Ellis had realized.

Raven's feet stuck in the deep mud. She sank to her calves. Another step and she sank almost to her knee.

"That's another danger of these wetlands. You can get stuck in the mud, even sink too deep to get out."

Ellis waded in, sinking to her calves. She grasped her daughter's hand and tried to pull. But she lost her grip on Raven's slippery hand, and the momentum made her fall backward into the rank marsh water.

Raven laughed.

"Very funny," Ellis said.

Raven laughed harder as Ellis struggled to rise out of the muck.

"I should have left you in there for the alligators."

Raven dragged her feet out of the mire and pulled Ellis's hand. When she heaved, her feet were too stuck to provide any leverage. She fell into the marsh next to Ellis, and they slumped into the putrid muck, laughing.

"How the hell did you get in here in the first place?" Ellis asked.

"When I felt myself sinking in the mud, I stretched out my body and swam to the deep water."

Ellis gave up trying to stand and crawled in a very undignified way out of the marsh. Raven did the same. They laughed at how ridiculous they were.

The mosquitoes were having a merry time, too. And the sun was setting. Ellis hadn't brought a flashlight.

"We'd better get back," she said.

Raven put on the T-shirt but didn't try to pull the pants up her wet legs. She slipped on her socks, seeming unperturbed by the mosquitoes hovering around her bare legs.

"You are a very good boy to stay out of the water," Ellis said to Quercus. She rubbed the big dome of his head, smearing it with mud. "Now we have to train Raven."

"I don't think I'll go in there again."

"Please don't."

Raven balanced on one foot and slid the other into her boot. "But where can you swim around here? I like water when it's hot like this."

"I know. I miss that, too. But there isn't anywhere to swim on this land."

There was still enough light to walk home. They'd gone a short distance when Raven shouted, "No! Quercus, no!"

She desperately tried to haul the dog away from something. Ellis looked down at an intricate arrangement of leaves and rocks. In the middle was a raccoon skull.

"What is that?" Ellis asked.

"Nothing."

Quercus wanted the skull.

"No!" Raven screamed.

"Quercus, sit!" Ellis said in her sternest voice.

He sat. Keith had shown her how to do that.

"Come!" Ellis said, beckoning the dog away from the skull.

Raven calmed as they left behind the *nothing* she had made. The arrangement of natural objects had looked eerily ritualized. Like some kind of offering. Ellis remembered Raven's strange talk of her kidnapping, as if she saw it as a divine event. Obviously, that was Audrey Lind's influence.

"Did you go to church when you lived in Washington?" Ellis asked as they walked.

"Why do people ask that?" she said.

"Who else asked?"

"Gram Bauhammer."

Of course she had. Ellis had never met anyone pushier about her beliefs than Mary Carol.

"I didn't go to church," Raven said.

"Did you practice any particular faith?"

After a pause, she said, "No."

Ellis sensed tension in her. She wondered why.

Quercus barked and bounded up the hill. He continued barking. Someone was there. It had to be Keith. The gate had been closed.

She told herself not to get excited, but her drubbing heart wouldn't listen. A month and a half ago, the day after Raven arrived, Keith had returned to collect his belongings. He'd told Ellis she needed time alone with her daughter. He'd refused to say more.

Now he was back. He must have calmed down enough to talk.

But what if he was there to say goodbye? Forever?

Ellis stopped walking. Two men were in her driveway petting Quercus. She couldn't see them well in the twilight, but whoever they were, they had climbed the fence to get in.

Ellis grabbed Raven's arm and pulled her backward. "Don't go up there!" she whispered.

"Why? Who is it?"

"It might be reporters."

Raven stared at the men.

"Last week, Sondra warned me that some reporters wanted to talk to you."

"Why is that so bad?"

She truly didn't know. She'd had no access to phones or computers. Her abductor had kept her away from the internet to make sure she never found out who she was. The girl had no idea of the mess the media could make of her life.

"Stay here," Ellis said. "You don't even have pants on."

"So what?"

"Just stay here."

Ellis climbed the walkway stairs Max had built to negotiate the slope. The two men turned around when they heard her footfalls. They were young, in their early twenties.

Ellis stopped walking. They stared back at her. "Mom?" Jasper said.

Mom. He'd called her that. After all these years.

She and the boys stood just yards apart. They were twenty now. Both looked a lot like Jonah, Jasper especially.

It all came rushing back. Those women she'd been, the bewildered college student taking final exams with pregnancy nausea; the new wife—Jonah rubbing his hands on her belly as he spoke to his sons inside; the woman screaming in the delivery room; the mother rocking, bandaging, promising there was no such thing as monsters; the addict who walked away from her little boys—her last words to them a terrible lie of maternal love that lasts *forever and ever.* They all came back at once, all those women crashing together within her.

It was different from when Viola had come back. The shock of seeing her daughter without warning had mercifully deadened her senses. As had Keith leaving. What little she'd felt through the numbness mostly had to do with the abduction. This felt so much worse, maybe because her boys hadn't been stolen as Viola had. Ellis had done the stealing. She had robbed herself of her boys.

And taken their mother from them. Why were they here, looking at her with the same ache she'd seen in their eyes the day she left?

She had to calm down. Find out why they'd come. Maybe Jonah had sent them with a message.

"Does Jonah know you're here?" she asked.

She berated herself. Those shouldn't have been her first words.

"No," Jasper said.

"Where does he think you are?"

"The Outer Banks," he said. "Last week I started summer break from college."

Raven came to Ellis's side. She was a sight, wet and muddy, her filthy T-shirt not covering her underpants. Her long legs looked gangly with nothing but her socks and big hiking boots. Ellis realized her own muddy appearance must look bizarre to her sons, and that wasn't how she wanted them to see her. Their last impressions had been bad enough.

"Hey, Raven," River greeted her, "or is it *Viola* now?"

"Raven," she replied.

River cast a sarcastic look at Ellis. Not much had changed since she last saw him. "You're okay calling her that?"

She wasn't. Ellis hated the name. But the young woman who had come back to her after sixteen years wasn't Viola Bauhammer. Ellis had no right to dictate her name. She'd conceded that after the first day.

"I guess not," River said when she didn't answer.

"Is everything all right?" Jasper asked.

"Yes." She looked down at her muddy clothes. "We must look pretty bad."

"I thought all Floridians looked like that," River said.

Jasper gave him a look.

"We were in the marsh," Raven said.

"In the marsh?" River said incredulously. "What, Friday night gator wrestling? Is that a thing around here?"

"We were hiking," Ellis said.

River snorted. For good reason. Why would Raven hike without her pants on?

"We need to clean up," Ellis said. "Do you want to come inside?"

What was she doing inviting them inside as if they were new neighbors come to introduce themselves? The civility of it all felt so off. But what else could she do?

"Our car is blocking the driveway by the gate," Jasper said.

"It's no problem," she said. She had no reason to believe Keith would return, now or ever.

The boys declined her offer of water or iced tea. They waited in the living room while Ellis and Raven cleaned up. Ellis rushed, too manic to compose herself.

She got to the living room before Raven, though she wasn't sure Raven would come out at all. She mostly kept to herself, especially in the evening. And she'd said she didn't like her New York relatives.

"I'm sorry about how you were greeted," she said. "You caught us at an odd moment."

"That's okay," River said. "Who won the match—you two or the alligator?"

"Thankfully, we won. Raven didn't know she shouldn't swim in the marsh. I sort of had to haul her out."

"You're kidding?" he said.

"She's from the north. She didn't understand the danger—or the unpleasantness."

The boys smiled.

Ellis was surprised when she opened her arms, inviting an embrace. "May I?"

Jasper went to her immediately and squeezed her tight. A man's embrace. The tears came when she thought of all the little-boy hugs she'd missed.

His eyes were wet when they released.

She looked at River. The last time she'd seen him, he'd refused to hug her goodbye.

"I'm not feelin' it," he said.

"River, what the hell?" Jasper said.

"It's okay. I understand," Ellis said.

"This is a cool place," River said. "I'd ask if you like it here, but I assume you do if you never came back."

"Yes, I like it, but I ended up here by accident, really." She thought of the stabbing, Keith driving her to Florida while she slept, the panic attacks that had held her captive in Gainesville for more than a year. The edge of it had been dulled by the whittle of years.

"Are you married?" River asked.

"No. What about your father?"

"Nope."

A strained silence.

"Do you have anything to drink around here?" River asked.

Jasper gave his brother a critical look.

"You mean an alcoholic drink?"

"Yeah."

"There might be a few beers out in the barn refrigerator."

"What, for the cows?"

"They're my boyfriend's."

"Will he mind if I hit his stash?"

"He doesn't live here anymore." She hadn't yet said that out loud. It was sinking in.

She got a flashlight and took them down the footpath that led to the barn.

"My business partner is a carpenter," Ellis said as she pushed open the barn door. "She made the barn into a guesthouse with a full kitchen and bath."

"This is great!" Jasper said.

"There's another bedroom up in the loft," she said. "But the only bathroom is down here."

"What do you use it for?" River asked.

"My boyfriend's sister, husband, and three kids came here at least once a year. They'd use this as their home base while visiting beaches or the Orlando theme parks."

"How long were you with him?" Jasper asked.

"He lived here for ten years."

"How long ago did you break up?"

"About six weeks ago."

River figured it out right away. "That was when Raven came."

"Yes."

"Why would he leave at a time like that?" Jasper asked.

She wanted to walk away from the question. The truth would hurt them. But she knew walking away caused a different kind of damage. Every time she looked in their eyes, she saw it.

"I never told him I had children," she said.

Yes, it hurt. A fresh glaze of pain spread into their gazes.

"So . . . you'd basically deleted us like files on your computer," River said.

"I guess I can see why he left," Jasper said.

"So can I," she said. She opened the refrigerator and motioned for River to look at the selection, a six-pack and three bottles of another brand. He grabbed the six-pack.

"You can't drink all of that if you plan to drive tonight," she said.

"I'm driving," Jasper said.

"But why drive?" River said. "Let's stay here."

"River . . . ," Jasper said.

"What?"

"She hasn't invited us."

"It's okay, isn't it?" River said. "We were going to find a hotel in Gainesville."

"Sit down," she said. "We need to talk."

River opened a beer and put the rest back in the refrigerator. The boys sat on the couch, and Ellis faced them on Keith's lounge chair, the one he used to watch football on the TV he'd bought for himself but pretended was a gift for her.

"You want to know why we're here," River said.

"I do," she said. "I also want to know why you lied to your father."

"Second question is easier," River said. He took a long drink. "We didn't tell him because he would have said we couldn't come here."

"Then why did you come?"

River looked at Jasper.

"It was your idea?" she asked Jasper.

"It was. Dad's lied to me all these years. He said he didn't know where you were. When Viola came home, I found out he'd known for a long time where you live. River knew, too."

"Internet," River said before taking another long pull on the bottle.

Jasper aimed a hard look at her. "Why would you ask why we're here? You're our mother."

Ellis hadn't had a drink since she quit in the mountains. But she wanted one of those beers.

Jasper said, "I'm here because I thought it was bullshit that Viola got to see you and we didn't. Dad says she's here to hide from reporters, but I know that's more lies. She lives with you now, doesn't she?"

"She does, but she doesn't want to. All she wants is to go back to Washington."

"Do you want her here?" he asked.

"That question is way too complicated to answer."

"Try."

"Okay. First of all, I'll say I'm relieved she's okay. All these years, I've had every imaginable fear about what happened to her. But it's not like this was some happy reunion. She doesn't want anything to do with me. Being here is like a prison sentence she has to serve until she can go back to her house in Washington. So . . . do I want her here? I don't know."

"I wonder what her house is like," River said. "Dad says she'll be really rich when she inherits."

"Are you serious?" Ellis said.

"You didn't know? That woman who took her is from some billionaire family in Chicago."

No wonder Audrey Lind successfully kept Viola hidden away all those years. She'd had limitless resources. And now Ellis understood why her sister had been so eager to drop Raven into the obscurity of the Florida woods. She didn't want the news of what her sister had done to penetrate her elite sphere.

River finished his beer quickly and got another from the refrigerator. "Can I ask a question now?" he asked.

"Go ahead."

"Are you still a doper?"

"Who told you that?"

"Gram, of course. And looking back, it's pretty obvious."

"I quit all that long ago."

"Too bad. I was hoping to hit you up for something good."

Ellis stood. "If you've come here to blame your problems on me, you can leave."

"But I can stay if I came here like Jasper to make nice? Or if I'm a poor abducted kid who doesn't know her ass from an alligator?"

"You know, I have a lot on my plate right now." Even as she said it, she was disgusted with herself.

"You've got a lot on your plate, and I'm hungry. Mind if we mooch some food before you kick our asses out of here?"

He was there to punish her. Clearly trying to rattle her with his obnoxious behavior. Maybe he wanted her to boot him out of her house so he could justify hating her. Hatred was an addictive emotion, and it thrived best with frequent injections that kept the high going. River hadn't had a fresh dose since he was a little boy. He didn't want her to give him a pill to dull his pain. He wanted a slap to increase it. And the sad thing was, he also believed he deserved to be slapped.

No, she wouldn't play into his self-hatred. "You're welcome to anything in my kitchen. And you can stay in this guesthouse as long as you want. But you have to tell Jonah where you are. He needs to know in case there's an emergency."

"He can call us," River said.

"He has the right to know where you are."

"He doesn't give a shit where I am. As long as I'm out of his house."

"Why do you say things like that?" Jasper said.

"I don't know," River said. "Sometimes truths just come bursting out of me."

"Let's go find you something to eat," Ellis said.

River gathered the remaining beers to bring with him. Ellis gave Jasper the remote to open the gate and showed him where to park and unload their luggage.

Raven was in the kitchen eating a vegetable-and-fried-seitan wrap she'd made for herself. She watched River stash his beers in the refrigerator.

"River and Jasper are staying overnight in the barn house," Ellis said.

Raven had no response. She slid her plate of food to the middle of the table. "Do you want the rest of this?" she asked.

"You should eat it. You've barely had anything today."

"I feel sick."

She often said that. She was losing weight too fast. In the bright kitchen lights, she looked gaunt and exhausted. Being away from Washington was wearing on her. Ellis wondered if she could intervene, try to help her get back there. But to do that, she'd have to talk to her legal guardian, and Ellis didn't want to be involved with Jonah in any way.

Jasper walked into the kitchen. "I put your bag in the guesthouse," he told River.

She didn't want to be involved with Jonah, yet here were the three children she'd made with him. In her kitchen. The room was suddenly small with the three young adults. Her house felt unfamiliar, like a house in a parallel world in which she'd never left Viola in the forest.

"Would you like what Raven is eating?" Ellis asked the boys.

Jasper studied the sandwich on her plate. "Is that meat?"

"Seitan. I switched from vegetarian to vegan."

"I'm vegan, too," Jasper said.

River drained the second bottle. "Your brainwashing worked," he said to Ellis, opening another beer. "He never got over the guilt you made us feel for eating meat."

"Lay off her!" Jasper said. "It was my choice. I never liked meat."

"That's the point of indoctrination," River said, "to make you think what you believe was your idea all along."

"You're acting like a total ass," Jasper said.

"Why would I have to act?" River said with a grin. He asked Raven, "I suppose you're a vegan, too?"

"No," she said.

"You eat meat?"

She nodded.

"Well, hell, no wonder you feel sick from eating that *shite*-tan thing. Let's go over to the barbecue place down the road."

"You're not driving," Ellis said. "That's your third beer in twenty minutes."

"Seriously?" he said. "You're going to play parent all of a sudden?"

"You're underage, and I gave you the beer. I could get in big trouble if you had an accident."

"Okay, that sounds like the mom I knew. It was more about you than concern for me."

"I told you to lay off," Jasper said, shoving his shoulder.

The blow made River stumble backward a few steps. He found his feet and threw a punch that Jasper barely dodged. Jasper grabbed him by the upper arms, shouting, "Stop it! Why are you doing this?"

"Why are you?" River yelled, shoving him back. "Why did you want to come here? We could be at the goddamn beach right now!"

They crashed into the baker's rack, toppling one of the very few possessions Ellis cared about, an antique apothecary jar Keith had given her for her birthday their first year together. Ellis had gradually filled it with little gifts of wildflowers Keith had brought from his walks on the property.

The jar exploded as it hit the floor. Parched flowers scattered in land mines of glass shards.

5

RAVEN

Raven cut her foot trying to help.

Ellis snapped at her for walking barefoot into the glass.

Jasper cut his hand.

Blood mixed in with the broken glass and dead flowers.

River did nothing, just leaned against the refrigerator, drinking his beer.

Ellis gave Jasper a box of Band-Aids and told him to clean his cut at the kitchen sink. She took Raven into the bathroom to look at the sole of her foot. "This is a bad cut," she said.

"I can do it myself," Raven said.

"Hold still," Ellis said. She cleaned and bandaged the cut and had Raven sit with her foot elevated on a couch pillow.

Ellis went to the kitchen, and Raven heard her thank Jasper for cleaning up the glass.

"I hope you don't mind that I threw the flowers away," Jasper said. "They were too mixed in with the glass to sort out."

"That's okay," Ellis said.

It wasn't okay. Raven rarely talked to Ellis, but she'd become familiar with her moods, and she could tell Ellis was badly stressed by the arrival of her sons. Raven wasn't happy about it either. She and Ellis had established a fragile balance. They both knew Raven would leave soon and there was no reason to try being friends. The absence of trouble and emotion between them was necessary for Raven as she grappled with everything Mama had done. All Raven wanted from Ellis was to be on her land until she could go home. Her closest companions were the grandparent oaks opening their giant limbs down to her, meadows that let her sleep on their flowered skirts, sandhill cranes bugling sweet music to her throughout the day.

But now these fighting boys had come and ruined everything. They had broken much more than the glass jar. Raven had felt it as soon as she saw them, everything in her life coming apart again, and she didn't think she could handle more breakage.

She heard thumping cabinet doors, River asking if there was anything stronger than beer. Ellis saying beer was all she had. She asked them to go in the living room while she cooked.

Jasper asked Raven if she was okay as he entered the room with his brother.

"It's nothing," she said. She lifted her cut foot off the pillow and sat up.

"Nothing?" River said, looking at her bandaged foot. "That's amazing. I guess you've already fixed it with your earth-spirit superpowers."

In her mind, Raven jumped off the couch and punched him much harder than Jasper had. In reality, she tried not to show any reaction. The person who deserved to be punched was her bigmouthed aunt.

River saw she was upset. "Yeah, we know," he said. "Our father told us about your kook religion."

"Shut up," Jasper said.

"I can say what I want, dickhead. What exactly can those earth spirits do?" he asked Raven.

"Nothing a person as lost as you could understand," she said.

"Good answer," Jasper said.

River was clearly angry that his brother had sided with her. He downed the rest of his beer and opened a new bottle.

"Have you figured out that the woman who stole you was insane?" he asked. "They tried to lock her up more than once, you know."

"You're the one who should be locked up."

"Maybe I should," he said. "And you'll be in the padded room right next to mine. And why is that? Because of that piece of shit who stole you. She wrecked a lot of lives! And for you to act like she was this great person really pisses off everyone in this family! You need to get with reality! She was a total wacko!"

Raven sprang up and shoved him in the chest. "Don't talk about her like that!"

Ellis pulled Raven away as Jasper grabbed River's arm. The boys were about to get into another fistfight.

"Stop this!" Ellis shouted. "All of you, stop!"

"All of us?" Jasper said. "It's River!"

"Go sit in that chair, River!" Ellis shouted.

"Oh my god," he said with a laugh. "I'm in time-out? Have you forgotten I'm not four?"

"I said sit!" she screamed. Her eyes were the same as Mama's when the storms thundered, her hand shaking as she pointed at the chair.

River complied.

"Why are you doing this?" Ellis asked, looking at each of them. "Why are you tearing each other apart instead of supporting each other?"

"It's River," Jasper said. "That's what he does."

"Yeah, it's what I do," River said. "And guess who taught me, *Mom*?"

"I never behaved like you do!"

"But you did a great job of tearing the family apart."

Ellis looked away from him, stared at the dark front windows.

Raven saw what she wanted. She wanted to be out there in the woods. She looked like a trapped animal. Raven knew how she felt. She supposed Ellis would leave the house.

But Ellis turned back to River. "Okay, let's talk about it. Is that what you want?"

"Yeah, let's talk about *it*," River mocked.

"What do you want to know?"

"You know what! Why did you leave two little kids who were already traumatized by their baby sister's abduction?"

His voice, the look in his eyes. And in Ellis's and Jasper's eyes. Raven saw some of what Mama had done to them. She felt even sicker than she had in the kitchen. She sank onto the couch.

"I was . . . I thought I was doing you more damage by staying," Ellis said. "At first your father had to make me take the pills. For the depression and guilt. Every second I was awake, I blamed myself for leaving my baby in the woods. What I'd done was broadcast on the news. All my friends and neighbors knew. Your grandmother never let me forget. Your father was angry with me . . ."

She wiped her fingers under her eyes. "Within a few weeks, I started drinking because the pills weren't enough. Then I added the pain medications they'd given me for my back. I couldn't stop. The more I took, the more I needed. I thought I was going to be like my mother. I thought I would be an addict for the rest of my life—and there was no way I'd put you through what I went through when I was little."

"I didn't know your mother was an addict," Jasper said.

Ellis was astonished Mary Carol and Jonah II hadn't told them. Possibly Jonah had finally drawn a line with them.

"What did she use?" River asked.

"Anything, but she got really bad when she started using heroin."

"Whoa," River said.

"What was your father like?" Jasper asked.

"I never knew who he was, and my mother refused to tell me."

"No stepdad or anything?"

"For a while, there was a man. Zane Waycott. He was like my dad. He was a chef at some of the same restaurants where my mother worked. He and I were really close—at least I thought we were. Then one day he just disappeared."

"Sounds familiar," River said.

"He didn't even say goodbye," Ellis said.

"If you think that day you said goodbye somehow helped, it didn't," River said. "It actually traumatized me pretty bad."

"If it makes you feel any better, I regretted leaving you," Ellis said.

"Then why didn't you come back?"

"So many reasons. The divorce, Irene—"

"Irene only stuck around for about three months," River said.

"It was a lot more than her and the divorce. Even after I got off the drugs and booze, I was sick with guilt about losing the baby. And by then, I'd been away for a long time. I was afraid coming back into your lives would hurt more than help."

"You could have come back," River said.

"Maybe. But something happened . . ."

"What?" Jasper asked.

Ellis looked too fragile to stand. She sat on the couch next to Raven.

"I was . . . attacked by two men in a campground. They stabbed me in the side."

"Holy shit," River whispered.

Tears dripped down her cheeks. "I almost let myself die from an infection. At first, I didn't go to a hospital. I thought maybe I deserved to die. But I was scared, too. I was afraid you and your father would find out."

"Why would that matter?" Jasper asked.

"I don't know! I was screwed up! Do you see why I left you? Even when I wasn't on drugs, I made bad decisions. I could barely keep myself alive, let alone take care of two little children. I loved you boys too much to come anywhere near you. To keep myself from wanting you, I made myself relive the day I left Viola in the woods. Over and over. It was like an actual circle of Hell."

It always came back to that. To the day Mama found the baby with raven hair and eyes. Her dream daughter. Her miracle.

Jasper had tears in his eyes. River stared forcefully at Raven. As if to say, *Do you see what that crazy lady who took you did to us?*

Ellis continued her story. "I had bad anxiety after the assault. For a while, I couldn't drive. I was having panic attacks."

Like Jackie after his father died.

"That was how I ended up in Gainesville," she said. "A friend from college lived there. I stayed with her for two years. She was the one who encouraged me to get into plant nursery work."

"And by then, no way were you coming back," River said.

"That's right," she said. "I felt better. I thought I was healing, and I supposed you two were. To come back to you then, to dredge it all up again, might have been a disaster for all of us. Or so I told myself."

She clasped her hands and looked down at them. "But it wasn't like you said before—as if my children were files on a computer I'd deleted."

"You thought about us?" Jasper asked.

She stared at her knotted hands. "Trees can do this amazing thing called Compartmentalization of Decay. When they get an injury, the cells around the wound change and put up a wall that contains the process of decay. Around that wall, a different kind of change in the cells forms another wall. Then a third wall. And a fourth."

She looked at Jasper and River. "Down the hill, there's a huge live oak that has a big hollow in its trunk, but the tree is thriving. The protective walls allowed the growth of wood to continue around the injury even as it turned hollow."

"So you're basically saying you're a rotten tree?" River said.

"I'm saying that's a better metaphor for what happened. I didn't discard you. You've always been there, at the core of me. But enclosed in a way that let me survive the pain."

"Shit, now I'm the rotten tree," River said.

"Not rotten. Go out there tomorrow and look at how beautiful that oak is."

He had no joke to follow.

"I'm not saying the walls I put up were good, and I'm not saying they were bad. This is simply how some people survive trauma. Maybe it's how this whole family got to where we are today."

"Sounds about right to me," River said. "A family of hollow trees." He drained his beer. "At this point, my stomach is so hollow, I'd eat shite-tan."

"I'd go back to cooking if y'all would stop fighting for five minutes," Ellis said.

"Oh my god, you say *y'all* now?" River said.

"Stay here a few more days, and it'll infect you, too."

"We need to get out of here," he said to Jasper.

"Not till we do the gator-wrestling thing," Jasper said.

Raven wondered what they were talking about. But for a moment, there was peace between them, and that was enough.

6

ELLIS

"Your daughter works as hard as you do," Tom said.

She did. Raven was very like her in that respect. She enjoyed physical work, especially as a way of managing stress. Raven was always moving—out walking, helping with the nursery plants, or cleaning, doing laundry, or cooking in the house. When she was inactive, she was engaged with schoolwork or a novel. Ellis sensed her perpetual need to keep active helped her cope with being thrown from one life into another she didn't want.

When they finished loading the plants into the truck, Max held up her hand for a high five, and Raven slapped it. Then they went off to the greenhouse to fertilize the plants.

"Great kid you have there," Tom said.

"Yes, she is."

"Where's Keith been?" he asked.

"He moved out," Ellis said.

Tom studied her. "Is that a good or bad thing?"

"It's just a thing."

"Want to talk about it over a beer?"

"I don't."

"So it's a bad thing. He's an ass if he's the one who left."

"I really don't want to talk about this," Ellis said.

He looked down the hill. "If this is your new guy, I'm feeling really old."

River was walking over from the barn house. He looked unusually alert for midmorning. He and Jasper had stayed in bed until past noon the previous two mornings since they'd arrived. Ellis suspected River had found a way to get drugs and alcohol in the nearby college town. He and Jasper had free use of the credit cards Jonah had given them.

"Tom, this is my son River," Ellis said.

They shook hands.

"Are you spending the summer here?" Tom asked him.

"I can't," River said. "I haven't learned how to breathe this much water with my air."

Tom laughed. "You live up north?"

"New York," River said. "I think people who live here must be hiding gills if they can survive these summers."

"The humidity definitely takes some getting used to," Tom said. "If you stick around and need work, my landscape crew is shorthanded."

"I can't imagine why," River said.

Tom looked as if the sarcasm was wearing on him. "Well, I'd better get going. See you next week, Ellis. Good to meet you, River."

"As if I'd dig around in the dirt all day," River scoffed after Tom started his truck.

"Why not? It might do you good."

"I'd rather swim with the alligators out back."

"What gets you up so early?" she asked.

"It's not that early. I was wondering where you were."

Ellis sensed tension in him.

"Do you need something?"

"Yeah. Maybe breakfast. If that's okay."

Since he and Jasper had arrived, River had driven into Gainesville or Ocala to get fast food for most of his meals. Jasper sometimes went with him, but he mostly ate with Ellis and Raven.

"No eggs or meat," she warned.

"I know."

He was definitely acting strange. She wondered what was going on.

While she was cooking, Jasper arrived in the kitchen. "Why are you already up?" he asked his brother.

"For the scrambled tofu and veggies, of course."

"Yeah, right," Jasper said.

"Want some?" Ellis asked Jasper.

"Sure. Thanks." He sat at the kitchen table with River.

Ellis made more when Raven came in. She had just enough ingredients for the three of them. She heated leftovers for herself.

She put the four plates on the table and sat down. The boys ate fast; Raven picked at her food as usual.

"Want to check out tubing at that spring?" Jasper asked.

"Maybe later," River replied.

"Do you want to come with us?" Jasper asked Raven.

"What is tubing?"

"You rent an inner tube and float down a river called the Ichetucknee. Apparently, it's one of the highlights of living around here."

"But don't get too excited," River said. "Bird-watching at Paynes Prairie was next on the list."

"Paynes Prairie is gorgeous," Ellis said.

"I'll take your word for it," River said.

His phone buzzed. He looked at it, then cast an odd glance at Ellis.

"What?" she said.

"Nothing."

"River . . . ," Jasper said.

River looked at him.

"What are you doing? You're acting weird."

"Which is typical, isn't it?" He got up and put his empty plate in the sink.

Outside, Quercus started barking.

Ellis went to the living room windows and watched a car drive slowly down the gravel road.

"Did one of you leave the gate open last night?" Ellis called.

They joined at the window and peered out at the car.

"I opened it," River said. "This morning."

Now she understood why he'd been tense. "Who is it? Jonah? Did you tell him to come here?"

River snorted. "If you think Dad drives a car like that, you really don't remember him well."

He was right. It was an old sedan.

She walked out onto the porch, and the kids followed. The man in the car was afraid to get out because Quercus was standing next to the driver's door, barking.

Ellis called Quercus to her side. He was much more obedient than his two predecessors.

The man got out of the car. He was probably in his sixties, balding and a little overweight. His face looked familiar. He stared at Ellis intently.

"Oh my god," Ellis said.

"Who is it?" Jasper asked.

"It's Zane."

"What the hell did you do?" Jasper whispered to River.

"I told him Ellis Abbey wanted to see him."

"How did you find him?" Ellis asked.

"Facebook. He was the only Zane Waycott. He doesn't live that far, in North Carolina. And he's still a chef."

"Why would you do this?" she asked.

"The way you talked about him, I assumed you needed closure." His smile was spiteful. "It feels pretty weird to see someone who ghosted you a long time ago, doesn't it?"

"You asshole!" Jasper hissed.

"If the sphincter fits . . . ," River said. He stepped back on the porch, smiling, arms crossed over his chest as he watched Zane's approach.

Zane walked as if in pain after the long drive. Age had made his face look harsher. Ellis remembered a softer look about him.

He stared at Raven as he came down the flagstone path. No doubt he saw Ellis's youth in her face. "Ellis . . . ," he said with apparent confusion. "I was told . . ." He looked at River. "Your son said you were dying and wanted to see me."

"Zane . . . ," Ellis said, walking to him. "It's good to see you."

"You too," he said distractedly.

"I'm not dying," she said.

"I see that." He shot a look at River. "I was told you had only hours to live. He said you were desperate to see me."

"I'm so sorry," Ellis said. "My son is . . . having some problems."

Zane strode toward River, his limp mostly gone. "What the hell is wrong with you? I've been driving all night!"

"You see?" River said to Ellis. "Now you know he really cares."

Zane balled a fist. "If you weren't her son . . ."

River looked about to go at it with him.

"Zane," Ellis said, "please come inside."

Zane and River continued to glower at each other.

"Come into the air-conditioning," Ellis said. "Do you like iced tea?"

"Yeah, sounds good," he said, averting his eyes from River.

Raven joined them, but Jasper dragged River away by his arm.

Ellis brought Zane iced tea in the living room.

"I'm truly sorry about what my son did," Ellis said. "I had no idea he contacted you."

"I can tell," he said.

"Our family is going through some problems."

"Is your husband here?"

"We're divorced."

He looked around. "This is nice. I imagined you living in a place like this. You used to go in that forest behind your mom's place."

"You called it the Wild Wood," she said.

"I remember," he said, smiling.

"I named my plant nursery *Wild Wood* after that place."

He sat in the stuffed chair, studying Ellis. "You and I could always cut through the bullshit, right? What's going on? Why did your son do this? There must be a reason."

"The long answer would be way too much information. The short answer is, I mentioned you during a conversation a few days ago."

"And . . . ?"

"He seemed to think I needed closure. At least that's what he said."

He gave Raven a look that indicated he'd rather not talk in front of her. But Raven stayed put. "I'm sorry I never came back," he said to Ellis. "I always thought I would. Your mother was like an addiction. Bad for me, but I couldn't stop."

"I know."

"When I finally broke free that last time, I knew I couldn't go back or I'd get sucked in again. Somehow, I finally got the willpower to stay away."

His words opened all the old wounds. He'd not once said anything about missing her.

"To make sure I never went back, I moved away," he said.

"I know. Mom heard from someone."

"I heard she died a few years later of an overdose."

Ellis nodded.

"Where did you go?"

He didn't know? He hadn't cared enough to find out if she had a safe place to live?

"I went to live with her father in Youngstown."

"Really? Him?"

"He wasn't the evil person she'd made him out to be. She hated him because he cut her off when she got out of control. He was a really nice guy."

"Figures. She always did exaggerate everything."

"Are you married?" Ellis asked.

"For eighteen years."

"Kids?"

"My wife had two kids from her first husband and didn't want more. That was okay with me." He picked up the iced tea and drank. "Is that other boy out there yours, too?"

"Yes."

He looked at Raven. "And I don't need to ask if this pretty lady is yours. You sure look like your mama. What's your name, darlin'?"

"Raven," she said.

"What are you, about seventeen?"

"Sixteen," she said.

"Do you live here or with your dad?"

"That's complicated," Ellis cut in.

He nodded. He leaned in as if to say something confidential, though Raven was right there. "Your boy River. That one's got more than a little of your mother in him, I think."

How could he say that? How could he not know how much that would hurt her? Was his goodness something she had imagined all those years?

He leaned back in his chair. "Now that I'm here, there's something I want to tell you. I felt bad about not letting you know before I left."

Ellis couldn't believe it. She would finally hear the words she'd craved all those years.

The front door opened. Jasper came in, River behind him.

"I'm sorry about what I did," River said. He didn't look sorry, and he glanced at Jasper with a slight smirk. His brother had somehow gotten him to apologize.

Jasper said, "When you leave, we'll follow you out and buy you a tank of gas at the station down the road."

More like Jonah would buy it when he paid Jasper's credit card bill.

"Thank you, but not necessary," Zane said.

"You're also welcome to use the guesthouse to rest for a while," Jasper said.

Zane grinned at Ellis. "Do I look that feeble nowadays?"

"You look good," she said. "What were you going to say? You said you felt bad about not telling me something."

"Right. About your father."

She hadn't expected anything about her father. When she was a girl, that topic had been so closed, her father may as well have never existed.

"Do you know who he is?" she asked.

His eyes changed. He looked more like the kind man Ellis remembered.

"Yeah, I knew your dad," he said softly. "Is it okay to talk about this in front of your kids?"

"I'm sure they'd like to know something about their grandfather."

"Unless he's a mass murderer," River said. "*That* I'd rather not know."

Zane ignored him. "I knew him for years before your mother did. I cooked with him. To this day, I think of him as my best friend."

"Your best friend? Why didn't you tell me?"

"Your mother wouldn't let me. He was a really good guy, Ellis. That's what I've always wanted to tell you."

"Mom told me she didn't know who my father was."

Zane glowered. "She meant that as an insult. Your father was Lucas Rosa. But he usually went by *Luke*."

So the father listed on her birth certificate was real. "Why isn't *Rosa* my last name?"

"Because your mother preferred it for your middle name—and she usually got her way with Luke. At least at first."

"Is that an Italian name?"

"Portuguese," Zane said. "Your dad came from a family of fishermen in Massachusetts."

"Interesting," River said. "No wonder Dad couldn't convince me to study law. My genes were calling me to a fish-slimed boat in the middle of the Atlantic."

Zane cast a critical look at River. "It's an honorable profession. And a dangerous one, even for experienced seamen. Luke's father and brother died at sea in a storm."

"How old was my father when that happened?" Ellis asked.

"Sixteen, and an orphan because his mom died when he was little. He lived with his grandmother for a couple of years, then went inland to live with a friend. We met at a restaurant in Pittsburgh when we were still prep cooks."

Zane smiled. "You'd never know Luke came from a hard life. He really knew how to have a good time." He studied her face. "You know, I think you look even more like him now than you did when you were little."

That was why Ellis looked so different from her mother. She'd gotten her features from her father. Now she could visualize his face.

"Does the name Ellis have to do with that family?" she asked.

He shook his head. "Your mom was a few months pregnant when Luke took her to see where he grew up. They camped all over the northeast and—"

"What? My mother camping?"

"She did a lot of stuff you never knew. Luke liked camping and turned her on to it. It's kind of interesting you called one of your kids

River—because that's how you got your name, from a river in the White Mountains where they camped."

"I'm named for a mountain river?"

He grinned. "I knew you'd like that. It drove me crazy I couldn't tell you any of this when you were a kid."

"What happened with my dad? Why was all of this kept secret?"

"To make sure you never asked questions like that, I guess. None of us was allowed to talk about it."

"Who wasn't allowed to talk about what?"

"You see? This is what your mother didn't want to happen."

"She isn't here. Tell me what I wasn't supposed to know."

"I guess you know her father kicked her out of his house."

"Yes."

"When that happened, she went to western Ohio with some guy, but it didn't work out. She moved in with a friend who got her a waitress job where she worked. In a smaller town like ours, all the restaurant people knew each other. Your mom hit our scene like a storm. She was wild, always had fun, crazy ideas. Every guy who met her fell for her."

Ellis had trouble imagining that.

Zane saw what she was thinking. "That was before the booze and drugs. She was really something to look at back then. *Striking*, I would call her looks. But there was only one of us she wanted, and that was Lucas Rosa."

"How old were they?"

"She was twenty-one and he was twenty-six. They were totally gone on each other. But boy could they go at it when they had a fight. They toned that down a little when your mom got pregnant. They rented a place and seemed really happy."

"They wanted to have a baby?"

"Yeah. They were into it. All of us were excited for them. You had twenty or so honorary aunts and uncles when you were born. You were the little princess of our parties—and we had a lot of parties."

Ellis remembered. Climbing into laps. "Come here to your auntie, sweetie." Arms lifting her. Someone swinging her around like an airplane. A smoky room. A man letting her drink out of his glass. "Don't get that baby drunk, you idiot!"

"How old was I when they broke up?"

"Three."

"What happened?"

He dragged in a slow breath and sighed. "Luke met someone else. He started going around behind your mom's back. One night when some of us were at their house, your mom was drunk and confronted him about it. He got mad but admitted to it. She told him to get out and never come back. Luke was really pissed about her yelling at him in front of everyone . . ."

Zane looked down at the glass of tea in his hands.

"What? What happened?"

"He jumped on his motorcycle and rode away. He'd only gone a half block when he sped past a stop sign and got hit." He paused, still gazing at the glass. "We heard the tires screeching. It was weird—we all knew right away what'd happened and ran over. We watched him die." He looked into her eyes. "You too. You were in my arms."

Ellis tried but couldn't remember. But she could still see the faces of her many babysitters, her "aunts and uncles," as Zane had called them. Now she understood they had been helping her mother after Lucas died.

"Your mom was never the same," he said. "She thought she'd killed him. But she never said that. She'd only say how much she hated him for going off with that other woman. All that love she still had for Luke became hate. It totally wrecked her."

"I guess I can see why she never told me about him."

"You were really rough for her; you looked so much like him. She was too hard on you. And when you got older, she sort of pretended you weren't there. But I guess I don't need to tell you that."

He didn't. Ellis had always assumed she'd had some deficit that made her mother hate her. But all along it had been about her father.

"When I started seeing her, I tried to be there for you, Ellis. I really tried. I owed that to your daddy. I loved that guy."

So there was the truth. Zane had come into her life because her mother, as he'd said earlier, was like an addiction for him. And he'd become her *almost father* because he had loved his friend, not her. Even worse, he had probably been taking care of her to appease that *striking* woman who'd first chosen his best friend instead of him.

Ellis glanced at River. His expression was inscrutable. He looked like he was trying to read her, too. As if they were playing a game of emotional poker. If she let him see that Zane had created a whole new level of pain for her, would he be glad he'd been its architect?

"All that love became hate," Zane had said. Was that what happened to River when Ellis left him?

Zane stretched up in his chair and rubbed his hands on his thighs. "Well . . . I'm glad I finally told you all that. It's bothered me some that you didn't know."

Bothered me some. Ellis almost laughed at the irony.

He grinned, blue eyes sparkling in that way Ellis had loved when she was little. "I'm glad you're not dying, Ellis."

"So am I," she said.

"You always were a funny one." He rose out of his chair. "I'd better get going."

She stood. "You're welcome to rest first."

"Thanks, but I've got somewhere to get to. Do you remember that friend of your mother's and mine called Rocky?"

"Of course."

"He's got a little place near Daytona Beach. I told him I was coming to Florida, and he's having me over. We're gonna go ocean fishing and have some bro time."

"Good thing I'm not dying slowly to keep you," she said.

He laughed. "Rocky'll be glad to hear it's not true. He said to tell you hello."

"Tell him the same."

"I will." He walked to the door, turned around. "Come here. I want a hug from Luke's pretty girl."

She was relieved to discover she wanted to embrace him. She felt no bitterness. Zane had taught her about love when her mother couldn't. What did it matter if he had or hadn't loved her back?

"Goodbye, Zane."

"Goodbye, Ellis. You take care now."

It had taken more than thirty years, but finally she'd heard him say it.

7

RAVEN

Seven ibis flew over her, and she stopped to listen. Raven never tired of hearing air whoosh through the wings of water birds. It was a new sound for her. Herons, egrets, ibis, cranes. They flew over Ellis's land all day. The big birds were one of her favorite things about living there.

But if she had to pick one favorite, it would be the old live oaks. Matriarchs of the woods, each had a different personality. Raven went to the one she loved most, an ancient fern-covered mama with an immense trunk and myriad twisted limbs snaking out like the fat strands of Medusa's hair.

Raven looked down at two Askings she'd made at the base of the tree. One was to bring her home to Washington. The other was to send her feelings out into the universe: "I love you, Jackie."

She sat between two humps of the oak's mossy roots and leaned against the massive trunk. She closed her eyes, tried to imagine what Jackie was doing.

"How can you stand these mosquitoes?"

She opened her eyes. River peered at her through a screen of young cabbage palms.

"Did you follow me here?"

"Sort of," he said.

"Why not just say yes?"

"Because that would sound creepy stalker, and I'm not. I had to go somewhere because they're all pissed at me up there." He pushed through the palms to get closer. "I saw you leave, and that looked like a good idea—until I started to stew in my own juices. How do people live in this steam bath?"

"You get used to it."

"You look like one of your earth spirits sitting there like that."

She had come to the tree because she felt sick and needed rest, but she'd get none of that now.

River noticed one of her Askings and walked over to it. "What's this? Offerings to the goddess tree?" When she didn't answer, he said, "Spirit got your tongue?"

"Why do you like to make people angry?"

"Because it's much more interesting than having people be happy with me."

She maybe understood. People who were happy with you would have higher expectations.

"Do you want to go do something? They're all looking daggers at me for bringing Zane. Even that scar-faced woman."

"Her name is Maxine. And she doesn't know about Zane."

"Mom probably told her."

"I doubt that. Maxine is deaf."

"Oh. That explains it."

"What?"

"How weird she acts."

Raven stood. "Just shut up, will you?"

"Whoa. What's this all about?"

"I like her."

Soon after Raven moved in, Maxine saw her vomit in the trees. She must have understood that Raven was homesick. Max sat next to her and gently wiped her mouth with a bandanna she had in her pocket. Then she wrapped one arm around her the way Reece did and stayed like that, just holding her for a while.

"So do you want to go somewhere?" he asked. "It's almost five o'clock. We could do an early dinner."

She felt sorry for him. He clearly didn't like to be alone, yet he compulsively provoked people into shunning him.

"Why did you lie to make Zane come here?" she asked.

"The truth?"

She nodded.

"I'd drunk no small amount of whiskey when I messaged him. This morning when he wrote back to say he was almost here, I honestly freaked out. But it was too late to do anything."

"You regret it?"

"I don't know. The guy didn't exactly seem bummed about ocean fishing. And my mother found out who her father was. Maybe I did them both a favor."

"I think it's good that Ellis found out who her father was, too."

He smiled. "Yeah? Great, one person in this family doesn't hate my guts."

"Except I don't like the lie you told to bring him here. That was mean."

"I know. It was. My drunk side is an even worse person than I am. But he's not the one who's asking you to dinner. I am. Do you like steak?"

"I love steak." She was reminded of Reece's birthday party.

"And you've been eating my mother's rabbit food? We need to get some high-quality protein into you." He added, "Not to be mean like my drunkard ego, but I was surprised by how wiped out you looked when I got here. Have you lost weight?"

"I don't know."

"I think a steak would do you good."

Maybe he was right. She was used to eating meat with Mama. And now she felt sick and tired all the time.

"I'm buying, of course," he said to encourage her. "Jesus, this sounds like a date and you're my sister." He put his hand to his throat and pretended to gag.

Just like Reece. Hiding his insecurity in humor.

"Okay, let's get a steak," she said.

He looked genuinely happy, and she felt better than she had for a long time.

He contemplated the tree. "How do we leave the blessed mother? Should I bow, maybe kiss her roots?"

She swatted his arm.

"Ow. You're mean," he said.

They walked back to the house to change. River told her to meet him at the car and avoid telling Jasper and Ellis about their plans. "I've had enough of their judgment for one day," he said.

Raven didn't understand why he'd be judged for going to dinner, but she agreed. Fortunately, Ellis wasn't in the house. She was probably at the nursery with Maxine.

Raven changed into a dress. It was one she'd worn to school and sometimes on dates with Jackie. It was too warm for Florida in June, but she put on sandals to make it more summery.

River wore slim-fitted pants, a short-sleeve button-down shirt, and slip-on shoes.

"What did you tell Jasper?" she asked in the car.

"Nothing—he was in the shower. Which means I haven't. Thank god for underarm deodorant."

He seemed to know his way around already. He got on the small highway that crossed over the Paynes Prairie wetlands, one of the few landmarks Raven knew from driving into Gainesville with Ellis a few times.

They drove to a restaurant he'd looked up that specialized in steaks. It was fancier than she expected. Men and women in crisp white uniforms seated them and took their orders.

River ordered whiskey on ice. He showed an ID when the waiter asked.

When the man left, she asked, "Is the drinking age lower than twenty-one here?"

"It's a fake ID," he said in a low voice. "I've had it for years. But don't tell Mom . . . my mom . . . Ellis . . . whatever."

He lit up when she laughed.

When the drink arrived, he held it up for a toast. "To my baby sister, who's once again tossed us into a stormy sea. May we find our way back to shore."

She tapped her water glass against his and drank. He downed more than half the whiskey.

"Finding the way back to shore is different for your family than it is for me," she said.

"You are our family."

"I'm not."

"You think you aren't, but you'll come around. Like Luke and Leia had to battle their dark origins."

"Who?"

"The Skywalkers. *Star Wars*."

Jackie had a *Star Wars* poster on his wall when he was little. But she still didn't understand the reference.

"You've never seen a Star Wars movie?"

"No."

"Wow." He finished the whiskey and asked a passing waiter to bring another. "How sheltered were you? Did you have a TV?"

"No."

"Phone?"

She shook her head.

"Jesus, how did you survive? Did you have any internet at all?"

"My mother used a phone and computer with internet to order supplies we needed. I was only allowed to use the computer for school assignments."

"Did you ever sneak and do some surfing?"

"She checked the computer history after I used it."

"Shit, that's messed up."

"It's smart. She said to give kids phones, internet, and video games when they're little is like giving them addictive drugs."

"Yeah, well, they give those to little kids, too."

"The father of a friend of mine was killed by someone who was reading a text while driving."

"That sucks. So you had friends out there?"

"I *have* friends out there."

"Do you know when you're going back?"

She shook her head. "My aunt and your father are in control of that, and no one tells me what's going on. All my aunt tells Ellis is the estate is still unsettled and I need to hide from reporters."

"She's hiding you to protect her own interests," he said.

"I know. But I agree with what she's doing. I don't want my mother to become a big news story and have people say bad things about her. I'll stay here for a while to stop that from happening."

He bit into a piece of buttered bread. "Is that the only reason you stay here? Aren't you at all glad you met your family?"

"I didn't know about any of you until a month and a half ago."

"Yeah, but now you do. Don't we mean anything to you?"

She tried to think of an answer that wouldn't sound too harsh. "A person can't suddenly feel close to people out of nothing. And none of you has made that easy for me." She wouldn't tell him that Maxine, unrelated to her, was the person she felt closest to since she'd come out east.

He smiled in his droll way. "I guess we aren't the most lovable family." He looked serious all of a sudden. "But there's a reason for that."

"I refuse to take the blame for everything that's wrong with your family."

"Of course you shouldn't. But you know who's to blame."

"You can't pin it all on my mother either. You heard what Zane said today. Ellis had problems in her family all the way back before she was born. I bet Jonah did, too. I saw what his mother is like."

"Yeah, Gram is a piece of work. To her, my mother is only slightly less evil than the Devil himself. My grandfather hated my mother, too."

"That was all there before I left your family."

"Yeah, but still. What Audrey Lind did forced our family skeletons out of the closet and turned them into flesh-eating zombies."

More and more, he reminded her of Reece. But maybe only because she missed Reece so much. Reece didn't have a drop of meanness in him, and River had plenty.

"Too bad you're a video virgin," he said. "I thought that was a pretty cool metaphor."

"I know what zombies are," she said. "They can't be skeletons."

"If you can have earth spirits in your world, I can have skeleton zombies in mine."

His second whiskey arrived. He drank it fast while they ate their salads, then ordered a third.

"I thought you said your drunk side wasn't asking me to dinner?" she said.

"I'm a big guy. It takes more than a little whiskey to get me drunk."

"Will you be able to drive us home?"

"I'm eating a full dinner. That will absorb it. I'll be fine."

She hoped so. He already seemed affected by the alcohol. As they ate, he talked animatedly about why he didn't believe in going to an expensive college like his brother. His bitter outlook on modern society and where it was headed reminded her of Mama. He even used the word *machine* to describe it once.

When they left the dark restaurant, he complained that the sun was still out. He wanted to go to a bar but said it was too early.

"I'm sixteen. I can't do that anyway."

"Oh, right."

That he'd forgotten she was underage worried her. He'd drunk three whiskeys and a glass of brandy.

"Let's do something else," he said. "I don't want to go back."

"We have to. They might be wondering where we are."

"They know where we are. Jasper sent me a bunch of texts asking why I went to dinner without him."

"Did you answer?"

"Nope."

"Why not?"

"Because Jasper is a pain in the ass."

Raven couldn't imagine Jackie and Huck acting like that toward each other.

In the car, River opened a small paper envelope. "Want to try some of this?"

"What is that?"

"Coke—cocaine."

The food she'd eaten seemed to rise up her throat. She had never seen anyone use cocaine.

"Want to try some?" he asked.

"No. And I don't think you should do that before you drive."

"I need to counterbalance the whiskey."

"You said it didn't make you drunk."

"It didn't. I just need a little pick-me-up." He had a tube in his hand.

"River . . . I don't want you to."

"Calm down. It's no big deal. Everyone does this."

He inhaled two lines of the white powder, and his eyes turned bright.

"Are you sure you don't want to try it? It feels really good."

"Stop asking," she said. "Are you sure you can drive?"

"Yep. I just need the perfect song . . ."

He took a long time choosing a song from his phone. He turned the volume on the car stereo too loud, but she said nothing.

Raven kept her attention on the road and his driving as he manically explained more about his reasons for hating the world. As they sped into the openness of the Paynes Prairie wetlands, he was looking at his phone to change the song. He glanced up at the cars parked along the highway.

"What's going on?" he asked.

"People come here to watch the sunset. Ellis told me it's a ritual around here."

"Let's do that. Do you want to do that?"

"I think we should go—"

"There's a pier over there," River said. "Let's park there."

He changed lanes sharply to get to the pier on the other side of the median. He still had his phone clutched in his hand when their car collided with another. He jerked the wheel to the right with one hand to get away from the grinding metal.

Everything turned upside down. Raven squeezed her eyes closed. When she opened them, they were in water. The car had rolled over the concrete ledge at the edge of the wetland. They were right side up again but sinking, her side of the car higher than River's.

"River! We have to get out! We're going underwater!"

His head was bloody, his eyes closed. She could tell he was unconscious.

She had to get him out before the car sank. The water wasn't up to her window yet, but she was afraid it would stop working when the water hit the mechanics. She pressed the button, relieved when it rolled down. Raven unbuckled her seat belt, trying not to panic at the sight of River's closed window receding under the water. She unbuckled him and pulled. He was dead weight.

"River!" she screamed as the water gushed into her window. "River!"

The water buoyed his body and helped her move him. But they were going under. Somehow she had to get him out through the window. Warm, sulfurous water poured over her. River's head was about to go under.

Everything vanished into a single thought—keeping him alive. She managed to drag most of his body out the window. But her head went under the water, and River's face had been under even longer. He was drowning. She had to get him to the air. She heaved her arm around his chest and struggled to get him to the surface. He was weighing her down, and she needed air. But she wouldn't let him go. She wouldn't, not ever. He was in Florida because of her. He was in that water because of her. If he died, she wanted to die with him.

Arms wrapped around her. Someone was in the water. But she was afraid they would make her let go of River and he'd sink. She clenched him tighter. As she was dragged to the surface, she sucked in a breath of air. "My brother!" she said. "Help him! He's hurt!"

"I have him!" a man said. "Let him go!"

Three men had jumped into the marsh. Another slid into the water and passed River up to the people standing at the concrete ledge. His body was completely limp, his face almost blue and streaked with blood.

He looked dead. She hadn't gotten him out in time.

The men in the water were helping her get out when someone shouted, "He's not breathing! Does anyone know CPR?"

A man and woman pushed through a large crowd. They knelt on either side of River. The man listened to River's chest. He said there was a heartbeat. Raven gasped a sob of relief. But when the woman opened River's slack mouth and breathed into it, nothing happened. He didn't wake up. He didn't move. He didn't breathe.

Beyond the cluster of cars and horrified faces, the prairie and water were impossibly beautiful. A flock of white egrets slowly flapped across pink clouds and blue sky.

Why had the spirits of that powerful piece of earth done this to one of their own?

Please let him live. Come to him now and make him breathe.

She willed the spirits to help him, but he did not breathe.

8

ELLIS

Jasper didn't want dinner. He just sulked in the guesthouse, eating snacks and watching TV. He was angry that his brother had taken the car while he was in the shower.

Ellis was surprised when she discovered Raven had gone with River. They hadn't left a note, and River wasn't answering Jasper's texts. As the sun sank lower, Ellis worried. But Jasper was sure they'd just gone to dinner without telling them. He said it was the kind of selfish thing River always did.

What was wrong with her children?

She was what was wrong with them. Her mother was what was wrong with them. And her father, who'd been so hotheaded he'd gotten himself killed over an argument. Her parents had wanted a baby when they clearly couldn't be responsible for another human being.

Some people shouldn't have children. Ellis had never thought she should or would. Then Jonah blew into her life and tossed up her plans for the future like so many dead leaves.

Quercus put his paws in her lap and licked her chin. He was the sweetest and most intuitive of the three dogs she'd had. Maybe because Keith had chosen him.

She ruffled his thick, furry mane. "You miss him, don't you?"

Seeing he had her attention, he ran for his ball. She rarely played with him. Keith had always done that. She got out of the rocking chair and threw the ball into the trees. Quercus fetched it. She threw again. On the fourth throw, the ball got stuck high in the spiky trunk of a cabbage palm. Quercus stared at it longingly.

Keith would get a ladder and bring the ball down, but she was too wiped to do that.

She went inside to get her phone and returned to her rocking chair. One was hers, the other Keith's.

She pressed his number. She didn't know why or what she would say. Just like that night in Ohio after she'd buried her phone and family pictures in the Wild Wood river.

"Hey there," he said when he picked up.

"Hey," she said.

"What's up?" he asked.

"The dog's ball is stuck up in a tree. Way up." It was a really asinine thing to say.

"That's too bad."

"Yeah."

An awful silence. She was afraid he'd say goodbye and that silence would go on forever.

"I don't think that's why you called," he said.

"It's not."

"Why did you?"

"I miss you. I'm wondering if you'll ever forgive me."

"I have. Sort of."

"You have?"

"Sort of. I can see why you didn't tell me about your kids. Feeling responsible for your child's abduction must be about as bad as it gets for a parent. Now I understand why you lived in campgrounds when I first met you. You were suffering from so much more than a divorce."

After a pause, he said, "But it's still tough for me, Ellis. I keep asking myself why you didn't trust me. Even when I trusted you enough to ask you to marry me and have our baby."

Tears dripped down her cheeks.

"Do you see how much that would hurt?" he asked.

"Yes."

After a silence, he said, "You're crying."

She tried to say yes, but it came out as a sob.

"Is everything okay over there?"

"Something happened today."

"What?"

"It's hard to explain."

"Try."

"There was a man who was like my father when I was little. He came here today."

"What happened?"

"I found out the truth about some things I'd never understood."

He waited, but she didn't know what more to say.

"The truth hurt?" he asked.

"More than I'd have thought after all these years."

"But aren't you glad you know?"

She was glad she knew who her father was, but discovering Zane hadn't really loved her or missed her still hurt.

"I think some truths are better left unsaid," she said.

"Not between people who truly care about each other," he said.

Ellis had cared; Zane hadn't. The love had been one sided. He hadn't cared enough to tell her about her father. Or even to say goodbye when he left. There had been no truth between them, and that hurt much more than the truths Zane had divulged.

She realized then why she'd called him.

"I love you, Keith."

There was no sound, but somehow she knew he was crying.

"Any chance you'd come over? I want to tell you about what happened today."

"This is good, Ellis."

"What is?"

"That you want to share the pain."

"I've got quite a bit, if you can stand it."

"I could have handled it, you know. All of it."

"I know."

"I'll be over in twenty minutes."

"Where are you?"

"I've been staying in Ben's guest room."

Ben was another park ranger who lived in nearby Ocala.

"You'd better hurry if you want to see the sunset. It looks like it'll be good."

"On my way."

He arrived before the sun went down. He hadn't yet closed his car door when they sank into each other's arms. Quercus butted and pawed at Keith until he pulled his attention away from Ellis. He knelt and hugged the dog. "I've missed you, too, you big, hairy old oak."

"How is your mom?" Ellis asked.

His mother had been depressed since Keith's father died a little over a year ago.

"She's better," he said. "She joined a senior club and made some new friends. I went up to see her last week."

"You went to Pennsylvania? Did you see your sister and the kids?"

"Of course."

"Did you talk about what happened with us?"

He nodded.

She'd known he would. Keith was close with his sister and mother, as he'd been with his father. And his sister's husband was like a true brother. Ellis had never seen such a harmonious family. She hadn't even believed such a thing existed.

"Do the kids know?" she asked.

"I think the abduction story might have been a bit much for them."

"What did the rest of the family think about it?"

"They remembered Senator Bauhammer. They were as shocked as I was to find out you were in that family."

"I guess they all hate me now?"

"How could you say that?"

"I lied to you all those years. Of course they hate me."

"Ellis, my sister started crying when she heard what you've been through."

Ellis could picture her doing that. She was the kind of compassionate, genuine person Ellis had always wanted to be. And she was a strong but tender mother, the parent Ellis had dreamed of when she was little.

"She told me I shouldn't have walked out on you," he said. "She said I couldn't imagine what it was like to lose a child and I should give you another chance."

Ellis blinked at the wetness in her eyes.

"And you know what my mom said?"

"What?"

"She said I was a fool to walk away from love." Now he fought tears. "My family said everything I needed to hear. Everything I wanted to hear. So here I am."

Was he saying he'd come back for good? She was too afraid to ask.

They walked hand in hand to the rocking chairs. She sat in hers, he in his. Quercus lay across Keith's feet to make sure he didn't go anywhere.

They watched the sky color behind the moss-tressed oaks, and she told him about her sons showing up unexpectedly, the fighting among the children, and River lying to Zane. She told him what Zane had said. The story about how her father had died. Why her mother had hated her.

"You really believe she hated you?" he asked.

"Well, she couldn't love me. Zane pretty much verified that."

He drew her out of her chair, tucked her against his chest. "And yet you have this great capacity to love. It's a testament to your strength, Ellis."

She drew back and looked in his eyes. "Why do you say I have a great capacity to love when I obviously fail at it?"

He smiled. "You love deeply, Ellis. It's trusting love that you fail at."

"Can I trust this? Will you stay?"

"I will. I've felt crazy missing you."

"Me too. Crazier than usual."

They kissed into the fall of darkness. Normally, they would have gone inside and made love, but everything felt new, and kissing better fit the mood of a fresh beginning. This time she wasn't a witch luring him into her dark wood. He knew everything, yet he said he would stay. She didn't need a spell anymore.

A flashlight beam shined on them. They broke apart and watched Jasper jog toward them from the barn house. "Mom!" he called. He stopped and took in Keith's presence for a second but didn't wait to be introduced. "River . . . River and Raven have been in a car accident. We have to go to the hospital!"

"Who told you this?"

"Dad called me. He said Raven told the hospital to call him."

"Is River okay?"

"I think it's bad. He's in the emergency room."

Keith insisted on driving. When they arrived at the stretch of Route 441 that crossed the prairie, they saw flashing lights on the other side of the road. Squad cars and a tow truck, police directing people around the scene of an accident.

"Is that where they crashed?" Ellis asked.

"I don't know," Jasper said. "I don't see our car over there."

Keith dropped them off at the emergency room entrance and went to park the car.

A doctor met Ellis and Jasper at the emergency room desk. "You're the mother of River Bauhammer and Raven Lind?" she asked.

"Yes. And this is their brother, Jasper. Did they both survive the accident?"

"So far, yes. River's situation is critical, but he's stabilized."

"I want to see him!" Jasper said.

"I know. But we're working on him."

"Doing what?" Ellis asked.

"The collision caused the car to roll over. It landed in water deep enough to submerge it."

Paynes Prairie. The accident they'd passed. Since the last big hurricane came inland, the water in the prairie had been deep.

"Your daughter probably saved River's life. He was unconscious, and she pulled him out of the car as it sank. But he wasn't breathing. He was under for at least a minute, and he has a head injury."

"Oh my god," Jasper said. Tears streamed down his cheeks.

"Two bystanders were able to resuscitate him at the scene," the doctor said. "That's good. We don't think he was without oxygen for more than a few minutes."

"Is he awake?" Ellis asked.

"He's in a coma. We're trying to determine the extent of the brain injury."

"He's breathing on his own?"

"He is. Does he have substance abuse problems that you know of?"

Ellis suspected he did, and Jasper confirmed.

"His blood has a high percentage of alcohol. Also narcotics. Raven verified he'd drunk whiskey and used cocaine before the accident."

"Where is she?" Ellis asked. "Is she okay?"

"I can't say for sure. She's a bit banged up, but she refuses to let us touch her. Literally. She says we're going to put drugs in her and hook her up to machines that will kill her. Were you aware that she has this phobia?"

"No, but I know where it came from," Ellis said.

"Some of that can come from shock," the doctor said. "Maybe you two can convince her to let us give her a sedative and examine her injuries."

Ellis doubted that. Raven was one to hold fast to her beliefs. She'd gotten a double dose of that trait, one from nature, the other from nurture.

The doctor took them to a room down the hall. Ellis hadn't expected her daughter to look so bad. She was curled in a ball on the floor, leaning against a wall in the corner. She was barefoot, her damp hair and dress streaked with mud. Drying wetland plants hung all over her. She looked like a pitiful aquatic creature that had been hauled up in a net and thrown ashore.

Raven removed her arms from her head when she heard them come in. She almost cried when she looked at Ellis, but her relief was overshadowed by her apparent mistrust of the doctor.

"We'd like privacy," Ellis told the doctor.

The doctor nodded, closing the door as she left.

Ellis couldn't help it. A profound ache of maternal love she hadn't known was still there propelled her toward this girl who would never call her *Mother*. She took Raven in her arms and pressed her to her chest. Raven sobbed against her.

Jasper wrapped his arms around his sister from behind. "Thank you for saving River," he said. "Thank you."

Jasper's crying prompted Ellis's tears. What a strange weeping lump of a family they were. Abbey, Lind, Bauhammer. Not one name in common. Not one experience shared for sixteen years. Suddenly knotted together more by pain than blood.

"I want to see River!" Raven wept. "They won't let me."

Ellis held her out in her arms. "They have to do tests."

"We have to watch what they do. They might kill him."

"We have to trust them. I know you were raised to be afraid of hospitals, but River needs treatment right now. We'll see him soon."

"I'm so scared he's going to die!" she said. "I tried to keep his head out of the water. I tried. But he went under. He wasn't breathing when they took him out."

"You saved him," Jasper said. "The doctor said you did."

"The people who breathed into him saved him," she said.

"They couldn't have done that if he'd gone down with the car," Jasper said.

"I shouldn't have let him drive," she wept. "He was drinking. He used cocaine. I could tell he wasn't right. But I thought if I watched him drive, nothing bad would happen."

Ellis thought of those many times she'd driven while under the influence of drugs. What a terrible risk she'd taken, and not only with her own life.

She held Raven again. "None of this is your fault. Not one thing, do you understand?"

A nurse came in. She wanted to take Raven's blood pressure and temperature, but she refused. Ellis saw no signs that Raven was in immediate need of medical treatment. She had some bruises and scrapes, but it was her emotional distress that was worrisome. Ellis didn't try to bully her into complying. She asked the nurse for clothing.

Jasper left while Ellis helped Raven change into a pair of hospital scrubs. Ellis scanned her body for signs that she might need the X-rays and CAT scans the doctor had suggested. She didn't see anything obvious, but when she mentioned the tests, Raven shook her head violently. She set a panicky gaze on the door, as if she were bracing to fly out.

"Okay, we'll wait and see how you are," Ellis said in the most soothing voice she could muster. "Everything is okay. No one will hurt you."

Ellis wet paper towels and wiped the dirt off her face. "Keith drove us here," she said. "Should I tell him to go home, or would you like to meet him?"

"He came back?"

"Yes, just before we found out about the accident."

"He came back for good?"

"I think so."

She studied Ellis's eyes. "You must be happy."

"I am. At least, I was."

"Where is he?"

"In the waiting room. I need to let him know what's going on."

"You'll come right back?"

"I will."

"You won't want him to leave," Raven said. "You can bring him in here."

Ellis found Keith and brought him into the examination room. Jasper and Raven were seated, Jasper's arms enveloping his sister. It nearly made Ellis cry again.

Raven stood to meet Keith. She shook his hand and said, "Nice to meet you, Mr. Gephardt." Audrey Lind must have been a stickler for manners.

They waited almost two hours before they were allowed to see River. He was still unconscious. His face was bruised and his head bandaged. He was attached to many machines—just what Raven feared—including a nasal cannula for supplemental oxygen. Jasper and Raven wept. Ellis was relieved he wasn't on a respirator. She softly kissed River's cheek, the first time since he was four years old.

Two hours later, River was moved to a patient room in the ICU.

An hour later, Jonah walked in.

Other than his present look of exhaustion and anxiety, he hadn't changed much. He was still slim and fit. He had the expected age sags and lines in his face, white wisps in his dark hair. The most notable difference was something new about his eyes. At first, Ellis couldn't grasp what it was. Then she understood. His gaze was layered. Beneath his

Glendy Vanderah

usual bright, blue-eyed confidence was a depth of sadness she'd never seen before.

"Dad!" Jasper said, running into his father's arms.

Jonah held him tight. Ellis still knew him well enough to see he was fighting tears.

Jasper didn't hold his back. "I'm sorry. It was my idea to come here. River didn't want to. This is my fault!"

"It's not your fault," Jonah said.

"Didn't you know they were in Florida?" Ellis asked him.

"I thought they were at the Outer Banks," he said.

"I told them to tell you. I insisted on it."

"I'm sorry," Jasper said. "We didn't want to make you angry."

Jonah walked to the bed, gently laid his hand on River's cheek. "I last talked to the doctor when my plane landed in Orlando. Any changes?"

"No," Ellis said. "They expect him to wake from the coma soon. The brain trauma was minor."

"She said he also took some water into his lungs."

"A small amount. That's why he's on oxygen and intravenous antibiotics."

Jonah turned to Raven, still wearing hospital scrubs. "You pulled him out of the car as it sank. The paramedics told the doctor you saved his life."

Raven said nothing. Ellis knew she believed the opposite.

Jonah put his hands on her shoulders. "You are a smart, brave girl." He took his daughter in his arms and pressed her to his heart. "Thank you. What a miracle you are."

She was crying when he let her go.

Jonah and Ellis at last fully acknowledged each other. Sixteen years of pain, guilt, blame, and anger crammed into their gazes. And maybe a little bit of love. Jonah embraced her, and she hugged him back. The strangest part was how easily her body remembered his. The smell of him, the way he held her, the soft sound of his breath in her ear. A thousand memories ignited in her nerve endings in the few seconds their bodies touched.

"Jonah, this is Keith Gephardt," Ellis said.

"Good to meet you, Keith," Jonah said as he shook his hand.

Keith had gotten a megadose of Ellis's past in the six hours since he'd returned. But he bore it well. He told Jonah he was sorry about the accident and offered him something to eat.

Jonah declined. He went to River and held his hand.

Ellis sat next to Keith. "Try to sleep a little," he said, tucking her to his chest.

"You're the one who needs it," she said. "You have to be at work soon."

"I don't. I told them I have a family emergency."

She pulled out from under his arm and looked into his eyes.

"You're my family," he said quietly, "and that means so are your children."

She returned to the nest of his arms, leaned her head against his heart, and fell asleep listening to its soft, steady rhythm.

According to the clock on the wall, she woke thirty-five minutes later. But the sleep renewed her as if she'd rested for hours. She craved coffee as she always did when she got up in the morning. She asked Keith if he wanted a cup, but he declined the offer.

Jonah had left the room. Jasper was asleep in the recliner. Raven stood over River.

"Any change?" Ellis asked her.

Raven shook her head. She looked about to drop from exhaustion. Just hours before, she'd pulled a large man out of a sinking car. Ellis couldn't imagine how she was still standing.

"You need to sleep," Ellis told her. "Would you like Keith to drive you home?"

"No."

"There's a couch out in the lounge. We could get you a pillow and blanket."

"I can't sleep until River wakes up," she said.

"You're making yourself sick," Ellis said. "River wouldn't want that."

She looked at River's face. "What River wants is to wake up. But this place makes him not want to."

"He doesn't know where he is," Ellis said. "He's unconscious."

Raven pressed her lips together, as if to keep her paranoid thoughts inside.

Ellis went in search of coffee and found Jonah at the counter ordering a cup.

"Keith seems like a good guy," Jonah said as they walked back to the ICU. "How long have you been together?"

"We've lived together for ten years."

"Wow, long time."

"What about you? Do you have a girlfriend?"

He stopped walking and faced her.

"What?" she asked.

He kept looking at her in a strange way. "I haven't told the boys yet . . ."

"Are you getting married?"

He looked around the lounge to make sure no one was listening. At that early hour, they were the only ones there. "I met someone seven months ago. He's the love of my life."

Her exhaustion slowed her ability to process his words. She just stood there staring at him.

He smiled wanly. "You look like you need to sit down."

She did. He sat across from her over a low table where they placed their coffee cups.

"I'm sorry," he said. "This wasn't the right time or place to say that. I'm tired . . ."

"For god's sake, don't apologize. I'm glad you told me. I'm really happy for you."

"You look surprised. I always thought you knew . . ."

A hundred reasons why she should have known sharpened her clarity. "Are you bisexual?"

"Gay."

"Do the boys know?"

"You're the first person I've told. Strange, isn't it?" He looked away, worked hard to keep his tears back. But when he looked at her, his eyes were wet. "As I said, I'm tired. I'm not myself."

"Don't say that! This is the truest I've ever seen you. It's beautiful, Jonah."

"Ellis, my god . . . you were always the beautiful one . . . what I've done to you . . ." He put his face in his hands.

"Jonah . . ."

He looked up at her.

"I understand why you had to deny it for so long. Your father. Your mother. That must have been torture."

"It was actual Hell. My father was one of the most vocal homophobes in the history of this country."

"And you knew when you were young?"

"Like you said, I denied it. I thought my attraction to men in high school was some perverse teen rebellion against my parents' beliefs. I told myself that into my twenties, but I never found a woman I could be with. Not until the night I met you at that party."

The Halloween party. Ellis dressed as a cloud, Jonah in the Zeus costume.

"For the first time in my life, I was attracted to a woman. I can't tell you what a relief it was. But it was so wrong. It was so goddamn wrong."

"What was?"

More tears dripped. "When I first saw you at the party, I thought you were a man. You were the most beautiful man I'd ever seen."

"I'd cut off all my hair."

"Yes, and your body was hidden in the cloud."

"Then you found out I was a woman. I was a woman you could be attracted to."

"Forgive me. I know you can't. I know it was wrong. But I did love you, Ellis. I really did. I'd never felt as much connection to anyone as I did with you."

Everything started coming into focus. He'd said he loved her too early in the relationship. He was needy, yet she clearly felt his emotional distance. He had trouble making love to her. That was how they'd gotten pregnant: one night she'd sacrificed protection to help along his fragile response.

"Weren't you at all attracted to Irene?" she asked.

"Irene was . . . Jesus, Ellis, how can I tell you these things?"

"Tell me. It's better than keeping it inside."

"There was a man, another lawyer. I suspected he was gay. But I couldn't go there. You know I couldn't. You, the kids, my mother, Senator Bauhammer . . . the whole country, for god's sake."

"So you went for your tennis instructor to try to kill your attraction to a man."

He nodded.

"I guess I wasn't looking at all like a beautiful man anymore—milk dripping out of my big boobs and all that."

Again, he nodded. "I thought having another baby would fix my problems, but it made it worse. You were such a beautiful mother. So gorgeous . . ."

"But pretty much the opposite of what you'd first found attractive about me."

He picked up his coffee, but his hand shook too hard to take a sip. He had to put it down. "Shit," he said and started crying again.

"I mean it when I say I forgive you," she said. "Believe it or not, I feel better now that I know. Irene really hurt when I found out, but now I get it."

"Do you get it?" he said with sudden vehemence. "You left Viola in the forest because you'd seen me with Irene. I'm the reason she was abducted. I'm the reason you resorted to drugs and booze. I'm the reason you left your sons. I'm the reason River is so screwed up." He pointed toward the elevator. "He's in that bed because of me. You took all the blame, but all along it was me!"

"Jonah, come on—"

"You know it's true! I've wrecked all these lives! Sometimes I don't think I can live with it! If I hadn't found Ryan when I did—" He stood abruptly and walked to the other side of the lounge.

Ellis went to him. "I'm glad you found someone to love. Loving Keith and being loved by him have been good for me. I hope you'll have that with Ryan."

"I hide it from the boys," he said bitterly. "I can't tell my mother. I sneak off with him. How much *good* is that doing me?"

"Then tell them."

"My mother? You know how she is. She lives in my house now, Ellis."

"So what? If she doesn't like it, she has plenty of money to move out. You've been living a lie all these years for what? For your parents' vile version of morality? Now that I know the truth, they're the ones I blame for Viola's abduction. It all goes back to them crushing the soul of a child."

"You can't blame them," he said. "Both of their parents indoctrinated them into those beliefs."

"And who raised their parents? And on and on all the way back? It's time to stop this cycle of hatred. Tell our boys you're in love. Bring Ryan over to the house. Let River and Jasper see who you are and who you love. I know it will be healing for them. And if Mary Carol tries to ruin it, kick her ass out of your house!"

He grinned. He looked ten years younger. "I'm glad you've still got your kick-ass side. I always loved that about you."

"Jonah . . . I'm so sorry I left you to raise our boys alone. I thought Irene would be helping you, and I had no idea how to—"

"Neither of us knew how to fix it. I think it was unfixable at that time. But now we can try again, can't we?"

"I would like that," she said.

He held out his hand. "Friends?"

"Absolutely." When she took his hand, he pulled her into a tight embrace.

"Let's get back," he said. "We should be there when he wakes up."

When the elevator opened on the ICU floor, Keith was right in front of it.

"I was looking for you," he said.

"Is everything okay?" she asked. "Did River wake up?"

"He's the same," Keith said. "It's Raven."

"What about her?"

"She's doing something strange. The nurses are upset. You need to get in there."

Ellis and Jonah hurried down the ICU corridor. They stopped in the doorway, taking in the bizarre scene of River's body covered in grass, flowers, and tree branches. A palm frond rose out of the pillows behind River's head like a green-rayed halo.

Raven appeared to have snapped, her guilt and exhaustion too much. She was carefully arranging the grass and flowers on River's blanket, occasionally holding a crushed leaf or flower near his nose filled with oxygen tubes. Jasper was looking at her as if she'd gone mad, as were two nurses.

"She left right after you did," Keith said quietly. "She came back with all this stuff hidden inside a plastic trash bag."

She had picked it from the landscape in front of the hospital. Ellis had brought her out there to give her a break from the tiny ER room earlier.

"Please tell her to stop," the younger of the two nurses said. "Those plants are from outside. He shouldn't be breathing that. This needs to be a sterile environment."

"Wrong," Raven said. "It's too sterile. People evolved with fresh air and dirt and plants. They can't feel good in a place like this. They can only feel sick. He needs to touch the earth to have a good reason to wake up."

The beauty of it nearly made Ellis cry.

"This is a great idea, Raven," she said, walking to the bed. "But usually people bring flowers to the hospital."

"That's what I'm doing."

"The flowers are supposed to come from a clean place. From a florist. And you put them in a vase, not on the sick person."

"He needs to have it close. To smell it and feel it."

A tiny spider crawled up the white blanket toward River's face. Ellis captured it in a plastic cup, placing another cup over it to keep it inside.

"You see?" the young nurse said. "There are bugs. If she doesn't stop, she'll have to leave."

"I will not!" Raven said. "Just go and let us take care of him the way we want to. Your machines aren't waking him up."

"The machines are monitoring him," the older nurse said in a kinder tone. "They aren't supposed to wake him up."

Raven crushed a leaf and smelled it before holding it near River's nose. "River, doesn't that smell good?" she said. "Do you smell it? River, wake up."

"This is ridiculous. I'm getting his doctor to stop this," the younger nurse said. She strode out of the room.

"Raven . . . ," Jonah said, "the doctor is probably going to want him to be clean. We'd better take it off now."

"Not till he wakes up," Raven said.

Jonah looked at Ellis. She didn't know what to do either.

A doctor came in. She looked tired, in no mood to negotiate with a teenage witch doctor.

"There are bugs crawling all over him," the nurse said.

"Come on, you know that's an exaggeration," Ellis said.

"We can't treat the patient with that on him. It's got to go," the doctor said.

"Can we just leave it there for a little longer?" Ellis said. "It's her way of dealing with the stress."

"Yeah, just leave it," Jasper said.

"I really don't see why it's a problem," Jonah said. He surreptitiously brushed an ant off the blanket, but the doctor saw.

"You can't bring dirt and insects into an ICU where there are sick people," she said.

"People bring dirt and insects in on their clothes and shoes," Keith said.

Raven tickled a grass stem on River's cheek. "Do you feel that, River?" she whispered in his ear. "Wake up."

"I'm sorry, but we have to take it off," the doctor said.

"You won't!" Raven said. "He's my brother, and my family said it's okay. Just go and leave us alone!"

Right then, River opened his eyes and coughed. He lifted his hand and looked at the taped IV needle with confusion. Then he started pulling the cannula tubes off his nose.

"I knew it!" Raven said. She leaned over the bed rail and kissed his cheek.

"Raven?"

"Yes! Do you feel better?"

He looked down at the piles of vegetation on him. "What the hell are you doing? Are you burying me?"

"Quite the opposite," Jonah said.

9

RAVEN

Keith threw the Frisbee to Raven, and she tossed it high, making River reach for it. He lobbed it back to Keith, who threw it long and low to Ellis, just returning from the nursery. She ran for it, but it landed short and she just missed. She threw it to River and joined the game.

River had taken off his shirt, and Raven appreciated how strong he was getting. For two months, he'd worked for Tom the landscaper and helped Ellis and Maxine with the nursery. He'd been alcohol- and drug-free for three months, since the day of the accident.

Raven looked at the watch Keith had loaned her. "We have to leave in twenty minutes," she called to River.

"Can't we skip it today?"

"No."

He threw the Frisbee forcefully at her head. He was good. But she was, too. She caught it and immediately flung it back at him.

"We'd better stop to give you time to clean up," Ellis said.

"Why would I need to clean up for a bunch of addicts?" River said.

Ellis and Keith walked away from the game. They wouldn't give him an excuse to be late for his Narcotics Anonymous meeting. On Wednesdays, Raven drove him to his NA meeting, and on Saturdays, she took him to an Alcoholics Anonymous meeting. She'd gotten her driver's license specifically to bring him to the meetings in Gainesville. His license had been revoked after the accident, and Ellis and Keith were usually too busy to take him.

River threw the Frisbee to her, and she didn't throw it back. "Go shower," she said.

"Jesus, you're a controlling bunch." He sat down in the grass and lay back with his arms under his head.

Raven walked toward him. "Fire ants."

"Shit!" He jumped to his feet.

"Just kidding."

"I'll give you fire ants!"

He grabbed her before she could run away. He lifted her off her feet, carried her to a fire ant mound near the driveway, and held her, head down, over it. Her hair nearly touched it.

"Stop it!" she shouted, laughing.

"Are you sorry?"

"Yes!"

"Will you say I don't have to go to the meeting today?"

"No."

"You'd take fire ants in the face for that?"

"Yes."

He tipped her back up onto her feet. "Your dedication to these stupid meetings is weird."

"They aren't stupid. My dedication is to you getting better, and that's not weird. Go put on a shirt and get in the car."

"Can we please not go today? I'm really not in the mood."

"You need to. With the hurricane coming, the Saturday meeting might be canceled."

"Show me how to pray to the hurricane earth spirit for that."

"Go!"

He grabbed the Frisbee off the ground, bopped her on top of the head with it, and went inside. He was such a child sometimes. But she loved his child side as much as she did him. She hadn't known him as a boy, and it was fun to see what she'd missed.

As usual, River stared at his phone during the drive into Gainesville. His phone was as much an addiction as the drugs and alcohol had been. She was glad she'd been raised without one.

"Check this out," he said, holding up the phone to her.

"I told you not to show me your phone when I'm driving."

"Just look for a second."

"No. You can tell me what it is."

"Jasper texted me a picture of our house with a 'For Sale' sign. My dad finally put it on the market today."

"So your grandmother really moved out."

"Yep. She lives in some fancy senior village now. And she says she's not leaving any of her money to my dad if he doesn't say he isn't gay."

"That's horrible."

"It's a typical Gram Hammer-'Em-Into-Submission move."

"Jonah won't give in to get the money."

"He won't. And I'm proud of him for finally standing up to her."

"Where will he live when he sells the house?"

"He and Ryan are looking for a place together."

"Are you sad to lose the house where you grew up?"

"Yes and no. I'll miss it, but I have a lot of bad associations."

Raven supposed most of that had to do with her abduction and Ellis leaving.

She pulled into the parking lot of the church where the meeting was held.

"Why don't you come in for some laughs?" River said.

"I have to read a book for school."

"Your loss," he said, getting out.

The first few times, Raven had gone in with him. But that was too much hand-holding. He had to want to get better on his own. As it was, she had to talk him into the meetings too often.

When he came out, he was in a quiet mood. And when River was quiet, it was hard not to notice. He remained silent as she drove to get dinner at a restaurant, as they often did after meetings.

While they waited for their food, she asked, "What did you talk about in the meeting today?"

"You, as a matter of fact," he said.

"What about me?"

"Your abduction. I'd never told them about that before."

"Do you remember it well?"

"Oh yeah, I remember it," he said in a biting tone.

"You were only four."

"Four and a half." He stared out the restaurant window. When he turned back to her, he said, "The thing is, I was more responsible than anyone has ever told you. At first, Mom took all the blame. Like, *all* of it. That was what screwed her up so bad. But, as you know, Dad told us he's to blame. I have to admit, that was a real shocker when he told us Mom had seen him kissing Irene that day."

It had been a shock. The day before Jonah and Jasper drove back to New York last summer, Jonah had sat his children down and told them Ellis saw him kiss his lover the day of the abduction. That was why she'd taken her children to the woods. She was comforted by the forest, and she'd gone there to think about what to do. She had decided to divorce Jonah, but she'd been so upset, she left her baby in the parking lot.

"Mom knows the truth, but she never talks about it," River said. "I was the one who distracted her and made her put you down in the parking lot. I spilled my tadpoles in the car, and I was being a total shit about it. I screamed my head off and made Mom put all the tadpoles back in the jar." Tears magnified his blue-gray irises. "She forgot she hadn't put you in the car because of me."

"You were a little boy. Of course you'd cry when your tadpoles spilled. It wasn't your fault."

"I was a little shit then, and I'm a big shit now. And if you think these meetings will change any of that, you're as deluded as everyone else. Right now, I want a drink so bad I'd get one if I still had my fake ID."

"No you wouldn't."

"You can't stop me! I'm a train wreck! Don't you see that?"

She went to his side of the booth and put her arms around him.

"Stop it!" he hissed. "You look like an idiot!"

She held on to him.

"Let me go!" he growled.

"No."

"You're even more screwed up by all of this than I am! You know that, right? You're a mess. You're acting crazy. Are you aware of that?"

People in the restaurant were looking at them. She didn't care. She wouldn't let him go.

"Oh my god! Okay, I get the point. Unconditional love is so awesome. Now get off me."

"Are you a train wreck?" she asked.

"No. I'm *The Little Engine That Could*. You can let me go."

She let go. "What is *The Little Engine That Could*?"

"A book my grandfather used to read to Jasper and me. It sucked. Now get on your side of the table."

She returned to her side.

"You need to back off," he said seriously.

"Why?"

"Because what you're doing just triggers the contrarian in me."

"What am I doing?"

"Caring too much."

"Do you really want me to care less?"

"Yes."

She leaned across the table. "The day of the accident, I didn't let you drown in that water, and I won't let you drown now. I hardly knew you that day, but I cared. I cared a lot whether you lived or died. You're my brother, and you're my friend. You can be as contrarian and mean to me as you want, but I'm still going to care."

"What if I throw you into an alligator pit?"

"You already did that."

He laughed. "Were there alligators that day? Did you see any?"

"I was too busy saving our lives to notice. But Ellis said there are a lot in that place."

"Would you have wrestled an alligator for me?"

"Yes."

"Would you battle Godzilla for me?"

"Yes."

"Do you know who Godzilla is?"

"No."

"You see? You really don't know what you're getting into with me."

Maybe she didn't. Who could know their future with a person they cared about? And even if they did somehow find out something bad was going to happen with that person, would they give up on them? Let them suffer alone? Love couldn't be removed like a thorn from a thumb.

Three days later, the hurricane hit and River's Saturday AA meeting was canceled. Good thing, because Ellis and Maxine needed their help getting nursery plants into shelter. Overnight, the storm's path had changed. It would skirt the eastern coast as it traveled northward, bringing much stronger winds inland than at first predicted. There was a possibility it would make landfall over the central part of the peninsula. Ellis said if that happened, the wind could cause damage to the nursery.

The rain and wind started late in the morning. Raven was soaked. And exhausted. She'd moved a lot of plants into the greenhouse and other protected parts of the nursery. Longleaf pine. Saw palmetto. Swamp milkweed. She pushed a fire bush toward River while she picked up a pot of grass with her favorite name. Fakahatchee.

"Look at that," River said.

She looked up at huge billows of gray and black clouds roiling in the eastern sky.

"It looks kind of like a funnel starting, doesn't it? Mom said hurricanes can make tornadoes."

The churning dark clouds looked enraged. Raven wondered what Mama would have thought of that sky. Would she see spirits in the clouds? Would she fear their fury? Raven had begun to doubt the spirits. She had felt them gradually leaving her since the day she'd blamed them for nearly killing her brother. Their disappearance hurt, made her feel terribly alone even when she was with her family. Mama had said that would happen if she lived in the outer world.

A slippery sensation stirred in her belly. She put her hand there, down low, not on her stomach. It happened again. As if a fish were swimming around inside her.

"Are you okay?" River asked.

The little creature inside her moved again. She pressed both hands on it. Rain driven by the wind pelted her face. River couldn't see her tears.

But Maxine stared at her. As if she knew. She often gazed intently at Raven like that. She came to Raven, put her hands on her arms, looked into her eyes.

"What's going on?" River said.

Maxine nodded toward the house to say he and Raven should go back. She made more gestures, indicating they had done enough. They should go home.

Ellis came over. "Yes, you two should go," she said. "Get a hot shower before we lose power."

"You'll for sure lose power?" River asked.

"In these rural areas, trees fall on the power lines in almost every big storm. And with a hurricane, it could be out for days, even weeks."

"We won't have water?"

"The pump runs on electricity, but Maxine will hook it up to a generator if we have a long power outage. Those will be cold showers, though. The water heater will go down."

"Cold showers?" River said. "No way." He jogged down to the barn house.

"Go on. We're about done," Ellis told Raven. "Thank you for your help."

Raven walked into the blowing rain. The tops of the oaks tossed madly in another gust. Her wet hair whipped her face, but she couldn't feel it. The wildness of the earth didn't touch her. She was insensible to it all.

Keith was home already. His supervisors had sent him home early, when it was still safe enough to drive. Raven liked Keith. He was one of the kindest people she'd ever met. But she didn't want to talk to him. She couldn't talk to anyone. She just wanted quiet.

She would go to the tree. Not the giant mother tree that was down in the bottomland. She would have no protection from the rain there. She would go to her second favorite tree, the one Ellis had talked about the day River and Jasper arrived. The oak that was partly hollow but still very much alive.

Raven walked down the hill to the tree. It was barely visible from the master bedroom window. She had to get inside before Keith saw her. She stood on the roots and climbed into the trunk's hole. She sat on the soft earthy floor of the little room. Ellis said the tree had put up four kinds of walls to protect itself from the spreading damage. Raven liked that, sitting in a tiny one-room cabin that the tree had made inside itself.

A gust of wind whined through the oak's hollow. But she stayed dry. She leaned against the tree wall. When she curled her body inward, her thighs pushed uncomfortably against her belly.

Because it was bigger.

She didn't want to think about it. She closed her eyes. She kept her attention on the outside drum of rain, whooshing treetops, creaking limbs, the moan of wind when it hit the hollow trunk just right.

"Raven!"

She opened her eyes. She had fallen asleep. Ellis was peering into the cavity doorway. She looked upset.

"How did you know I was in here?"

"Max," Ellis said loudly over the wind.

"How did she know?"

Ellis handed a wet piece of paper down to her. It was from the little notebooks Ellis and Maxine used to say things they couldn't translate into gestures.

The first line said, *Do you know where Raven is?*

Maxine answered, *She's not in the house?*

No. And not in the barn house. I'm worried.

Look inside the hollow oak.

What???

Look there, Maxine wrote. *You need to talk to her. Really TALK to her.*

Raven crumpled the note and let it fall.

"What did she mean?" Ellis asked. "Is something wrong?"

Is something wrong? Her whole life had been a giant wrong.

"Please talk to me," Ellis said. "You can tell me."

Raven wiped her hands down her face.

"Why are you crying, sweetheart?" Ellis said. "Please tell me."

She would have to tell her. And better now when no one else was there to hear.

"My mother—Audrey . . ."

Ellis looked surprised that she'd called her by her first name. She'd never done that before.

"She tricked me," Raven said. "She lied to me."

Ellis had nothing to say. Because of course Audrey had lied. Everyone knew that. Even Raven had come to understand Mama had told her lies. But she used to think they were necessary lies. Good lies.

She sat up higher inside the tree. "Do you know what I used to believe?"

Ellis leaned into the tree to listen over the wind and rain.

"I believed my father was the spirit of a raven. She told me I was a miracle made by an earth spirit that embodied all ravens that had ever lived on Earth. He created me with her spirit. I actually believed I was only half-human."

Ellis was trying not to cry.

"No one knows my real name," Raven said. "It isn't Raven Lind."

"What is your name?" Ellis asked.

"Daughter of Raven. I didn't have a human last name because I was the child of an earth spirit. My mother mostly called me *Daughter*."

"Why don't you come out and we'll talk in the barn? River is having lunch with Keith and Max in the house."

Raven heard her, but the words didn't register. "Do you know what else she told me? She said a person who's half-human can't make a baby. Have you ever heard of *reproductive isolation*, when two unlike species can't make offspring?"

"Yes," Ellis said.

"It was all a trick," Raven said. "She wanted another baby. She kept telling me to have sex with boys I met at school."

Tears dripped down Ellis's cheeks.

"She said my father the raven would want me to enjoy the act of sex. She said I didn't have to worry about making a baby. She kept me locked up all those years, but suddenly she let me go out with boys anytime I wanted."

Raven picked up the crumpled paper and opened it. "Maxine knew. I'm such an idiot."

"What are you saying?" Ellis asked.

"Do you know what happened when we were in the nursery a little while ago?"

"What?"

"I felt a baby move inside me. A baby. There's a baby inside me."

The despicable crime was right there for her to see, reflected in Ellis's horrified reaction.

A sob burst out of Raven. Out of her very soul. And another. She could hardly talk through the crying. "It isn't mine. It's hers. It's Audrey Lind's baby. She worked on getting that baby since I was a little girl. I grew up too fast. She always said that. And she kept saying she wanted another baby. I have this horrible person's baby inside me!"

Raven covered her face and cried against the tree. She smelled so good. A Mother Tree. The kind of tree you could ask for things. Or so she had been taught.

Dear Mother Tree, make me hollow like you are. Take the baby away. Take Mama out of me. Make the place where she was into a pretty little room like you have. I want to live there forever.

Hands lifted her. Strong arms. Ellis was pulling her out of the hollow, and Raven didn't stop her.

Ellis pressed Raven against her body. Raven thought she must remember the sweet smell and feel of her mother from when she was a baby. Because Ellis was exactly what she wanted. Better even than the tree.

Raven had never cried so hard.

"You'll be okay," Ellis said. "Go ahead and cry. You need to. It's good to let it out. I love you so much. I love you. My sweet baby. Everything will be all right."

A quieter cycle of the hurricane hushed the woods. The gusts calmed, and rain pattered gently.

Raven wiped her hands over her face. It felt swollen.

Ellis placed her hands on Raven's cheeks. "Sweetheart . . . are you sure? Are you certain you felt a baby? Could it be—"

"It's a baby. Maxine knew. She saw me throwing up one day. I thought I was sick from missing Washington."

She had vomited the day Sondra came to her house with her sister's letter. That had made Raven think it was normal to be sick with unhappiness.

"You haven't had your period?"

"I got a few spots once. I thought my body had changed from everything that happened. Especially after the car accident."

"Do you mind if I look?"

Raven pushed back against the tree and lifted her shirt.

Ellis caressed the bulge. She was trying not to cry. "I thought you were finally gaining weight. But this definitely looks like a baby. If you felt the baby move for the first time, you must be about six months along."

"It happened at the end of March."

Spring break from school. She and Jackie had made love many times that week. What would he say if he found out? She'd told him she couldn't get pregnant.

She was crying again.

"It's okay. It's okay. We'll figure this out. Who is the father?"

"Jackie. Jack Danner."

"Is he a boyfriend . . . a friend . . . ?"

"He's my boyfriend. But maybe he gave up on me by now. And he'll think I tricked him like Mama did. I told him I couldn't have babies."

"He'll understand, won't he? How long had you been together?"

"I've known him since I was seven. I love him more than anyone in the world."

Ellis looked astonished. "Why didn't you tell me this? Have you had any contact with him?"

Raven shook her head.

"You poor girl! You should have asked to use my phone. Or we could have bought you your own."

"I've never been allowed to use phones. Mama always said they were bad. And River is addicted to his."

Ellis unzipped her raincoat pocket and took out her phone. "As you know, I'm not keen on phones either. But this . . . this is definitely a situation where a phone is very good. You're going to call him right now."

"Here?"

"We only get good phone reception outside because of the metal roof on the house and barn. And the rain has let up. You'd better hurry before more rain blows through." She held the phone out to her. "I'll leave to give you privacy."

"I don't know his number."

"What are his parents' names? I'll call information."

"His mother is Rose Danner. His father died."

"Does his mother work on Saturdays?"

"No, she's a teacher."

"Shoot, I just realized something." She slid the phone back into her pocket. "I need to tell you something before you call. I want you to hear it from me, not from Jack or his mother."

"What?"

"There's been a lot going on out there. I haven't told you because I didn't want to upset you. But you've been told enough lies."

"They found her body?"

"Yes. They had to do an autopsy to make sure there wasn't foul play."

Raven imagined doctors cutting up Mama's body. It made her sick. She squeezed her eyes closed and put her hands over them to stop seeing it.

"They had to know what killed her," Ellis said. "They were worried Sondra or someone else might have been involved in her death."

Raven opened her eyes. "Aunt Sondra?"

"There's been an investigation to make sure she didn't aid her sister's crime."

"Did they find out what killed Audrey?"

"She had heart disease—similar to what killed her mother. But she probably died of hypothermia. She removed her clothing, lay down in a hollow she'd excavated, and pulled dead leaves over her body to hide it."

Raven easily saw her doing that. Vividly. More tears mixed with the rain on her face.

"I'm sorry," Ellis said. "I'm sorry I had to tell you that. But we've seen what hiding the truth has done to our family."

"Where is Audrey now?" Raven asked.

"I don't know."

Raven was surprised she wasn't more upset that she didn't know where the body was. She didn't know what she felt about Audrey Lind. What River had told her at lunch on Wednesday haunted her. To think that poor little boy blamed himself all those years for the abduction. For what Audrey Lind had done. It tore at Raven's heart.

Ellis held her by the shoulders. "Your boyfriend and his mother will probably know these things. The story of what Audrey did has been a big deal in their community. It's on the TV news and in all the papers. That's why no one talks about you going back. I doubt you'd want to be out there right now."

Raven could easily envision it. Everyone at school talking about it. Poor Jackie. How strange that must be for him.

"Maybe we could fly Jack out here for a visit," Ellis said. "I'm tight on money, but Sondra can easily pay out of your inheritance."

"He could come here?"

"Is he in school?"

"He's a senior in high school."

"That could be a problem. But ask him, if we can get him on the phone." She huddled closer. "We'd better call. Here comes more rain."

Ellis typed things into the phone and finally spoke to someone. She asked Raven the town and road. Then she said, "Yes, please connect me." She handed Raven the phone. "It's ringing. Wait for her to answer."

"Hello?" Ms. Danner said.

It was strange to hear her voice through the metal-and-glass machine in her hand.

"This is Raven," she said.

"Raven! Oh gosh. Oh dear. I'm tearing up. Hold on a minute."

Raven started crying, too.

Ellis walked away to give her privacy.

After a few sniffles, Ms. Danner said, "How are you, darling?"

"I'm okay. I miss you."

"Boy, do we miss you! Where are you calling from?"

"Florida. I live with my mom now."

My mom. She couldn't believe she'd said that. Ms. Danner started crying again.

"Let me get Jackie," she said. "He's upstairs."

The flutters in Raven's stomach weren't the baby.

The wind blew hard again. She was afraid she wouldn't be able to hear Jackie. She climbed inside the tree while Ms. Danner called Jackie to the phone.

"Raven?" Jackie said.

"Yes." The word came out as a sob.

"Where are you?" He was trying not to cry.

"Florida. At my mother's house."

"Is that okay? Do you like it there?"

"It's getting better. It was really hard at first."

"I can imagine."

"I've missed you so much," she said.

"Me too."

"How's school?" she asked.

"Horrible without you."

"Is everyone talking about me?"

"Yes. And that makes it worse. I even had a reporter try to ask me questions about you."

"I'm sorry."

"It's not your fault!"

"Jackie . . . ?"

"What?"

"Do you think you could fly out here? My mother said my inheritance from Audrey could pay for it."

"Yeah! When?"

"Now."

"Now? Like, today?"

"No. But after we get the ticket."

"I'd have to ask my mom about missing school."

"I need to talk to you. I have to tell you something."

"What?"

She wanted to see him when she told him. And touch him.

"Raven, tell me! What's wrong?"

She had to tell him. Maybe it was better that she couldn't see him if he got angry.

"Audrey Lind—the woman who stole me—she told me lies. She told me I'm different from other people."

"Well, you are," he said, trying to be cheerful. "In the best ways possible."

"She told me my body is different. She said it wouldn't make babies."

Silence.

She slid down the tree to the ground. "I'm pregnant with our baby."

"Oh my god," he whispered.

"I didn't know until today. I felt it move. She lied to me. I'm sorry, Jackie. I'm sorry."

"Don't apologize! It was her."

"Are you upset?"

"I'm surprised, but not mad, if that's what you mean. I'm more worried about you—that you have to go through this . . . on top of everything else . . ." He went quiet, too emotional to speak.

She couldn't either.

"I'm coming out there," he said. "I can miss some school. I'm sure my mom will be okay with that."

"She can come, too, if she wants. And maybe Huck and Reece. I can get tickets for everyone."

"Huck's too busy at college to take time off. And Reece . . ."

"What?"

"There's sad news. His mother died in July. He lives with us now."

"Reece lives at your house?"

"He didn't have anywhere else to go. He doesn't have enough money to rent a place. He's really down."

"Please bring him!"

"I wish I could. But he has two jobs now. He's trying to save money for college."

Ellis peered into the tree. "The wind is really picking up out here," she said. "I want you to get out of this tree. It's making me very nervous."

"Who is that?" Jackie said.

"Ellis. My mother."

"What did she say about the wind?"

"There's a hurricane here."

"I saw that on the news. I had no idea you were in it."

"Please come out," Ellis said.

Raven heard the roar of the wind, felt it shudder the tree walls.

"I have to go," Raven said. "I'm inside a hollow tree, and the wind is really strong."

"You're inside a tree? In a hurricane?"

"Yes."

"I have to tell Reece this. He'll love it."

"Give him a big hug for me."

"I will—even if I get teased."

"I love you, Jackie."

Silence, maybe because he was crying.

"I was afraid I'd never hear you say that again," he said. "I was afraid to keep being in love with you."

"You are still?"

"I love you as much as ever."

"I can't wait to see you."

"I know. Give the baby a kiss for me."

"That might be difficult."

"It was a joke. Get out of that tree before it blows down."

She handed the phone to Ellis and climbed out of the oak into the squall of rain and wind.

"How did he take the news?" Ellis asked as they walked to the house.

"He's not upset. He said he loves me."

Ellis took her hand and squeezed it. "I'm happy for you. Did you ask him if he wants to visit?"

"He's coming. As soon as we get tickets."

A strong gust made branches snap overhead. They ran back to the house, laughing at how drenched they were as they arrived on the porch.

"Talking to Jack has done you good," Ellis said. "I'm glad I'll get to meet him soon."

"You'll love him. He's the sweetest person."

"Raven . . ." She put her hand softly on her cheek. "I see how much you love him. And out of that love came this baby. You and he and your love made this child. Nothing and no one else. Do you understand?"

"I'll try to."

She kissed Raven's cheek.

"Do you mind if I start calling you *Mom*?"

"I would love that," her mother said.

They were both going to cry. They looked out at the Wild Wood. The wind had stopped, and sunlight suddenly slanted through the oak canopies. Rain dripping out of sparkled leaves and drapes of moss looked like glitter in the steamy, straight-edged shafts of light. It was the most magical the earth had ever appeared to Raven.

"Wow, look at that," her mother said.

"Is the storm already over?" she asked.

"No, we have hours to go," she said. "The hurricane's swirling center sends out bands of squalls that make the weather change rapidly."

Even as she spoke, racing gray clouds scuttled the sunlight, plunging the Wild Wood into mysterious darkness. With a precipitousness that captured Raven's breath, the wind returned with unrestrained fury, whipping branches, moss, and leaves into reckless flight.

"You see?" her mother said. "The tempest has returned."

"I think it's beautiful," Raven said.

Her mother laughed and hugged her arm around her. "You've got a lot of me in you, girl."

She did. She had often felt something, a strength of heart and soul that kept her going when Audrey was too sick to take care of her. When she'd wandered as a lonely half-spirit child in the woods. When she'd vowed she would never let go of Jackie, Huck, and Reece once she'd found them. She used to think that power had come from the raven spirit. Now she knew much of her strength had passed to her from Ellis. From this woman watching the storm with her. This mother who could hold her in her arms. Who could cry with her, talk to her, and understand her.

She was half-Ellis. Not half-spirit. And she'd never felt stronger.

10

ELLIS

The baby moved beneath her hands. Something hard jutted against her palm. An elbow. Maybe a knee.

"She likes it," Raven said.

Raven always referred to the baby as a girl, though she was only guessing.

"She can see the sunlight through your skin," Ellis said. "Maybe that's why she's so active."

"That must be beautiful."

Ellis poured more massage oil onto her belly and gently rubbed her hands over Raven's taut, sun-warmed skin. Raven relaxed against the pillows.

Ellis looked out at the muted colors of the field, thought of the new life soon to emerge from the roots of the hibernating grasses and flowers. She wondered where the baby would be when the first flowers bloomed. Raven and Jackie still hadn't decided whether to keep the baby or give it up for adoption. Or maybe they had decided and hadn't told anyone. Ellis stayed out of their decision. Raven and Jackie were remarkably mature teenagers. They didn't need advice, and Ellis wanted them to feel confident about whatever they decided.

Ellis pulled Keith's soft flannel shirt down over Raven's belly. He had offered his shirts when Raven refused to buy maternity clothes. But in recent weeks, she'd grown out of most of Keith's clothing.

Ellis took off Raven's socks and massaged her feet with the oil.

"That feels great," Raven said.

"Your dad used to massage my feet when I was pregnant with the boys."

"Not with me?"

"No. Things weren't going well with us by that time."

"Mom . . . ?"

Ellis looked up at her. She had tears in her eyes.

"What's wrong, sweetheart?" Ellis asked.

"I'm really sorry about that day I said I wasn't meant to be yours and Dad's. That was the meanest thing ever to say to a mother. Especially one whose baby was stolen."

"You don't have to apologize. You were indoctrinated into another way of thinking by Audrey from the time you were a baby."

"It was still mean. I should have known that."

"You only think that because your healing has been so rapid. How far you've come since that day is a testament to your incredible strength of spirit."

"Sometimes I don't think I've come far. Have you noticed I never ask to go back to Washington anymore?"

Ellis had noticed but didn't want to ask about it.

"Do you know why? I'm afraid Audrey's spirit lives on that land. I'm scared of how angry she is with me for everything I've done. I'm even afraid there are earth spirits there that side with her." Tears ran down her cheeks. "I love my house and those woods and fields, but I'm too frightened to go there. I don't think I ever will again."

Ellis wrapped Raven in her arms. "I'm not surprised you feel that way after everything that's happened. Give yourself more time to recover."

"I let Sondra and the police do everything she didn't want. They dug up her body. They did an autopsy on her. I don't even know where she is right now."

Ellis wiped her tears. "That was all out of your control. And I'll tell you where she is. Her spirit lives in your memories. And those are controlled only by you. Try to let go of the bad and keep the good of her within you."

Raven looked astonished. "Do you think she had good in her?"

"You're a beautiful person. She must have had good qualities."

"I can't believe you would say that."

"It's not easy. But I understand that she was sick. And I saw right away that you must have been raised with kindness. All those years, I was afraid you were being treated cruelly."

"She was cruel sometimes. Just telling me I was the daughter of an earth spirit was a mean thing to do."

"It wasn't intended to be mean if she believed it."

"She did believe it. But I think sometimes she realized what she'd done and felt bad about it. It was one of those times that she mentioned the name Bauhammer."

"Poor woman. What pain she must have endured. I'm glad she had the comfort of her earth spirits."

"But they're why she took me."

"Her sickness is why she took you. And who knows? Maybe the nurturing she saw in the earth helped her take care of you."

Raven stared thoughtfully at the distant trees.

"Do you know what I think about her earth spirits?" Ellis said.

"What?"

"I think her deep appreciation of nature was altered, became exaggerated by her illness."

"That's probably true. She told me she and her mother would go to the Montana wilderness to help her feel better when she was sick. She said that was where she learned to speak to the earth spirits."

"She was using nature to heal herself. I did that intuitively when I was a little girl, and consciously after your abduction."

"What did you do after I was abducted?"

"I went to the western mountains to recover. That was how I eventually stopped using drugs and alcohol. Nature has incredible healing power. Audrey felt that, but she began to believe she could manipulate that power to act on her behalf."

"She did. That's what she thought she could do."

"There is a kind of spirit in mountains, trees, and rivers. I feel that same as Audrey did. But I let the spirits be themselves. To project my being onto theirs could only diminish them."

Raven looked at her curiously. "You see earth spirits?"

Ellis picked a few blades of grass. "This grass is making food for itself from sunlight. And that food feeds many creatures. I believe photosynthesis is a kind of miracle. The poet Walt Whitman called a leaf of grass 'the journey-work of the stars.'"

Ellis laid the blades of grass in Raven's palm. "I don't need to see actual earth spirits in this field to find a million things that inspire me. When Audrey said you were born of a raven spirit, she turned your birth into a sudden act of magic that wasn't half as miraculous as the truth. Imagine all the incredible events that had to happen for you to be here. The astrophysical, geological, and evolutionary processes that made you—and all life on earth—are the great wonders of our universe."

Ellis kissed her daughter's cheek. "You really are a miracle, you know." She rested her hand on Raven's baby bump. "And here you are making another."

"I think it's a miracle that we found each other again," Raven said. "Do you ever think that?"

"It's one of the most amazing miracles ever," Ellis said.

Raven returned the kiss to Ellis's cheek. The first kiss her daughter had given her. Ellis looked out at the field to keep from crying.

Together, they watched three crows flap over the field. When one of the crows called, Raven said, "Fish crow, right?"

"Yes. I love that sound."

"So do I."

Raven pushed up her sleeve to look at her watch. "Jackie's plane landed in Gainesville a half hour ago."

"We'd better get up to the house."

"I can't believe this day is finally here," Raven said. "This week is going to be wild."

"Wild" was an understatement. Soon seven people would arrive to spend their December holiday with them. The guesthouse would be packed with River, Jasper, Huck, and Reece in the downstairs room and Jonah and Ryan in the loft bedroom. They would all have to share one bathroom. There'd been lots of jokes about peeing in the woods.

The main house would be less crowded with five people and two bathrooms: Jackie with Raven, Jackie's mother in the master bedroom, and Keith and Ellis sleeping on the screened porch. Ellis assumed most of the barn guests would be at the main house during the day or walking the trails. The weather was supposed to be warm.

Keith walked down the trail to meet them. "I was wondering when you'd come up. They'll be here soon. Come look at what we did."

When they arrived at the house, Ellis understood why Keith had sent them down to the field. He, River, and Max had brought pots of native pines, hollies, and magnolias down from the nursery. They'd put them on the porch and around the house, lacing miniature white lights in their branches. They'd strung the biggest loblolly pine from the nursery with lights and red ribbons and placed it in the living room.

"This is beautiful," Ellis said. "Who bought the lights and ribbons?"

"I did," Keith said.

"I should have known. You always wanted a Christmas tree."

"And now we're both happy. The tree is native and didn't have to die. I'm going to plant that one on our property—as a memory of our first holiday with the kids."

With the kids. She kissed him and whispered, "You're adorably sentimental, you know that?"

"I don't mind wearing the adorably sentimental pants in this family."

"Speaking of pants, you'd better change," she said, noting how muddy he was from moving the plants. River and Max were, too. Ellis put her hand on her heart to tell Max how much she loved the decorations. She squeezed River's hand and said, "Thank you," and for once he didn't make a sarcastic joke. He was getting more comfortable with being loved.

The rental car with Jackie and Huck, their mother, and Reece arrived twenty minutes later. When Reece saw Raven, he said, "She looks like a balloon that's about to pop. How could you do this to her, Jackie?"

"Do you want me to draw you a few diagrams?" Jackie said.

"Please no. Your PDA was always graphic enough."

"The baby might have been conceived on your birthday," Raven told Reece. "Remember the party we had?"

"I remember," he said. "But too much information. You're making me blush in front of all these people I don't know."

"Yeah, right," Huck said. "It would take a lot more than that to embarrass you."

Ellis and Rose greeted each other with a tight hug. Ellis had gotten to know Jackie and his mother during their two visits in autumn. Ellis had felt immediate kinship with Rose. They had a lot in common: divorce, rural living, sons close in age, veganism, reverence for the natural world, and, of course, Raven and their coming grandchild.

In October, during their first walk alone together, Rose had abruptly begun crying. "I should have known," she wept. "I saw something wasn't right with Raven and her mother."

"You can't take any of the blame for what Audrey Lind did," Ellis said.

Her tears kept coming. "I should have called the police. There were times I almost did."

"What would the police have done when Raven showed no signs of abuse?"

"I know. That was why I never called. I had no proof of anything bad going on, just a gut feeling. But still . . . I wish I'd done something."

"You did do something," Ellis said. "You gave my daughter love. You helped her feel less isolated. You gave her the courage to ask for school. She's told me that you, your sons, and Reece changed her life."

Rose's hazel eyes had gleamed. "She said that?"

"In my most hopeful moments after the abduction, I dreamed of a compassionate person like you helping her. It's as if those hopes took wing, found her, and steered her to your family. I'll never be able to express how grateful I am . . ."

She and Rose had embraced, both crying, and from that moment they'd been as close as friends who'd known each other for many years.

And during this holiday, Ellis would get to know the other two boys who had changed her daughter's life. Already, she could tell Huck and Reece would be as easy to like as Jackie.

After the guests were shown their rooms, Raven and Jackie disappeared into the woods. No one tried to find them when a late lunch was put out. They had a lot to talk about.

During lunch, Rose asked, "Have you made any progress convincing Raven to go to a hospital for the birth?"

"She absolutely refuses," Ellis said. "She wouldn't agree to a midwife either. She said she and Jackie have studied how to deliver a baby on the internet."

"Oh my god! Seriously?" Reece said.

"This worries me," Rose said.

"I know. But what can I do? Drag her? Audrey made her phobic about hospitals."

Keith said, "We're hoping she'll go into labor while Jonah and Ryan are here. Ryan is a doctor."

"What kind?" Rose asked.

"A surgeon. He doesn't normally deliver babies, but he knows how."

Ellis said, "I told Jonah to warn Ryan that he might have a working vacation."

Everyone laughed. Ellis laughed with them, though she dreaded her daughter's labor. She never would trust fate. It always did what it wanted. Fate didn't give a damn how good a person was, or how innocent a baby, before it swept them away.

Shortly after Raven and Jackie returned home, Jonah, Jasper, and Ryan arrived. Ryan was four years older than Jonah, but he had a youthful appearance that made him seem younger. He was tall and fit, had blond hair and blue eyes, and wore glasses with aqua frames. He hugged Ellis and kissed her cheek as if he'd known her all his life.

He whispered in her ear, "I brushed up on my delivery skills. I'm ready. But that will be our secret."

"Thank you," she whispered back. "She still says Jackie is going to deliver the baby."

Ryan grinned. "Brave boy."

They put two tables together in the living room for dinner. Keith turned down the lights to better see the Christmas tree. He also lit a fire, though it was still warm outside. For "ambience," he said.

Ellis loved how full her house felt. With family, new friends, laughter, healing. She nearly cried during dinner more than once.

Dinner cleanup went fast with everyone's help, even Quercus, who licked many plates clean. The group was in a lively mood. Everyone except River. Ellis recognized the fraught look in his eyes.

She took him by the hand and led him to the front porch. "You want a drink, don't you?"

"Is it that obvious?"

"To me it is."

"I want one so bad I'm about dying. If I had a driver's license, I'd probably be gone by now."

"I'm sorry to hear that. You've been doing so well."

"It's all of this," he said, gesturing at the lights on the holly tree. "I haven't had a sober Christmas since I was maybe Raven's age. Normally I go through the whole season in one long stupor. And now I'm finally twenty-one and I'm supposed to be sober? How ridiculous is that? Can't I see what it's like to order a drink legally, just for once?"

"You're making up excuses."

"I almost asked Reece or Huck to take me."

"Raven would be devastated if you did that."

"I know," he said.

"Wait here."

She went inside, grabbed a bottle from the refrigerator, and popped the cap. She brought it to River.

He stared at the brown bottle. "Is that a beer?"

"It's a little recovery secret I learned from a guy in a campground."

Caleb reading "Song of the Open Road" in her tent. She always thought of that night when she bought kombucha. Caleb had recommended it to help her stay sober. Back then, the drink wasn't as easy to find in stores as it was now.

She put the bottle in River's hand.

He looked at the label. "I've never tried kombucha."

"The guy I met told me it helps when you're craving a drink. It's fermented and fizzy like a beer, and holding a cold brown bottle helps."

River tried it. "Pretty good."

"It has a little alcohol in it from the fermentation process. Not enough to get you even tipsy, though. I have quite a bit in the refrigerator. Hidden in the back."

"Did you buy it for me?"

"For both of us. I didn't drink hard for long, but even after all these years, the Christmas season makes me want a drink sometimes."

He took another sip. "You're right. Raven will be a wreck if I get drunk tonight."

"You have to do it for yourself."

"I know. But she helps. And so do you. That's why I stayed here. If I'd gone back to Dad's house, I knew I'd drink again. And my dealer lives up there."

"You can do this," Ellis said. "I know you can."

He guzzled more of the kombucha. "Can I say something that's totally out of character?"

"Sure."

"I'm really glad you and my sister are in my life again."

"Can I hug you while you're out of character?"

"Okay. But hurry before the real me comes back."

She hugged him and kissed his cheek. Sixteen years since he'd let her. She was having a record day for kisses.

Jasper leaned his head out the front door. "Raven wants to say something to all of us."

"Coming," Ellis said.

"She must have decided what she's doing with the baby," River said.

"I suppose so."

"I want her to keep it," he said.

"I hope you haven't told her that."

"I haven't. I know it's her decision. But I don't want my first niece or nephew living with some stranger."

"We need to support whatever she's decided."

"Yeah, I will."

They went inside. Raven was standing between the Christmas tree and fireplace. Everyone was seated on chairs and the couch facing her. Ryan moved over so Ellis could sit between him and Keith.

Raven said, "Having all the people I love in one room is the best thing that's ever happened in my life." She went silent, wiped her eyes. "Sorry . . . pregnancy hormones," she said, and everyone laughed.

"I have two things I want to say." She looked at Reece. "I want to say them now because Reece can only be here for a few days. He has two jobs, and one of his bosses said he'd be fired if he doesn't get back on the twenty-sixth."

"The day after Christmas?" Jasper said.

River said, "That sucks."

"First is something that Jackie says will be difficult for him."

Ellis wondered about the playful way they were looking at each other.

"I've decided I want to be called by my legal name, Viola Abbey Bauhammer, from now on."

Ellis hadn't expected that. Keith clasped her hand.

Raven—Viola—continued. "I honestly don't like what the name Bauhammer stands for in the world—because of my grandfather—but I hope the rest of us Bauhammers can change that."

"We will," Jasper said.

Jonah's eyes shined.

Viola looked at Ellis. "It will be hard for me to get used to *Viola*," she said. "But I want to—to honor my mother."

Ellis and her daughter locked gazes, a powerful exchange that seemed to transcend their sixteen years apart. As if Viola had always been right there with her.

"My mother has been dedicated to the conservation of plants since she majored in botany in college," Viola said. "She named me for the genus of violets, one of her favorite spring flowers. Jackie wants to be an ecologist—maybe even a botanist—and he says the name Viola is as cool as Raven."

"Can I still call you Bird Girl?" Reece asked.

"You'd better," she said, eliciting laughter around the room.

"The other thing I wanted to talk about is my house in Washington. I now own it. I also own the cabin in Montana where I spent my summers. All of you are welcome to use my houses. I know these places brought pain to many of you, and now I hope they'll bring you joy."

"Thank you," Jonah said. "That's a beautiful idea."

Again, Viola looked at Reece. "But if you want to stay in my house in Washington, you'll have to arrange it with Reece."

"With me? Why?" Reece said.

"Because I'm hiring you to be the caretaker of the house." She lifted an envelope off the fireplace mantel and handed it to him. "Your payment for the first year is in this envelope."

"A year?" he said.

"Yes, open it."

Reece slid a check out of the envelope. "No way. I can't take this."

"You aren't *taking* it," she said. "You're working for it."

"Doing what?"

"I've decided to stay in Florida for a while, and I need someone to take care of the house. I trust you, and you're really good at fixing things. You're the perfect person."

"*Live* there?" he said.

"Live there, but only until you get into college to study writing like you always wanted. I know you want to go to the school in Seattle where Huck goes. When that happens, you can drive down to the house once a month to check on it. You can use Audrey's truck to do that, by the way. It will basically be yours."

Reece gaped at her.

"Have you ever seen him speechless?" she asked Jackie.

"Never," he said.

"Raven . . . ," Reece said.

"Viola," she corrected.

"This is way too much money for a year of doing what you said."

"It's what I think the job is worth. It'll cover tuition and dorm for a year at the University of Washington."

"You can't just give me this much money."

"Yes I can. I'm ridiculously rich, and rich people do things like this." Everyone laughed.

"It's true, Reece," Jonah said. "Some of my wealthy clients have done much stranger things with their money."

"Like what?"

"Like bequeath a million to maintain their pets' graves to the end of time."

"Wow," Reece said.

"I think Viola's use of money is a bit more practical than that, don't you?"

"Yeah, but—"

"Do you want me to hire someone else?" she asked.

"No. Get over here." Reece engulfed Viola in his arms.

"Woo-hoo!" Huck cheered, jumping up with his arms in the air. "Party at Reece's house!"

"No parties!" Viola said.

Jackie and Huck laughed and grabbed Reece. Their mother was next. Jonah embraced Viola and spoke quietly to her.

"That's quite a girl you've got there," Ryan said.

"I know," Ellis said, wiping her eyes.

She realized Max didn't know what was going on. She took out her pad of paper and wrote a summary of everything Viola had said.

She's a blessing, Max wrote.

Ellis nodded.

She didn't say anything about the baby.

Maybe still undecided.

That baby's coming any minute. She better decide.

All true, but Ellis didn't want to push the teens. It was a life-changing decision. They had to be certain.

The party in the living room lasted another hour. Jonah and Ryan left first. They looked like they very much wanted to be alone. Ellis had never seen Jonah so happy and relaxed.

Not wanting to disturb the lovers, the five boys and Viola got a card game going in the main house. Max headed home, and Rose went to bed. Ellis and Keith made love in their porch bed, then fell asleep to the murmur of the young people's laughter. The happy sounds of her family and friends were every bit as satisfying as listening to owls and tree ducks.

On Christmas Eve morning, Viola and Jackie were up earliest. They ate and went for a walk. The others who'd stayed up late to play cards didn't rise until around noon.

Keith and Rose took charge of lunch while Ellis showed newcomers Ryan, Huck, and Reece around the nursery. Afterward, everyone played Frisbee, football, and a long tournament at the horseshoe pits Max and Keith had built over the summer. River had been playing for months and was the ringer of the group, even better than Max.

The sunset was covered by clouds. Darkness and a scent of imminent rain enveloped the Wild Wood. Ellis hadn't seen Viola or Jackie all day. She asked if anyone else had. Rose said her son had come into the kitchen to get food and drinks at around one o'clock. He said he and Viola were having a picnic, but Viola wasn't with him.

Ellis and Keith went out front to talk privately. "Are you thinking what I am?" Keith asked.

"Yes. No way would she miss being with friends and family on Christmas Eve. Especially Reece, when he has to leave soon."

"He doesn't have to leave for those jobs now," Keith said.

"He's leaving. He told me he won't leave his employers shorthanded over the holidays."

"Good guy," Keith said.

"He is, and Viola adores him. She wouldn't miss this time with him."

Keith looked out at the back acres. "So she's somewhere out there having the baby?"

"Sounds like her, doesn't it?" Ellis said.

"I'm afraid so."

Jonah and Ryan were coming down the path from the barn house. "No one has seen Viola all day," Ellis said. "Jackie came to the kitchen to get lunch without her and disappeared."

"Oh boy," Ryan said.

"You think she's in labor?" Jonah asked.

Ellis nodded.

"Poor Jackie," Ryan said. "I wouldn't want to deliver a baby at night in the woods."

"And it's starting to rain," Keith said.

"Good thing it's warm," Ryan said.

"It feels warm to us because we're from New York," Jonah said. "It's midsixties, and it will feel colder if she's wet."

"We'd better hand out flashlights and start searching," Keith said.

"She won't want that," Ellis said.

"I think we should talk to Rose and see what she thinks," Jonah said. "She knows Jackie better than we do."

Rose was in the kitchen with Huck and Reece.

"I see by all your faces you've come to the same conclusion I have," she said.

"Yes," Jonah said, "and we're trying to decide whether to go look for them."

"She's having the baby?" Reece said.

Huck turned off all the burners on the stove. "We have to find them. No way can we let Jackie do that alone in the dark."

Jasper and River had come in from the living room. "Viola won't like that," River said.

"I don't care," Huck said. "We can't let her call the shots just because a mentally ill person made her afraid of hospitals. If something bad happens, my brother will never forgive himself. Raven . . . Viola . . . should never have asked this of him."

"I agree," Reece said. "That woman, Audrey, used to force Viola to make promises that were horrible for her. We can't let her get in the habit of doing that to people."

His words hit Ellis viscerally. He was right. Her daughter was manipulating Jackie the way her abductor had controlled her. Jackie was only seventeen. To ask him to do this alone was absurd.

"Okay, we're decided," Jonah said. "Let's find flashlights. Ryan, get your bag."

Maxine came into the kitchen with a stack of waterproof tarps, blankets, and towels. She urgently nodded at the door to say they should get going.

"Apparently Max figured out she's having the baby long ahead of us," Keith said.

While Ryan ran for his medical bag, they searched the house for flashlights. Viola's was gone from her bed stand, and Max had one from her truck. That left only three for nine people.

They were in the living room deciding how to search the property when the back door opened.

"She's home!" Jonah said.

"No," Jackie said breathlessly, striding into the room. He was wet and had clearly been running fast. He looked desperate.

"What happened?" Reece asked.

Jackie tried to talk while he caught his breath. "The baby . . . it's coming. It's too dark to see anything . . . and now . . . it's raining. She's in so much pain . . . I'm kind of freaking out."

"Oh, Jackie!" his mother said.

"Has her water broken?" Ryan asked.

"Yes. Not long ago. She's been in labor all day."

"Where is she? How far?" Ellis asked.

"She's in that little circle you keep mowed to have picnics. At the edge between the big field and woods."

Where Ellis had massaged her the day before.

"You're a doctor," Jackie said to Ryan. "You would be able to see if everything is going right, wouldn't you?"

"I can do my best," Ryan said.

"Will you go look at her?" Jackie asked. "She won't come to the house. She wants to see the stars."

"Of course I'll go," Ryan said.

Jackie pointed at the blankets and tarps Max was holding. "Those are a good idea. She's soaked, and I'm afraid she's getting too cold."

"Let's go," Ellis said.

"I have to run ahead. I need to get back to her," Jackie said before he jogged out of the room.

Ellis led the group. Max took up the rear to illuminate the trail from behind. The ones who didn't have flashlights carried supplies.

The rain changed from a mist to a steady drizzle. No one spoke. A great horned owl softly hooted from the northern woods.

"Be careful of the roots," Ellis said as they entered the forest trail.

Ahead, she heard Jackie's voice. When they arrived at the edge of the field, Viola was on her hands and knees, wearing only a man's shirt, having a strong contraction.

Ellis knelt at her side. "I'm here, sweetheart."

"Mom!" she gasped. "It hurts! I didn't think it would hurt this much."

"Let Rose and me help." She beckoned Jackie's mother to sit on her other side. They rubbed her lower back. "How does that feel?"

She squeezed her eyes and groaned. She couldn't answer. Her contractions were almost continuous. But she was unusually quiet.

Max was trying to get the rest of the group to take the edges of a tarp she'd opened. Keith understood. The blanket Viola was on was soaked and muddy. "Hold the tarp up, and we'll make a clean, dry place for her," Keith said.

River, Jasper, Huck, and Reece each took a corner of the tarp to make a canopy while Max and Keith spread another tarp and two blankets beneath it. "Will she let us move her?" Keith asked Jackie.

"I don't know."

Max heard none of that. She went to Viola, put her hands on her cheeks, and looked closely into her eyes. She gestured at the dry blanket. Viola gave no answer, and Max didn't wait for one. She wrapped her arms around Viola's chest, lifted her fully off the ground, and carefully set her down on the clean blanket without getting her muddy boots on it. She stripped off Viola's soaked shirt and gently dressed her in a clean, dry flannel. Viola seemed in too much misery to notice.

Ellis, Jackie, and Rose took off their shoes and moved to the dry blanket. Jonah joined them.

"Will she let me examine her?" Ryan asked Ellis.

"Ryan is going to make sure everything is okay," Ellis told Viola. "Jackie will feel better."

She nodded slightly.

They positioned her on her back to make it easier for Ryan to see. He took off his shoes and sat next to Jackie. Before he did anything, he said to Jackie, "You're doing a great job. Tell me where she is."

"She's fully dilated, and she has the urge to push."

"Did you discuss pain help?" he asked.

"Yes. She doesn't want it."

"Then I won't give her anything unless she asks." He listened to Viola's chest with his stethoscope, then to the baby's heartbeat. "Mama and baby sound perfect," he said.

Ellis felt like she could breathe again.

Ryan used his flashlight to see the baby's progress as Viola bore down with another contraction. "Jackie, do you see? That's the baby's head."

Jackie looked as dazed as any new father.

"Everything looks good," Ryan said. "She just needs to push."

Viola continued to be quiet through the pushing.

"You can scream all you want, Viola," Ryan said.

"She doesn't," Jackie said. "This is how she's been."

"We don't care if you sound like a squealing warthog," River said.

"And we promise not to take videos," Reece said.

"Shut . . . up!" Viola said, almost laughing through the contraction. The four young men holding the tarp snickered.

Ellis and Rose helped Viola into a squat. But that meant they couldn't see what was happening with the baby.

"I need to see the stars," Viola said. "Move that blanket or whatever it is."

"It's raining," Ellis said. "There won't be stars."

"Actually, there are," River said.

They pulled the tarp back a little. The sky was clearing to the east, though rain still pattered on the tarp. A gibbous waxing moon was rising above the trees. Fleeting billows of clouds drifted like gray smoke over the lopsided orb of moonlight. Bright stars shined here and there as the clouds moved over them.

Jackie kissed Viola's cheek. "Look. Isn't that beautiful?"

"Yes. Yes . . ." She wept, staring at the moon and clouds as she pushed. She kept her eyes on the dreamlike scene. It helped calm her. Ellis felt her focus, get control of the pain.

Rain beat a soft rhythm on the tarp. No one spoke. Everyone sensed silence was best for her.

Viola bore down again and again in her quiet way. The rain patter gradually diminished. The moon rose above the trees, silvering the dry grasses and wildflowers of the dormant winter field.

A flock of black-bellied tree ducks called as they flew over the eastern fields. Their nocturnal whistles were one of the loveliest sounds of that land, like children of Pan playing ethereal music on instruments fashioned from marsh reeds.

Viola closed her eyes, surely listening to the birds, as she pushed her baby closer to the earth.

"Jackie," Ryan said softly. He shined his light beneath Viola. "Get ready."

Jackie prepared to take the baby into his hands. With two last grueling pushes, the baby slid onto his palms.

"Go to it," Ryan said. He handed him a small towel and the bulb suction.

"Is she okay?" Viola said. "Jackie . . . ?"

Jackie laid the infant on the blanket and gently wiped its face. He expertly suctioned the nose. The baby made a soft cry.

Ellis could feel collective relief in the group.

"It's a girl," Jackie said in a shaking voice. "She's getting pink. She looks good."

Keith propped Viola up with folded blankets so she could see the baby. The tarp came down. River, Jasper, Huck, and Reece leaned down to look.

"She's as quiet as our Bird Girl," Reece said.

Viola laughed through soft sobs.

"She is quiet," Jackie said to Ryan. "Does she look okay to you?"

"Some babies are quiet. Let me take a look."

Ryan checked her over and listened to her heart. She began to cry louder. "There, you see? She wants nothing to do with me. She wants Daddy and Mama."

Ellis wasn't sure he should say that. If they'd decided to give the baby up for adoption, encouraging bonding might be painful.

Ryan helped Jackie wrap the baby in a clean towel, and Jackie laid her on Viola's chest. Viola wept and kissed her. Ryan gave Jackie more gentle guidance through the process of cutting the umbilical cord.

"Congratulations, Jackie," Ryan said. "Great job."

"Really great," Jonah said.

Huck patted his brother's shoulder. "Yeah, awesome."

"So what's her name?" Reece asked.

He shouldn't ask, but Ellis hated to ruin the moment by saying that.

"She is Daughter of the Miraculous Universe," Viola said.

Silence.

"Okay," River said. "Interesting name."

"*Really* interesting," Reece said.

"Be quiet," Huck whispered.

"It makes a cute acronym," Reece said. "DOTMU."

"We can call her *Dot* for short," River said.

Jackie was smiling, seemingly unperturbed by the odd name.

"Is that really what you're calling her?" Jasper asked.

Viola snorted a laugh. "I was joking. I knew you would all believe me."

"Thank god!" Reece said, and everyone laughed.

Ellis said, "Before you name her, what are your plans? Are you keeping her?"

"I'm going to name her," Viola said. "Jackie and I have already chosen her middle name. Tell them, Jackie."

Jackie looked at his mother. "Her middle name is for you, *Rose*."

"And it's close to my mother's middle name, *Rosa*," Viola said. "My grandfather's family name."

Rose's tears shined in the flashlight glow. "I like that. Both families represented in one name."

Jackie stroked his fingers on the baby's cheek. "Did you think of a first name?" he asked Viola.

"I did," she said. "I thought of it when the moon was shining on this field. My mother seeded these native flowers and grasses many years ago when I was far away from her." She looked down at the infant in her arms. "She'll be named for where she was born. Her name is Meadow. Meadow Rose."

"I really like that," Jackie said.

"It's a gorgeous name," Ellis said. "And it's the name of a North American wildflower—an unusual species because it's considered a thornless rose."

River bent down and gently held the baby's tiny fist. "I'd rather she have some thorns."

"You would," his brother said.

"Well, she's damn pretty without them," River said.

"You done good, Bird Girl," Reece said. "It's a great name."

"Thank you," Viola said. She carefully placed the baby in Ellis's arms. "Mom, you get to decide whether her last name is Abbey or Gephardt."

Ellis and Keith looked at each other, too stunned to speak.

"We want you two to raise her," Jackie said. "And don't ask if we're sure. We are."

"I can verify that," Rose said. "They decided weeks ago. It's been tough to keep it secret."

"Won't it be difficult for you to have her in the family?" Keith asked.

"It makes it less difficult," Jackie said. "We didn't want her to leave the family."

"We'll tell her the truth about everything," Viola said. "She'll call Jackie and me *Dad* and *Mom* and Ellis and Keith *Grandma* and *Grandpa*. We'll just be a little different from most families."

"We're both hoping to get into the University of Florida so we'll be nearby," Jackie said. "I've already sent in my application."

"He'll definitely get in," Huck said. "He has a great application."

"What do you think, Grandma?" Jonah asked Ellis.

"I'm . . . I'm honestly afraid for Viola and Jackie. I know how painful it is to lose a baby."

"We aren't losing her," Viola said. "We'll be in her life. You know Jackie and I are too young to raise a baby. We have to finish high school. We want to go to college. She'll be raised by two of my favorite people on earth—in this beautiful place. And with River, Jasper, and Huck for uncles. And Dad for a grandfather and Ms. Danner for a grandmother."

"Don't I get to be an uncle?" Reece asked.

"You're officially an uncle," Viola said.

"And Ryan is officially a grandfather," Jackie said.

Jonah laughed and patted Ryan's shoulder.

"And Maxine will be her aunt," Viola said. "Do you see, Mom? We could never have found a better adoptive family."

Ellis looked down at the baby in her arms. In her little round face, she saw newborn Viola. Viola who had come back to her less than nine months ago. Daughter of the Miraculous Universe, indeed.

A hush fell over the group as they waited for Ellis to answer. She stroked her fingers on the petal-soft cheek of Meadow Rose. A magnificent sensation overcame her. As if her heart had been a bud that was suddenly blooming, growing so big, it might not fit inside her body.

Ellis looked around at them all. She wasn't the only one with tears on her face. "I do see," she told Viola. "This is a beautiful family. You chose well."

"Ellis . . . ," Keith said.

"Yes?"

"I'll ask you one more time. Will you marry me?"

She hesitated, but her silence had nothing to do with indecision. It was a moment of wonder. Because she was certain of her answer. Absolutely certain.

"Yes, I'll marry you."

The family's cheers and laughter rang out over the fields, through the forests, to the marshes. Ellis imagined the sound rippling farther. To the woods of New York, to the Ellis River where her parents had been happy and in love, to the little campgrounds of Ohio, to every western peak she had stood upon, to the Washington creek that had brought Viola to Jackie. And there was her family, in her little Wild Wood, at the heart of all that spreading joy.

ACKNOWLEDGMENTS

First, I want to thank my readers. Connecting with you through my characters and stories has been one of the greatest gifts of my life.

Thank you, Carly Watters, for encouraging me to write this story when we first discussed it. I'm grateful for your expertise, and your enthusiastic support of my writing.

Curtis Russell, thank you for adeptly taking the helm while Carly was on maternity leave.

Thank you, Alicia Clancy, for believing in this book and enriching it with your editorial gifts. Your *komorebi* brings a beautiful touch to the story.

Laura Chasen, I'm deeply grateful for your knowledgeable, perceptive, and compassionate style of editing. More thanks to Danielle Marshall and her crew at Lake Union Publishing: Gabriella Dumpit, Nicole Burns-Ascue, Shasti O'Leary, Stacy Abrams, and Rosanna Brockley.

Lots of gratitude to Gary Gillette, MD; Ernestine Lee, MD; Richard Chasen, MD; and Jennifer Tucker, NP, for bestowing your medical expertise. Additional thanks, Karen Gillette and Laura Chasen, for your help.

Thank you, Suzie Byrne, for your friendship and big heart.

Karl Vanderah, thanks for helping when I called with random story difficulties.

Stephanie Robinson, I'm sorry your childhood town got cut, but let's pretend Keith grew up in Brockway.

Endless gratitude to every piece of earth I've ever loved—especially the wildish little realm behind my childhood house that helped me in so many ways.

Cailley, William, and Grant, I'm grateful for the love and laughter you've brought to my world. And to the worlds I create.

Scott, a hundred times *thank you*. You're always there with a light when the power goes out. I can't imagine finding my way to this story without you.

ABOUT THE AUTHOR

Photo © 2017 Ashley Nicole Johnson Photography

Glendy Vanderah is the *Wall Street Journal, Washington Post*, and Amazon Charts bestselling author of *Where the Forest Meets the Stars*. Glendy worked as an avian biologist before she became a writer. Originally from Chicago, she now lives in rural Florida with her husband and as many birds, butterflies, and wildflowers as she can lure to her land. For more information, visit www.glendyvanderah.com.